EIDETIC
TRANSUBSTANTIATION

A NOVEL

WILLIAM J. PALMER

ANAPHORA LITERARY PRESS

QUANAH, TEXAS

ANAPHORA LITERARY PRESS
1108 W 3rd Street
Quanah, TX 79252
https://anaphoraliterary.com

Book design by Anna Faktorovich, Ph.D.

Cover Images: "Paris. The Eiffel Tower is a most uncanny structure…" photo by Lewis Wickes Hine, March 1919. American National Red Cross photograph collection: Library of Congress Prints and Photographs Division Washington, D.C.
"John F. Kennedy motorcade, Dallas, Texas, Nov. 22, 1963" photo by Victor Hugo King: Library of Congress Prints and Photographs Division Washington, D.C., LC-USZ62-134844.
"Man with pointer in front of a projected slide showing an aerial photograph with label 'MRBM Field Launch Site San Cristobal #1 14 October 1962', at a discussion on Cuba at the State Department, Washington, D.C./ WKL" photo by Warren K. Leffler: U.S. News & World Report magazine photograph collection: Library of Congress Prints and Photographs Division Washington, D.C., LC-DIG-ds-07185.

Published in 2019 by Anaphora Literary Press

Eidetic Transubstantiation: A Novel
William J. Palmer—1st edition.

Library of Congress Control Number: 2019914326

Library Cataloging Information
Palmer, William J., 1943-, author.
    Eidetic transubstantiation : A novel / William J. Palmer
    252 p. ; 9 in.
    ISBN 978-1-68114-514-3 (softcover : alk. paper)
    ISBN 978-1-68114-515-0 (hardcover : alk. paper)
    ISBN 978-1-68114-516-7 (e-book)
1. Fiction—Thrillers—Espionage. 2. Fiction—Historical—General.
3. Philosophy—Movements—Existentialism.
PN3311-3503: Literature: Prose fiction
813: American fiction in English

For Maryann

Special Thanks to Tracy Collins-Pfeiffer, Kirk Cerny, and Anna Faktorovich for their help in bringing this novel to fruition

Other Works by William J. Palmer

Fiction—Novels

The Detective and Mr. Dickens
The Highwayman and Mr. Dickens
The Hoydens and Mr. Dickens
The Dons and Mr. Dickens
The Wabash Trilogy:
The Wabash Baseball Blues
The Redneck Mafia
Civic Theater
The Uses of Money
Two Cities

Non-Fiction—Books

The Fiction of John Fowles
Dickens and New Historicism
The Films of the Seventies: A Social History
The Films of the Eighties
The Films of the Nineties: The Decade of Spin

CHAPTER 1: CUBA

When it all began very few people knew about my gift. My bosses in the military knew about it. I was no more than a minor functionary in the Pentagon photo room, day after day, staring at, sometimes through powerful magnifiers, aerial photographs. Russia, Vietnam, Cuba, China, troop movements, naval fleet operations, pictures from the air of the ground or the sea from 10,000 feet, everything miniaturized, roll after roll of film, shots sequenced every four seconds.

August 1962 and American U-2 spy planes are criss-crossing the globe taking these aerial photographs. We are supposedly engaged in a Cold War with the Commies so our military establishment, the Military-Industrial Complex as Ike had named it, was forced to shoot aerial photographs rather than shooting guns and rockets and bombs and missiles. I had often thought that for the Generals (on both sides) Cold Wars must be really frustrating because they offered very few opportunities for them to trot out their wartime hardware and see what it could do. However, though it probably got the Generals little satisfaction, the U-2 spy planes were one piece of hardware that was pretty much one hundred percent effective. Flying miles above the earth manned with cameras that could photograph very clearly a carbuncle on a Commie's ass, the U-2's kept the Pentagon pretty fully appraised of what their Cold War enemies were up to.

But, nevertheless, photographs, sequences of stills, were yet just bits of information that needed to be analyzed, placed in the proper context. Remember, this was the 1960's. We didn't have the instant replay, stop-action, zoom-zoom technology that we have now in the 21st Century to interpret whether an NFL football player actually caught a pass or stepped out of bounds or reached the ball over the goal line. What we had was me and the other minor functionaries like me in the NPIC (the National Photographic Interpretation Center) which was under the command of one Air Force General Edward Lansdale who in turn was running the Pentagon Photo Room under the aegis of the CIA, America's fledgling spy agency, offspring of the OSS of World War II.

So that was what I was doing, interpreting, analyzing, actually pecking out reports on my typewriter, that day in 1962 when the photo reels from Cuba first came in. Actually, it was all pretty absurd because I was a 23 year-old civilian analyst for the Air Force, the CIA, whoever, and, though neither I nor the Generals or any of the other denizens of the Cold War in the Pentagon knew or even imagined it, but one of the most important photo sequences of the whole Cold War had just plopped down on the desk of this nobody next to his hand-cranked magnification viewer.

That day was really like any other in the photo room, but when I started looking at this new set of aerial photographs it really wasn't like any other at all. When I threaded them through and first sat down to my viewer, I'm sure I was thinking: *No big deal! More Cuba.* Spy planes had been flying over Cuba every week for two years ever since Castro took over. To tell the truth, the Cuban pictures they kept giving me were among the most boring of all the film sequences that showed up on my desk. BORING! Sugar cane plantations. Brown tobacco fields. Dusty mountain roads. Desolate beaches. Miles and miles of rain forest jungle. Yes, really boring, and then, all of a sudden, that day, they weren't. You see, I'm an Eidetic and that is why I was in that photo room in the first place on that day in 1962 when the flyover pictures from Cuba came in.

My special gift, my Eidetic Memory, was the whole reason I was recruited by those Air Force Intel guys right after I finished by undergraduate degree in criminology from Purdue University followed by my Ph.D. degree in Foreign Service from Georgetown, all at the ripe old age of 22. Yes, I was definitely a prodigy. Not only did I have those two academic majors but I also had full minors (and very powerful interests) in History and Literature. Plus, I had picked up three foreign languages—Spanish, Portuguese, French—along the way. Most Ph.D. studies focused on one subject for their graduate studies, but thanks to my Eidetic Memory I was able to branch out into a number of different subjects and ultimately draw them all together in a dissertation on the Peloponnesian Wars the likes of which the Georgetown graduate school had never envisioned. Needless to say, I was the youngest Ph.D. that ever matriculated out of the university and probably still am to this day sixty years later. At least I like to think so. But of course, time and the younger generations tend to ultimately catch up with you.

Somehow, the military, Air Force intelligence to be specific, found out about my gift. They probably got me on their radar thanks to my high school and college friend Lenny who had gone in the Secret Service right after we graduated from Purdue. Lenny was one of the few people in my life who knew about my special talent and, who knows, maybe he bragged on me and some Air Force recruiter took note. Lenny loved bragging about my strange talent and often took bar bets with the aid of my Eidetic Memory. More about Lenny later.

So, you see, my special gift, my Eidetic Memory, was the whole reason I was recruited by the Intel wonks to look at their pictures. As it turned out it was a pretty good move on their parts. I not only saw things in ways that other people couldn't, but I remembered exactly, absolutely, totally accurately, every single thing that I saw. Thus, I was able to compare and contrast pictures in ways no one else they had could. Like I said, they hired me right out of grad school and I went with them because they offered me three times the salary that I could get as an assistant professor teaching whatever at any American university or a lower level diplomat in the American foreign service somewhere overseas. Little did I know what I was getting into.

So that is how I got to the day in 1962 when the aerial photos from Cuba first got dropped on my desk. When I first started running them through my viewer, after no more than fifty frames, I knew that something was wrong. The spy plane fly-over always started filming over those parts of the island where there were military encampments. It's not as if Castro had a real army or any real military establishments like Russia or China had. His guerilla forces were just starting to put themselves together as an army. Mostly they were still living in tent encampments, though some had started building real barracks to house themselves. Anyway, from the very start of this sequence of photos, a military encampment in the jungle outside of a fairly large farming town, Santa Clara, showed up and I immediately sensed that something looked really different. Then I looked at another encampment outside Ciego de Avila and the same anomalies hit me in the eyes there. These photos were quite different from the photos of the same places from a week before.

Ruts etched the bare ground of the jungle clearing that hadn't been there before. The jungle protruded further into the clearing than in the earlier photos. The protruding jungle was a different shade of black and white, darker, tighter, deader, too regular, not random. I had seen that shade of grey, that configuration before. Camouflage nets covered with cut palm fronds. Fake jungle. Hiding something. The ruts. Made by vehicles, heavy vehicles. Tanks? No. Cubans didn't have tanks. What were the camouflage nets hiding? I had to stop and think on that. I realized that I was only about fifty or sixty frames into the canisters of films. There had to be more information buried in those pictures, images that would answer my questions.

So, I stopped for a moment to think, to compose my thoughts. I realized that as an analyst that was what I did. I was composing some sort of narrative out of those photos. Suddenly my Criminology classes came back to me. Ferreting out clues, putting evidence together, trying to solve a mystery, catch a killer, track down a criminal who didn't want to be caught. I was composing a narrative out of those pictures, looking at them and trying to imagine what was going on in that jungle clearing, in that crude military encampment on that skinny little island so far away from my closed room in Washington. Little did I ever imagine that in the twenty-first century whole battles, military operations, in Afghanistan, Syria, Iraq, would be fought with deadly drones on computer screens (which are the offspring of my aerial photos of the 1960's) from small closed rooms like this by military nerds like me.

I broke out of my reverie and went back to the photos. The spy plane had banked out over the ocean and was coming back for another run and was filming all the way down the length of the island. As it passed over Ciego de Avila I saw movement in the photos. Strange shapes. I cranked one photo after another slowly through my viewer, simulating movement in the jungle clearing. Conical shapes. As the photos sequenced I turned up the magnification and suddenly realized that I was looking at wheeled vehicles, large two-pronged flat-bedded vehicles. Those weren't harmless Cuban trucks making those ruts. They were Russian double tracked missile launchers. I had seen them many times in our aerial photos from fly-overs of Russian military bases.

One thing I'll never forget. (But, of course with my particular species of memory I never forget anything anyway.) That one thing was the way I felt when I first realized what I was looking at. Exhilaration certainly, an adrenalin rush. Triumph partially, as I realized that I was well on my way to solving a mystery. A real eagerness to start composing my narrative for the Generals. All of these positive emotions sort of rushed upon me as I realized what those objects in the aerial photos actually were. When I had finished my silent celebrating, I went back to the photo sequences and now the conical shapes, the Russian missile launchers, were gone, withdrawn, disappeared, wheeled back into their hiding places beneath the camouflage netting. Evidently the fly-over had with blind luck been clicking away when they were out in the open. Then the reality of what I had seen burst upon me and slowly sank in. Now my exhilaration was gone and fear suddenly set in, almost a sense of doom. *Why are they hiding them?* I realized. *What are they doing there?* Those weren't really legitimate questions because I already knew the answers. The Russians were setting up missile launching sites in the jungles of Cuba, no more than ninety miles from the American mainland, from Florida. That's how I remember it all, that first dawn of recognition. It all came to be known as the Cuban Missile Crisis and I was certainly in on the ground floor of it.

After I had cranked through all of the aerial footage from those U-2 passes, I had accumulated some more evidence to shore up my Cuba narrative. The spy plane pictures, for me, supplied clear photographic evidence of medium range (SS-4) and intermediate range (R-14) ballistic missile launching facilities. I was absolutely certain of this conclusion because I already knew by heart and could flawlessly identify the ordinance that I had detected in the photos from my watching of the same machines sitting unhidden in aerial photos of Russian military bases. And remember, with my Eidetic Memory I never forget anything, any image, any detail, once I have seen it. As I sat at my typewriter composing my report for the higher-ups, what I came to think of as my Cuba narrative, it suddenly hit me that I was the first one, at that point in time the only one, who knew what the Russkies were up to in Cuba. I tried to write an absolutely truthful account for the Generals of what I had seen in the aerial photos followed by my analysis of my discovery's meanings, my Cuba narrative.

(Actually, that is what I hope this whole book will be, my truthful account of the journey my Eidetic Memory took me on over the course of my fairly long and often memorable, certainly rememberable, life. It was pretty much there, that day in August 1962, that the power and the effect of my Eidetic Memory really kicked in. That day, now more than fifty-five years ago, was where it all started.)

I typed up my report in the kind of detail that only an Eidetic can reproduce from memory and I immediately walked it over to the OD, a Captain, and told him that it was really pretty important and he should probably read it right away. About thirty minutes later said Captain marched up to my desk and in a shaky, rather uncommanding voice, ordered me to come with him. Being a civilian and not really needing to follow orders from my military bosses the way that real soldiers snapped to attention, I started straightening the papers next to the typewriter on my desk (actually two carbon copies of the very report that the Captain was holding in his slightly trembling hand). Evidently not moving fast enough for him, he barked at the top of his voice: "Dammit Edwards, move it, follow me, NOW!" This time I did as I was told.

As we marched double-time out of the photo lab and through the maze of Pentagon hallways, he briefed me on where we were going. It was pretty scary.

"We're going to take your report directly to General Lansdale," he actually stammered as he said it. "You are going to talk him through it. First tell him quickly who you are and how you found this information. Then, and this is the important part, tell him exactly what it means and how you reached your conclusion that the Russians are putting missiles into Cuba."

That was it. We knocked at a windowless door and at the gruff response "ENTER" we went in. Behind a desk much smaller than I expected it to be, strewn with thick files and reports under manila covers just like mine, sat General Edward Lansdale of both Air Force Intelligence and the CIA. My Captain saluted him, though his hand was still unsteady, while I stood awkwardly shifting from one foot to another behind the Captain.

"What have you got?" Lansdale opened the interrogation. "It must be important, or at least you think so, if you walked it over here to me."

"Yes sir, I really think so sir, too important to wait sir," my Captain actually stammered out his response, nervous as a golfer in a glass factory. As I picture this scene now so many years later it strikes me as strange how afraid my Captain was of Lansdale, how cowed he was in the General's presence. I had no idea then, but I do now, who Lansdale really was. After I met him that morning, I asked my military colleagues who knew. I came away from those conversations very impressed, in fact somewhat awed. Lansdale was the Eminence Gris of the American spy community post WW II and the OSS of Wild Bill Donovan. Later on, long after the Vietnam War was over and Lansdale was dead, books would be written about Lansdale's spy presence during the Vietnam War which supposedly we hadn't really gotten into on that morning in 1962.

"What have you got there?" Lansdale's voice was like sandpaper.

"This is Michael Edwards, one of our photo, aerial photo, analysts, sir. This is his report of our most recent fly-over of Cuba," and then as if he had momentarily forgotten he added on yet another superfluous "sir."

"So?"

My Captain was momentarily tongue-tied as if he was afraid that Lansdale might kill the messenger, the bearer of this really bad news.

When the OD didn't say anything right away, I decided to speak up. Actually, I was totally confident in what was in my report so I had no problem stating my facts.

"The Russians are setting up missile facilities in Cuba, General," I said and I think he sensed both the excitement and the urgency in my voice.

"Who are you?" he barked as if he had forgotten what the Captain had just told him. The fact probably was that he also was momentarily stunned by what I had just told him.

"Michael Edwards, sir. Civilian photo analyst."

Finally, the OD found his voice. I don't think he liked me taking over the conversation. But he was a fair man and what he said reflected well on both me and my discovery. "It's all in Edwards' report there," the Captain said. "He is our very best analyst. He never misses a thing,"

"At ease, men. Sit down." And he directed us to two straight-backed chairs against the wall.

We sat and waited while he read through the five pages of my report. As he read, his lips pursed and I'm not sure his eyes ever blinked. He was one of the most intense human beings I had ever observed in my short life. It was as if—in his eyes, in the tightening lines in his face, in the shifting and stiffening of his body language, in his hand grasping the paper and his fingers skating over the lines of my words—he was already laying the groundwork for dealing with this national threat.

"Well now," he finished. "let's go gentlemen. I need to see these pictures for myself" and he was up from his desk and through the office door like a fullback powering into the line.

We followed him back to the photo lab and he sat down at my desk and started cranking at my magnification viewer.

"You, Edwards," he actually remembered my name, "here," and he firmly patted my desk off of his right shoulder, "tell me what you see, point it all out to me, how you reached your conclusions. And Captain

Bankston, while we are looking at these pictures would you go get Mister Edwards' personnel file for me."

We looked at the pictures for a good half hour. Almost immediately we changed positions. I sat at the desk and did the cranking and General Lansdale leaned over my right shoulder as I stopped and pointed out the important details in the pictures, some of them so subtle that only I could see them right away and had to point them out and explain them to the General.

My Captain left and pretty quickly returned with my personnel file. He stood respectfully at ease behind us as I pointed and talked the General through the aerial photos. Finally, he had seen enough to fully understand what I had written in my report. He had barely spoken the whole time but for an occasional "uh huh" or an "I see" or an "okay." He straightened up from leaning over my shoulder and stepped back, his hand on the back of his balding head, thinking.

"You're absolutely sure those are medium and intermediate range launchers?" He was addressing me, but it was more as if he was talking to himself.

"Yes sir. I am. I've seen them hundreds of times since I came on board in my fly-over photos of Russia. I can tell you the exact missiles they are built for."

I hadn't realized it but he had brought my report with him and still had it in his hand. Then he took my personnel folder from Captain Bankston and turned to go. But then he turned back to us and nodded quickly. "Good work, men. Yes, very good work." And then he was gone.

"Wow, he's a scary piece of work," I said to Captain Bankston after the General had left the photo room.

"Scary is sure the right word," he assented. Then he added his "well done" to the General's and thought for a moment, "Let's not talk about this to anyone else in here," he finally said, "until we see how it plays out." The gravity in his voice reignited that fear, that vague sense of doom, that I had felt when I first started seeing things in the pictures.

Our meeting with General Lansdale ended at 0900. He walked back into the Photo Room at 1330 that afternoon.

"You two, come with me." He ordered. Me and the Captain jumped up and followed him into the Pentagon maze like a couple of pull-toys.

He led us a merry chase through the hallways all the way to the far side of that huge sprawling building, passing through three different "TOP SECRET" and "RESTRICTED," armed-Marine-guarded, portals into what everyone called the "spookiest" area of the building, into the lair of the C.I.A.

Please pardon me for being a little melodramatic at this point in my narrative, but for a civilian like me the whole Pentagon itself and especially the "RESTRICTED" areas that were labeled "TOP SECRET" and had loaded guns in the hands of hard-faced, head-shaved, totally unsmiling Marines guarding them really were scary, intimidating, pretty much to be avoided. And yet here we were being led down these corridors of fear in the depths of the building.

"We are meeting with Mister John McCone, the head of the CIA," General Lansdale announced as he knocked on another window-less door at the end of our forced march through the Pentagon tunnels. "Your report caught his eye, or I should say it really caught his attention, and we have been working over it ever since I left your photo room this morning. Edwards, fair warning, this meeting is going to focus almost entirely on you. Be ready to answer each question he asks straight up. This is important. Your report and you, well your qualifications not you in person, will be going to the President this evening."

That said, and a "come in" reply from within to Lansdale's knock propelled the three of us into the CIA's inner sanctum.

"Ah, gentlemen," McCone greeted us not rising from his desk.

There was only one other chair in the office so we all three remained standing. General Lansdale made the introductions, pointing out that I had written the report under the Captain's command and that Bankston had seen fit to bring it immediately to his, Lansdale's, attention.

"Yes, so I've been told, Okay, gentlemen, follow me and we'll go somewhere a bit more comfortable." And thus, we adjourned down yet another hallway to a conference room with a long table and rather comfortable padded chairs. McCone sat at the head of the table with Lansdale to his immediate right while the Captain and I sat on the next two chairs, together on McCone's left side. And so, we got down to business.

McC: I've read your report Edwards. Excellent work, really excellent. Very alert, both of you. (and thus, he included Captain Bankston in the compliment.)

Me and CB: Thank you sir.

McC: First of all, and I can't emphasize this enough. So far the four of us know about this and I want it to stay that way for now. DO YOU UNDERSTAND! (he punctuated this last with a slight raising and thickening of his voice and a penetrating stare and his "DO YOU UNDERSTAND!" clearly was not a question,)

Me and CB: Yes sir, absolutely sir. (the two of us nodding our heads like a couple of kewpie dolls.)

McC: I'm going to brief the President this evening in the White House so you can see why secrecy is so important and this all has to stay with us for now.

Lansdale took this opportunity to enter the conversation.

L: For tonight and tomorrow you two are going to be joined at the hip. Bankston, I want you to go back to your office and arm yourself. Edwards, I want you to go back to your desk, pick up the Cuba reels and your magnification viewer and be ready to deliver them to the White House first thing tomorrow morning. Do not let them out of your sight. Sleep with them under your bed. You two will sleep here at the Pentagon tonight. Captain, you are going to be his bodyguard. Take good care of him.

I know that I was speechless and the wide-eyed, open-mouthed expression on Bankston's face was evidence that he was just as speechless as I was.

McC: Good. That's settled. Now Mister Edwards, I've been looking with great interest at your personnel file. It says that you have a special aptitude for your job as a photo analyst, that you possess a special intellectual gift, an Eidetic Memory.

Me: Yes sir, that's right, I do sir. I mean, yes, I have it, that kind of memory. (I was babbling like a fool,)

McC: That's outstanding. I must admit that when I read about this memory thing in your file that I had no idea what it meant, had never even heard of it before. So, I looked it up in the Encyclopedia Brittanica. Really fascinating. If you can do all the things the encyclopedia says you can do then you could prove a real asset to us in the whole affair. Seems to me your talents are probably being wasted in our photo room…(he paused, then went on to correct himself)… but of course that's not true since you are indeed the one who discovered these missile launchers from the photos in the first place. Thank god you were there.

Me: Yes sir, I'm glad I was there too. (and from the bottom of my heart I wished I was back there now doing my boring job, nobody bothering me, my personnel file still gathering dust.)

McC: Yes, this Eidetic thing really is a special sort of gift, isn't it?

Me: (I just nodded.)

McC: (changing the subject drastically) Have you ever parachuted from a plane at night Edwards?

Me: God no!

McC: Are you a good swimmer?

Me: Yes. Pretty much. Probably.

McC: Your personnel file says you speak fluent Spanish. Is that right?

Me: Yes sir. I speak four languages besides English. I'm good with languages.

McC. You are a young guy. Twenty-two your file says. You seem fit. Are you fit Edwards?

Me: Yes sir. I think so. Pretty fit.

McC: Have you ever camped out? Overnight say? In the woods?

Me: Yes sir. I was a Boy Scout sir, but I found it really boring so I quit.

McCone had a good laugh at that and glanced at Lansdale as he did.

McC: We'll I'm pretty sure that what we have in mind you will not find boring. Have you ever heard of the Pathfinders? Of the CIA's 'Pathfinder' program? Of course, you haven't because it is 'Top Secret.' But it is an interesting approach to intelligence gathering.

Me: No sir, I've never heard of it. (Then I felt rather stupid because he had already answered his own question for me.)

McC: Actually, it is General Lansdale's program. I'll let him explain it.

L: It goes all the way back to WWII and the OSS and the French Resistance. And right now it goes back to you and your personnel file and your special memory gift. Have you ever seen that grcat old Hitchcock movie *The 39 Steps*, Edwards?

This whole meeting had turned into an interrogation of my personnel file and my Eidetic Memory. The ricocheting questions were setting my head aspin and leaving me wondering where all of this was going. And now we were talking about old movies. It was getting really bizarre. But strangely enough, the Hitchcock movie he had asked me about was actually one I had indeed seen in an undergraduate film studies class. It had been indelibly etched (just like everything else) in my Eidetic Memory bank. And, all of a sudden, I thought I knew where this whole colloquy was going, what McCone and Lansdale had in store for me.

Me: Yes, I have seen *The 39 Steps*.

L: Really. I hadn't expected that you had. I thought I might have to explain it to you. Do you remember its plot?

Me.: Yes sir. I remember everything.

L: Then you remember the spy character, Mr. Memory.

Me: Yes, I do. He doesn't have to copy or film stolen secret documents. He can just recognize them at a glance.

L: Yes, that's it. That's what we want you to do for us. But not documents. Rather landscapes, terrain, ordinance, machines. Whatever you observe down to the smallest detail.

McC: Edwards, we want you to be our 'Pathfinder.' We want to put you into Cuba to be our eyes, ears, boots on the ground, around those missile launcher sites. We are especially interested in the numbers down there. How many launchers? How many missiles? How many Russians? The Cubans don't know how to fire missiles.

L: The Pathfinders are only in the field in time-sensitive situations, when we need accurate intel right now, immediately. We only use Pathfinders for two or three days. They collect all the intel they can in that short time and then we exfiltrate them out. They don't take notes or pictures or anything that will tip anyone off that they are spies. They just watch and listen and collect intel in their memories. Thus, it is essential that they don't get captured or killed. Then they come back and tell it all to us. With your memory you will make a perfect Pathfinder.

McC: You see, Edwards, we don't have time to train you for this. That's why I asked you all those questions before. You see, we want to drop you into Cuba tomorrow if the President okay's it.

It seems that it had all already been decided. I was to be their "Pathfinder." They had put it all to me in a way that I could hardly refuse. Only then did they ask me if I would do it.

McC: You'll do it for us, won't you Edwards? The president himself will be reading your file tonight.

L: When you come back, your whole situation with us, your job, your pay scale, your whole government status will be changed. Totally enhanced. Totally.

McC: He's right Edwards, your whole life will be transformed after you complete this mission. You will have performed an extraordinary service to your country. You will be a Cold War hero of the first order.

I, of course, had not the slightest idea what a "Cold War hero of the first order" might be or exactly what my "extraordinary service to my country" might entail or even exactly what my "mission" might be, but they had me in so deep that I knew there was no way I could refuse. I couldn't even envision how my life would be so drastically changed if I did their bidding, completed their mission in Cuba. All I knew is that almost immediately I heard myself saying…

Me: Yes, I'll do it.

McC: Excellent Edwards. I knew you would come through for us and the President of your country.

L: You are the perfect man for this job, for the Pathfinders program. With your memory you are invaluable to us.

McC: OK, you two, go back to your photo room and pack up. If the President approves our plan you will be briefed and supplied at 0800 tomorrow morning. Dismissed. (that last from McCone rather threw me as it implied that I was now in the military under his command).

Captain Bankston and I went back to the Photo Room and packed everything up. We slept in a worker's dormitory that night with the film close at hand. The next morning an armed Marine arrived at 0730 to escort us and our files to our destination in "Spookland" as the CIA section was commonly designated by the rest of the less spooky denizens of the Pentagon. McCone and Lansdale were waiting for us behind a table in a nondescript conference room. On the table were a pile of clothes, a tattered backpack, and a badly stained and torn wide brimmed straw hat. A map of Cuba also laid out on the table with areas circled and roads marked.

L: Here Edwards, change into these clothes. Starting now you are a Cuban fieldworker looking for work on a tobacco plantation. The whole time you are in Cuba you will be on foot except for one journey by bus between the two circled areas on the map. (which he thumped with a decisive finger).

McC: You will not have a single thing on your person that will expose your identity as an American spy. You will simply be a common laborer looking for work.

L: Inevitably as you pass close by the missile launching facilities you will be stopped and questioned. Here is a script for you to help you answer any questions you might be asked. Memorize it. (I think he failed to realize how obtuse his last words were. I read it through once and handed it back to him. Both he and McCone looked at me unbelievingly. Their realization of what I had just done gave me great satisfaction).

Once I had changed into the Cuban peasant clothing, we turned to the maps.

McC: From your report, there are the two areas that we would like you to approach and observe. Count everything. OK? The numbers of ordinance and men will be especially valuable to us.

L: We will drop you by fast boat here. (he tapped a place on the north east coast near the town of Santa Clara and traced his finger on a road inland toward the first circled area on the map). You will go on foot to here and observe this first launch site. Then you will back track to the town of Santa Clara and take the first west bound bus to the area of Ciego de Avila where the second launch site is located.

This time General Lansdale didn't make the same mistake of telling me to memorize the map. He must have realized that I had already done that long minutes ago when we first turned to look closely at it.

L (continued): Exactly three days after we drop you ashore return to the same beach and our boat will pick you up at exactly 2100 hours. If you are not there the first night the boat will return the next night at the same time. If you are not there then, we will assume that you are either dead or arrested.

And with that heartening note my briefing was done. They turned to Captain Bankston and ordered him to escort me to the boat, then to the drop point on the beach in Cuba, then to remain with the boat in Key West, then to pick me up on my exfiltration night. With that the two of us were once again dismissed and told to catch our plane, an Air Force cargo craft, at 1400 hours for our shuttle to Key West from whence my great adventure was to begin.

Great adventure or not, perfectly adopted for the job or not, frankly I was terrified. I told Captain Bankston I just wanted to be alone for awhile before the car to the airstrip picked us up. He took me to a small enclosed garden. He never let me out of his sight, standing inside the glass door, as I stepped out into the August sunlight of the little garden and walked across to a stone bench set against a concrete wall with anemic ivy trying to grow up it.

The sun was warm and welcoming. The air humid and heavy. The skin of my face felt the high summer air. It was the only skin uncovered by the peasant costume they had tricked me out in. *Good lord what have I gotten myself into.* I thought. *Those damn aerial photos.* I still wasn't absolutely certain what I had found. *What does it mean? How important is it? Why have they got such screaming hard-ons for it?* I wish I had never seen those pictures. As I sat on the bench in the August sun I wished I had never heard of Eidetic Memory. I wished I had never gotten this strange gift. On the outside, as Captain Bankston kept his eye on me, I looked fine, just sitting enjoying the summer sunshine, but inside I was in a five-alarm panic. *How did I get myself into this mess?* Then it came to me. *Lenny! This was all Lenny's fault. He was the one who had gotten me involved with the Air Force, with the aerial photos, now with the spooks. If it hadn't been for Lenny I never would have been here in this mess.* As soon as I placed the blame on my best friend, I knew that I was wrong. It really wasn't Lenny's fault at all. It was my own fault, me and my damn freakish memory. Being Eidetic was a gift alright, but it could also be a curse. Then Captain Bankston opened the door and motioned to me. I grabbed my backpack and he escorted me to the car that took us to the airport and the plane that took us to Key West that took us to the long sleek fast boat that fired its powerful engines and sent us skating across the waves to Cuba.

My three days in Cuba from the moment I waded ashore from that fast boat until I ran into the sea and jumped back aboard were the tensest, most terrifying, most alert and sensually cognizant days of my life. Cuba was a hot, sun-baked, mosquito and bottle fly infested hell on earth made all the worse by the constant throbbing threat within my mind of imminent capture and torture and execution at the hands of brutal mustachioed monsters of the Cuban version of the Russian KGB. At least that was the whole scenario that my runaway imagination conjured up to plague me the whole time I was on the island. In reality it was nothing like that. My three days as a Pathfinder mainly consisted of a lot of hiking along inferno-hot dusty roads or under a fetid canopy of dried out palm forest or through grey rocky hillsides. I saw a number of tobacco plantations and fields of sugar cane, but my actual spying time looking at the missile launching emplacements consisted of mere minutes.

When I got to the first site some ten miles outside of the town of Santa Clara, I at first simply walked by it on the road, registered what I saw, and kept on going for at least another mile. Luckily, I could see almost the whole site from the road. What I saw was a large clearing of graded dirt with a wire fence around it. Not a chain-link fence or an electric metal fence or even a barbed wire fence, but just a plain three strand wire fence that wouldn't even keep the cows in or the coyotes out back home. In other words, it was all pretty primitive which told me that the builders of the site were in a hurry to get on with the other kinds of construction that I observed: the framing and pouring of concrete slabs, the digging of post holes for the hanging of camouflage netting, the cutting of palm fronds off of the trees around the encampment, the building of a pole barn back in the jungle probably to house the troops that would staff the site. The soldiers in residence were outnumbered by the workmen. I presumed that the workmen were some of Castro's rebels who knew how to work construction. The soldiers were of two identities. In brown unmarked shirts and short pants, some wearing red berets and carrying carbines (or having them propped against trees nearby) were more formal members of Castro's army. In heavier black shirts with chevrons on the sleeves, some even with medals pinned to their breasts, were what clearly were Russian soldiers. I counted as many as I could on my first pass then confirmed my count on my second pass two hours later: 27 workmen. 16 Cuban Army soldiers, 10 Russians. They seemed to be building five flat concrete slabs approximately 10 yards square. And, most importantly, I could see the dark shadows of three large vehicles or machines parked back under the trees and camouflaged by palm fronds. These I presumed were the launchers I had seen on the aerial photos. After my two passes, I fled the site like a thief leaving the scene of his crime, walking as fast as I could without running and drawing attention to myself. The whole time as I fled that site sirens and armed police were converging upon me inside my head. When I reached the town, a really rather large, spread-out town, of Santa Clara, I finally breathed a little easier. I was no longer alone on the road, vulnerable to being discovered for what I really was. My first foray as a Pathfinder had been pretty successful I thought. I hadn't been stopped or searched or discovered or arrested and I had actually gathered the intel that I thought McCone and Lansdale (and I would learn much later President Kennedy) wanted. That evening I took a bus out of Santa Clara and rode bumpily on rutted roads through the night to Ciego del Avila, another burgeoning town much like Santa Clara. This day did not go as smoothly as had my first.

This day started well with a good breakfast of eggs and beans and tortillas in a tiny bodega in the town. My hike to the launch site on the map they had shown me back in Washington was longer than the first day's march from my landing point on the beach to the building site, about fifteen miles I calculated using the sun as my timepiece. When I got to the vicinity of the site it was literally out of sight. It was hidden down a newly cleared, heavily rutted, dirt road into the overhanging jungle. I knew I couldn't approach the site down that road. It was clearly the only way in or out of the site and would surely be guarded by soldiers with rifles who would shoot anyone on sight who didn't belong. In other words, me. This was how my mind was working, quite clearly I felt (if perhaps somewhat melodramatically). They probably wouldn't shoot me on sight. They would probably just capture me so they could torture me horribly, and then shoot me. So, I didn't go down that road.

Instead, I struck off into the jungle. Not such a big deal you may think. Well, then you've never tried, under pressure of discovery and death, to make your way through a Cuban jungle without benefit of a machete or even a Swiss Army knife. It was unbelievably slow going and, on the way, while being attacked by every species of biting insect endemic to the Cuban jungle, my eyes kept scanning the ground, the trees, the thick foliage on every side for panthers, jaguars, crocodiles and snakes ready to leap out or slither out at me. It seemed forever, but I finally saw a clearing ahead of me. I found a vantage point, hugged a thick palm tree trunk, and started to count. 5 missile launchers under camouflage netting, 8 concrete pads all looking to be finished and ready for use, an open-sided building filled with cots covered by mosquito netting. Five Castro Army soldiers carrying carbines sitting on tree stumps around the encampment. 12 Russians in various stages of repose as if in waiting for some order to be given, for something to happen that would propel them into action. My counting done I retraced my steps through that hellish jungle and regained the main road back into Ciego del Avila.

My mission was basically accomplished. My intel was eternally stored in my Eidetic Memory. Feeling safe for the first time since I landed on this cursed island, I finally had the time and the leisure (if that is what you can call being an American spy behind the lines in a hostile country) to actually think about and analyze what I had seen, the intel I had actually collected. The one thing that leapt to the surface of my mind strangely enough was something that wasn't there. As I trudged that dusty road back to the town I realized that on either side of the launching sites I had never seen any missiles. That could only mean that they weren't here yet. Probably that was what the Russians at the second, more finished, site were waiting for. I slept that night under a bridge abutment in Ciego del Avila and the next morning took the first bus to Santa Clara. Leaving the bus, I never even paused before heading out of town. I arrived at the beach five hours before my pick-up time. I curled under a sun-warmed rock on the shore and waited. My boat arrived right on time and I ran to it through the surf like a man running toward salvation and his well-earned place in heaven. It was as if the whole world around me had been transformed and I was a new person, freed, alive, a survivor, transubstantiated.

I was back in the Pentagon in Washington in a matter of hours, showered, back in my own clothes, all the bites and welts on my skin tended to by the military doctors, ready for my debriefing with Mc-Cone and Lansdale. It lasted for two hours. I poured out to them every image, every sound, every number, every single perception of Cuba that was etched on my memory. Actually, I think they were somewhat amazed at what they got. They recorded it all on a tape recorder which was immediately transcribed by a security-cleared Pentagon typist into reports I imagined to be distributed to the President and his advisors. At the end of it, McCone looked at Lansdale and then turned to me.

McC: Edwards, well done, amazing, we've never had a Pathfinder debriefing like this one before. Simply amazing. Stand down now. Rest up. Relax. We will get back to you later if we need you again.

And that was it. I didn't hear from them again for weeks, after the Cuban Missile Crisis was done and gone. But I never went back to the Photo Room again either.

CHAPTER 2: CETOLOGY

I'd like to tell you that my Cuba Pathfinder expedition was some kind of Hemingway adventure of the sort they make highly suspenseful movies about, all spy skulking and death-defying escapes and heart-stopping checkpoint interrogations and face-offs with ruthless Russian KGB agents. But it wasn't at all. The whole mission was actually un-eventful. In my peasant disguise I was pretty much invisible like all the rest of the poor people there. I was never stopped, never questioned. I barely talked to any other people. Hardly used my good Spanish at all. Invisible. Isn't that what a good spy is supposed to be? The second day I actually slept on the bus with children and chickens squawking all around me.

I think that it all just happened so fast that it never really sank in what I was doing. When it was all over, I thought that there truly must be something wrong with me. Down there I wasn't really afraid or tense or even all that excited. My pulse wasn't racing all the time. I wasn't always looking over my shoulder. I was just doing what I was told, watching and counting, as fast as I could so I could get the hell out of that mosquito-infested hell hole. I must say though that I was really glad to see that fast boat come plunging and bouncing over the dark waves into shore the night of my pick-up.

And also, after it was all over and I thought back on what I had done, I realized that the real adventure was my finding the missile launchers in the photos in the first place. Probably a lot of military guys, certainly my friend Lenny, had the qualifications to be a much better Pathfinder spy than I, but I couldn't help thinking that maybe I was the only one who had the precise qualifications to find those Rus-sian missile launchers. I could see them in my mind's eye thanks to the connections between the past and the present that only my Eidetic Memory could make. I was the only one who could see that those deep ruts weren't there the week before, that the jungle was a different shade of black and white than it had been, that the blocky shapes in the pho-tos were actually what they actually were. That was my adventure and I realized that it was all due to this strange gift, this eerie way of seeing and remembering what I was blessed with.

Of course, all that said, I had already placed the blame for this whole mess or adventure or transubstantiating epiphany of a moment (to use James Joyce's word) on my old buddy Lenny, who, unbeknownst to me, was about to come back, unbidden, into my life in a big way. Lenny had been the one, after grad school, who, over beers, had convinced me to go into government work rather than be an assistant professor or a junior diplomat. Lenny was the one who talked me into that photo lab where my Eidetic Memory could work out on the monkey bars of those worldwide aerial photographs. So maybe this is as good a time as any to tell you about Lenny and the strange sort of wizardly effect he has had on my life. Yes, in a way, Lenny was like a wizard for me, able to wave his magic wand, plant things in my mind that would ultimately guide my actions. In fact, it was Lenny who first discovered that I had my Eidetic Memory.

Lenny and I grew up together, went to high school and college together, right up until about age seventeen. That was when I started pulling away from him academically and he started scrambling to keep up. I graduated from high school in two years. It took Lenny three and a half to get out. We did both end up at Purdue together, were roommates for a year actually, though he was only a sophomore when I graduated and decided to go to Georgetown and study International Relations in the school of Foreign Service. I guess we had a sort of intellectual competition going, but due to my special gift Lenny never really had much of a chance. My Eidetic Memory made it a drastically uphill playing field for him. I should also add that in high school Lenny had been a star football and basketball player. I was the local nerd, egghead, brainiac, whatever all the generations since our 1950's might have labeled my kind of person. But Lenny and I had grown up on farms right next to each other and, despite his impressive athlete's physique and his BMOC popularity in high school and college, we had always been the closest of friends and that never changed. Nonetheless, Lenny was (and is) a really pretty smart guy. When we were in school he was always reading. He was the only student I ever met in those college years who actually read all of the books on our professors' "suggested reading lists," those long bibliographies attached to their syllabi that were there to support the "required reading list" for the course. Hell, most of the students in my classes didn't even read the required texts. But Lenny did. As a result, he was a fountain of esoteric knowledge, of interesting facts and events and people. He knew all kinds of stuff that you wouldn't expect ordinary college students to know. In fact, Lenny was how I found out about my gift. Lenny was the one who defined it for me, named it for me, made me see for the first time why I was so different from everyone else, why I had such an easy time in school while everyone else actually had to study, why I seemed to look at and register the world around us so differently than everyone else. Until Lenny named it, my gift, I'll tell you honestly, I had no clue. I really had no idea that I had it. I didn't even know what it was until one day in college when I was on a long bike ride with Lenny and two of our other friends.

The four of us college pals—me, Al, Reggie, and of course Lenny—all took off on our bikes one sunny spring afternoon from the University to ride the country roads to a catfish house about ten miles away. Fried catfish, you see, was one of Indiana's two state delicacies, the other being fried oversized pork tenderloins. As you might have noticed, "fried" seems to be the major form of gourmet preparation practiced in restaurants in the state of Indiana. As those delightfully droll Hoosiers say: "If you don't fry it, it ain't cooked!" That might well be the Indiana state motto contending only with the Latin phrase "Yocalis Cow Tippus" which hangs from the rearview mirrors of every rusty pick-up truck statewide. But I digress. Upon our arrival at our catfish house, we planned to drink beer and stuff ourselves with the Indiana State fish most of the afternoon, and then pedal unsteadily back. We got there about two o'clock and immediately upon looking at the menu Reggie realized he didn't have his glasses.

"How the hell could you lose your glasses?" Lenny barked at him.

"Yeah," Al joined the fun, "couldn't you see that you couldn't see?"

"Bite me! I'll bet they fell off my bike seat while I was putting a new tube in that flat tire,"

About halfway into the ride Reggie's front tire had hit something sharp and blown out. No big deal. We all replaced tubes in our English bikes all the time. This was, of course, before the age of mountain bikes and heavy-duty inner tubes.

Me: I remember that, you pulled over next to the second telephone pole right after we made that sharp left turn off of the road that runs along the river. Your tire went flat and you pulled your bike over. You lowered the kick stand and bended down to check out the tire. Your glass case fell out of your shirt pocket then. You picked it up off the ground and sat it on the bike seat. My question is why weren't you wearing your glasses.?

R: I had on my sunglasses. I remember it all now.

Me: It was right in front of a faded white farmhouse with a red brick chimney and a blue shingle roof. (I could see it clear as day) Second telephone pole from the turn.

L: Faded white? Really? (Lenny mocked me)

R: Crap, now I have to ride back there and find them. It's gotta be four or five miles.

L: Aw hell, Reggie, I'll ride with you. (Lenny, to the surprise of all of us, volunteered) Won't take us long. I want to check something out anyway.

The two of them set off pedaling and Al and I ordered our beers. Lenny was right. It didn't take them long at all. But what happened next changed my whole life, answered a lot of questions I had been asking myself for years, explained why school, even college, had come so easy to me.

As we sat there drinking beer and eating catfish on a picnic table outside the place as the afternoon glittered around us, Lenny looked at me in a strange, actually pretty creepy, way.

L: You know Mikey, it was exactly like you said. Second pole. House with blue roof. The whole deal. Fucking exactly. Reggie's glass case was sitting right there on the ground.

Me: So?

Lenny seemed to think that whole event was something out of the ordinary. He didn't say anything for a minute. He was thinking it through.

L: I've been taking this psychology class this semester just for the hell of it, (let me just cut in here to say that Lenny and I were both Criminology majors so Psyche wouldn't have been that far out of our ballpark) and we spent about two weeks just talking about the different kinds of memory.

All of us around the table between sips of beer were wondering where this was going.

L: Mikey, you've got an Eidetic Memory.

Me: What the hell is that?

Honestly. I had no idea. Until he said that, I had never even heard the term before.

By this time Lenny was sort of lost in a reverie, in another world, not really listening to me? "That really explains a lot," Lenny said to himself, out loud but not to us.

Me: Earth to Lenny, what did you say I've got?

L: You've got an Eidetic Memory. That's why I rode back with Reggie. I wanted to check it out.

Me: Is that good? What is it?

A: Here we go. (Al rolled his eyes)

R: You had to ask. (Reggie poked me)

You see, we could all see it coming, one of Lenny's lectures. Lenny knew all kinds of weird shit that he had found in books that nobody else had even the slightest inclination to read. And he loved to lecture on the esoterica that he picked up and that none of us particularly cared about. But, as he perked up and entered lecture mode this time, he actually had my full attention. Al and Reggie had pretty much gone back to their beers because this particular lecture of Lenny's seemed aimed directly at me.

L: My Psych prof ran us through the whole memory playbook in that class. There are all sorts of kinds of memory—long term, short term, implicit, explicit, episodic, semantic, sensory—and that's not even all of them.

Al leaning in with an exaggerated yawn.

Reggie loudly simulating snoring.

But Lenny and I just ignored them and they went back to their beers.

L: A lot of people talk about 'Photographic Memory' but very few people know about 'Eidetic Memory.' In fact, the two are often confused. I don't really understand it, but Eidetic Memory is like a hundred times more powerful than Photographic Memory.

Today, in the 21st Century, we'd probably say that Eidetic Memory is like Photographic Memory on steroids, but there weren't any steroids back then so that metaphor just wasn't available. But here is the even more interesting, or perhaps eerie, extension of Lenny's long-ago lecture on the different kinds of memory. When I first got the idea for writing this book I went and googled "kinds of memory" and I found one that Lenny hadn't mentioned that day at the picnic table with the guys and the fish and the beer. There is a more recently explored kind of memory they call "Highly Superior Autobiographical Memory (HSAM)." People with this type remember in detail everything they did on any certain day in their past life. Now, as I write, I think I realize that not only am I an Eidetic but I also have HSAM available to me for this particular writing task. But back to that bike ride to the fish house.

Me: And you think I've got this?

L: I'm dead certain you've got it. You're an Eidetic, Mikey. You're a memory freak. You see things differently than everyone else. You remember everything you see or hear or touch or smell in perfect detail.

At that moment, across the picnic table from the boys, I realized that I had remembered the scene on the road with the pole and the farmhouse and Reggie's glasses in perfect detail and, even weirder, I could call up that scene in my mind again and actually see it in all that same detail as I had seen it in my memory. Maybe Lenny was right. Maybe I was one of those Eidetic freaks. It took me a while to get used to that idea. In fact, later, after we got back that afternoon, I went to the Encyclopedia Britannica (the same source that Mr. McCone would consult about me years later) and to Webster's Dictionary and this is what I found:

Eidetic: 1) relating to or denoting mental images having universal vividness or detail as if actually visible. 2) (noun) a person able to form or recall Eidetic images.

As I would come to know after that day of Lenny's big discovery, Mr. Webster and Mr. Britannica's definitions of my gift certainly didn't do justice to it. In a rather short time as I graduated from college then got my Ph.D. at Georgetown I not only constantly experienced the power of my Eidetic Memory, but I also studied it, challenged it, constantly tested it against the world around me, against the people I met, against the books I read, and the things I observed. Thus, by the time I took that job with the government in the Pentagon photo room I was pretty aware of just what my Eidetic Memory could do, what kind of power it had. It was like an extremely powerful pair of binoculars that increased my awareness of everything around me.

Awareness. That is a pretty good place to start. Have you ever noticed how most people, wandering haplessly through the world, are almost totally unaware. Most people just don't pay attention at all—to the world, to others, to their own sensations, to what they see and hear and touch and taste. Distracted? Daydreaming? Tunnel-visioned? They just don't register the whole complex panorama of the reality that surrounds them. Like Lenny and Al and Reggie. When we stopped to fix that tire back on the road, none of them saw the telephone poles or the farmhouse. None of them registered the colors or the movements of the others. In other words, none of them collected the necessary data for memory to accurately recreate the scene. But me! Today, more than fifty years later, I can still see that scene on the road as if I was still there, as if it was only yesterday. That is what Eidetic Memory is all about. It pays attention to everything. It is really almost all-seeing and is certainly all-remembering. It sort of possesses approximate powers to those powers that are usually only attributed to God.

Memories. They are the connections to the past that everyone has. But mine were so much better more detailed than anyone else's. And my memories had a half-life like radium and the accuracy, the zoom capability, of the most expensive camera. An Eidetic Memory is like a Wellsian time machine or a Star Trek transporter. It can move you back and forth in time—present to past and past back to present. Unfortunately, it hasn't the power to thrust you into the future. And beyond that weakness, Eidetic Memory is incapable of forgetting. With an ordinary memory, time, often a really short span of time, offers one the power to forget. An ordinary memory allows one to simply erase, as off of one of those chalk-dusted blackboards that we had in every schoolroom back in the fifties and sixties of the last century. But Eidetic Memory won't allow one to forget anything, no erasure here. One's memories are always there in total visual detail. An Eidetic doesn't possess the luxury that most people have of just turning off your mind, of conveniently forgetting.

So, you see, an Eidetic Memory can be both a blessing and a curse. Certainly, Eidetic Memory possesses a kind of super awareness. It is susceptible to all of the good and bad that is generated out of the rush of everyday life. It pays close attention to everything but I am not sure that is always such a good thing. Yes, it is totally and astutely aware of all that goes on around it, but its problem is that it can't erase any of it, clean the blackboard. A problem with being Eidetic is that you are always tied to, anchored in, knee deep in the past. This could be really useful (as in my aerial photos discovery or my ability to remember every word my professors spoke or the text books I read), but, as I said, it can also be a curse. There are times when I wish I could just shut off my memory, wipe clean all the images that pulse through it. Don't get me wrong. I am well aware of how lucky I am to have my special power. And yet I can't help wishing sometimes that every minute, every second of my past life, wasn't so graphically clear. So that is why I acknowledge that my freakish memory is also at times a curse.

And I find it really ironic that my Eidetic Memory was diagnosed that summer afternoon on that bike ride by, of all people, Lenny. When I say 'diagnosed' I make it sound like Lenny had defined a disease. But rather, what Lenny saw in me was not anything like a disease, but was just something I had, like a birthmark, something that was there and wasn't going away and that I had no control over. And it was certainly ironic in that my friend Lenny had just recently discovered a new word and had found a living example of it in his best friend. When he gave me my Eidetic Memory, gave it a name, he meant it as a very positive thing, a real compliment. And, as he said right at the moment he named it. It really did explain a lot.

One thing it explained, and the more I thought about it came through to me loud and clear, was how very different I was from everyone else. It explained my awkwardness around other people, my tense awareness of everything that was going on around me, my absolute need to spend periods of every day alone in a dark room with as little stimulus as possible around me. Let me give you a very clear example. I am a terrible driver. If I could advise you, don't ever get in a car driven by an Eidetic. An Eidetic driver can never be satisfied with keeping his eyes on the road, is not capable of focusing solely on the traffic lane lines on the roadway. The Eidetic driver's eye and head are constantly panning, as if on a swivel, back and forth, one side to another, being sure not to miss anything in front, beside, even behind (which takes both eyes off the road even with the mirrors). The result is an erratic bobbing and weaving, caroming, progress along the street or, heaven forbid, a crowded highway. I realized the danger to myself and others of this Eidetic handicap quite early on and decided that the acute awareness of the world around me that my Eidetic Memory demanded in some ways (automobile driving being one of them) had to be accommodated because it simply couldn't be denied, wasn't going away. So, I started taking the bus, and I have ever since. Of course, as I moved to bigger cities, the bus became the subway and the subway became the commuter train, and ultimately, way back here in the 21st Century, I became totally reliant on Uber to get me where I wanted to be when I needed to be there. Public transportation of all these sorts allowed me to sit quietly and swivel my head and eyes as much as my Eidetic awareness demanded without fear of fender-benders, road rage from cut-off other drivers, or, god forbid, head-on collisions causing fiery conflagrations and multi-car pile-ups with high loss of other innocent people's lives. However, I must admit that there did come a time when I did take up driving on a rather extended level. It had to do with both geography and circumstance. The geography was the American west and the circumstance was my flight from the government east. But I get ahead of myself.

I'm sorry. I'm sure that this chapter reads like those boring "Cetology" chapters in *Moby Dick*. You know, those chapters interspersed with the voyage of *The Pequod* that told you everything you would ever want to know about a whale's mammoth penis. But I feel now, more than fifty years later, that I clearly understand (as I really didn't way back then) what my gift is and how it works and its power (for better or for worse). I'm just trying to give you a sense, before I go back to the twisted trail of my life, a sense of the process I had to go through in coming to understanding my Eidetic existence. It all started with that first discovery on that bike ride with my buddy Lenny and it has progressed to now as I sit here fifty-some years later trying to write this book. OK, yes, boring "Cetology" perhaps, but "PAY ATTENTION!" This chapter (and perhaps others like it down the road in this manuscript) is important for what this whole story is about.

Oh, the hell with it! I'll tell you what it is mostly about right now. It's about how memory is our only powerful weapon against death. OK, there you have it. Oh damn, strike that sentence. It is incomprehensible this early in my narrative anyway. All you have read so far are two anecdotes about me and my memory "strolling down the avenue" as the old song goes. But so far you have no idea of the utterly transubstantiating effect my memory would have on my life. Neither did I at that point. On that far-off day when Lenny got all excited about my gift, I had not the slightest inkling of how it would change my life, not just once or twice, but in the course of my multiple lives in the fifty-some years since.

Suffice to say this story that I am trying to set down at this late date is my memory piece, my remembrance of things past. Just like *Moby Dick* is Ismael's memory piece, or *The Rhyme of the Ancient Mariner* or *Heart of Darkness* or *The Great Gatsby* or *Dancing at Lugnasa* or *Great Expectations* or hundreds of other literary narratives or movies, like *Apocalypse Now* or *Little Big Man*, where a narrator looks back into the past and creates or recreates himself as a character in a story. The story may approach truth or may deconstruct into fiction, but no matter how it hits paper it is still a memory piece and memory (for better or worse) is still at work. But no matter what form it takes, every memory piece ends up searching the past to find out what impelled the direction that the central character's life took. That narrator, whether reliable or unreliable, is still aware that everything in the past totally changed the direction of his or her life. Now, imagine how a memory piece written by an Eidetic might take shape. Imagine its accuracy, its attention to detail, its total awareness of everything around its story, its central character, its style. Now that would be some memory piece. That would be a really reliable narrator.

CHAPTER 3: DALLAS

After I got back from Cuba, for the next ten days or so, I really did nothing, except for one meeting that I will never forget. That was dumb. I never forget anything. What I meant to say was except for one meeting that was especially memorable. Lansdale and McCone, in best cloak-and-dagger tradecraft, led me through some steam tunnels under Pennsylvania Avenue and right into the basement of the White House. I was ushered into a conference room with a bunch of men in grey and black suits and a bunch of generals in full uniform heavily be-medaled. And right there, sitting at the head of the table in person he was, President Kennedy himself. Mr. McCone gave me a general introduction to the room and then the President himself spoke right to me: "Mr. Edwards, I've heard a lot about you in the last few days and I've decided that you could be a living model for 'what you can do for your country' from my Inauguration speech." He spoke slowly in that broadly accented, patrician, New England, dialect, and then he started a round of applause for me that everyone in the room joined in on.

When the clapping receded, the President nodded to McCone and my real purpose for being there took center stage: "Mr. Edwards, we would like you to look at some more photographs for us and give us your analysis."

Then the Chief of Staff of the Navy spoke up: "Mr. Edwards. These are aerial photos of a convoy of Russian ships that are steaming at full speed for Cuba." And he motioned for me to take a position at the table on his right shoulder where about fifteen photos were already lined up. "It's as you can see," the Admiral continued, "they are cargo frigates and on their decks are a number of sets of tarp-covered material. Naturally, we can't see through the tarps to identify what they are hiding though we certainly have out suspicions. So," and he paused, "we hoped that your sharp eyes and your special skills might be able to get us a bit closer to identifying what's under those tarps."

I nodded. I still hadn't uttered a single word since I entered the room. All of those people probably thought that I was either a mute or a hillbilly so backward that I couldn't put a simple sentence together.

In reality, I was just stunned, overwhelmed. For God's sake, I was in the same room as the President. Thank god they gave me a job to do because it covered up my terror. I bent to the familiar task of reading their aerial photos. Doing that jolted me back on track. To my relief, as I took in the line-up of ship photos, I stepped back into my element, found some comfort in doing something that I knew I could do well, that I knew no one else could do as well as me. Finally, I found my voice.

"Since they are all Russian ships sailing toward Cuba I'm sure you must suspect that they are carrying missiles to arm those rocket launchers that are already in place," I stated the obvious. "Does anyone have a ruler?"

People shuffled around, pulling out drawers in the table, until finally one man ran out of the room and returned almost immediately waving a common foot-long classroom ruler probably yanked from some nearby secretary's desk drawer.

Again, I bent to the photos and took a number of measurements of the tarp-covered stacks on the decks of the ships. On a handy note pad I made some rudimentary calculations to determine the photo's scale and the tarp's relation to it. Then I was ready to give them this information. Let me preface that information by saying that it was not at all a guess on my part. I was absolutely certain.

"These two ships have stacked two deep and four across two stacks each of Russian SS-4 medium range missiles. These two ships here, you see, have stacks that are shorter in length and wider, probably six across. They too are two-deep stacked. These I am certain are R-14 intermediate range missiles. So, doing the math, these four ships have 16 SS-4s and 24 R-14s. By my measurements calculated to scale of the photos, I am very certain that is what you've got beneath those tarps."

Only then did I look up from my task and let my eyes rather quickly glance around the room at my listeners. They were quiet. Some of their mouths were open. Some of their eyes were wide and staring. Some others were looking at each other sort of unbelieving. I think they might have thought that I had some form of x-ray vision of the sort only Superman possessed.

"OK then, Mr. Edwards, really we can't thank you enough. You have done a great service to your country," it was the Admiral speaking and it was clear he was dismissing me. I even started to back away from the table in hopes of quickly making my escape out the door.

"Mr. Edwards," President Kennedy's voice stopped me in my tracks, "after this whole Cuban mess is over we will be in contact with you again. Well done."

And that was it. Mr. McCone stayed in the room and General Lansdale took me back to my hotel, and the Cuban Missile Crisis wended its complex way toward resolution.

As I said earlier, aside from that one brief meeting, after I got back from my Pathfinder incursion in Cuba, for the next ten days or so I really did nothing. The CIA set me and Captain Bankston up in a really nice Washington hotel, and we waited. Why the Captain had to be there with me I don't really know unless the CIA wanted to make sure that I didn't talk to anyone about all of this stuff that was going on. There still had been no news coverage or public discussion of nuclear weapons in Cuba. That hotel had a library and I ended up reading some spy novels, James Bond novels, those novels with all of their gimmicks and gizmos and gadgets, their fast cars and loose women, their constant suspense and danger and engagement often hand-to-hand, with the enemy spies. I had immediate first-hand experience that this spy game was nothing like that. Rather, from just having come back from Cuba, I knew that spying was a plodding, silent, physically dirty, even bug-infested game. My spy experience was like hiking through hell with nowhere to sleep at night. But mostly it was all about being alone in a hostile world. I must admit though that James Bond would have liked the fast boat that got me to Cuba and back.

It was almost a month after my trip to Cuba and about ten days after the so-called Cuban Missile Crisis was resolved (thanks to President Kennedy's negotiation skills and his naval blockade) that my buddy Lenny came looking for me. By this time, I was just sitting around waiting at a desk in the Air Force assignment office of the Pentagon. After that whole Cuba adventure, I had become a sort of Intel superstar and I had to participate in a number of debriefing meetings with all sorts of military types some of whom wanted me to join their photo-spying operations. It seems that the different military services and the CIA were all pretty good at collecting photo intel and developing their pictures, but they weren't very good at understanding them. That's where I came in. All the military spooks fully believed that I was the only one capable of analyzing and interpreting their visual data. Maybe they were right. Who knows? As for me, I just thought it was all pretty stupid. Actually, how I came to be the focus of so much attention to this day remains as much a mystery to me as what my beloved wife saw in me or where my Eidetic Memory came from. After a while I actually got a little homesick for my old desk in the Air Force photo room. And then Lenny showed up, the proverbial bad penny.

Lenny and I went down to the cafeteria and had an extremely interesting lunch. I found out what he was doing and he let me know that he knew absolutely everything about what I had been doing. I guess it is about time that I tell you all about Lenny because he was the one who got me into all of this military stuff in the first place. Like I said before, he was really a pretty smart guy plus he was big, all of 6'4" and probably 230, and a very good all-sport athlete. I graduated from Purdue before he did and we sort of lost track of each other for a while when I went off to get my Ph.D. at Georgetown. During that time, by hook or by crook, Lenny ended up in the U.S. Secret Service, that branch of the government who are the "Guardians," the body guards of the country's decision-makers. They are, of course, best known for protecting the President. Lenny likes to poke fun at his job, calls the Secret Service the "guard dogs of government,"

Anyway, about a year before, right at the end of my Ph.D. studies I ran into Lenny in a bar in Georgetown. He told me about his job, his fortuitous rise through the ranks of the Secret Service to a position of some responsibility. As far as I could understand, by his shadowy description of it, he was in charge of evaluating and assigning Secret Service agents to different guard dog teams. He was what today in corporate jabberwock is called HR. He was a personnel policeman, an agent overseer, a scheduler and people planner. Whatever. I had no clear idea at all what he was. I am not sure that he even knew what his precise job description was. As time went on though I realized that perhaps he was really a very talented "fixer" and "handler." As we talked, he emphasized how there was all kinds of opportunity in government work and how good the pay was. He also went back to his favorite subject, my Eidetic Memory. He was sure that once they read about that on my application that the government jobs would be coming out of the woodwork after me. I hate to say it, but he was right. He guided me through the application process, even talked to a few people on my behalf, and within a couple of weeks I was going though orientation in the Air Force photo lab in the Pentagon.

And now he was back sitting me down in that cafeteria and talking to me about coming to work for him in the Secret Service. But that wasn't all. He wasn't there on his own volition. The word had come down, all the way from the President, that the Secret Service should go and get me. Of course, on the bubble of my Cuba notoriety, Lenny had made no secret of the fact that he and the super spy of the Cuban Crisis were high school buddies and best friends. So, as Lenny represented it, the President himself had sent him to get me. "It's an important job," Lenny argued. "C'mon, sign up with us." I'm pretty sure that is not how it happened at all, but then it was Lenny after all.

And so, within weeks, my time in limbo was over and I was undergoing training (especially in the use of firearms which I abhor) and classroom orientation in the U.S. Secret Service. My teachers realized fairly quickly that I was capable of absorbing their information instantaneously and spitting it back at them verbatim without the slightest hesitation. So, after about two weeks of the orientation process, they gave up on coaching me and sent me away for assignment. That is where things got interesting. Lenny and his boss, a Marine Major Cameron, called me in for a meeting. They had an assignment that they felt was directly tailored to my special Eidetic talent and to my analytic experience with the Air Force. I caught my breath for a long minute when the first thing they told me was that I was being assigned to the President's Secret Service team. *Oh shit*, I thought, *I'm going to be guarding the President.*

"In fact," Major Cameron clapped me on the shoulder and said, "The President asked for you himself."

"You're going to be his team's 'eye-in-the-sky and on the ground,'" Lenny dropped the second major bomb of this interview.

"Ooookay…?" I stared at the two of them, "and that means?"

"Whenever the President goes anywhere for a public outdoor event," the Major jumped in, "beforehand, a day or two before, a Marine helicopter does a flyover putting airborne eyes on all that will be going on around the President's route. It will be you and the pilot in the chopper. Then, the day of, you will be the 'Scout,' the 'Point Man,' the eyes of the Secret Service out in front. You'll be about two hundred yards in front of the President's motorcade on the back of a motorcycle checking out all of the possible trouble spots that you spotted from the air before."

"Don't you see Mikey," Lenny couldn't restrain himself. "It is the perfect job for you. With your Eidetic Memory, with your ability to analyze visual material right away, on the spot. It's perfect. This job has your name written all over it."

With that, we all sort of settled down for a couple of minutes. I picked at my cafeteria meat loaf; Lenny and the Major took sips of their coffee.

"Yeah. Wow. That sounds great," I finally said. But, I'll tell you, my heart was racing and the weight of responsibility was already starting to descend on my shoulders. I told myself that Lenny was right. I would be especially good at watching crowds, seeing things, people, sharp movements, suspicious terrain, stuff that no one else would be able to see and interpret. But guarding the President? Whoa! Now that was a pretty big order of business.

But all of that is just background to this particular chapter in my life. The real story begins here and its importance will be immediately obvious. I had been in the helicopter for almost seven months including almost forty previous presidential trips with motorcades when we pulled into Dallas two days before President Kennedy's arrival. My job actually was not that far removed from looking at aerial photos back in my days in the photo lab. Now, however, from the chopper or from the motorcycle I was still looking at a kind of photos, but they were not stills. They were in constant motion, the motion of the chopper through the air or bike on the road, the motion of the subjects of observation and all surrounding them on the ground. Lenny had been right. Thank god for my freakish visual memory. It allowed me to mediate between the shifting realities of my flight through the air and the movement of all of the coursing entities on the ground.

As I said, we set down in Dallas two days before President Kennedy's arrival. My pilot, and to this day so far removed from that day in Dallas my close friend, was Marine Sergeant Ron Reed. That helicopter was like a really comfortable pair of boots that he put on every day, as was the motorcycle that we rode together like the old-west Cavalry scouts. To this day I think that if he felt like it he could have flown that chopper through the goal post of a football field blindfolded or jumped that motorcycle over the curb and into a hill climb without ever thinking twice.

We spent those two days before Air Force One got there prepping as we always did for one of the President's motorcades. We had a complete checklist that we ran through, but by far the most important item on that list was our orientation fly-over. We always did it on the day before the motorcade, at the precise time of the motorcade, at the exact speed of the motorcade, and of course, over the assigned route of the motorcade. For me, the main purpose of the fly-over was to closely observe the terrain below, the areas of possible concealment along the route, the buildings lining the parade route whose windows we knew on the day of the motorcade would be packed with people straining for a glimpse of the President. In doing this, my job was to capture the route firmly in my infallible memory so that when the time came I could detect any anomalies, any suspicious people or actions, and sudden movements toward the parade route, actually anything out of the ordinary at all that caught my attention and that hadn't been there or hadn't been normal during the fly-over. After that fly-over I mapped out a whole report of "alerts" for the Secret Service agents riding on the running boards of the President's car, possible places where an assailant or assailants might exploit. To me, a little hill on the right side of the highway on the President's route seemed like a definite place to keep a close eye on. It was about 400 yards after the President's car turned the corner into the Dealey Plaza and right before an expressway overpass. I knew that the next day that hill would be crowded with people eager for a good vantage point for seeing and waving to President Kennedy and Jackie as they drove slowly by. I remarked to Reed that we needed to closely check out that hill the next day as we led the motorcade.

Little did I imagine that day before the President's arrival that within twenty-four hours the scene that I was observing in the fly-over would be indelibly etched in the minds of a generation of Americans and other people all over the world. By the next day every person in America would know that scene by heart—the black cars, the famous riders in the cars, the street, the crowd, the grassy knoll, the overpass—everyone in America would view that whole scene of President Kennedy's assassination over and over on television. It wouldn't take an Eidetic Memory to call up that scene that would unfold the next day in Dallas. It would be called up in detail in the public imagination for years to come. But tomorrow, the fateful day, I would have a view right in the middle of it all that no one else had. A lot of good it did! Even my powers couldn't save him!

After completing the orientation fly-over, I had a clear idea of the route of the motorcade in all of its twists and turns, it's really rather unthreatening, or so I thought, terrain. Reed and I were ready to saddle-up and lead the parade the next day even as the bullet for the President was being loaded. On the big day, now on our motorcycle, we would take the point, him driving, me up behind. My job was watching, checking out all the trouble spots we had marked the day before, scanning the crowds. On motorcade day Reed and I were the first boots on the ground so to speak. My job was to look for changes from the day before, things like a possible gunman moving quickly through the crowd toward the roadway or perhaps someone close to the roadway with a suspicious package that might be a bomb, to spot any possible threats and immediately warn the President's car. No hesitation. Shout that warning into the earbuds of the Secret Service agents riding on the running boards of the car so that they could take immediate evasive action, speed up the car, swerve it, cover up the President and the First Lady. Reed and I had done this dozens of times before. We had actually issued "MAYDAYS" six or seven times. Mostly they were false alarms but in guarding the President of the United States it never hurt to be careful.

The big day arrived like any other. Air Force One landed and the stairs unfolded. The President and Mrs. Kennedy and the Vice-President Johnson and Mrs. Johnson came down waving and were met by a small delegation of dignitaries including Governor Connelly and his wife who would be riding in the car with the Kennedys. I was on the motorcycle off to the side of Air Force One's taxiway. The black convertible limos with the running boards in the back for my Secret Service colleagues were pulled right up on the tarmac ready for the President and his entourage to enter as soon as he completed his obligatory hand-shaking of the gaggle of Texas dignitaries—two of them actually in cowboy hats—who had trotted out to meet him. Reed was already revving up the engines of our motorcycle in preparation, as we always did, for leading the motorcade when everyone in the official party was finally saddled up and ready to roll out of the airport to downtown Dallas.

When the President and the First Lady finally finished their review of the assembled dignitaries and got into the back seat of the black convertible limo (Governor and Mrs. Connolly were in the front), Reed gently twisted the accelerator and the whole show was underway. Our MO was always the same. We rode pretty slowly at about 200 yards out front with me constantly on the lookout for anything out of the ordinary anywhere around us, especially in the crowds next to the roadway or in the windows of the buildings along the route. I was especially attentive to any of the potential trouble spots I had noted in our flyover the day before. I was in contact on an open channel with the headsets of every one of the Secret Service agents on the ground, on the running boards of the cars, those stationed along the sidewalks of the motorcade route. I always maintained silence unless I saw anything I didn't like. If I ever saw anything threatening (and in my forty previous motorcades I had only been forced to break radio silence seven times), I immediately screamed "MAYDAY" into my mic and as fast as I could talk started directing my Secret Service colleagues in two different maneuvers. First, I would tell the agents on the running boards to cover up the President and the First Lady. In other words, jump on top of them and shield them with their bodies. Second, I would direct the other agents on the ground in the direction of the threat. Also, in this second phase of my warning, the drivers of the motorcade vehicles would immediately speed up and drive away from the perceived threat.

As I said, seven times before I had "MAYDAYed" those procedures into place. Five times they had been false alarms, suspicious movements in the crowd, weapon-like objects in the hands of spectators or poking out of windows, things like that which turned out to be non-threatening. But two other times we had actually spotted would-be assassins and neutralized them before the motorcade reached a position of vulnerability. Neither of those failed assassination attempts were ever publicized. The Secret Service, as befits its name, likes to keep its secrets. But the effects of these situations sent us a really powerful message that assassins were out there and it was our job to ferret them out. So, ideally, I never broke radio silence, was quite careful to not "cry wolf." Worst case scenario, I was frantically screaming desperate "MAYDAYs" into my colleagues ears non-stop.

And so, that day in Dallas, we rolled and the motorcade followed behind us. It was a beautiful day. Full Texas sunshine. Shirtsleeves weather for November which certainly wasn't what the President and Mrs. Kennedy had left behind in Washington. Vice-President Johnson and his Lady Bird in the second car were, I'm sure, excited to be coming home. Believe me, there was certainly some question who was the most beloved politician in that motorcade that sunny day in Dallas.

The trip into the city from the airport was uneventful, and didn't even present much for me to look at. There were people along the route waving but the landscape was nothing but barren desert with perhaps a few warehouse-type buildings. But when we reached the city limits it was a completely different story. The streets were lined with spectators three and four deep. The small hills along the way sported many more Presidential enthusiasts, people in lawn chairs, children and adults waving for all their worth at the motorcade passing in front and below them. Every window of every building along the route held more wavers hanging out over the motorcade. It was a truly enthusiastic crowd as the President and their favorite son the Vice-President passed before them waving like sun-kings at their loyal subjects.

Behind Reed on the bike I was having a bit of trouble seeing out due to the bright glare of the sunlight. The glare gave a kind of pulsing, fragmenting effect to my line of vision down the motorcade route. I changed to a darker pair of sunglasses and that helped some, but I couldn't help blinking as I peered out at the crowds flanking the black limos making their way slowly along. As the cars made their turn behind us onto the downhill stretch through the city plaza absolutely jammed with people, movement behind a white parking lot fence off to the right ahead of us at the very top of a grassy knoll caught my attention. It was one of the trouble spots I had noted, potential cover for a shooter perhaps. Yesterday, at the top of the hill was a white fence. In the chopper Reed and I had done a pass over the hill to see what was behind that fence which looked to be about eight feet high made of white-washed wood. Behind the fence was a gravel parking lot that the fence closed off from the Dealey Plaza. Yesterday the lot was totally empty so we figured that it must be locked up for some reason or else cars or maybe trucks would be parked there.

Today, when we approached that little grassy hill in front of and below that white fence right next to the roadway, it was filled with people. Families sitting on blankets with picnic lunches waiting for the motorcade to pass, people taking time off from their jobs in the buildings around the plaza to get a glimpse of the President, a man with a movie camera standing and filming the scene from halfway up the hill. But something was different from the day before. As we approached I spotted heads looking over that clapboard fence. I counted four. It set off an alarm in my Eidetic Memory, sort of the same way those ruts in that Cuban jungle had a year before. *What were those people doing there? The fence was eight feet high. They had to be standing on something. How did they get into that closed parking lot? Just them.* It was just too suspicious to ignore.

"MAYDAY! MAYDAY! White fence on top of grassy hill. Four men," I screamed into my headset mic. But just as I did I heard the shots. They exploded from behind us. I was totally confused. I had called "MAYDAY!" on a threat in front of the motorcade, yet the shots, I counted three, simultaneously, came from behind us. They yanked my head back from the four men who had triggered my alarm. I learned later that the shots had come from the upper windows of a non-descript brick building that we had just passed. I had flagged it on my vulnerable positions map, but the men on the hill behind the fence had distracted me and I had failed to check it out. I had screamed my "MAYDAY!" warning, but it was for the wrong threat. I had screamed "MAYDAY," but it was too late. The damage had been done. The running board agents had leapt into action at my first "MAYDAY," but they hadn't been fast enough. They hadn't been on the running boards, but had been walking beside and behind the President's car. The President was hit. My swiveling head caught him slumping to the left into Mrs. Kennedy's lap and my Secret Service colleague finally covering both of them up as the limos picked up speed and raced away under a nearby overpass and out of sight. Reed also gunned our motorcycle to keep up with the racing motorcade. And just like that it was over.

I had been too late. I had missed something I should have seen. I had been distracted by one situation away from another. Whether the four men I had seen were also assassins, whether they even had a rifle, whether they would have gotten off any shots at the motorcade, I would never know. The reality was that the single shooter in the high window had definitely gotten off some shots at the President. At that time, as we followed the limos to the hospital, I was heartsick, inconsolably guilty. I couldn't believe that I had missed the shooter's rifle poking out of that window. Oh, I had shouted "MAYDAY" alright, but not for that shooter. Who knows? The blink of an eye. The momentary glare of sunlight. Four men at a fence. I had been looking the wrong way and our President was dead.

In the aftermath nobody blamed me. After all, I had shouted "MAYDAY," warned of the danger. But a warning shout can't stop a bullet. And no one knew just why I was shouting my warning anyway. But I did. I actually blamed myself for a long time for President Kennedy's death. I also wrote down every single thing that I had seen in my debriefing report. And Ron Reed's report totally supported mine though he had not seen the four men at the fence. But nobody blamed us. As I said, we had issued a warning scream almost simultaneously with the gunshots. Only I blamed myself. Only I was guilty. As I played that scenario over and over in my mind, I convinced myself that from the fly-by the day before I should have known that the upper windows of that building were the perfect spot for an assassin with a rifle. I should have known as we flew by that building on the day of the motorcade to glue my eyes to its windows and never blink. I should have known, but I didn't. And that is what fueled my guilt for months and years and even now, half a century later.

But what happened after the assassination, after the state funeral, after President Johnson had taken over, also still is imbedded unavoidably in my unstinting memory. The slow, stumbling, controversial, inconclusive findings of the Warren Commission, the investigative body for studying the assassination, still bother me to this day because of my own contribution to the Commission's findings. Correction: my own *non-contribution* to those findings.

When the Warren Commission convened, I of course, was called along with some 550 other witnesses. As it turned out, the Commission would take almost a full year to complete its investigation of the assassination, to interview all of those witnesses, to view and study the more than 3000 exhibits of evidence collected in relation to the assassination. My testimony, such as it was, turned out to be a mere droplet in the ocean of material that the Commission collected. My interview appointment wasn't even scheduled until May 1964. But what I found strange, what still nags at my memory, was what happened to me at the time that I was scheduled to testify. In the weeks before my scheduled appearance before that Commission's investigations I was very nervous about my testimony, uncertain about what I was going to say. I was still really shaken by what had happened in Dallas, already plagued by guilt over what I perceived as my negligence and poor judgement in the whole assassination moment. I was intent on trying to get my mind straight for my interview. But then the weirdness began.

First, to refresh my memory, which I really didn't need to do, but which indicated my lack of confidence, my insecurity, my lack of understanding of what had happened that day and of the images recurring constantly in my mind of all that I had seen that day, first of all I went looking for my debriefing report. The one that I had written out right after Reed and I landed that afternoon after escorting the President's motorcade to the hospital. My report, strangely, was nowhere to be found. I went to the Secret Service library where such reports were customarily filed and it wasn't there. I went to Lenny and asked him if my report had been moved somewhere else due to its sensitive nature. He assured me he knew of no such change in procedure.

L: I didn't even know it was sensitive.

I asked him if the Warren Commission had requisitioned my report. Again he denied any knowledge of any such request concerning my report.

L: It just must have gotten misfiled, Mikey. It'll probably turn up sooner or later. Hell, with your memory you sure don't need any old report to tell you what you saw or didn't.

Me: But I'd like to take it into the interview anyway. As backup, you know, in case they don't understand about my memory, so I can show it to them as written right after the event that day, not six months later, like now.

L: Aw Mikey, you're blowing this all up out of proportion. Do you know how many people they are interviewing? Hundreds. Everybody says it's all just a big farce. Everybody knows that Oswald shot the President. Nothing you have to say is going to change any of that. Anyway, you're not the agent they're interested in. All that shit is raining down on the guys with the cars in the President's immediate detail.

When I left Lenny's office, I wasn't any more confident about my upcoming interview, but I did stop thinking about my missing report. Lenny's total lack of interest in its disappearance actually reassured me. Misfiled? Why not? The Pentagon was an awfully big place. I was sure that pieces of paper got lost every single day there. But what happened next struck me as even more weird.

Now it was only two days before my appointment with the Commission investigators and I was called into Lenny's Secret Service office and there was General Lansdale from my Cuban Missile Crisis days sitting right to the side of Lenny's desk. He wasn't in uniform as he always had been before. Instead, he was wearing a dark brown, sort of dingy plaid, raincoat and a dark fedora that looked like it had been through a war. Lenny just sat there behind the desk not saying a word, sort of sheepish, as if he had gotten caught in a lie.

"Edwards, hello, I hope you remember me," Lansdale greeted me as soon as I walked through the door, jumping to his feet and extending his hand for a shake.

Me: Of course, I do General.

I replied shaking his hand while all the while thinking *How Stupid! Doesn't he remember that I remember everything?* (I have always found it strange, no, just a little bit annoying, how people forget that I'm Eidetic and not like them or everybody else.) But my surprise at seeing him in Lenny's office must have been somewhat evident. As we stood there awkwardly opposite each other with Lenny behind the desk looking like he wanted to climb into one of the desk's drawers, my mind was racing: *What is he doing here? Does he want me, god forbid, for another of his Pathfinder assignments? Why is Lenny acting so strangely? Good lord, what have I gotten myself into now?* My first impulse was to flee, to turn tail and run out of the office and lose myself in the maze of Pentagon corridors. Instead, I outright lied through my teeth right to Lansdale's face.

Me: General, good to see you again.

Ln: Yes, well yes.

Lansdale sat back down.

I pulled a chair from beside the other side of Lenny's desk and sat down facing Lansdale. Still Lenny hadn't said a word. It was as if he wasn't even there except that it was his office. From the look that I saw on his face I think he really would rather not have been there at all.

Ln: Mr. Edwards, Mr. McCone and I have heard very good things about your work here with the Secret Service."

Why did I of a sudden feel that I was no longer really in the Secret Service, in a position of protecting people, but had been suddenly yanked back to Spookland, dragged down into the dragon's lair of the CIA?

Ln: We have read your whole helicopter surveillance of the assassination report. Very thorough. Very well done.

Well that answers my question about where my report disappeared to, I quickly realized. I glanced over at Lenny and, still looking sheepish, he shrugged at me with both his shoulders and his hands.

Ln: However, Mr. McCone and I would like for you to be deathly ill on the day that you are scheduled to appear before the Warren Commission interviewers. We, Mr. McCone and I, wouldn't ask this of you if it wasn't a matter of the most sensitive national security. Rest assured that when you miss this interview you will not be called back. We will make sure of that. And you are not the only witness of whom we are making this request. The only reason we are doing this is that we fear that the Commission's investigation is not enough concerned with national security and might be touching upon some very sensitive areas of that security. Also, the Secret Service is being raked over the coals for their failure to protect the President that day. Rumors of drinking the night before and charges of very slow reactions to the shots at the President are flying in the Warren Commission. We see no reason to include the CIA in the attacks that the Commission is making on the Secret Service.

I just stared at him, trying to process what he had said, not really understanding at all. *What the heck did the CIA have to do with it,* I thought. My deer-in-the-headlights look just spurred Lansdale on in his oily attempt to reassure me that doing his bidding was really in the best interest of the American way.

Ln: Mr. McCone just doesn't want to give the wrong impression. Things are already so very confusing over there in the Commission. We, the CIA, had agents all over the motorcade site, there to help protect the President. It is just a question of protecting their identities.

Lansdale seemed to think that his words of reassurance did the trick because his tone completely changed at that point. He hadn't even considered asking for my opinion of his "deathly ill" request. He just took it for granted that having heard him out was my consent to do what he had just, in no uncertain terms, told me to do.

And so I nodded stupidly, mute, stupefied out of words. And I did what he told me to do. And to this day, fifty years later, I still regret it. But that is yet another arc to my story.

Two days later. On the day of my scheduled interview, I phoned in my sickness excuse and went into hiding (my own decision, not the CIA's) for four days in a small B&B in Maryland. I never heard anything from the Warren Commission again. I never talked to any of their investigators. I checked and my report from that day in Dallas never surfaced as one of the 3000 exhibits that the Warren Commission studied. I have no idea where that report disappeared to. At one point certainly McCone, Lansdale and the CIA had their spooky little hands on it, but it never appeared again. The Warren Commission report on the Kennedy assassination came out some months later, almost a year to the day of the assassination itself. The Commission report was 800 pages of text, but the collected materials of the Commission deliberations and findings were ultimately published to the tune of 3000 pages. I wasn't in it. And maybe that is a good thing. The Warren Commission report did focus on the perceived failure to act, to move fast enough, to protect the President of the Secret Service agents on the ground, in the cars of the motorcade. That report, it seems, has laid nothing to rest about the assassination event at all. Over the years, right up to the present when the final redacted documents were released, the Warren Commission report has engendered nothing but controversy and confusion. That report has generated enough conspiracy theories to outnumber the voluminous pages of the Commission report itself. The report steadfastly argued that Lee Harvey Oswald acted alone, but since that argument was made, to quote Cecil B. DeMille's favorite tag line, "a cast of thousands" of assassins, conspirators, motived persons of interest, and, yes, spooks, have emerged from the quagmire of Warren Commission material to cast doubt on everything that the Commission did.

As I think back on them now from this long, long distance in time in my life, these events of the assassination and its aftermath, even the whole Cuban affair earlier, seem more and more like a dream, immaterial, as if perhaps they never really happened simply because I still don't fully understand them. And it seems that I am not alone. Does anyone then or now or across the years really know what happened that day in Dallas so long ago?

But, because of my ruthless memory, I know that none of it was a dream at all. I saw what I saw from my perch on the motorcycle that day and I am certain that no one else saw the assassination from my point of view. And in light of later events I know for certain that no one else (except perhaps for Lansdale and McCone) ever became aware of what I saw, what nags at my memory, what is locked like a desperate prisoner longing to escape in my consciousness. Even now, fifty years too late, I still ask myself: *Why wasn't my view of the assassination ever explored? Did anyone ever really want to understand it all?*

But then I expand my neuromania. I start worrying that perhaps not just those episodes but my whole life has been but a dream indelibly etched in my freakish memory. Perhaps now, in my trying to write it all down, is my belated attempt to wake up from that dream and set my memory free in space, time and reality.

CHAPTER 4: CETOLOGY AGAIN

Whale ho! Sorry, that was just my droll way of giving you readers a heads up that another *Moby Dick*-like Cetology chapter is coming. It will be a sort of defining chapter where I'll try to put into perspective the real powers of my Eidetic Memory. At the end of the last chapter, I used the work "freakish" as an adjective describing my Eidetic powers. That is a pretty good descriptive term for Eidetic Memory, but not for me. Yes, my memory is indeed "freakish," but I certainly don't think I am. I am actually pretty ordinary. Well, perhaps that's sort of hard to stomach about a person who before the age of twenty-five has been intimately involved in two of the major historical events of the American twentieth century. You may think that this book is starting to read like *Forrest Gump,* but really it isn't. Forrest was a total naïf, blissfully unaware of what was going on around him, floating through life with little or no sense of the historic significance or the personal formation of all the earthshaking events going on around him. But this book is totally different. For better or worse, my Eidetic Memory makes me aware to the nth degree of absolutely everything that is going on around me, every day, every minute. Forrest didn't understand his life at all. Fortunately, or unfortunately for me, I understand mine all too well and it sure hasn't been like sticking one's hand into a box of candy. So, I may not be Forrest Gump, but I'm also not the fearless Pathfinder super-spy that Lansdale tried to make me out to be. On the outside, I am really a pretty nondescript American CIA and Secret Service agent going about doing his job. Yikes, I guess that really doesn't sound very ordinary, but stop and think about it. The jobs I did for the CIA (looking at aerial photos) and for the Secret Service (riding in a helicopter and on a motorcycle) were really rather mundane, assembly-line, boring, day-to-day-repetitive-action jobs, certainly not "freakish" as James Bond and Jason Bourne and Superman and Spiderman and all those other comic book heroes across the years were. But inside, in my interior world of Eidetic Memory, yes, I was definitely "freakish." And after the whole experience of President Kennedy's assassination I was acutely aware of my "freakishness" and how my Eidetic powers had pretty much taken over my life.

One day recently as I was working at writing down this memory-driven work of whatever it is—memoir? Autobiography? Existential self-reflection? Dream?—I unwrapped a piece of Dove dark chocolate and popped it into my mouth. Imprisoned in a cell of writer's block that day, I absentmindedly glanced at the shiny, pressed-aluminum wrapper and the saying emblazoned on it caught my eye. "Keep life moving forward, looking backward is only for time travelers." Now don't get me wrong. I don't usually find my deeper thoughts in candy bar wrappers as my friend Forrest did. But I was struck by how opposite to my own situation that saying was. At first, I didn't agree with what it was saying at all, for obvious reasons. Thanks to my Eidetic Memory and my really advanced age, now, at the time of this writing, pretty much my every waking moment is dedicated to looking backwards. But then I realized that there was more to that quote then its seeming denigration of memory. It was that silly candy wrapper that gave me a whole new view of myself, of my life, of this manuscript that I was struggling to get down on paper. I was a time traveler alright. I was "freakish" alright. And my Eidetic Memory was my time machine.

I recently saw a movie on television called *Nostalgia*. It focused on a guy who sold sports memorabilia and his friends, all of whom need to encounter some triggers out of the past—letters in an old trunk, a photograph in a relative's house, the death of a former lover—in order to remember. Actually, I found that movie not only cliched but really amusing from the point of view of my own situation. For an Eidetic, the past is always there. No matter how far back—fifty, thirty, twenty, ten years past—the past strains at my memory, resides as clear as the reflection on the surface of a pristine mountain lake. In other words, I can see my past so clearly that it might as well be right outside my window when I look out each morning, right dead in front of me as I sit on my rocker on my front porch, right there sharp as the tip of my pen against the background of the blank white paper as I sit here working to write about it. Pretty cool, I thought, a time-traveler, that's what I am. Yes, pretty cool. Yikes, in my mind I even talk like I'm back in the sixties, the time I was just writing about.

Just imagine if you could remember, could call up in perfect detail and living color every act, every scene, every word, every success, every failure, every person, place or thing that you had ever encountered and experienced in your life. Imagine, if you remember every single kiss you had with the girls you fell in puppy love with in high school and even college. Just imagine if you could remember in graphic detail every single touch, caress, coupling, with every single woman of erotic desire in all the many years of your life. Imagine if you could remember exactly every word of every book you ever read. Imagine if you could look at a complete page of numbers, say on a spreadsheet or trade invoice or restaurant bill, and recite them precisely after one glance. And just imagine, what if you could remember exactly every word in every conversation that you ever had? What if you could remember every landscape, every view that you ever looked at, in graphic detail—colors, textures, all senses primed and alert and effortlessly recoverable, always easily available? What if you remembered every joke you had ever heard? What if you remembered every town you ever drove through, every dive bar and gas station and bodega and 7-11 you ever stopped at? Just imagine remembering every highway you've ever driven, every rest area you ever stopped at, what kind of urinals—metal troughs, ceiling to floor porcelain walls with drains at the bottom, five- foot high coffin-like porcelain stand-ups, little kids low egg-shaped wall-mounted, regular waist-high wall-mounted—each rest area sported for one's peeing pleasure? How would you feel if you remembered every pizza, sub, burger, fast-food sandwich you ever purchased and which ones gave you the worst heartburn? Imagine if you remember the name, the label, the taste of every wine you ever sipped. What would it be like for you if others were consistently amazed at your powers of recall of what they said, what they did, where they were, what they wore, who they were with, whatever? Just imagine if you could remember every single first in your life, the first time you experienced love or hate or fear or triumph or defeat. What if you clearly remember the first calculus problem or complex equation you solved? Or the first time you cooked your own full meal or rode your bike or discovered a great work of literature like your favorites: Conrad's *Heart of Darkness* or Fitzgerald's *The Great Gatsby* or Camus' *The Stranger*? Or what about music? Wouldn't people be completely amazed if they knew that after hearing a song only once you could recite all the lyrics? No, sing *a cappella* all of the Beatles' songs, or the sixties hits from *American Graffiti* or Arlo Guthrie's *The City of New Orleans* or Kris Kristofferson's *Me and Bobbi McGee* or the Eagles' *Take it Easy,* or so many more. Really, how would you feel if you could remember every time your feelings were hurt, or you felt slighted or jilted or neglected or intimidated or mistrusted or deceived or exhilarated?

An Eidetic's mind, going all the way back to the sixties, is a huge pile of file cards scrupulously alphabetized, organized, readily available. Or, in today's terms, twenty-first century terms, it is like the digital memory of a search engine like Google or Bing that can call up in the blink of an eye whatever information you need. Back in my day, the sixties of Cuba and Dallas, my Eidetic Memory was just about the most powerful search engine anyone could have. And for me it was effortless, as effortless as tapping your Google app nowadays. In the sixties, seventies, eighties and nineties the world was not yet digitized, but I pretty much was, at least within my own fields of experience and the world my memory consumed every day. But most of all, can you imagine what it would be like to remember every single thing that you saw and be able to immediately replicate those images in the most accurate and precise detail? That's what my Eidetic Memory could do, function like the most sophisticated digital camera, capturing color and line and depth and texture and expression and delight and movement in the most precise detail, and then retaining that image forever for possible future recall. My relentless memory never missed a trick. If I had been a detective then, rather than later, I never would have missed a clue: a shoe without a mate, a pair of panties under the picnic table, hair matted in a drain, a hotel ball-point pen, a golf ball, a stapler, ruts in a clearing, men behind a wall, a woman I could have loved being led off to prison. That, dear reader, is what being Eidetic is like. That, you poor put-upon receiver of too much information (TMI) in this Cetology chapter, is the remarkably "freakish" power of my memory.

But think about your own powers of memory, how your memory links you to your own past life. Memory can be a double-edged sword. It can take us to places of nostalgic bliss. Glen Campbell, the Country and Western singer who just died a few years ago, sang about "the rivers of your memory" that keeps you "always gentle on my mind." Fine, but memory can also force us into reliving psychological nightmares. Yes, definitely, memory can be both a blessing and a curse. For me, the Kennedy assassination as it infected my memory, burrowed into my consciousness like some poisonous mite, was the first real Eidetic curse that I experienced. There would be several more, but for me (and for the whole country) the Kennedy assassination was exactly this kind of cursed memory. In 1963 the Kennedy's were blessed, America was blessed, poets compared that time and place to the rebirth of Camelot.

Then, in the blink of an eye, to some extent the blink in my own eye, it all disintegrated, and became my own personal curse, the nation's most tragic memory.

All memory really is, after all, is one's struggle to stay alive, one's struggle to recapture the vitality, the exhileration, the successes of the past in the hope they can reinvigorate the dwindling present, maybe even offer some hope for the future. But the only problem is that memory often calls up the bad along with the good, the failures along with the successes, the losses, the defeats, the tragedies. And, what if a person's memory is much more acute, much more aware, much more detailed, precise, and even visually high contrast. That's me. Being Eidetic is certainly no walk in the park. My vision, since the fifties, has been in HD (high definition) before that technology was ever even dreamed. What if every funeral, every betrayal, every lie you ever told, every failure of courage, every sin of omission, every vile act that you ever committed, was indelibly etched into "the river of your memory" and was a long way from being "gentle on your mind?"

Ordinary people with normal ranges of memory have consoling powers of forgetfulness. But an Eidetic can never forget anything, is totally incapable of leaving the past alone. His mind races with memories, the old is writ in marble in his mind, the new flooding in. Often, many times every day, I wish for my all-powerful memory to fail, to forget, but it never does, it can't. As I lie down to sleep at night, like Jake Barnes in Hemingway's novel, I stare through the darkness to the ceiling and I try to forget, to shut down my memory, to draw the curtain of darkness over the insistence of the past, and inevitably I fail. Eidetics don't sleep very well!

Which brings me to another debilitating effect of being Eidetic. It causes one to exist in a constant state of heightened awareness. Memory isn't the only heightened sense that Eidetics possess. Probably 95% of the human race are generally unaware of almost everything that happens around them, especially peripherally. Let's call them Muggles (OK, I know, but it is a pretty convenient name for most of the human race). And then there are Eidetics. This particular awareness tic of Eidetic Memory is much more complicated than at first it might seem. In fact, an Eidetic's heightened awareness sends out debilitating ripples into a number of other areas of an Eidetic's life. Heightened awareness gives one a nagging sense of insecurity that they are missing things that are happening around them that they should be seeing or remembering as was the case with me on the motorcycle not seeing Oswald's window. Hence, it is very hard for an Eidetic to relax, to focus on the straight ahead and the narrow view of reality. An Eidetic's head and eyes are on an incessant swivel, left and right, over one's shoulders, trying to take in and register everything. For example, it is not really a good idea to let an Eidetic drive you. If you think texting on cell phones is a driving distraction, take a ride with an Eidetic sometime.

In other words, heightened awareness is yet another kind of Eidetic obsession. Eidetic Memory is like watching a movie in a highly sophisticated way. Normal people only see the action in the center of the screen, the dominant image. The Eidetic certainly sees that, but also sees everything around the edges of the screen where equally important images often reside. This would come in handy for me later when I became a film critic. An Eidetic's eyes and memory can't let go of the complex panorama going on around him: the pretty girl walking along the sidewalk as you are driving by, the hawk circling in the sky above as you are driving below, the sign waver on the corner dressed like the Statue of Liberty as you are pulling up to the stop light behind cars, or the men by the white fence while the rifle is poking out of the sixth floor window above the President's motorcade.

Conversely to the Eidetic's blessing or curse of heightened awareness is the Eidetic's ability to compress his attention span into a single glance, a quick read through, and instantaneous registering of something amiss in his view, like ruts from heavy machinery in a jungle clearing in Cuba. Again, the Muggles, 95% of the human race, have very short attention spans. Paying close attention is simply not a widespread ability of most people. But for the Eidetic, paying attention via his heightened awareness is attained in the mere blink of an eye and retained in the computer-like filing system of his memory. In Ray Bradbury's futurist novel *Fahrenheit 451* people spend their lives memorizing their books in order to preserve then for posterity much in the way that ancient monks in the dark ages hand-copied extant manuscripts in order to preserve the world's knowledge for the generations to come. For an Eidetic though, in the shortest span of attention, he can memorize whole books, documents, columns of numbers, whatever, and retain them for life. So you see, everything around him, everything that has been brought to his attention, is always there for a person having the powers of Eidetic Memory. When one gets along in years like me that is a pretty heavy load of files to be carrying around, really rather overwhelming. So, you see, being an Eidetic is not all just a sunlit walk along the verdant path of the past.

Don't get me wrong, being Eidetic is a tremendous gift, the possession of a set of powers that very few others have or even understand. But it certainly isn't just a set of powers to be constantly nurtured and enthusiastically anticipated. In my life it thrust me into situations of high responsibility—from looking at aerial photos to guarding a President—that at the time at such a young age (my early twenties) I could hardly understand much less predict how important my Eidetic participation might be. But, in those dark months after the Kennedy assassination, I came to realize that my unflagging memory of that event was but a droplet in the Collective Memory of that terrible day, the Collective Memory of the nation and of a whole generation.

Think of all the books and movies you have ever seen—from Forrest on his bus-stop bench to Rose on the Titanic saying "I can still remember the smell of the paint in the ballroom" to Marlow in either *Heart of Darkness* or *Apocalypse Now* to the other Marlowe in *The Big Sleep* or to Michael standing to the side of the stage in that marvelous memory play *Dancing at Lughnasa*—that are offered from a voice-over, first-person perspective (like this book that I am writing) which thrusts you the reader or moviegoer back into the past.

Actually, the movies work rather well as a metaphor for Eidetic Memory. Both that intensely visual memory and the movie screen offer full color images of the past in intimate (actually larger than life) detail and total accuracy. First person memories told by a voice-over narrator are almost always presented in Eidetic detail. If I was just a normal person with the sort of flawed, barely aware, inattentive memory that most normal people blithely live their lives with, this book would be a very different sort of narrative. My problem, back then however, barely in my twenties, is that I didn't fully understand my powers in relation to the less acute powers of the rest of the world's population. I was operating under the illusion that I was radically different from everyone else. And I was. But that did not mean that I was apart from the Collective Memory of everyone else. In fact, I was an important part of the Collective Memory because I possessed memory material that no one else remembered.

A book I read back in the Seventies, long after the Missile Crisis and the Kennedy Assassination, a book about baseball, a memory book titled *The Boys of Summer* by Roger Kahn about the Jackie Robinson

Brooklyn Dodgers, ended with a paeon to memory:

Who will remember? Is that the mind's last, soundless, dying cry? *Who will remember?* There was no rustling of old crowds as my long wrenching, joyous voyage ended, only the question, "Who will remember?"

I am just sailing out (in this book) upon what will be my own "long, wrenching, joyous voyage" but for me that question is a rather easy one to answer. We, the Eidetics, will always remember. And we, the Eidetics, know better than anyone else, how important memory is for it is the total essence of our lives.

And yet still it nags at my mind, the often dream-like qualities of my memories that once you wake up from them take on a sinister quality of mystery. How real are my memories? How accurate are those graphic details that leap out at me as I remember? Do I really understand all the implications of memories? These were the questions that nagged at me, that thrust me into a vortex of doubt. These questions whirled around my memories and made me realize that perhaps my memories of all these events were either not real at all, only psychological creations, like dreams. Or (and then I remember that I really am Eidetic) at worst my memories aren't the complete version of the events that my hubris, my pride in my magical powers, had made me so confident that they were. In those early days of the Missile Crisis and the Assassination I had come to believe that because my Eidetic Memory was so powerful and that I retained everything I saw or heard or touched with a kind of god-like omniscience that I was in control of reality. But the more I thought about it I realized that certainly was not the case.

What is wrong with this account thus far is that my perfect memories were only a small piece of those events that they figured in. I needed to prescribe myself a strong dose of humility and its companion, reality. I realized that I hadn't been present at all the machinations and deceptions and strategies that swirled around these tumultuous historical events. I wasn't privy to the CIA scheming of McCone and Lansdale. I was right in the middle of the President's assassination, but I was never involved in the Warren Commission hearings. I don't know why. I should have at least been called in to provide my two cents to those deliberations as to what really happened that day in Dallas. And those doubts raised all sorts of new questions in my mind. Were my memories of those events some sort of a threat to the official version that ultimately asserted their claim to reality? Was memory ever capable of recapturing reality? Or, could memory only recreate an incomplete simulacra of what really happened? And finally, does the fact that my memory, my exceptional power of re-creation, was still not powerful enough to bring understanding, or make one comfortable with their understanding of reality? In other words, no matter what powers we level at the past can we ever find reality through them?

Dear reader, you must forgive me for this long Cetological chapter. An Eidetic always sees way too much, thinks much too much, and, in this case, writes down way too much. We need to leave these nagging doubts behind and get on with life.

CHAPTER 5: BERKELEY

After the assassination of President Kennedy and the sharp criticism we got from the Warren Commission for our perceived failures in guarding the President in Dallas, the morale of the Secret Service hit an all-time low. We were accused of drinking too much, of womanizing, of working sleep-deprived, of not setting up the motorcade cars properly with their running boards out. The Warren Commission stabbed us in the gut and twisted their knife. It became clear that Earl Warren had found his fall guys and he used us to deflect attention from the fact that his Commission left a myriad of unanswered questions about what really happened that day in Dallas.

As for me, if the Service was really down a year after the assassination when the Commission report came out, I was even further down. The things that the Commission report focused upon—the drinking the night before, the slow reaction of the agents, the limo driver's freezing at the wheel, the running boards not being there, the culture of womanizing—were of no concern to me. I had done or been aware of or committed none of those sins. Reed and I had always played it straight, done our jobs. I had not even been included in any of the criticism. And yet I felt terrible about what I, and I alone, perceived as my contribution to that whole fiasco, my failure in a job that I and others thought I was extraordinarily qualified to do. I had been looking the opposite way when the shooter, Oswald, was poking his gun out of that window behind me. For the longest time I thought that I had been distracted and my President had died. But then I was told by Lansdale and McCone not to testify before the Commission. And yet, I had been the only one to give a "MAYDAY" warning that day seconds before the shots were fired even if it was for the wrong perceived threat. And worse yet. I had, at their orders, never been allowed to give my side of the story. And I didn't know why?

The more I thought about it all, the more I wondered if I had really been distracted at all. I had seen what I had thought was a real threat and I had reacted quickly and aggressively. Unfortunately, in doing so I had missed the real threat in the high window. I even speculated that the perceived threat I had reacted to might even have been a diversion. Or maybe it was a backup assassination team in case Oswald's marksmanship failed. All of this was roiling in my overheated mind. It got so that I was having trouble sleeping. On the job, in the helicopter, riding point, I was constantly doubting my judgement, seeing things that might be threats, could turn into threats, until almost everything became a threat to President Johnson. I was existing in a life of growing paranoia over my ability to function as the President's protector. Finally, I couldn't take my insecurity in my job, my doubting of my ability to function at the highest level necessary, and I resolved to quit the Secret Service. When I told him, Lenny didn't take it well.

I had decided to start a new phase in my life, but of course I had to sit down with Lenny and tell him why I had to leave government service. I met him in a coffee shop near the White House, late morning in April 1965, a spring rain coming tentatively down, the sidewalks glistening outside our window, a pretty nice day, welcome, signaling the end of winter. As we sat there on our first sips of coffee, I saw no reason to beat around the bush.

Me: Lenny, I wanted to tell you first, I'm going to resign from the Service.

L: Quit! What the hell?

Me: I need to do something else, get on with my life. I know you got me these jobs and I'm really grateful. That's why I'm telling you.

L: Why? You're great at this job. Everyone respects you.

Me: You know why. It's what's bothering everyone else around here.

L: The Assassination, right?

Me: Yeah, definitely. I just haven't figured out a way to deal with it. I'm losing sleep, flashbacks. It just keeps nagging at me. The doubt. The guilt.

L: Fuck Mikey. Deal with it. We're all working at doing that. You can't quit. My god, you're a superstar, a hero around here. Everybody knows you're a straight-arrow. You called the Mayday in Dallas. You almost saved the President.

Me: Yeah, almost. That's the problem.

L: Mikey, c'mon. Everybody knows about you and admires you. Damn, you saved us from the Russians in '62. You were a Pathfinder. They're the CIA elite.

Me: Lenny—I was a Pathfinder for three days and all I did was count ordinance. Nobody even knew I was in Cuba.

L: Look, Mike, you know that you are special. You can do things that no one else can do. You are especially suited to this job.

Me: Yeah, well, maybe, maybe not.

L: (raising his voice) Where the hell do you think you're going to put the Eidetic Memory of yours to work? (here his voice got plaintive) Where are you ever going to make as much of a difference as you can make here? Think about it. This is where you belong. You can't quit. Please, don't do it.

Me: I have to Lenny. I need to start a new phase in my life. I need to become someone else. Most of all I need to find a way to get that damned assassination out of my mind.

Of course, that was obviously a vain hope. Nothing ever leaves an Eidetic's head. I knew that I was incapable of forgetting, but at that point in my life I still hadn't found a way to deal with my bad memories. That would take years, and still wouldn't accomplish my significant kind of erasure. As for Lenny, despite all his arguments, he understood my situation all too well. Later he told me that even he had been thinking of doing the same, quitting the Service, but he had decided he wouldn't do it, that he would stick it out and work hard to forget. Unfortunately. that wasn't an option for me. The other thing that I realized really bugged Lenny was his worry about me wasting my Eidetic powers. I guess I never really understood how very much in awe of them and protective of them Lenny really was. And so, I quit the Secret Service, even moved out of Washington, went home to Indiana where Lenny and I had grown up.

Ah, Indiana. Maybe I should spend some time there with you, my reader, before we move on with my life story, my ramblings through memory. I've already told you one version of my origin story, that bicycle ride where my Eidetic Memory got named by Lenny. I guess you could say that all that went before that day was just backstory. But that's not really true. There are all sorts of different kinds of origins. I have since come to believe that every person at different times in their life comes to experience these new beginnings, has a new origin story. Moments like my bike ride experience and Lenny's revelation are like what Joyce called an "epiphany" perhaps, or what Wordsworth called a "spot of time" or, perhaps best of all, when that angel knocked St. Paul off of his horse on the road.

I just realized that I am sixty or seventy pages into this book and you only know one thing about me. Granted it's a pretty important controlling aspect of my life, but I would like to think that I am much more than just an Eidetic. Granted there aren't very many of us around. Probably some Eidetics don't even realize that they have special powers. I was in my twenties before I even knew what the word meant. And some Eidetics probably don't want people to know because they don't want to be seen as different or weird, or they don't want normal people to know how much information they retain and possess forever, or they don't want their special powers to be used for the wrong purposes. You readers know what I've done in my government work using the power of my Eidetic Memory, but you don't really know much about me at all—what I look like, what I think about, how I grew up (no, not on the planet Krypton), how I was in school, in college, all the backstory that led up to my work with the government that I was now leaving. Most autobiographical memoirists begin with their origin story—when and where they were born, their parents, their family life, their schooling, blah, blah, blah. No reader really cares about all that crap. I can do my first fifteen years in one quick list: born 1942 in Indiana, happily married parents, only child, father a small farmer, mother a retail store clerk, yes, of course, first in my high school class, bookworm, not an athlete.

However, there are a few things that I do think are important. First of all, despite all that you have been reading thus far, I really am pretty normal, average, just by looking at me you would never guess that I have this special power. Secondly, I'm not this total loner, happy in my voyeuristic isolation, my roles as a watcher of the world, as these early chapters might infer. Yes, I spent three years pretty much alone, looking at aerial photographs, peering out of the windshield of a Marine helicopter, but despite that perception I get along with people well. I became fast friends with Captain Bankston and Ron Reed my work colleagues. I had all kinds of friends in college and grad school besides Lenny. In fact, jumping ahead ten years, I got married which is a whole other story that I will tell later. So, you see, I am not like Forest Gump at all.

I always knew growing up that I had a good memory. I won all the spelling bees in grade school, got A's on every test I took, remembered all sorts of arcane facts, events, dates, people. Nobody could touch me in quiz show questions or especially anything involved with images like movie scenes or landscapes seen out of car windows. When I got to college it was more of the same. I never had to take a note either when sitting in class or when reading my text books. Then Lenny named me an Eidetic, outed me as the LGBT people would say these days. Grad school was more of the same. I skated through, had earned my Ph.D. by age 22, pretty fast. But really, I was a grad student like all the others. I studied, I went to class and listened, I read a lot on my own in subjects that interested me, mostly in literature and history.

Then, out of grad school, Lenny took me under his wing and I went into government work. Thanks to Lenny I felt like I was putting my special talent to good use. Then it all came apart and, to steal a metaphor from *Star Wars* years later, the dark side of my Eidetic Memory asserted itself. And that is why I left the Secret Service. Now it is well into the 21st Century and I am looking back and I realize that trying to run away from my Eidetic Memory was really a futile exercise. Nonetheless, I tried and tried for quite a long time. Hence the next phase of my memory piece. Let's call them the hippie years. Or the semi-hippie years. Or maybe the failed hippie years. Or actually the phony hippie years.

In my three years of government employment, well paid employment, I had earned enough money in 1966 terms to, I figured, last me about three years. Nowadays, in 2018, it would probably last me about three months. But back then I was actually pretty well off. The first thing I did was buy a Volkswagen bus. They were all the rage in the late sixties. I decked it out with curtains for the back windows, a stereo music system, and a mattress on the floor in the back where I had taken out the seats. Then I just got in it and headed for Indiana and home. Mom and Dad were really happy to see me when I drove into the barnyard out of a clear blue Indiana sky. And Indiana was fine for a while. But after Washington and my work experiences it got really old and unutterably boring. A wild and crazy night in my part of Indiana was driving the twenty miles into West Lafayette and hitting the college bars. I guess I looked plenty young enough to be there and no one, not even the bouncers who checked ID's at the doors, ever really questioned why someone my age was there drinking beer and ogling the coeds. But after a while I just didn't feel comfortable doing that anymore. I lasted about six months in Indiana and then I decided to go roaming.

I had never really been to an ocean or to the beach so I decided that my first stop would be California, Los Angeles and the Pacific Ocean beaches. I had spent enough time, actually too much time, in the east.

The west seemed a much more promising, relaxing, laid-back place to go to the beach. Oh, I had been to beaches in Cuba at night and I had flown over beaches in places like Miami and North Carolina, but I had never really just sat on a beach and tanned and looked out at the ocean seeing all the way to the horizon across the surface of an endless sea. Actually, I really never imagined what a spell the beach would cast over me. The beach and its attendant ocean hypnotized me, became a source of a thousand and one delights, put a new spin on my head that until this day, about sixty years later, still draws me toward the beach, the ocean, the far horizon. For six months that year I camped on Venice Beach. Well actually, I camped in the bus in a parking lot on the beach. In those days Venice was L.A.'s version of the Haight in San Francisco. It was the hippie sanctuary, the last stop before Mexico on the marijuana, peyote, magic mushroom, highway to hell or heaven. Just walking down the boardwalk you could get a contact high. That boardwalk along the sand was an unending parade of beards and sandals and serapes and bell bottoms and fuzzy vests and fuzzy minds and the constantly patrolling but not really arresting fuzz. I lasted about six months there before I decided to move on. That would be my longest stay anywhere on my Volkswagen pilgrimage along the west coast. I went to Tijuana for the Day of the Dead and instead of elating me it depressed me. I went to Easter Sunday services on a cliff overlooking the ocean near San Diego, but I didn't feel resurrected. Have I mentioned thus far that I was a semi-devout Catholic, had been all my life. Later, I touched down in the Haight, but instead of a summer of love it was a summer of disappointment. Big Sur showed some promise but ultimately meditation didn't work for me either. I spent a good month in Seattle until I started to feel mildewed. And then Lenny showed up.

Me: How did you track me down?

L: Your mom told me where you were.

Damn, ratted out by my own mother! Those damn postcards.

L: And she gave me your license plate number.

Terrific!

No just kidding, actually I was sort of glad to see Lenny. You see, I was getting bored again. My peripatetic wanderings up and down the Pacific Ocean beaches were starting to wear me out. I was even thinking of unparking the bus and getting an apartment somewhere. I was sick of bathing in the ocean and using public restrooms. And I looked around me there in the late sixties and all I saw was confusion, anger at the war, the government, the whole screwed-up situation. And now Lenny was back and I had no idea if his materializing out of thin air was going to make my life better or worse.

L: Mikey, I've got a job for you that is perfect. (Thus Lenny started his seduction) With your memory you are exactly what we need.

Me: Who is 'we' Lenny? The Secret Service? I can't go back there.

L: Yeah, I know. I've moved over to the FBI. You'd be working for them but no one will ever know.

Me: Whew. You mean J. Edgar Hoover? I've heard some really bad shit about him.

L: Believe me (he laughed), it's all true.

Me: What do you mean that no one will ever know?

L: We want you to work undercover. You'd be sort of like a Pathfinder again but this time you'd be working here at home, for the FBI. And it really pays well.

Me: What do you mean undercover? Where undercover?

L: We want you to go back to college, pretend to be a grad student, gather intel on all these protestors. Don't you see, you are perfect for this. You know the territory because you've been a student all your life. You look the part what with your beard and that bus you drive. And you have that marvelous memory that never forgets anything, names, addresses, conversations. It's the perfect job for you.

Me: What college? Where?

L: Berkeley. Right down the road here in California.

I have to say that I was really skeptical, actually fearful is probably a better word. Not fearful of the job itself or the situation I would be putting myself into. But rather fearful that Lenny was pulling me back in again. Government work hadn't really worked out for me before and this certainly didn't seem very promising either. I didn't think of it then at the time, but Lenny never used any of the usual arguments: that I would be doing it for my country, making a contribution to the national defense, protecting something important. None of that. All Lenny argued was that I was the perfect candidate for the job. Like I said, I didn't realize it then but thinking back on it I do now—it wasn't much of an argument. So why did I decide to do it? I was about out of money. I was tired of my wandering without any destination or objective. And, I guess I was sort of lost and needed somewhere to go. So I let Lenny talk me into it.

That somewhere turned out to be Berkeley alright. It had been the origin and the center of almost every protest movement of the sixties from the Free Speech Movement to Civil Rights to the Anti-Vietnam War protests which were still at their height all over America. As I think back on it now, Lenny was like a shadow, dogging my footsteps. He seemed to move with ease from one government company to another government company to yet another. But he always seemed to end up with me, leading me from one Eidetic-driven task to another. He was my trainer and my handler for this next (and illegal I found out later) FBI job of what came to be called "domestic surveillance." That was just a fancy name for my undercover assignment. Infiltrating and spying on these college kids was just like going undercover with the mob or with a drug ring or as a vice cop entrapping prostitutes. You get the picture. It was not really all that glamorous. Lenny was like a Mr. Fixit figure for these various government agencies. I never really got a good sense of what his job description was. He was the guy familiar with the tools of government who could make everything work at the most basic level. He was like a master political electrician or carpenter or plumber. In fact, a few years later, in the Watergate fiasco, the term "plumbers" was actually applied to the bungling burglars who got caught with their fingers in the Democratic Party headquarters. Anyway, Lenny gave me the necessary tradecraft, dressed me for the role, gave me a pep talk, patted me on the butt, and sent me off to spy on the radicals.

When I got to Berkeley, Mario Savio was long gone, but others, like Tom Hayden, had taken his place and I worked my way pretty quickly right in with them. For a while I just drifted, hanging around on the fringes of these campus radical groups, moving from one to another, smoking pot (it was everywhere I went), fucking (everybody was fucking like stoned rabbits), and looking for the right connection, the person who would be my key to open the door to the most radical groups. It seemed as if I slept with every college girl I met. These sure weren't sorority girls. They were nasty free love hippies. Many of them had lost their cherries and honed their sexual techniques in the Haight. They just couldn't get enough fucking. The days didn't seem long enough to cram into all the sex they wanted. Who was I to argue? In for a dime, in for a dollar. But all of these girls were giving it away for free. Lenny had warned me that there was a good chance that a lot of sex would be involved and boy was he right. He also said that I would get a bonus every three months. He called it my combat pay.

Like I said, when I got to Berkeley, I took my time, looking for an opening, hoping to unlock the door to some serious intel. Nobody ever suspected that I was an FBI spy. They were much more worried about narcs than about government undercover agents. If I had ever turned down a joint, they would have fingered me right away. But I got good at being a pot-head just like them and that made me OK. And then, after a while, I was regularly screwing one of their own.

Victoria was a real piece of work as well as a real piece of ass. Her specialties were protest marches and every possible form of sexual congress that one could imagine. But despite those attributes, she was the one girl I met who could get me into the most radical of the organizer's groups. Actually, she was hilarious. She was like a fireman. She would bang my brains out then leap out of bed right into her clothes it seemed and rush off to raise political hell. I'd stumble after her and when I finally caught up she would laugh and say, "what took you so long, legs not work?"

Again, like I said, by the time I got to Berkeley I think the original radical scene had pretty much seen its day. What really amazed me was that the intel I put out to Lenny—names, addresses, meeting topics, numbers of feckless conspirators—I really couldn't judge to be very valuable. And yet the FBI kept paying me handsomely for it. In fact, it all seemed utterly worthless to me until one day Victoria introduced me into one rather interesting group. "These people are the real thing," Victoria assured me. They called themselves the Students for a New Society, the SNS, probably an intentional echo of Berkeley's old SDS and SLA. They embraced the similarly rehashed ideals of burning it all down and starting over that had set so many fires in the sixties already. I had been in Berkeley for more than a year when I infiltrated the SNS and, to tell you the truth, the whole scene was getting pretty old for me. Then one day I walked in with Victoria to one of their apartments and they were actually in the act of building a bomb. They were using a magazine article they had found in some radical journal from years before that supposedly told them step-by-step how to do it. No one was lighting up joints or smoking in that apartment. That was how I knew right away that these dudes and their ladies were for real. Victoria introduced me around as one of their own and no one seemed suspicious. They just went right on with their handling of what looked like plastic explosives and their running of thin wires.

Wow, I thought, they're really going to do this. And suddenly I realized that Victoria had finally put me on to something worthwhile, something that might actually grab the attention of my handlers, something that might actually mean something important, save some lives, be a meaningful contribution, whatever. Except, for me, there was one real problem. You see, in my pot-induced haze, I nurtured a certainty that the worthless intel that I was feeding to the FBI would never have any consequences, or that I was collecting my government salary plus combat pay and that my feeding at the public trough wasn't hurting anyone. Amidst all that denial I had become pretty much a sympathizer with all of these idealistic young radicals, a fellow traveler if not a true believer, but nonetheless understanding of why they felt they needed to save the world from the very government I was so secretly working for. Up to this point, when I walked into that bomb factory apartment, I had comfortably rationalized that I was just messing around and getting paid for it. But now everything had changed. I was right in the middle of their anti-war war against the powers that be. I was right on the verge of betraying them, sending them all to prison. And I did.

Two days after I made my report to Lenny, I was told to stay away from that apartment the next day. That morning, when Victoria and I had completed our morning boff, she had jumped right out of bed and into her jeans and combat boots. I pled exhaustion and said I would follow her along to the apartment once I caught my breath.

"I'm getting coffee and heading over there," she said. "See you there."

I managed to control my guilt and curiosity for about an hour. I even, in that time, convinced myself that I might have some real feelings for Victoria. So, I decided to go over there and try to get her out before the FBI charged in. Of course, I was too late. When I got to the apartment three unmarked paddy wagons were pulled up in front. The bomb workers, including my Victoria, were being led out in handcuffs by bullet-proof-vested, sunglass-hidden, side-arm-packing agents. All that was missing were the Gestapo jack boots. And I realized that I, I alone, had made it all happen. A small crowd had gathered to watch the criminals paraded out to the paddy wagons. I stood to the rear of that crowd, perhaps still unbelieving of my role as the Judas Goat who was sending all of these far-from-innocent yet so young people off to prison. When they led Victoria out, she was cursing and spitting at her captors. I tried to duck down behind the people in front of me, but my body just wouldn't obey. In a sense it betrayed me. In that split second

I think I realized that I would never see Victoria again, that we would never share another joint or another bed, that I had completely ruined her life. I tried to duck away, but I couldn't take my eyes off of her and she saw me standing there watching her being led off. Her eyes fixed on me and I knew that she knew. I will never forget the look of hurt and terrible realization that froze her face and her gaze upon me. Then her look changed instantly, like her jumping out of bed like a fireman after sex. Her look changed to a glare of contempt and hatred. As she disappeared into that paddy wagon I also felt a tremendous weight of relief being lifted off of my shoulders, like Sisyphus relieved of his rock. I realized that my time at Berkeley was over. Victoria would surely tell her cohorts that she suspected that I was their betrayer. I should have heeded Lenny's order to stay away that day. But as the paddy wagon pulled away and the crowd dispersed, I was glad I had come. I was glad that my cover was blown. I was glad that now I could get my real identity back. The only problem was that I still didn't really know what exactly my real identity was.

You see, I had pretty much been grappling with my identity ever since I had gone undercover at Berkeley. It was ironic to me that my FBI cover identity was more real than Michael Edwards was. I didn't know who I was. I had moved through those two fateful government jobs like some kind of puppet, doing what the men pulling the strings told me to do. Then this FBI job at Berkeley had just exacerbated that feeling of being cast in someone else's image, of being just a human puppet in the FBI's puppet show. After a couple of months at Berkeley it got even worse. My cover identity was starting to obliterate my real identity. When I would get high, I would fantasize about really being the radical hippie free-loving anarchic political rebel that I was pretending to be.

I didn't really have much to do at Berkeley. I wasn't a student so I didn't have classes to go to or tests to take. So, when I wasn't stoned or wasn't chasing hippie sluts, I started reading. It was the era of Existentialism and the popular books of the day that the students were all reading seemed to be dealing with exactly the problem that was bothering me. Self, identity, freedom, choice, were all the buzz words of that dominant sixties philosophy and they were exactly the issues that I was struggling with in the doldrums of my double life. I started out with Hesse. Everyone was reading him. *Steppenwolf. Siddhartha.* He was the poet of lost identity, the guru of the questioning self. And then Sartre.

He was the high priest of Existentialism. He made the rules, laid down the roadmap to selfhood. His "Existence precedes Essence" was the mantra of the whole Existential sixties. I tried to read *Being and Nothingness,* but got lost in its verbose and jargoned philosophical arguments. But then I found his much more available essay "Existentialism is a Humanism" and he started to make sense to me. Next I discovered Camus and he became my existential guide. *The Myth of Sisyphus. The Stranger.* They were so clear, so conversant with my own confusion about myself. But remember, all this time, while I was exploring these concepts of self and identity, I was leading a double life. The problem was that now that my double life was over I felt as if I didn't have any life at all. Michael Edwards had never really surfaced as an existential being yet. I was totally essence-dominated, pulled this way and that by others, a passenger at life not the driver. About the only thing I was driving was my Volkswagen bus and with very little delay I put Berkeley in its rear-view mirror.

CHAPTER 6: MORE CETOLOGY

D riving out of Berkeley, I had no destination, no roadmap for the rest of my life. I had no connection to any real world. There were no people I could go to for shelter or understanding. My parents on the farm didn't count. They had never really understood my precociousness, my difference from all the other children in the school. They especially didn't understand my strange power of memory and enhanced sight, and I didn't want to burden them with my problems anyway, those nice aging farm people. Ironically, the only real friend I had was Lenny and I had just run out on him, fled his influence in my hippied-up Volkswagen bus. I found myself wandering through the West looking for something to hang on to.

OK. That's enough. Now I'm just whining over my situation. Yes, without a doubt I was really messed up. Sure, I was lost. Definitely, I was extremely guilty over the Judas role I had played for more than a year and a half in Berkeley. I was all of those things as I fled Berkeley. But as I drove east toward the California line I suddenly realized that my immediate problem was that I was out of grass.

Driving east, however, I couldn't think of any place else to go except back home to Indiana. I knew I could never stay there to live, never settle into my parents' bucolic life. As I drove, I thought about my parents and that triggered a lot of overly vivid memories. Perhaps then this is a good point in this feckless narrative to go back in time and remember my growing up with them in Indiana. Actually, amateur autobiographer that I am, I now suddenly realize that remembering at least one important aspect of those long-gone days of childhood will prove really useful for what was about to happen next in my, at this point, aimless life.

I also realize now that this book I am writing has really given you readers very little to go on about my life before the Cuban Missile Crisis and the Kennedy Assassination. I was in my early twenties when those two dramatic events consumed my power of Eidetic Memory. I had lost my identity, my existential selfhood, in an unconsidered servitude to others, to the state, to Lenny's magnetic influence, to the C.I.A., to the Secret Service, whatever. But finally, driving east, I asked my memory for help, for something out of the past that I could cling to, buoy myself up with. I was pushing thirty and the sixties were receding in my rear-view mirror. Ironically as I drove, my nagging memory transported me back to my childhood.

My parents were devout Catholics. After my dad survived World War II and got out of the Army and came home to Indiana to take over his father's farm, the Catholic Church played a major part in our lives. In fact, as I look back analytically on it now, when I was growing up the Catholic Church actually defined the circadian rhythms of our lives in that small farming community. We celebrated the hell out of Christmas, Lent, Good Friday, Easter, all of the Roman Catholic holidays that comprised the year, the changes of the seasons, the events in the life of Jesus and the Apostles way back then.

I didn't go to a Catholic school because we didn't have one out there in the country. But after Mass every Sunday I went to Catholic catechism classes. I started with them when I was in the first grade and, for some reason that Lenny never understood, stuck with them all through high school. I think I was drawn in because they were good stories set in a far-off time. Of course, after the first few years they weren't really catechism classes. They were Bible-reading sessions with the local parish priest one evening a week complimented by the Sunday sermons which I got into the habit of listening closely to, of depositing in my memory, of critiquing weekly. So, on Fridays when Lenny, who was also Catholic, sort of, was ordering hamburgers at the local diner in town, I would be eating fish stick sandwiches that tasted like cow patties and settling in to read my Bible in preparation for Sunday's gospel and sermon. Then, when I got to college, I continued to go to Mass every Sunday (something that Lenny could never understand) especially to listen to the sermons of the priests who ran the college Catholic church and Newman Center. Their sermons were, naturally, more academic, more theological, as befitted the more intellectual atmosphere of the university as compared to my former rural cornfield Catholic Church. I guess it was just a matter of habit that I would get out of bed on Sunday mornings, leaving Lenny snoring contentedly in our dorm room, and go to Mass.

OK, call it backstory. Call it foreshadowing. Call it whatever the hell you want. But because I'm the narrator of this memory piece and a cranky old man to boot who thinks that at this juncture it is important,

I'm going to tell you about my growing up. No, about my growing up Catholic. You see, it has a lot to do, as I see it, with the structure of this book, with my memory story, with the strange structure of my life. And you, as readers, should realize what a trustworthy and reliable narrator I am. My Eidetic Memory would stand for nothing else.

So, after I fled Berkeley and was driving east all alone and was thinking seriously about my identity problems, about how thus far in my life "essence," the controlling world outside my "self," had always preceded my "existence," that is when I harkened back to my early Catholic upbringing. My Eidetic Memory was on full power. One moment I was driving away from one life and the next moment my remarkable memory was transporting me back in time to my grade school, high school, college days going to Mass. It was then that my memory fixed upon one governing Catholic concept that had always intrigued me. "Transubstantiation." When I first started thinking about it back in my catechism days, I thought it was a really cool word. But when I started thinking about it driving east that day, I started thinking that it was an idea I could really embrace, an idea I could use to understand what my Eidetic Memory had done with my life (and what perhaps it could do for my life in the future). But wait, I am getting rather ahead of myself in the retelling of my story. Driving east that far off day I think "Transubstantiation" sort of came to my rescue out of the existential funk that I was in.

Transubstantiation. The high point of the Mass. The miracle that the priests pull off every Sunday. Christ's great metaphor. Actually, in its intonation at the Consecration, the Transubstantiation is really rather poetic. Listen:

Take this all of you and eat of it,
For this is my body,
Which will be given up for you.

Take this all of you, and drink from it,
For this is the chalice of my blood,
The blood of the new and eternal covenant,
Which will be poured out for you and for many,
For the forgiveness of sins.
Do this in memory of me.

That last poetic line, the invocation of "memory," I realized was what really reverberated for me. That was it, Memory. That last line signaled the controlling theme of Christ's Transubstantiation poem. Memory was the whole motive of that Christian alchemy, bread into body, wine into blood, that metaphoric miracle to always be remembered. Memory was the whole reason for the choreography of the Transubstantiating ceremony, first at the biblical Last Supper, and then repeated every single day all around the world at the focal point of the Mass. It was as if there at the Last Supper the Ur-Priest was sending a message of memory to be repeated every day for centuries. Remember. Remember me. Isn't that what we all want? Isn't that our only leverage against death?

Jesus wasn't so dumb. He knew when he said that in the upper room that night of the Last Supper that he was going to die in the next few days. In fact, he knew from the very start that memory would be mankind's tool for overcoming his death by crucifixion, for believing in and marveling at his resurrection and ascending into heaven as his story goes, his great enduring memory piece. He also seemed to be saying that memory is, or could be, everyone's personal means of defeating death. It certainly is everyone's means of bringing our dead back to life. In fact. memory is itself a miracle, like the raising of Lazarus or Jesus' own Resurrection. It has the miraculous power of reassuring us of our own existence as formed out of our personal past and the pasts of all of those that we remember, both living and dead.

As I drove east and my Eidetic Memory pulsed Catholic, I realized that the whole ritual of Transubstantiation is itself a poetic memory piece. Jesus's poem, his ode to "memory," as recited by the priest in the Mass, is actually a quote from the biblical narrative of the Last Supper. I realized that from the beginning, from my days as an altar boy, age eight, nine, ten, when I would kneel in front of the priest as he stood at the altar raising first the host, the bread, and then the chalice, the wine, I had been drawn to the ritual of the Transubstantiation. *What a neat trick,* I remember me thinking way back then. I think that even then, at that young age, I always doubted the bread actually became the body of Christ and the wine His blood. And yet I still was caught up with the idea of it all.

Forget Jesus, it was the idea that the very substance of something could be transformed into something completely different. Remember the ancient alchemists? They embraced the same idea except their substances were much less common or available to all, much more commercial and capitalist. Back then I wasn't yet conversant with the concept of metaphor so the idea existed as something I thought might be really capable of happening. Later driving east out of Berkeley, I started seriously analyzing the metaphor of Transubstantiation. My question was: *If it is Christ's great metaphor, then a metaphor for what? Just what does it represent, this miraculous changing of the essence of the bread and wine? Is it sending a certain message to all of us later generations?*

Ideas are rather fragile things. Often, they exist only to be disproved. Existentialism is a good example. It had really a rather long shelf life. Conceived in the 1940s as an antidote for Nazism and Communism and all of the other Essence-imposing forces of the mid-twentieth-century, it spoke to a lot of disciples throughout the sixties, seventies and even the eighties of the last century. But then the naysayers, the deconstructionists, the technocracies, rose up to replace it. Certainly, ideas are fragile things. But Transubstantiation as an idea kept alive by the ritual of the Mass has survived for over 2000 years pretty much unedited, intact. The poem, the metaphor, recited every time the Mass has been celebrated over the centuries, has held up, offering itself, like the bread and the wine, for interpretation, for a constant recurring Transubstantiation. It resurfaced in my memory as I was driving east in my bus that day so long ago. It resurrected itself just for me one might say. It became the idea I saw as a means of finally placing my existence before the essence that I had become.

Traversing time, much later in life, long after my flight into the desert from Berkeley, I listened one evening to Leonard Bernstein's *Mass.* When it reached that moment of Transubstantiation at its center, I immediately remembered my own journey to Transubstantiation so many years before. My priest always ended the whole Transubstantiation ceremony with the unadorned declaration: "The mystery of faith." That should have been a tipoff for me as to how to take the whole thing. But, again, I was still too young to really figure it out. All I knew then was that this Transubstantiation thing really was a pretty cool idea. But then, fleeing Berkeley, my mind reeling in a chaos of non-existence, suddenly my memory seized on this idea of Transubstantiation and I started to mold it to my own confused situation. *Perhaps the very substance of reality could be changed if one believed.* I knew I was secularizing the whole idea, but to me that seemed irrelevant. *The principle of Transubstantiation didn't have to just be a God-trick. Why couldn't it just as well be a Man-trick? After all, Jesus was both God and Man wasn't he?* I thought of the existential literature that I had been reading. Those existentialists were trying to perform the same Transubstantiating trick, changing an essence-dominated life into a life of existence where the true self came to the fore.

That was when I really started to relax, somewhere around Salt Lake City, and came down off of the guilt-stressed, utterly disconnected cross that the whole Berkeley episode had nailed me to. OK, I know that I just went too far with that metaphor. Sorry, I got carried away. When I left Berkeley, I felt like I was completely empty, hollow. I had sold myself to the FBI, a Judas at the Last Supper. But then, strangely, I had found hope in this whole metaphor of Transubstantiation. I wanted to go to Mass to listen to the priest recite the words. Have you any idea how hard it is to find a Catholic Church in Salt Lake City, Utah? But I finally found one and went to Mass and the words were still the same as they had always been. The poem to memory was as magical as when it had first been recited at the Last Supper. Leaving Salt Lake my freakish memory skated over all of the transubstantive evolutions of my life over the years and I reveled over the mystery as it had unfolded. That moment, listening to Bernstein's miraculous crescendo, became an indicator for me of just how my Eidetic Memory had changed my life, my lives, over the years. How that Memory had presided over my personal collection of separate selves. But once again I get ahead of myself in this amateur autobiography.

I know that I have been rambling on about Transubstantiation now for a number of pages but I felt that I had to do it for two reasons. First, like that whale-obsessed narrator of *Moby Dick* constantly returning to his "Cetology's," I will paraphrase a contemporary cliché of self-enlightenment: Transubstantiation was for me "the whale in the room" and I felt I had to deal with it. I realized that as my life story progressed that idea, not in its religious application but in its secular presence, would become my way of explaining my constantly evolving consciousness and life experience. But secondly, my reflection upon Transubstantiation became a stabilizing stream of thought. It gave me hope that despite this identity-less, hollow, black hole of regret that the whole Berkeley experience had sucked me into, maybe I could transubstantiate myself into a person that I could stomach. I drove east and then south. Somehow, I ended up at the North Rim of the Grand Canyon. As I stared into that unbelievably great abyss, which in my self-pity I compared to my own situation, everything quite suddenly came together for me. My resilient memory all of a sudden started to recharge itself as if it had been plugged into some brooding power source emanating, perhaps, from that surging river so far below. I realized that all we can really be certain of is our past, the information that our memories call up for us. We can't control the future at all, can't even really see what is coming at us. But our past could put us into an orbit, a pattern pushing us toward a transubstantiating future. I'm sorry, reader, I realize that I am raving almost metaphysically, but it should signal you about how truly messed up, lost, up in the air, I was that day looking down into the Grand Canyon.

Oh, and one other narrative touchstone that I am sure that you readers will find of interest. Finally, I have come to a part of my story that Lenny had nothing whatsoever to do with. I had fled Berkeley and by the time I hit the Nevada line I had decided that I'd had enough of the West. I honestly didn't know where I was headed except that it was back East, probably home to Indiana, at least for a while. In other words, my life was all pretty much up in the air, as I drove away from Lenny, the FBI, Berkeley, Victoria, and my days as J. Edgar Hoover's Judas goat.

I was completely alone with my thoughts as I headed east. It was just me running away, no road maps, just highway signs. Reno, Tahoe, Salt Lake City. Along the way I would stop for gas and cokes and gas-station pies and look out at the desolate wastelandscapes around me and wonder who I was and where I was going and what was before me. Believe me, all that was behind me was, to my great chagrin, indelibly lodged in my vivid visual memory. And, as I drove, that was when my muddled head fixed on the idea of Transubstantiation. And that's when I pulled into the Grand Canyon Park, North Rim. I was tired, almost dozing off, when I passed a sign for it and I thought *Why Not?* I took a nap in the bus for a while, then when I woke up and looked out I realized that I was in a really different and special kind of place. What happened next is the episode that I said earlier Lenny had nothing to do with. If anybody had anything to do with it, it was God.

I had gotten out of the bus and was leaning on a metal railing at the edge of a massive stone outcropping overlooking the canyon. The view was the likes of which I had never seen before or even presumed to imagine. I guess there is a real reason they call it the "Grand" Canyon. Stretched out before me for what looked like miles across its great expanse was a massive landscape of depth crenellated with maze-like passages worn into the rock by centuries of glacial sculpting. While most western United States landscapes stretch out under a big sky and rise to a high horizon, this landscape descended sharply, brutally, darkly into a deep, deep abyss, almost hellish in its plunging depth to a rocky floor below. As I stared straight down over the railing, it reminded me of the descriptions of the lairs of dragons in Tolkien's *Lord of the Rings* that I had read in high school. And down below in the gorge, snaking through the brooding passageways of rock, was the river. It was the Colorado River I learned later, though I wasn't in Colorado at all. But to me it was more like the River Styx wending its way through that hellish rockscape below.

But I am waxing melodramatic in the service of the stunningly powerful effect of my first impression of that amazing place. It was an impression that worked powerfully upon my ragged, guilty and discouraged consciousness. Yes, I certainly have gone overboard with my description, but when an Eidetic sees something as memorable as this, he sees it in ways that no one else does or can. He sees it in perfect detail in terms of color, texture, shape, line, like an art expert studying through a magnifying glass the brush strokes of a priceless oil painting. That scene, my first view of the Grand Canyon, throbs in my oversensitive memory. In reality I was looking out on a striking panorama of sky, air, layers of earth tones, and of course that greenish-blue water far below. The rock passages through and across the canyon were brown and red and orange and moss green. The sky above was also layered in bright blue close-up to me to a shadowy grey out over the center of the canyon to a blue-black gathering above the south rim far, far away.

As I said before, I was leaning against an iron railing looking out over the edge of the Canyon when a voice behind broke into my reverie.

"It's really beautiful isn't it?"

I turned to see who it was talking to me and there she was. But I never got a chance to answer her question because at that very moment a bolt of lightning and a crash of thunder yanked both of our attentions back across the canyon. Somehow a dark rain cloud had formed out over the canyon's far rim and was moving steadily toward us accompanied by some bolts of lightning stabbing down into the canyon. The sight of it froze me for a minute. I remember thinking that it reminded me of a scene in a John Ford western that I really liked, *She*

Wore a Yellow Ribbon, where the cavalry is riding in formation across a western landscape with dark mesas in the background when suddenly a thunderstorm erupts around them and they are attacked by lightning bolts thrusting at them like jagged bayonets.

I turned back to the woman who addressed me and I remembered thinking that she was really pretty in a hippie kind of way, glasses, very curly hair like a fluffy halo all around her face, wearing a poncho or fringed jacket.

"Yes it is, really amazing," I finally replied to her. "But it looks like it is going to rain."

"I know, that dark cloud and that lightning is sort of coming right at us, isn't it?"

In the brief moments of this conversation the wind picked up and the gathering storm seemed rushing upon us. I was still holding a hand against the wind to the railing as I started to answer the question.

"Yeah, we better…"

Suddenly, I was jolted backwards through the air landing hard on my back on the stone floor. I must have blacked out for a few moments because when I came to the women was kneeling over me, cradling my head, and sort of gasping out words at me.

"Oh Jesus, are you all right? Are you OK? Oh my God."

At first, hearing her, I thought that she thought I was Jesus and she was praying to me. But quickly I realized that her words were just figures of alarmed speech, that she had been jolted out of her comfort zone just as I had. Though, admittedly, my jolt, which had thrown me about six feet through the air to land hard, was a lot more jolting than her jolt of surprise.

As I woke up, I found myself looking into the face of this extraordinary nut-brown, sun-freckled, curly-haired angel. It was at that moment that my whole life changed. It took long moments sitting there on the ground with her ministering to my stunned self for me to re-attach myself to reality. When I finally did clear my mind, I realized that it was that stupid iron railing that had done it. Evidently the electricity building violently up in the lightning and thunder storm had found a friendly conductor in that iron railing which had in turn sent a bolt of electricity into me strong enough to launch me into the air and slam dunk me. The cold rain pelting down on us then quickly revived me. She helped me to my feet and together we ran to my bus which just happened to be the vehicle parked closest to the spot of my near electrocution. Uninvited she scrambled into the bus with me and we both sat back, me behind the steering wheel, she in the passenger seat, large droplets of rain coursing out of our hair and down over our faces, huge windblown splashes of downpour pelting the windshield, and together breathed a huge sigh of relief.

"Oh, I'm so glad you're OK," she looked up at me right into my face. "that really scared me,"

"Shocked the hell out of me too." I replied, not realizing exactly how appropriate (and stupid) what I said really was.

At that she laughed.

And realizing the unintentional joke that I had made, so did I.

Looking back on that scene now, as I have many times over the years since, all I could ever think of was Saint Paul being knocked off his horse on the road to Damascus that I had read about from back in my Catholic grade school catechism days. When I said that was when my whole life changed, I really meant it. Her name was Nicole and, in a sense, she was like that angel who helped Saint Paul up off the ground that biblical day by the roadside. When I woke up and looked into her face, strangely enough I knew right away that she was the one. It was right then and there that my life finally started to change, to take on some new substance, to look for a new path, a new existence to use Sartre's word, or even better, to transubstantiate. It was as if, out on that rock, like Sisyphus, I realized that I still could be happy despite all of the baggage I was carrying around, despite all of the regrets that my powerful Eidetic Memory had stored up and weighted me down with.

But, enough philosophy and theology, there I was sitting in the front seat of my VW bus dripping away with this lovely woman, who I didn't even know but who I already had decided that I was in love with. Then the rain stopped and the sun burst out like it had been there all the time just waiting for us. I had never been very successful with women until I got to Berkeley and all of those free-love, sex-crazed hippie girls. Then what Victoria and I had wasn't really a relationship. She was both a bodyguard against the raging sexual hungers that most of the women we hung out with had and she was an *entre* into the most entrenched circles of the Berkeley radicals. Though what Victoria and I had wasn't really a relationship, it was the closest thing to one that I had ever had. But now, here I was, thinking in really extravagant terms, after an acquaintance of roughly four minutes, about having a real relationship with this total stranger who I had just met by flying through the air into her arms.

She: I hope you don't mind me following you in here out of the rain.

She finally broke the awkward silence. I hadn't said anything because I was still sort of only half back from my recent fly-by.

She: I guess I wanted to make sure you were OK, after what just happened out there you know.

Me: No, no problem. It was really raining out there. Yes, I'm fine. The rain sort of woke me up, you know, got my head sort of back straight. Looks like the sun is actually out now.

She : Yes, well, I'll be going then. I'm glad you're OK. That sort of really scared me.

Me: No, wait, don't go. I want to thank you. For taking care of me, you know. Where did you come from anyway? It's like you appeared out of nowhere.

She laughed at that, a smiling lilting laugh that made her look and sound even more like an angel.

She: I came on that tour bus over there, (she pointed) with all of those old people.

Me: Really?

She: Yeah, I didn't know what I was getting into. Most of them have canes and walkers. I mean, it's depressing. That's why I was out on this point where you were. I signed on to the tour in Vegas because I really wanted to see the Grand Canyon.

Me: My name is Mike, Michael Edwards, Mike.

I held out my hand for her to shake like an A-1 doofus.

She: Nicole, Nicole McKee.

And she gave me a firm handshake as if she didn't think I was an idiot at all.

Her touch was electric. I didn't want to let her hand go. But I did, immediately, as if I had been shocked for the second time that morning. I looked at her and my mind began to race. *How do I keep her here? How do I make her want to stay? What do I say? How do I keep her from thinking I'm some sort of creep?*

I might add that I really like her name. Nicole. It pulsed with Paris, with French romance, with a hint of all those French philosophers that I had been reading in Berkeley.

That was it, my prompt.

Me: Nicole. What a nice name. Are you French?"

N: No, no. My parents are Scotch-Irish, I think. But my mom told me she always wanted to go to France and that's probably why she picked my name.

Me: Nicole.

I said it again as if I was tasting it with my tongue.

Me: It really is a cool name.

Then I realized that I was making the whole conversation awkward again and I was afraid that she was about to bolt.

N: Well, I better get back to the bus before it leaves without me.

Me: Yes, of course."

She started to open the door and climb down out of the bus.

Me: Wait! (she could probably hear the panic in my voice) Are you going back to Vegas on that tour bus?

N: Yes, it is just a day trip.

And that is when I took the plunge, just decided to work without a net, risk everything on the off chance that maybe I could project some sort of completely unreasoned and undeserved trust.

Me: I'm driving to Vegas this afternoon. Instead of getting back on that bus with all those old people would you like to ride with me?

She thought about it for a long minute. Her lips pursed. Her nose crinkled up. Then her brilliant blue eyes went wide and she smiled back at me.

N: Why yes, I think I'd like that.

So she climbed back into the passenger seat next to me and off we went.

I will pick them back up in Las Vegas that evening in a page or so, but now I just want to return briefly to the real subject of this Cetology chapter, that "whale in the room," Transubstantiation, that I had been thinking so strangely about as I drove toward my taking flight at the Grand Canyon. If you remember, before we were so electrostatically interrupted, I had just separated the whole Mass ceremony of Transubstantiation from its religious moorings, gave it a small "t": signaling its secularization. Then I applied it to my own existential longing for a new life, a new identity, a new substance to my existence. Have you ever noticed how so many biblical stories and more modern literary ones take place on the road? St Paul, who I mentioned earlier. The Good Samaritan. Mary and Joseph and the Magi all traveling toward Bethlehem. Or later, the picaresque novel from Don Quixote to Mr. Pickwick to Jack Kerouac to the Hobbits, even to Queequeg and

Starbuck and Captain Ahab (though theirs was a watery road). The road and the experiences, obstacles, adventures, they encountered on the way changed all of their lives, transubstantiated them. Literature is packed with examples of just these sorts of life-changing experiences. Lord Jim fighting to redeem himself after abandoning the Patna. Marlow meeting Kurtz in the Congo. Thoreau first discovering Walden Pond. Nick Carraway's first meeting with Gatsby. Pip first being seduced into his great expectations. For better or for worse, as a blessing or a curse, these life-changing moments are everywhere in literature. It is as if St. Paul is being knocked off his horse over and over again. I'm in no way saying that what happened back there at the Grand Canyon was any sort of religious experience. What I'm really only saying is that I can definitely identify that moment as the sharp signal of a tectonic shift in my life, a moment that my Eidetic Memory would come to realize had happened before. When I saw those ruts in the Cuban clearing or when I spotted those men by the fence that morning in Dallas or when Victoria in Berkeley had looked right at me as she was being led away in handcuffs, those were all transubstantiating moments though I hadn't really recognized them as such at the time. No none of those were religious experiences. However, as I thought back on them, I realized that transubstantiation could be secular as well as religious. To me, it became perfectly clear that over a lifetime our body and blood could reconstitute itself a number of times. One didn't need grass or peyote or magic mushrooms to experience the spiritual high of secular transubstantiation. All one needed to do was wake up from a bad dream and see the face of an angel.

"Good morning America, how are you?" Arlo Guthrie rasped out of my Volkswagen bus's radio as Nicole and I drove toward Las Vegas. The sun was up, the mountain air was clean, the road was almost all downhill, and that seemed like a really appropriate song for our journey. Most people refer to Las Vegas as sin city, but for Nicole and I Vegas would be fun city, bright lights city. And yes, what some might look at as sin, but what Nicole and I were pretty sure was making love.

Our lives are like our shoes. We try them on, break them in, walk around in them for a while, get completely comfortable in them. That's how it was for me and Nicole that first night in Vegas. We walked the streets, talked non-stop, bathed in the bright lights all around us. We change the paths of our lives constantly and sometimes we don't even know we are doing it. I think the neon pathways of that city in the desert just went to our heads that night, and it happened so fast. Vegas back then wasn't like it is today in the 21st Century. Oh, the lights were bright and the hotels were plush and the names on the marquees—Sinatra, Dean Martin, Wayne Newton, the magicians and the lion tamers and the comedians—were impressive, seductive, but it was nothing like today. No Eiffel Tower. No Pyramid of Giza. No water ballet. No Pirate battle. No Stratosphere. No Trump Tower. No bronze statue of Elvis. Time and memory are such co-conspirators. Vegas is such a good example of how time and memory paint impressionistic pictures of the past, complex shimmering images of an ancient age, so long ago but so close at hand. Things were different then. The mob, real gangsters, were running Vegas. I, we, were different then. Men and women trusted each other, for better or for worse. Feminism was just starting to grow-teeth. Free love was a delicious appetite that was in full flower. Vegas was an erotic Babylon that offered tremendous potential for illicit action and radical departure from the norms of the fifties puritanical society that had been washed away by Vietnam and Watergate and the precarious instability of seventies American society. Vegas was sexual and inviting, sexual license or sexual freedom, whatever one wished to call it. It was a gleaming, hot, neon-lit, excess-dripping valley of beckoning sin. It was all of those things and more.

But for us the bright lights and the day for night atmosphere were all we needed. I had plenty of money left over from my sojourn undercover in Berkeley. I took Nicole out to dinner at a really fancy hotel/casino. After we ate, we played some slot machines and drank some free drinks that the waitresses in really short skirts for those days brought around. Then we got a really fancy hotel room, in a place called *The Frontier*. I remember it had a huge picture of Wayne Newton on its marquee. Nicole really liked that room with its huge king-sized bed and its modernistic stuffed couches and easy chairs. It even had a Jacuzzi tub that we could fill up and play in if we wanted.

As soon as we got into the room Nicole moved into my arms and we started kissing, our first kiss. It was all so relaxed, so natural, just so right. No desperation like it had been in high school. No manipulation or using like it had been with Victoria in Berkeley. I have to admit that Nicole spun my head in a whole new direction. Her kiss literally switched off my Eidetic Memory, made me forget all that had come before. Her kiss triggered my first conscious transubstantiation, my first non-Lenny life choice. This time there was nobody to answer to but the two of us, the two of us together, wanting each other, the door closed behind, the bed like our own special world beckoning before us. That magnificent room beckoning us into a whole new life, maybe the way that the river flowing before them held out such promise of freedom for Huck and Jim in Twain's novel. Oh yes, that first night in Vegas we made love, stepped out of our old walking shoes, threw off our socks, and let our naked feet lead us across the plush deep pile carpet into a whole new dimension. That king-size bed was our raft, that plush carpet was our river. Finding each other was our break for freedom and a new life.

Making love with Nicole was a kind of miracle for me. She melted my whole being down into the bodies and blood of our love-making. When we made love it was so clean, so pure. I think you 21st-century readers probably get my point. There was no hurry about our love-making, no urgency, no sense of having to prove oneself. In fact, we didn't want it ever to be finished. We were so together, so one with each other. There was no real before or after, just a perfect now.

Nicole came to my rescue at exactly the right time. I had very little idea of who she was or where she had come from. She didn't know me from Adam. And yet we came together as lovers as naturally, as powerfully, as suddenly as that bolt of lightning over the Grand Canyon that had launched me into her arms. For three days we roamed the streets of Las Vegas taking in the sights, laughing at the people, mocking the monstrosities, eating well, drinking silly umbrella drinks, blinking at the nighttime neon, and, of course, spending most of our time in that wonderful king-size bed in that garish hotel, morning, noon, and night.

If any memory rises to the high level of Eidetic magnification, it has to be the memory of one's first soul-enveloping love. Not just finding a soulmate but falling under the spell of a soul sorceress. That was what I found in Las Vegas in Nicole. Perhaps it was because I was lost and she found me. Perhaps it was because I was ready to shed my past life and go in a completely different direction. Perhaps it was because I was just trapped in the numbing reality of years of anti-existential nausea. But Nicole was my doorway back into life, my guide to happiness in that neon wonderland, that emerald Oz, that hopeful Camelot, that absurd *faux* world which as time went on into the 21st century would build its Eiffel Tower, its Great Pyramid, its stratospheric skyscrapers, it's miniature New York, its pirate ships, its dancing waters, its shimmering simulacrums of the whole world lined up along one wide boulevard. I know that all of those places weren't there in the seventies. I think *Circus Circus* was probably as good as it got back then. But we didn't care. As we explored all the byways of Las Vegas, we were drawn to the city's excesses like two lovers dancing in a dream.

And we made love. For three days we made love to each other in every possible way. If you did the old journalist's 5 Ws test on our love-making we would pass with flying colors. We were two people finding each other for the first time (who), definitely coming together, as one, often orgasming at the same time (what), in our king-size bed in the Frontier, in the shower and the jacuzzi tub, (where), at every hour of the day and night, groping each other, caressing each other, fondling, feeling, touching, loving, the whole time we were with each other(when), and of course (why).

Actually, I'm not really sure that we really knew "why" we were doing it, but we didn't care one bit. Making love in that ridiculous city, that simulacra of reality, that absurd imitation of life, we found each other and it set us free from the past, liberated us from the gifts and the guilts of memory. To put it in terms of my transubstantive metaphor, in those three days in Vegas we turned the unleavened bread and the insipid wine of our deadened pasts into orgasmically joined bodies and sexually boiling blood. I think, looking back at it now from this great distance, that neither one of us even thought of it as anything as mundane as just "fucking." No, we were making love in the most soul-changing traditions of the past, like the great lovers Dante and Beatrice, Eloise and Abelard, Romeo and Juliet, Caesar and Cleopatra, Gatsby and Daisy, Scarlett and Rhett,(but in a much less romantic setting than all of they).

Ah, but all of those love stories came to sad endings, didn't they? And after those three days we realized that we too had to return to reality. Nicole had to go home, back to her job, which I found out was a high school English teacher in Denver. The last thing she had planned for on her tour bus vacation to Las Vegas was three days non-stop love-making with a mysterious stranger literally thrown into her arms by god. She had a plane ticket, but it was only a one-day drive to Denver and neither one of us wanted our absurd, comical, neon idyll to end, so I talked her into letting me drive her there. Years later, watching TV, I saw a commercial for Las Vegas whose tag line went: "What happens in Vegas stays in Vegas." Back then, in our case, that *risqué* slogan didn't really hold true. Little did we know it at the time, but when we left our magical three days in Vegas we had an extra passenger coming along for the ride.

It was in another magical place called Canyonlands in eastern Utah looking out over a river-carved filigree of rock channels that I asked Nicole to marry me. When I actually said it out loud (*I had been thinking about it all the way up on our drive from Vegas*), it hit Nicole standing on the edge of that canyon every bit as hard as that lightning bolt that hit me on the edge of the Grand Canyon four days earlier. She, being much much saner than me, flinched, stepped back one step, thought about it for a long silent awkward minute, and then said:

N: Oh Mike, no, no, we've only known each other for four days. We have to see where this goes. If it goes well, if it goes past Denver, ask me again, when I'm not totally flustered, when reality has set back in."

Well, of course, I was disappointed. But as I think about it now that first proposal was born out of the hot rush of blood that had been our time in Vegas. Somebody once said or wrote, whatever, that "love is not the place you've come to, it's the place you go from." For Nicole and me Vegas in all of its superficial, fake, *faux*, foolish splendor was that place. It didn't make any difference that it was all phony. For us it was the special place where we found each other and we were soon to realize would be even more special for us because it was where we made our baby.

Too soon I had to drop Nicole off in Denver. She had to go back to work the next day. She lived in an apartment in a building. I didn't go in with her. We stood at the curb and said our goodbye. She shot the elephant there in the street:

N: Mike, when I said 'no' to you yesterday, it was the right thing to do. But it wasn't the end of it. Let's think about it. You drive back to Indiana, see your parents, get back on the farm. I'll go back to work. Let what we have cool. Then let's talk again. Then let's see where we are."

We kissed right there in the street between my hippie bus and her solid brick building, a long lingering kiss that neither one of us wanted to end. But end it did and I drove away. She waved me all the way down the street to the corner.

Driving cross-country toward Indiana seemed so surreal to me as if I was trapped inside a dream. It was as if all of my life was simply a dream laid out in Eidetic chapters. It was a dream like Scrooge had in that old Christmas story. There was the guilty past dominated by memory. There was the orgiastic present with all my feelings for Nicole rushing in on me, spinning my mind in a vortex of hot pulsing emotions. And then there was the frightening, or maybe fulfilling and freeing, future with Nicole. As I drove, the Eidetic aspect of my past story, my life plot, kicked in. *Would this dream of love that I was in end and Nicole fade like one of Scrooge's ghostly visions? Was my whole life thus far just a dream that I periodically woke up from before falling back into a new dream? Was my life destined to be a succession of Eidetic chapters like this book that I am writing now from my memory's observation post in the future? Is that what memory really is—a map of self-transubstantiation?* It is interesting to think back on it now writing from my vantage point in the finished future, to see that you live many different lives within a lifetime.

You know how you know that you are really in love? It is when you just flat can't stop thinking about the other person, when you literally seize up in your throat because you miss her so much, want to be with her so bad. You know that you are truly in love when your lover's voice echoes in your memory like the haunting melody from the most beautiful song you have ever heard. Driving cross-country I was driving away from Nicole, but actually it was as if I was driving more toward her than away. She was all I could think about. *Nicole. Nicole. Where is she? What is she doing? Is she thinking of me? Was our Las Vegas idyll real or just a dream?* She had totally inhabited my mind. Good Lord, I was almost thirty years old and I had fallen in love for the first time. I had to laugh at myself as the miles piled up behind me and the future, invisible, stretched out ahead. I was a real case of arrested development. Or perhaps I was just at a stop-over on my journey to Eidetic transubstantiation.

CHAPTER 7: ACADEMIA

I turned thirty and my rootless hippie life-style sputtered out just like the engine on my VW bus. In those days thirty was the age after which no one could be trusted. The bus made one more trip west, to be with Nicole, and sputtered out, burping and coughing, just as I was driving back into Denver. My restless sojourn at the farm in Indiana with my parents had only lasted six weeks when Nicole called me to tell me that she was pregnant. Though that news had shocked my parents, it didn't really make any difference to me. I had already decided that I had to go back to Denver to be with her. Those seven months waiting for our baby to be born were some of the happiest Nicole and I ever had. It was just the two of us doing everything together. My FBI blood money was still coming in thanks to the typical government bureaucracy that took months to figure out how to expunge me from their books (a task a good accountant could have sorted out in about fifteen minutes). So the checks kept showing up and I kept cashing them and my so-called handlers never noticed for months that I wasn't still in Berkeley. Nicole and I hiked in Colorado's mountains and visited Denver's museums and even went to the big Stock Show and Rodeo that passed through town every May. That extravaganza was the harbinger of spring for that cowboy town backed right up against the front range of those magnificent Rocky Mountains. It was a glorious time for us, a time of young love and togetherness and freedom.

Then, at the end of those seven months, our daughter Grace came along, smoothly, entering our lives with a quick yelp, then a calm contented smile, and the opening of two of the bluest, most beautiful eyes that Nicole and I had ever imagined. She was perfect and she became our guide into a very different kind of happiness and a whole new perspective on our lives. Just as up until then Lenny had been my guide, leading me along the paths of my inferno and purgatorio, so did Grace lead Nicole and I into the paradise of parenthood. We named her after my grandmother Grace (never Gracie, never never like that addled woman on sixties television) no, Grace, as in "saving grace" and "amazing grace" and "gracefulness" and "the grace of god" and all of our little family of three's "good graces." Grace had always been my personal favorite name. Yes, it was my grandma's name who had been really nice to me when I was a little kid, but it was more than that. To me Grace meant that you were special in the eyes of god, calm and pure and full of grace, a child of heaven.

I sold the bus and traded in my hippie lifestyle for a family life with Nicole and Grace. And I started looking for a job. I quickly decided that the heavy dark cloud that had been hovering over me, stalking me since grad school, was finally going to have to be acknowledged. I decided that maybe a job as a professor was the path I should have taken in the first place right after I got my Ph.D. Academia beckoned and I took the bait like a largemouth clamping on a noisy spinner or a sexy repalla. Thus, my academic career flowed over me just as our hippie life was ebbing away.

Remember, I had a bachelors and a masters degree in "Criminology" from Purdue University and a Ph.D. degree in "Foreign Service" from Georgetown, so I was pretty well qualified to do a lot of different stuff in an academic setting. Despite the Criminology degree, I had never really considered being a cop, but then (thanks to Lenny) I had ended up at the FBI anyway. And I never really considered going into the Foreign Service, but I was so good at learning foreign languages (thanks of course to my Eidetic Memory) that it seemed a really logical choice for graduate study for me. If you really want to know the truth, I traded my hippie lifestyle for a truly happy family life and an academic job so boring that at least once a month I contemplated hanging myself in the garage. But there was always Nicole and Grace to pull me out of my black ops days. Actually, when I made out my job resume for an academic position, I really had high hopes that I would be starting an exciting new life totally different from the three lives under Lenny's evil influence that I had led up to this point. Boy was I wrong on that!

There may be no more boring an existence than a life in academia. "Academia"—it sounds like some sort of a disease doesn't it? Like nausea or myasthenia or clamydia or neurosthenia or amnesia the disease of the memory. I don't know what I was thinking, but I threw myself wholeheartedly into academia as if it was the solution to all my problems. I had a wife now and a child on the way and I needed a steady job. Like an idiot I convinced myself that academia was the place for me. And it was. And I thrived in that fetid swamp of intellectual boredom. And worse yet, I toiled there for twelve whole years. I got tenure right away after three and a half years. Ah tenure, academia's version of a life sentence though there was the chance of periodic parole. Those paroles were called "sabbaticals" and I got one—a half year off with full pay—after six years on the job. It was free money to do research in my field of expertise. Yeah, right! Nicole and I packed up Grace and fled academia for the beaches in California. We just drove until we dead-ended into the ocean. I had seen a sign that said "Beach Towns" just outside of L.A. and steered toward it. We rented a cottage right on the sand in Newport Beach, the Balboa Peninsula, just south of L.A. For two people who had just been paroled, Newport was like going back to the garden of Eden, an American Eden made up of sun and sand and surf but especially of freedom outside of the confines of jobs and faculty meetings and pseudo-sophisticated cocktail parties and teaching schedules and tenure committees.

But I am getting far ahead of myself in this narrative section focused on our descent into academia. First a word about "Tenure." Supposedly, Tenure is the Holy Grail of academia. Tenure is the equivalent of a guaranteed, lifetime, no-trade contract for a baseball player or a soccer star or an NBA freak. Tenure is supposedly academia's way of encouraging one to buy into the whole ivory tower life of the pipe-wielding, tweed-jacketed, elbow-patched, sherry-sipping academic world of pot-bellied pretention. In truth, Tenure is a really cleverly devised trap. Tenure is academia's way of castrating its constituents, of unsexing its utopian residents, of disarming any militant ambitions that an up-and-coming professor might bring to the fray of academic politics and publishing. In academia, Tenure is the ultimate lock-down, the solitary confinement that starves the intellect and wastes away the desire to accomplish anything even tangentially related to life in the outside world. Young professors pass through the gates of academia full of eager desires to do important work and contribute to the intellectual progress of knowledge and perhaps, in some fields, even society. Young professors charge toward Tenure, joust their way through the staged tournaments of academia like young knights hoping to be invited to sit at King Arthur's Round Table. Then, when they are finally granted Tenure, they suddenly, like Twain's Connecticut Yankee, are set back down out of their feckless dream and locked up in the gray boring prison of academic reality. Tenure shoots its recipients up with the irresistible drug of complacency. Tenure is indeed addictive. It is an open invitation to do nothing for the rest of your life (and get paid for it).

It seems like a blessing at first, a kind of freedom, but sooner or later you realize that you have lost your bearings, your ambition. Your ideas aren't coming to you anymore. You have lost touch with the realities of the outside world. You exist in an airless void, a black hole, a vacuum of your own making. Sartre and Camus would have hated the whole idea of Tenure. Baudrillard would have recognized it as a massive ironic joke.

I got Tenure really quickly, but once again I am getting a short way ahead of myself. I left off with you looking over my shoulder as I was making out my job application for academia. I didn't know the first thing about making out a resume for a job in academia so I just made it up as I went along. I listed my education—Purdue and Georgetown—my degrees—BA, MS, Ph.D.—my other academic interests besides Criminology and Foreign Service—History, Literature, languages (4), movies. By the way, while making up this resume I found out that in academia a resume isn't called a resume but rather a CV which stands for "Curriculum Vitae" which is Latin for "Life List" or something like that. At any rate, on my un-resume or CV or whatever, the thing that I did that was very un-resume was write two descriptive paragraphs about my work with the CIA in the Cuba affair and my work with the Secret Service for President Kennedy. I didn't write a paragraph about my year on the Berkeley campus as a stool pigeon for the FBI. I rightly figured that particular job experience probably wouldn't sit very well with academic hiring committees. It must have been an OK resume or CV or whatever, but probably it was so successful because I just had the right stuff (to echo Tom Wolfe) at the right time and place. You see, in 1972 when I started sending out my job applications, Purdue University, my old alma mater, had just decided to create a Forensics arm of their Criminology department where I had been one of their star undergraduates ten years before.

Anyway, I dutifully sent out my CVs. I should say "we" sent them out together because Nicole typed all twenty of them on our portable Olivetti typewriter using carbon paper to make copies so we would know who to and for what job we were applying. I only sent out twenty CVs because there just weren't that may universities then that had Criminology Departments. Michigan State was the pioneer in that field and therefore the most famous, but my old school, Purdue, back in Indiana, was a real up-and-comer in the field. Purdue was advertising for an Assistant Professor in Forensics to create a teaching lab as part of their established Criminology Department.

I didn't know squat about Forensics, but that is where my Eidetic Memory really came in handy. Over a period of four days I camped in the public library in downtown Denver and read everything I could find about the emerging Science of "Crime Scene Forensics." And, of course, I remembered every word of it as if my mind was some sort of player piano and the Forensics roll just kept spinning through it over and over again. Nonetheless, for whatever reason, and despite the fact that I was totally unqualified to fill the position they were advertising, Purdue University bit on my application and sent me money to take the Greyhound Bus back to Indiana for an interview.

That interview was hilarious, a complete joke. Much later I found out that I was the only candidate that the department head interviewed for the job because he had gone "gaga" over the fact that I had actually been in the same room with JFK. I also later found out from his secretary talking out of school one afternoon over beers in a campus bar that the department head actually thought I was CIA and had romanticized me in his imagination into some sort of dangerous ex-spy. Well, actually, I really was CIA…FOR THREE DAYS! My point is that the interview that I had traveled for across about a thousand miles in that pungent bus was a complete farce. I'm sure that the Criminology Department chairman who interviewed me had been so captivated by my CV that he had already made up his mind before I ever got there. I'm sure he would have hired me even if I showed up for his interview without any pants on.

As I said earlier, in my application I had described my Cuba Mission for the CIA and my Secret Service tour with President Kennedy. Remember, this was 1972 and the assassinations of 1968, and even the assassination of President Kennedy, were still festering wounds in the memories of all Americans. And those wounds weren't even close to healing.

"What was President Kennedy like? Gosh, what was it like to work for him, see him every day?" the Department Head asked me, hero-worship the pulsing undercurrent in his voice.

I told him that the President had always been very nice to me, hand-picked me for the job I did after my part in the Cuban Missile Crisis which had been the great triumph of his administration's foreign policy. I didn't tell him about the heavy burden of guilt that I still carried secretly within concerning my part in that fateful day in Dallas.

DH: And that Cuban Missile Crisis, I'm really interested? You were taken on by the CIA and sneaked into Cuba in the middle of the night? Fascinating. What did you do after they got you into Cuba?

Me: I counted.

I don't think that was the answer he expected at all.

DH: What do you mean?

Me: I counted.

I rather enjoyed watching him trying to figure out what I was talking about. I let him twist in the wind for a few more seconds.

Me: I counted machines. Rocket launchers. I counted people. Russian troops. Cuban troops. I computed the dimensions of their camp sites.

DH: Ah, you counted.

He said that as if he actually understood what my mission to Cuba was all about.

Anyway, the interview was a joke and the Department Head hired me on the spot and I took the job without the slightest hesitation. Indeed, I took the job eagerly, optimistically, little imagining how much I would grow to hate it. But I shouldn't be so hard on poor old Purdue University. Granted, it certainly didn't project the high ivied pretensions of the more storied universities of that era. Purdue was totally, and contentedly, actually quite proudly, red brick, more a trade school than a university, its major majors being Engineering and Agriculture. It took students in and four years later egested them out into the work force no real worse for wear. It was more an assembly line than a university in the classical sense, proud that it offered a conservative rather than a liberal education. But Purdue offered me and my little family one thing that made the job perfect for that time and that place in my life. Security.

I took the job without even thinking because I knew that at Purdue, in Indiana, far away from Lenny's evil influence, Nicole and Grace would be safe. For one thing, it was a great job for me because it was close to my parents' farm and Grace would have Grandpa and Grandma to dote over her. My parents would prove to be enthusiastic baby sitters for Grace to the point that she often spent as much time out at the farm as she did in our little apartment in West Lafayette. Grace just loved the farm, riding on the tractor with my dad, picking strawberries and making pies with my mom. She learned to milk a cow and gather eggs from the henhouse. But best of all she was always out and about in the fresh country air. Purdue was a pretty good deal in that sense of closeness to family, to a stable support system.

For another thing, it was a great job for me because it gave me *carte blanche* to create my own Forensics Lab, actually build from the ground up to all my very own specifications. It was my own little fiefdom inside the Criminology Department. I designed my Forensics Lab as if it was a movie studio with sound stages and sets for simulating crime scenes. I had three basic stages. The smallest was a bedroom which I imagined would be great for reproducing rapes, domestic violence, jewel thefts. It had a sliding door for illegal entry, breakaway windows for cat burglars to plunder, and all the requisite drapes and carpets and dresser drawers and jewelry boxes and, of course, the bed itself, for the collecting of the culpatory evidence that bedroom invaders always leave lying around or sticking to. My second stage, the biggest, highest-ceilinged room, was initially bare and designed for whatever larger multi-use the crime *du jour* demanded. It could be a bank or a school or a restaurant or a business office or a night club. My third stage was outside the back door of the building. It was an urban alley complete with dumpsters, homeless encampment furniture (a mattress, a tent, shopping carts), doorways in brick walls, and, of course, all chain-link fenced-in so its set decoration, its filthy ambiance, could not be disturbed.

Besides these three crime scene sets, off the main hallway of the Criminology Department building (which we shared with the English Department) I was given two smaller rooms that would have been faculty offices if they hadn't been given to me for the staging of my smaller crime scenes or for use as simulated interview rooms. Then there was one more special room. Actually, it was a small narrow room, little more than a broom closet, that was being used for storage. I cleaned it out, painted it a toxic hospital-scrubs green, put a six-foot long, two-foot wide narrow table in there, and it became my autopsy theater. I had made a connection with a young doctor from the local health clinic who had done an autopsy in med school. He was not only entertained but delighted at my proposition for him to become my *faux* Coroner. He said that he could even get a teaching credit for it from his clinic and also put it on his resume. Once a semester he would spend three classes leading my students through the autopsy dissection of a cadaver that the university (and my ever-helpful, worshipfully-supportive Department Head) supplied for me. I would have loved to have heard how this particular rather morbid expenditure was justified to the university accountants or the Board of Trustees. I also enjoyed counting how many of my students lost their lunch during his first autopsy class. I gave a McDonald's coupon for a Big Mac to every student who made it through that first autopsy class without throwing up. My class was at One PM and after that first autopsy experience the majority of the class fasted before turning up for the others.

Years later, probably about 2004 or 2005, one of my granddaughters introduced me to an elaborate computer game that she was quite seriously playing. It was called *Sims* and involved creating a whole world populated by computer people called "avatars" that lived out their lives at the whim of the game player. As she introduced me to her avatars and led me on a tour through the city laid out on her computer screen, I couldn't help but think back on my early days in academia when I was setting up my Forensics Lab. I realized that what that computer game was doing was exactly what I had done thirty years before, creating a world of simulation and trying to make it mirror reality. I had to chuckle though. The one thing that my Lab world of the seventies and the real crime scene worlds of the 21st century shared was the very first supply purchase that I made back then. I ordered three big boxes of yellow crime scene tape.

But there were a number of other really positive things about Purdue University that triggered my snap decision to take the job. I knew the town and was confident that it would be a nice safe place for Grace to grow up just as long as she never brought home a boyfriend like Lenny. The campus, while a bit on the red brick, functional, unspectacular side (let's face it, if it hadn't been a university it could have been a state prison), with all of its buildings looking exactly the same, still had wide sidewalks and green grass and a spectacular student union built out of granite. We rented an apartment a five-minute walk from the campus.

Also, this particular university offered a number of things that really complimented my own interests. As I might have mentioned earlier, I was really good with languages and the Purdue Campus was a virtual melting pot of foreign exchange students. Because of its excellent reputation as an Engineering and Agricultural school, countries all over the word sent their best and their brightest to Purdue in the hope that those students would someday return home and become leaders in the nation-building of their own countries. Walking out onto the campus on any day was like suddenly being transported to Mexico City or Brazil or Korea. The polyglot of languages that I encountered was like music to my Eidetic ears.

And, oh yes, then of course there was the excellent sweet corn that was sold on street corners out of farmer's carts all summer long. Not a bad place at all perhaps for a normal midwestern person. As for me, I grew to hate it and from almost the very beginning started hoping for a way out. But Nicole and Grace were happy and prospering here amidst the corn fields on the banks of the Wabash River, so I tried my best to keep my restlessness under control.

I must admit, however, that the one thing that acted as my saving grace (besides my own Grace), the one thing that gave me interludes of relief from the stultifying boredom of academia, was the teaching. Before I ever entered my Forensics Lab and greeted my first roster of students, I had decided that my classes were going to be completely hands-on (like my high school Biology class where we were forced to dissect frogs). I wanted my classes to as closely as possible simulate the processes of doing Forensic collection of evidence at crime scenes and then sitting down and analyzing it. During the summer, after I took the job and before classes began, I drove from West Lafayette to East Lansing to check out Michigan State's Criminology Department and their Forensics Lab that had only been in existence for two years. Boy was I glad that I did! The people at Michigan State were unbelievably accommodating. It was obvious that they were really proud of their department and their new Forensics Lab. That trip cued me to what kind of supplies I needed for my Lab. I had already worked out the architecture for my crime scene movie sets but that trip to Michigan State filled in the details of what I would need to fill those sets with realistic props and materials. I came away with a long list of things to order. And to my great surprise, as I drove back to Purdue, I realized that I was actually having fun putting together my little simulated world. *Maybe academia isn't going to be so bad after all,* I thought. Of course, it turned out that I was quite wrong. But then, at first, it seemed like it might be a lot better than it turned out to be.

Another surprise awaited me when I got back on campus and the school year began. I was completely taken by surprise at how nervous I was before I went into my classroom that first day. I mean flop-sweat nervous, wanting-to-flee nervous, deathly- fear nervous, almost pants-peeing nervous. I had no idea why I was suddenly so intimidated, where this attack of stage fright had come from. My Eidetic Memory remembered every detail of my first day of classes as an undergraduate in this same building fourteen years before, sitting at my desk waiting for the teacher to come in. But it was completely different now. Then I had just been a relaxed curious student, now I was the one under the gun, the one expected to lead, to produce, to teach. As I stood outside the door to my brand spanking new Lab, I was scared to death. I suddenly realized that the Lab facility that I had spent the better part of the summer building couldn't teach itself no matter how hands-on it was. Standing outside my Lab's door that first day of classes my mind was racing. *What am I doing here? What will I say to them? Am I prepared? Do I know enough? Oh lord why did I take this job?* I was a real mess.

Of course, once I got up the nerve to open the door and go in, my Eidetic Memory saved me as it always does. It was just a first day case of the jitters, but I will always remember it as the first vague sense that maybe academia really wasn't for me. To my credit, though, I didn't let on to anyone (not to Nicole, not to my colleagues, maybe not yet even to myself) my acute doubts about this latest transubstantiation of my being. Teaching proved remarkably easy for me and after a while I realized that I really enjoyed it. My Forensic Lab proved to be quite well conceived and both myself and my students had fun in it. For them, I think, the Lab was a break from the boring classrooms of the rest of the university comprised of a bunch of desks and a blackboard. Our classroom was like walking into a crime movie. Instead of listening to lectures, we searched for clues. Instead of reading text books, we dusted for fingerprints. Instead of working out math problems, we calculated the trajectories of bullets fired. Instead of studying theories of reality, we analyzed the murdered bodies and the spilled blood of crime scene victims. Years later television would produce a whole group of shows based on exactly what we were doing in my Forensics Lab way back in 1972 and call it "CSI."

My next twelve years, my academia transubstantiation, went by in a blur probably because those years were so normal, so domestic, so uneventful, no missile crisis, no assassination, no undercover work, just college teaching and family life. Grace grew and prospered. After a while Nicole went back to teaching high school English. I settled into an intellectually passive existence, my life a warm bath of days and months and years that all ran together because they were all so unobtrusively the same. But worse of all, my Eidetic Memory became locked in the boredom of academia.

Like Picasso I had entered a kind of blue period in my life, muted in the dull glow of acquiescence that I realized I somehow had to fight, but that I didn't really at first know how to go about fighting. I realized fairly early in my so-called academic career that I was bogged down, stuck to the ankles and slowly sinking in a quicksand of conformity, of conventionality, into a world that I really didn't like, but worse of all of a world of my own making. Yes, probably as early as my second semester, my Eidetic Memory, like an annoying insect buzzing around my head, started prodding me for some challenges, some material or some situation, that it could apply itself to. But academia just didn't offer much in the way of challenges. Days, months, years were all pretty much the same. Time wasn't measured by the calendar or the seasons, but rather by semesters. Progress wasn't linked to any real-world accomplishment, but rather by mid-terms and finals, published papers and conference presentations, life organized on paper.

After a while I tried to construct some memory exercises to sort of keep my Eidetic hand in, but I had real trouble when looking closely at my life in academia finding any material that was really memorable. Then I hit on the one important thing that I figured was going to be really worth remembering from this blue period in my life. That material was Nicole and Grace and the family life that the three of us built together. They were the antidote to the disease of academia that I had contracted. They had become the core of my identity and they were the neural pathway to keeping my Eidetic Memory alive. Through Nicole and Grace I found a whole new way of deciphering the world, my life, our reality. Just as I had researched and built my state-of-the-art Forensics Lab, I set out to build a perfect world for Nicole and Grace to live in. I bought an old rambling farmhouse just a ways out of town abutting right up against a large cornfield on one side and a grove of trees with a small creek running through it on the other side. Nicole and Grace furnished it with all sorts of stuff that seemed to randomly catch their eye at farm auctions and garage sales. Remembering my own growing up on my mom and dad's farm, I put a new roof on the house and bought a riding mower to deal with the lawn that consisted of some grass but mostly weeds. Harkening back to my days at Berkeley, I grew my own marijuana in a small plot down by the creek bank. For a while these domestic creations satisfied my need to fight off the boredom of academia, but soon I ran out of projects around the house and Nicole and Grace were off at school all the time and I was left alone with my life once more turning a Picasso-esque blue.

About my fourth year at the university, just to entertain myself, put a little spice into my teaching regimen, I talked my department head into letting me supplement my Forensic Science offerings with a movie course. *Crime and Evidence* I called it, echoing Dostoevsky. I had always been a movie fan ever since I was a kid going to the Saturday matinees way back in the fifties. I think movies were a place where I could lose myself and enter other worlds where life was more exciting, more cinemascopic and more technicolor then the farm and the corn and the small town at the crossroads where we lived that was comprised of a gas station, a diner, a mom-and-pop grocery store, a seed and implement dealer, and most important of all a movie theater that might later become the inspiration for *The Last Picture Show*. I argued to my Department Head, that *Crime and Evidence* would be both a history of the whole development of clue-collecting and deductive analyzing of crime scenes plus an opportunity for the students to see other detectives other than themselves doing the hard work and the intellectual applications of Criminology. The Department Head, still, I think, intoxicated by the fact that I had once been in the same room with JFK, bought my argument hook, line and cinema. He gave me an enthusiastic go-ahead for the course.

Once I got serious about it, *Crime and Evidence* really sort of created itself. God knows there was certainly plenty of material available for it. It was almost the nineteen-eighties and there were more good crime movies around than I could ever include in the course. There was one problem though. VCRs and videotapes and DVDs hadn't been invented yet and made available to the general public so I had to get my movies on large cumbersome celluloid reels and feed them through skeletal clacking projectors that failed on an annoyingly regular basis. I learned to thread film, to splice film, to store film to keep it from deteriorating, but most important where to buy films or rent films or borrow films from other universities.

My course syllabus was chronological and historical. I started the class with Sherlock Holmes. I mean who else? Clearly, he was the greatest Forensic Scientist and evidence analyst who ever populated the pages of countless books and movies. By 1978 when my *Crime and Evidence* course took on its first case, there must have already been at least thirty or forty Sherlock Holmes films to choose from. Over the years I probably screened most of them for my class. Raymond Chandler's Philip Marlowe was the next obvious choice and *The Big Sleep* with

Humphrey Bogart prowling crime scene after crime scene was perfect for my class. Holmes and Marlowe were a good match on the front of the course because both of them solved their cases via sharp eyes and even sharper analytic skills. From the 1940s an obvious choice was *Double Indemnity* with Edward G. Robinson as its relentless insurance investigator. I also used an excellent film noir, *Out of the Past,* because it showed my students how a missing person search went. The 1950s and 1960s not only were especially fertile for the great crime films, but also took my class into foreign films. Jules Dassin's *Night and the City, Rififi* and *Topkapi* were all films that over the years I forced my students to watch with subtitles. They loved them and for some it was probably more reading than they had done the whole rest of their lives. From the fifties, of course, I had to include Hitchcock. *Strangers on a Train* and *Dial M for Murder* were perfect to demonstrate the unraveling of so-called perfect crimes. But perhaps the best Forensics film of all time from that era was *In the Heat of the Night* with its cerebral detective, Mister Tibbs, being a definite match in matters of evidence collection and deduction for Sherlock Holmes. And I brought the course right up into the Seventies with *Chinatown.*

Anyway, after I taught *Crime and Evidence* for two successive semesters in 1978, the word got around campus and when school came back in session in 1979, I had 200 students enrolled in my movie class and twice the number of Forensic Science majors as we had the year before. My movies class had to be installed in the university's largest amphitheater classroom. Needless to say, my department head was ecstatic. If I had been one of his favorite professors before, now I was clearly approaching superhero status. It was really pretty funny. I had just conceived that film class to break up the boredom and here it was taking on this larger than life of its own. What the heck, I asked the department head to give me three teaching assistants to help me deal with my hordes of Forensic moviegoers and he didn't even blink. I recruited the grad students from the English Department Film Studies program and my little Forensic fiefdom found itself even more firmly buttressed.

One spin-off from my *Crime and Evidence* movie course was my side-line career as the film critic for the local newspaper. Someone there heard about the popularity on campus of my course and offered me a part-time gig writing movie reviews. It was a pretty good deal. I got to go to the movies for free and they paid me fifty dollars for every review I wrote which was usually one a week. Nicole called it my beer money. And once again my Eidetic Memory really came in handy. I didn't have to sit in the dark taking notes like all the other film critics. I just watched the movie and remembered every single scene, image, line of dialogue of it. I really enjoyed that film course and it went on to become a staple of the Criminology Department. But nonetheless, pretty soon the boredom of cornfield academia started to eat away at my psyche once again.

About my seventh year at the university, just back from my first sabbatical at the beach, fully entrapped in tenure, my Forensic Lab and my film course both going strong, my student evaluations and resultant teaching awards jumping off the charts, the same old question that I had asked myself in my early years in academia raised its ugly head once again. *What am I doing here?* I was almost forty and compared with what I had done in my twenties my life in academia was like sleepwalking. I needed something to perk me up, something to draw my attention away from the boredom of academia and put some meaning beyond just going to work and teaching every day. The Criminology Department shared a campus building with the English Department and over the years I hung out a lot with some of the English Department people, both professors and grad students. We would meet at a bar most Friday afternoons and talk about anything and everything. I had even hired some of the English Department grad students to be teaching assistants for my film course. Of course, one of our main topics of conversation was books—the books they were reading, the books the faculty were writing. It was in that bar drinking beer with those people, who were clearly much more committed to academia than I was, that I got the idea that maybe I should hunker down and write a book. But not just any book, a book that would lift my mind and my spirits out of the blue period that I seemed to be sinking deeper into with each passing year.

The more I thought about it, the more I realized that the subject of my research project, the governing idea for my book, had been staring me right in the face all of my life. Memory. It just so happened that right about that time I was reading a popular science fiction novel by Kurt Vonnegut, *The Sirens of Titan*, and I realized that it was a book all about memory. Then one of the English profs that I had discussed my book idea with suggested another popular sci-fi novel, *Fahrenheit 451*, that was also about memory, about people memorizing books in order to preserve them for future generations. That was when I really started looking around me and realized just how many memory books there were and, even more, how there was a whole history of memory exploration that stretched out across the centuries.

But for me, obviously, there was one even stronger motivation. That was the study in depth of the very guiding power of my own life. I decided to try to write a history or psychology or philosophy or whatever of "memory." I realized that it had very little to do with my academic specialty or the subjects of my Forensics teaching, but that didn't deter me, in fact never even entered my consideration. Forensics had grown old for me anyway. The Forensics of Sherlock Holmes and Mister Tibbs were starting to be supplanted by computers. I saw a future in which the human deductive element would be taken over by machines just as would probably all of American life. And those machines might possibly possess memories even better than mine.

As I wrote earlier, my idea for my book on memory really began with my reading of futuristic fiction, Vonnegut's *The Sirens of Titan* and Bradbury's *Fahrenheit 451*. They predicted a bleak future where human action and agency was supplanted by machines which was exactly the future that I saw coming for Forensics. But about that time one of the films that I chose for my film class I realized also was a pertinent memory document, Hitchcock's *The 39 Steps*. Now it was 1980 and ironically *The 39 Steps* had actually been mentioned by either Lansdale or McCone way back in 1960 when they were recruiting me and my Eidetic Memory into the CIA at the time of the missile crisis. Mr. Memory, an Eidetic just like me, was Hitchcock's spy who had memorized the coded British defense initiatives known as "the 39 steps." Those "steps" were what Hitchcock liked to call a "maguffin," something, anything, it didn't matter what it was, that the spies in his movies desired, wanted to get their hands on or keep their enemies hands off, and thus chased after the whole movie. Of course, the "maguffin" was nothing more than a plot device that Hitchcock employed, but in *The 39 Steps* his "maguffin" was a bit more complicated than uranium for building an atom bomb (*Notorious*) or a piece of microfilm containing sensitive information (*North By Northwest*) or a bomb-rigging enemy agent (*Saboteur*). The "maguffin" in *The 39 Steps* was actually the material captured in a man's Eidetic Memory. As I played that film in my class, I decided that writing a book about the tremendous importance of memory in the unfolding plot of human history might be a really useful thing to do.

My book actually started taking shape in my mind as I watched Hitchcock's film reel out in the darkness of my classroom. I decided that I would definitely have a chapter on "memory movies and memory books." Vague ideas for the other chapters like "the theories and philosophies of memory" or "the historic impacts of memory" or "heroes of memory" or "the political and/or diplomatic uses of memory." Slogans like "Remember the Maine" and "Tippecanoe and Tyler Too" and "Remember, it's not what your country can do for you, but what you can do for your country," or, of course, Christ's "Do this in memory of me," all kept popping up in my mind as I envisioned the make-up of my great memory book.

Of course, that book never got written. Oh, I worked on it for a while. The first chapter I started writing was my survey and critical analysis of all the books and movies about memory. I got about halfway through that chapter when I happened to be reading Freud's *On Dreams* and I got sidetracked into starting another chapter on the psychological importance of our memory powers. But I never finished that chapter either. As I tried to write this book, I slowly started to realize that it was little more than an academic exercise. At best I was only refreshing the memories of my imagined prospective readers on all the documents and assertions of the past on the subject of memory. I wasn't stimulating their own memories which for 95% of human beings lie 95% dormant 95% of the time in their lives. The more I thought about it, the more I realized that the people around me never really were aware of, never really observed, what was going on around them. In my Forensic movie class, I had tried to get the students to see not just what was going on in the center of the frame but what was around the edges of the frame, what was happening in the background as well as in the foreground of the film images that they were watching. Very few of my students really got it. And I realized that very few people in general ever saw anything other than what was right in front of them. They just weren't like me. They weren't at all driven to take in everything that their peripheral vision could encompass. So, after trying to bring it to life in words for almost two years, I suddenly abandoned my memory book, walked my pen away from it (we didn't have laptops in those days), and let it die a natural death.

I should have known that I'd never finish my academic study of memory. I had entered upon the planning and conceptualization of this research project with great enthusiasm. But like my whole dabbling in academia this project soon sank into boredom and languished in a growing doubt about its function and contribution to the body of human knowledge. Just like my recurring question about academia—*"Why am I here?"*—I asked pretty much the same question about my book—*"Why am I writing this?"* Come to think of it, perhaps I should be asking that same question about this book here that I am writing and you are reading. But I'm pretty sure I know why I am writing this book. My time is getting short. I want to get all my memories down before my own living memory starts to fade. I'm sort of like the wanderers in *Fahrenheit 451* who want to get their chosen books memorized before the final copies are destroyed.

And so, my twelve years in academia, twelve years of classes that soon became routine, twelve years of soporific faculty meetings, stultifying cocktail parties, Ph.D. dissertations that put you to sleep in their first ten pages, passed by like sludge inching its way down a sewer ditch. In other words, just like this chapter on my life in academia in this book that you are reading, those twelve years were sort of the doldrums of my life.

But those years in academia were by no means totally wasted. Me and Nicole and Grace were happy despite the cornfield boredom of our Indiana lives. I don't think I had ever been as happy or as stable as I was then. We were happy as a family. Me and Nicole were in balance in our lives. We were happy as parents and lovers. Grace grew and prospered as a carefree child, a curious student, a healthy happy free spirit on our little country estate with her grandparents nearby on their farm. And despite all of my whining and disdain even academia wasn't all as bad as my restless mind made it out to be. Our lives moved along, slow, bucolic, seemingly harmless, admittedly boring (for me), but above all safe.

I know as I read back over what I have written in this chapter that I have stressed a midwestern sense of security that I felt there, safely tenured in academia. For a long time, twelve years, our life was normal and loving because we were so together as a family. But I should have known that it could never last forever. Suddenly, it all came to pieces in the blink of an eye.

Early on in this manuscript I wrote of how my Eidetic Memory is both a blessing and a curse. Certainly, my guilt over President Kennedy's death nagged at me all the time, but that was nothing compared to what I am forced to write about now. This new curse returns in my memory every day, clear in graphic detail, indelibly embedded, Eidetically unflagging.

Late November. Thanksgiving coming soon.

Two snows already.

Road icy.

Nicole had just cleared the town.

Close to home.

At the bottom of a pretty high hill.

Close to the turnoff.

Semi crests the hill.

Going too fast.

Thinking back on it now, trying to write it down even from a distance of so many years, so many other lives, it is still really hard. The words just don't seem to want to come. Writing about the death of your soulmate, the one you loved more than anyone else is like, like… OK, like biting down on that piece of rawhide in those old western movies when a bullet had to be removed, yes, like "biting the bullet" so to speak, coming to grips with your pain. But no cowboy or soldier ever bit the bullet. Bullets are too small. You see, even as I write I am avoiding writing. Running away from that terrible reality that my cursed memory keeps replaying in my mind's eye. Dodging the memory of it. Trying to find the words to describe it. Fleeing into my present problem while avoiding the past reality of Nicole's last moments,

At the crest of the hill the semi starts to slide.

Black ice. Invisible.

Nicole's Volkswagen bug just starting up the hill.

Semi trying to brake.

Nicole looking up and seeing it.

Semi starting to jackknife.

Nicole looking frantically for someplace to go out of its way.

Semi going full sideways.

Semi sliding fast.

No escape from it.

Terrible impact.

That trailer, sliding sideways down that hill, must have swatted Nicole's car like the bug that it was, batted it into the air, off of the road, into the trees, crushed it into a twisted tangle of metal, and Nicole was gone before it ever came to rest. I didn't see any of that. I wasn't at the side of the road watching it all happen. My Forensics experience indelibly painted the images of that terrible crash in my unforgiving memory: the skid marks, the black ice, the positions of the vehicles, her car wedged between and wrapped around two trees, listening to the distraught truck driver's words, and, oh my god, looking into the wreckage of Nicole's car at her poor twisted bloodied body. My relentless memory, my cursed memory, images of every second of that horrible day. The accident that I didn't see pulses just as fiercely in my mind's eye as its whole terrible aftermath.

Yes, even when I started this memoir all of those chapters ago, I knew it would be hard to write about this, about losing Nicole, At the time, immediately afterwards, I had spells when I couldn't even breathe when I had to face the reality of it. My throat would close up and my heart would start to throb and totally uncontrolled tears would start to stream down my face in rivulets. Now I am trying to put that whole terrible episode of my life into words and my pen doesn't really want to work either, is seizing up on me. What can I really say? In a second, a breath, a blink, she was gone and my life changed forever, took a turn so sharp off course, so swift, that it might as well have been me in that car wreck. In fact, for the longest time, I sincerely wished it had been me.

CHAPTER 8: PARIS

Ah, Chapter 8. As I sit here almost two decades into the twenty-first century trying to write this crazy memory book, Chapter 8 suddenly seems ridiculously appropriate for this particular stage in my life. Chapter 8! No, Section 8! In the code language of the U.S. Army that means "eligible for a mentally incompetent discharge" or in other words "crazy," maybe "shell shocked," "battle fatigued," or "catch-22ed." Ever since WWI Section 8 has been a way for soldiers to escape the horrors of war, a way out of the trenches, the fox holes, the rice paddies, the desert storms, the booby-trapped roads of America's battlefields. Yessir, at this point in this book, Chapter 8, my Section 8, is an acutely appropriate place to be. I had my own horrors that I was frantically looking for a way to escape. It was 1982 and I had just turned 40 years old and I had days when I wished that I was dead. Oh yes, I was a perfect candidate for a Section 8.

And so, after Nicole's death, Grace and I fled to Paris.

Well, it really wasn't as simple as that last sentence may make it seem. After Nicole's accident, Indiana, the Midwest, the America of out-of-control semis and twisted wreckage and unthinkable death became a vortex of sickening images and haunting dreams. Everywhere I looked I saw Nicole. I'd see a woman walking down the street and I would think it was her. I'd see a teacher helping schoolchildren off of a bus and I'd think for a moment it was her. I knew it was my mind playing tricks on me. I knew I was in denial, hoping that she wasn't really gone.

Worst of all was our home, hers and Grace's and my safe little haven from the rest of the world. Everywhere there that I looked I saw Nicole, in our farmyard, in our garden, coming up our lane toward me with a smile on her face and her arms out for a hug. I felt guilty when I realized how little I had valued the small, simple things in our life together—washing the dishes, sitting at the kitchen table having coffee, eating dinner and talking about our day, walking hand-in-hand across the fields and through the woods around our little farmhouse, watching Grace together in her school plays and her softball games, being together every day and, regretfully, taking each other for granted.

But now she was gone and deep down I knew I could never bring her back no matter how many mind tricks I tried to play on myself. As each day, week, month, passed she became more insubstantial in my mind. Her image would be there for a second, then she would just de-materialize, fade into nothingness like a wisp of smoke. It got so that I didn't know what to do, how to cope with her being gone in reality and yet still so very much in my torturous memory. And so, I ran.

I fled to Paris. But even running away isn't all that easy. It took me almost a year to get on that plane to Europe. Long before we left, I knew I wanted to leave. But I had to sell the house. That was part of my running away. It was a haunted house now. Nicole's ghost roamed its hallways and rooms. The house sat unwanted on the market for months until a new Assistant Professor at the university bought it for him and his young gamily, a wife and a daughter just like my family had once been. They wanted to keep a horse for their little girl to learn to ride. When I turned the keys over, I hoped that they found the same happiness that we had found in that house and that they had much better luck in the long run.

Then I had to decide whether to resign from the university or take a leave of absence for a year which was the longest they would allow a professor to be gone. I finally chose the leave of absence even though I was almost certain that I would never return to academia or to Indiana even.

Then Grace had to finish her school year and I had to somehow convince her that she wanted to leave all of her friends, her sports, her grandparents, her creek and her woods to flee with me to a big city in a foreign country across the world. I laid out a number of arguing points for Grace. I promised her we would only be gone a year (when I knew deep down that I never wanted to come back), and that she could learn to speak perfect French (hoping that perhaps she would discover the same facility for languages that I had), and that she could go to the best private school in all of Europe where she would live and learn during the week and then spend all of her weekends and holidays with me touring the country (this being probably the one promise I made to her that I had the best chance of keeping).

So, I sold the farm, had an auction sale in the farmyard and sold al-most all of the furniture and implements. Then I took Nicole's clothes to Good Will. That last made me feel the most guilty and sad. I felt like

I was obliterating Nicole's whole existence, putting her out of our lives as if she had never been there. But then one day I was sitting alone on a bench in the farmyard as we were in the process of packing and getting ready to go and Grace came up to me from behind, tapped me on the shoulder, startled me out of my troubled thoughts.

Grace: Whatcha doin'dad?

Why not? I thought. *Why not just tell her the truth?*

Me: Thinking about your mom, missing her.

Grace thought for a moment, then she sat down beside me on the bench.

G: You know dad, when I'm missing her, I think of her as our guardian angel, watching over us, taking care of us.

Suddenly I felt as if the sun had come out from behind the black cloud that had hung over me since Nicole's death. *Out of the mouths of babes,* I thought. God bless her.

Me: Oh Grace, you are so, so, very right. And she'll always be there for us, guiding us, alive in our memories.

I didn't realize it exactly at the time but when I said that I was right.

With Grace's words, Nicole no longer remained a ghost haunting me, but rather became a partner in my ongoing life, a standard for me to live up to, a counselor in all of my decisions as she had been for all of those years we had together. From then on, whenever I had a life decision to make, I invariably asked myself the question, "*What would Nicole tell me to do?*"

"Why Paris?" You might ask. Well, certainly one reason, probably the overriding reason, was that it had always been a romantic ideal for Nicole and she had always wanted to go there. After all, her parents had given her a French name. I guess that, amongst all of my other guilts, was guilt that she had never made it there. And I didn't want to feel guilty that way about Grace. Maybe I thought of Grace as a kind of surrogate for Nicole. Maybe if I took Grace to Paris, Nicole, thanks to some strange magic, would be going along with us. Pretty illogical that, wouldn't you say? But there was no logic to any of this. I remember Nicole sitting in our family room listening to a Judy Collins record. Revolving on the turntable, it spun out the words: "*My father always promised us that we would go to France/ We'd go boating on the Seine and I would learn to dance.*" Listening to that song, Nicole's eyes would glaze over and she'd get this far-away look on her face that told me that the song had transported her to the romantic Paris of her dreams.

But that certainly wasn't the only reason. Europe, the old world, seemed like a good place for me to escape to. I was sick of America, sick of the Washington East, sick of the Hippie West, even sick of my mistakenly safe home grounds in the Midwest that had so brutally betrayed me. Europe seemed like a place where I could disappear, a much more manageable world where nobody knew me at all and I could be alone with my guilts, my regrets, and my all-encompassing sadness over the loss of Nicole. In other words, a place where I could be alone with my memories and not have to share them with anyone. Europe seemed like the answer. It wasn't even written then, but later on I sort of snapped to attention whenever that Jimmy Buffett song—*"He went to Paris looking for answers to questions that bothered him so."*—came on. *Boy, that sure was me back in 1984* I always think. And the irony of it all is like the man in the song. I didn't find any answers either.

What I didn't realize at the time, and what didn't really figure in my decision to flee America, was that despite my brooding gloom, I still hadn't given in to despair. I was only lost. I was acutely aware of that. But though I didn't realize it then, I still had hope, and its name was Grace. Almost instinctively I wanted to get Grace, who was only thirteen years old then, out of an American society that, again in the illogic of my grieving mind, had been responsible for the death of her mother and the love of my life. I hoped that maybe Paris might be a happier place where we both could throw off our sadness. Of course, I was wrong. My unstinting memory was never going to allow that to happen.

And so, I packed Grace and myself up in four heavy square suitcases (roller bags hadn't been invented yet) that we lugged to the airport, and we jetted off to France. It took almost a week to find an *Ecole* where Grace could live in. She was skeptical, but I told her it would be just like one of her favorite children's books.

In a high house in Paris
All covered with vines,
Lived twelve little girls
In two straight lines.
And the youngest of these was
Madeline.

Grace was not the youngest in the *Ecole des Saint-Michel*, and the school wasn't run by nuns, but it seemed a rather comfortable boarding school and almost immediately Grace took to it as if Indiana was well behind her.

After I got her settled there, I went looking for an apartment in the neighborhood of the school. We had been living in a cheap hotel for the first week. The *appartement* that I found was near Grace's *Ecole* in the *6th Arondissement* which is the French word for district or neighborhood. That neighborhood's more familiar name was the *Latin Quarter* and it was the area closely surrounding the Sorbonne, the great Parisian university. I was already pretty fluent in French thanks to my Eidetic Memory and Grace was easily picking up French word for word as we went along that first week. Once she got into her school and made friends, she was talking like a born Parisian. Thus, Paris greeted us with busy work, but once Grace was well-placed and I was alone in our little,*appartement,* I had a chance to look around me and try to figure out what I had gotten myself into. At first Paris, for me, was little more than a view from my balcony. Our studio *appartement* was on the sixth floor of an ancient tenement on the *Rue des Victor-Cousin.* It was within walking distance of the *Sant-Germain des Pres* of Sartre and Camus and just off the *Sant-Germain* opposite the *Sorbonne* and the Luxemburg gardens on the fragile border between the *Sant-Germain des Pres* and the *Latin Quarter.* Our balcony was postage stamp size with a with a rusty iron railing, but it was high and provide an unobstructed view of the fantastical roofscapes of Paris. They were a kaleidoscopic theater of shifting light on mansard windows and protruding chimney pots on a crenellation of rooftops reaching all the way to the quais on the Left Bank of the *Seine* and the towers of *Notre Dame.*

The *Latin Quarter* was the student area for the *Sorbonne* that I could look down on from my balcony. Ours was a residential neighborhood, a low-cost neighborhood, a somewhat run-down, Bohemian one might say, old neighborhood, whose best, most exciting, most famous days were behind it. Paris, the boulevard *Sant-Germain*, the *Latin Quarter*, the Left Bank (*La Rive Gauche*), still then were all about dead or dying painters and writers and photographers and dancers and actors. I knew nothing about any of them or the places they once haunted in the very neighborhood that Grace and I had set down in, but in a couple of weeks of roaming around, their names, the places where they ate and drank and conversed and made love took up residence in my memory just as we had taken up residence in their historical footprint. I had rented our *appartement* in the *Latin Quarter* because it was cheap. Little did I know, in fact I was totally unaware, that our residence was right in the middle of where Existentialism was born.

I was drawn to the haunts of Sartre and Camus and Simone de Beauvoir that I had become entranced with during my time at Berkeley. Indeed, the Existentialists were the one lasting positive thing that I brought away from that Judas-like Berkeley experience. Our apartment was but a short walk to the *Café des Deux Magots* at the corner of *Place St-Germai*n *des Pres* and *Boulevard St-Germain*. Directly behind *des Deux Magots* is the *Le Café la Flore*. Both were the main watering places of the Existentialists of the 1940s and 1950s. Comically, to me, "Rendezvous of the Intellectual Elite" is stamped on every bill issued at *des Deux Magots*. By the time Grace and I got to Paris, Existentialism was on the wane and Sartre and Camus and de Beauvoir had become tourist attractions for the cafes much like "George Washington Slept Here" was in America. But though the 6th may once have been the *arrondissement* of the "Intellectual Elite," it also, and still was when we got there, the residential neighborhood of the hard-working classes of Paris as well as the thread-bare students of the Sorbonne. In fact, sitting at the small sidewalk tables of *des Deux Magots* or *Le Café de Flore*, a panorama of all of the classes of Paris life paraded before you from the lovely and confident *Parisiennes* to the short-skirted, high heeled *demoiselles* to the baker's wives to the carpenters and iron mongers to the long-haired, pony-tailed, black-bereted students to the bumbling tourists from all across the world.

In those days, Paris was an expatriate melting pot. There were exiles from everywhere: all over Europe, America, Africa, from the Middle East of Cairo and Riyadh and Tehran and, of course, Jerusalem. And Asians from China, Korea, Japan, even Viet Nam, which was just struggling back to life after its bombed-out Sixties and Seventies.

Almost from the beginning the city had a guilty allure for me. Academia had been my blue period and Nicole's death had been my black hole of despair. After a rather short while Paris became my distraction, my way of setting my memory off on the run away from my debilitating past. Nicole's presence was still upon me, but in Paris as time went on it didn't seem to hang so heavily. For me, when we first arrived and got settled and Grace was in school and I was alone during the week, Paris wasn't really a happy place, but it was a new place, a different place, an interesting place. I especially found the *Seine* to be a calming and consoling presence. That river flowed so gently, so unhurried, through the city. A serene beauty emanated from its graceful bridges and its majestic islands. From my balcony I could look down upon the elegant arc of the *Seine* from a high distance. But from a bench on the *quai* I could look at the river flowing past me close up. Either way it had a calming influence.

But, once again, I get ahead of myself. Grace seemed quite happy in her school and within the course of a few short weeks she was speaking gleeful French with her new-found school friends and with equal glee correcting her father's flawed and stumbling French. I did, however, spring one word upon her that I culled from my little French-English paperback dictionary. That word was "*flaneur.*"

G: What's a *flaneur*? Sounds like some kind of pancake.

Me: (Reverting to my professorial lecturing mode) A *flaneur* is a walker of the streets of Paris. We are going to be *flaneurs* Grace.

G: What is such a big deal about a streetwalker that it has to have a special name?

Me: First of all, not a streetwalker.

I couldn't help but smile at my little joke that Grace certainly couldn't understand, although as time went on, we would be accosted by a number of Parisian *demoiselles* and naturally Grace would become curious or at least become suspicious of their motives in approaching me.

Me: A walker of the streets with no immediate destination.

G: But how is that different from a streetwalker?

Me: It just is.

Clearly Grace didn't like that answer at all, but she let it go and I went on with my lecture.

Me: A Parisian *flaneur* is a person who walks through Paris at his or her ease and looks at everything to see what the city will bring.

G: Is a *flaneur* always walking?

Me: No. Not at all. He can be sitting on a bench and watching, like the people in the sidewalk cafes, or he can be leaning against a lamp-post and watching, or even, (and I thought of myself) standing on his balcony and watching the world go by.

G: So, on the weekends when I come home from school, (I could see that Grace was working it out in her mind) you and I will become *flaneurs*?

Me: Yes, exactly.

G: Will we be able to stop at a *patisserie* along the way?

Me: Of course, (I laughed) Things like that will be the fun of it.

And so we became *flaneurs*. Grace and I on the weekends. Me alone during the week. Actually, when I was alone, I was more just an aimless wanderer fleeing from my memories. I tried to sight-see, but it did me no good because in my aimless wandering all I could think about was Nicole, wishing she was here with me. Nonetheless, my ever-persistant memory worked at taking in and remembering in graphic detail all that I saw and heard and ran into around me. Finally, I sat myself down and told my grieving, heart-broken self that I needed to let Paris rescue me from drowning in my sadness. My first week in Paris, a pseudo-*flaneur* alone, I walked to seek out Sartre and Camus and Simone de Beauvoir. I got a sidewalk table at *des Deux Magots*. It would be, it turned out, my home base in Paris. But chasing those long-dead Existentialists around Paris, reading their books again, only made me feel sad. I guess that as I sat at my table in that tourist-trap café I felt sad that I had missed them, couldn't sit and talk to them over my espresso, could never really be part of that "Intellectual Elite" that my café bill so loved to brag about. I realized that my personal substance had to get out, walk, and immerse myself in a Paris of my own. And so, I set out to become a real *flaneur*.

Why had I come to Paris? That question still haunted me. So I set out to answer it, on my own, Grace safely in school. Paris is a city of bridges. That was one of my first realizations as I walked the *quays* along the Left Bank. The bridges all along the elegant curve of the River Seine from the Eiffel Tower to the prow of the ship-shaped *Ile-de-la-Cite* are the city's connectors. The bridges are arching stone pathways between the bohemian, working-class Left Bank and the wealthier, more up-scale Right Bank with its *Belle Epoch* four-star hotels and restauran-tes—The Ritz, Maxim's, Prunier's, Droucant's—and the sidewalk cafes and *quai*-side kiosks and tunnel-like "*passages*" selling anything and everything—books, antiques, curios, jewelry—of the Left Bank. The Right Bank seemed to me the *serieux* section of Paris, all banks and of-fice buildings, Commerce and Capitalism, suits and dark lace-up shoes. The Left Bank just seemed more welcoming, more open and thought-ful, more artistic and alive, younger. Actually, I rarely ventured over the bridges to the Right Bank. I just felt more at home in Grace and my comfortable *6th Arondissement* neighborhood with the *boulangeries* sell-ing warm fresh *baguettes,* its *cav a vins* selling the sweet cheap *rose*'s and *cabernets*, the *patisseries,* the *charcuteries* setting pork cutlets.

After the bridges, Paris is also a marvelous, totally various, medita-tive and restful city of *parcs* and benches. As I walked the city, I would invariably come upon the open iron gates to any number of secret *parcs* and gardens. My Eidetic Memory served me really well as I walked. It etched a perfect map upon my mind of the beautiful places that I stumbled upon, a map that as time went on allowed me to return to my favorite green retreats and tree-lined *esplanades* again and again. To the south across from the towering tinker-toy Eiffel Tower stretched the majestic *Esplanade des Invalides* lined with its perfectly matched linden trees like sentries guarding its arrow-straight walkways. Within easy walking distance of our tiny *appartement* along the *Boulevard Sant-Michel* sat the luxurious, perfectly manicured Luxembourg Gardens with its straight lines of clipped lime trees and green grass and a multitude of available benches where one could sit and watch the passing parade of walkers on the shaded paths, or the tennis players rallying, or the lovers embracing on the steps of the old iron bandstand, or the children sailing their toy boats in the central fountain, or the frozen faces of the statues on the terraces or in the fountains. Oh, the Luxembourg Gardens were like a living panorama for the Eidetic *flaneur* like myself. But as time went by, as I started carrying a notebook and sharpened pencil on my walks in the city, I tended to seek out the smaller, quieter, more hidden, secret *parcs* to spend my time and jot down my thoughts. But again, I get ahead of myself. I will tell you more about my notebook later.

On the weekends, with Grace as my companion in *flaneurie,* we were much more American tourists visiting all of the more famous landmarks of Paris. We started out close to home crossing the *Petit Pont* to the *Ile-de-Cite* and the great gothic cathedral of *Notre Dame.* Oh, how Grace loved *Notre Dame* both inside and outside. Outside, its flying buttresses and monstrous gargoyles fascinated her, brought her pointer finger to incessant life. There, there, there, she would make sure that I missed none of the horrendous monstrosities of the cathedral's walls and roof lines. Inside, Grace was struck speechless by the church's massive arched ceiling and great stone pillars, its apses and altars and its field of worshipping pews. We tip-toed the aisles of *Notre Dame* in homage to the sacred place that it was, little thinking that some 35 years later it would be doomed to burn and crash.

But of course, Grace next had to climb to the top of the Eiffel Tower and look down on the whole city through the iron bars of its grillwork. For Grace that was like climbing Paris's mountain. For me, it held no romantic association whatsoever. It was certainly imposing, but in a cold, metallic, lifeless way like an overblown erector set. I never warmed to Paris's most famous landmark and frankly I was quite happy that Grace never asked to go there again. I guess once was quite enough for her also. Happily, as we walked the city on our touristy weekends in our early Parisian days, Grace and I explored much more interesting venues of all sorts. We had a guidebook that Grace took early possession of and when we would seek out a museum or a church or a famous building she enjoyed reading aloud to me its history, its notoriety, its famous *habitues,* its relevance to this city steeped in history. It was through that guidebook that she discovered one of our greatest Parisian treasures.

It was early 1985 when we first discovered the *Jeu de Paume,* "*Jeu de Paume*" is the French word for the sport of Tennis, and the building actually once housed real tennis courts. But in 1985 it was the small museum for Impressionist art, very much the anti-*Louvre.* Grace and I had spent days prowling the gloomy halls of the great *Louvre* with its arrow-peppered martyrs, its epic battle scenes and epicurean dinners, its kings and princes and their elaborately gowned and collared ladies, its mythic recreations of Leda and her swan, the Minotaur, Narcissus and all the other monsters of Medieval and Renaissance art, and, of course, poor enigmatic Mona Lisa, eternally puzzled by the legions constantly staring adoringly at her. We came to hate the *Louvre,* but instantly fell in love with the *Jeu de Paume.* It was a rather low long thin building on the north corner of the *Tuileries Gardens* next to the *Palace de la Concorde* about as far from and dwarfed by the massive buildings of the *Louvre.* Indeed, it was a place to escape to from the *Louvre* and that is how Grace and I found it. It was a nice small manageable museum and its walls were hung with the kind of pictures that Grace and I immediately fell in love with. Again, we knew little about them or about art then but, as the saying goes, we knew what we liked and the Impressionists for us were fresh air and brilliant light after the overwhelming gloom of the *Louvre.* Together we discovered our first Impressionists and their Post-Impressionist brethren here—Degas, Seurat, Cezanne, Monet, Morrisette, Van Gogh, Gauguin, and all their *simpatico* colleagues—and they would be our favorites forever after. Today, in the 21st Century, the Impressionists are no longer housed in their own little museum and the *Jeu de Paume* is a photography museum (not nearly as interesting as it was then). Our Impressionists were moved to the *Musee d'Orsay* in 1986. But in 1985 we found the *Jeu de*

Paume and it has brought great happiness to us.

By this time my voracious memory had pretty much memorized our guidebook and I felt that I could answer almost any question that Grace posed for me as we prowled the streets and neighborhoods, bridges and cathedrals and *parcs* of Paris.

G: Who was this Hemingway person?

She asked me one afternoon as we were walking in Montparnasse.

Me: Where did you hear about him?

G: His name was on a building back there, a wooden sign hanging on the iron fence.

Me: He was an American writer, short stories and novels. A very famous one. He lived here in Paris with some other famous writers for a while after WWI and WWII. He won the Nobel Prize in Literature.

G: Is that a big deal.

Me: Oh yes. It sure is.

G: What other writers did he live with?

Me: Well, he didn't live with him. They just all lived in Paris at the same time and they hung out together. They were called expatriates because they came here from America to write.

G: Are we expatriates then too.

Me: Yes, I guess we are. We've come here from America too.

G: Are you going to write dad?

Well, there it was. I had sort of been thinking about it, about writing something, about putting down on paper all of the stuff that lay festering in my infectious memory. But when Grace asked that question it brought the whole possibility of me trying to be a writer like Hemingway or Fitzgerald or James Joyce or any of those other writers who had come to Paris so long ago in flight from America. Back at Purdue University I tried to write a book and it had turned out badly. But, in another sense, I was an expatriate in the clearest sense of the word. Like Rick in *Casablanca* I was running away from America because of the terrible trauma that I couldn't face, like Hemingway and Fitzgerald trying to purge WWI out of their consciousness, like Picasso trying to find in art a way to express his restless desire for total creativity, originality. Then I realized that though they were all expatriates, ultimately they all went back home.

G: Are you going to write dad?

Grace's question hung in the air, a pregnant possibility that in a very vague, unformed way I had actually been considering.

Me: Maybe. Someday. I don't know.

G: Well, (Grace looked right up at me and passed judgement) I don't think these American writers could ever be as interesting or as wonderful as the painters and their pictures in the *Jue de Paume*.

And that was that. I thought that if I ever did write something (like this book perhaps) that it really wouldn't impress Grace very much. It was the Impressionists for her. But there was one other artist that Grace developed a real fondness for and that was Toulouse Lautrec. By a strange coincidence Grace's infatuation with Toulouse Lautrec came after my own visit to one of Lautrec's favorite sources of inspiration, the famous, perhaps infamous, *Moulin Rouge* night club in *Montmartre*. Of course, our little guidebook recommended it as a must-see venue for visitors to Paris and that had tempted my curiosity. And I must confess that a *risqué* evening at the birthplace of the Can-Can was the better part of the temptation. I had really felt not a great deal of interest in women or sex since Nicole's death. No interest at all back in Indiana. But Paris was different. After prowling its streets in the evenings and sitting alone at sidewalk tables in its cafes for a month or two, there was no way I could miss the city's open and unashamed sexuality.

Actually, as I observed it from my position of celibate aloneness then and as I think about it now some forty years later, I realize that I have never been in any city where the art and action of love is so openly expressed. As I walked the city in those first few weeks, I couldn't help but notice how the enthusiasm for full-bodied physical contact seemed characteristically Parisian. Everywhere I looked there seemed to be intensely engaged lovers. Lovers on park benches, on the grass, in taxis, on the Metro, on roof tops, in window seats, at café tables, all around me. Here in 2019 the Parisian passion for public kissing, embracing, heavy petting, in the abbreviated argot of cell phones texting, would simply be called PDA. But for the Parisians it certainly was much more complex than that. Or perhaps I just made it so from my voyeuristic position on the outside looking on at their eager and happy public expressions of desire. I very quickly realized that Paris is a totally feminine city. The women of Paris, the *Parisiennes*, are certainly beautiful, oozing class, but also very sharp, intelligent and definitely openminded, especially sexually. After all, French kissing wasn't called that for no reason. For some wonderful reason Parisian women like to show others, everyone, the world, how they feel, whether it is strong feelings for a lover, for a work of art, for a perfect meal, for political causes, for high-heeled shoes, for whatever captures their attention, gets their juices flowing. *Parisiennes* are openly expressive and public passion may be their most expressive tendency. And no one can deny that it is a fun and healthy one.

But one other aspect of Parisian sexuality also made itself quite evident to me soon after Grace and I arrived in the city. After we got settled and I began haunting the Left Bank cafes, sitting at sidewalk tables nursing my glasses of red wine in the evenings, the *desmoiselles,* the prostitutes, began appearing out of the night approaching my table without hesitation, smiling and greeting me. "Monsieur," asking me if I would like their company, if I would buy them a drink, if I would "*Voule vous couche*" with them.

Perhaps then, after a few months of this constant observation of public passion, it seemed perfectly natural for me to be tempted toward a night of decadence at the *Moulin Rouge.* Truth be told, though certainly energetic, even athletic, I found their Can-Can to be rather tame. They seemed to me a vulgar version of the classy Radio City Music Hall Rockettes, a sort of working-class, or perhaps criminal-class, kick line. Anyway, I went and my sexual curiosity was rewarded with the same feeling of guilty semi-arousal that my waving off of the *desmoiselles* who approached me in the cafes caused me. I couldn't go with them because I felt as if it would be a betrayal of what Nicole and I had shared. Sadly, I began to handle this guilty return of my dormant sexuality on my own.

But the one good take-away of my visit to the *Moulin Rouge* was my immersion in the life and work of Toulouse Lautrec, which Grace soon discovered from our museum-going. While waiting for the Can-Can to commence that night I had wandered around the club taking in the *fin-de-siecle* ambiance. Just looking at the decorations on the walls, the framed Lautrec prints and posters, identified the place not only as a mini-shrine to Lautrec but to the whole Post-Impressionist period. The master of ceremonies for the evening's Can-Can told how the *desmoiselles*, the prostitutes who worked out of the club back in the 1880s, had inspired the Can-Can dance as they often drew would-be customers into their clutches by pulling up their skirts and showing them their knickers. Evidently, as portrayed in his paintings, those *desmoiselles* also powerfully inspired Lautrec as so many of his works were of the prostitutes whom he frequented. Walking around the club that night as the Lautrec prostitute paintings unfolded before me, I didn't anticipate the awkward questions that within a few weeks my fourteen-year-old art enthusiast daughter would pose as she became enamored of Lautrec's body of work.

That is not to say that Grace had not already started posing awkward questions. More than once when the two of us were sitting at an outside café table a prostitute had approached us and was about to speak to me when, upon noticing the young age of my companion, decide against her proposition and, once even with a soft pat on Grace's head, retreated in search of another likely customer.

G: Who was that lady? Did you know her? What did she want? Didn't she act strangely?

It was at times like that when Grace would hit me with a barrage of those sorts of questions that I really longed for Nicole.

And so Grace became enamored with Lautrec's works. That interest sent her to our little guidebook which not only gave her background on Lautrec but introduced her to all of Lautrec's Post-Impressionist compatriots in the decadent ambiance of the *Moulin Rouge*. I never told her that I had actually visited that very den of iniquity, but I was well prepared to carry on a conversation with her about the art history that she was discovering. This particular conversation took place as we sat on a bench on the Seine across from *Notre Dame*.

G: Who was Van Gogh? This says that he was Toulouse's best friend.

Me: He was. They often argued about the subject matter of their art.

G: And Cezanne, and Gauguin. (she pronounced it" gow-gain")

Me: Yes, they were friends and fellow artists at the same time, all living in *Montmartre*.

G: Oh, can we go to this *Montmartre* some day?

Me: Yes, of course, but we certainly can't walk there. We'll have to take a bus.

G: Or could we take a taxi, A taxi would be fun.

Me: OK. A taxi it is.

G: And Degas? Who was he? The book says that Degas's ballet dancers greatly influenced Lautrec's paintings of the prostitutes at the *Moulin Rouge*.

At that I think I visibly flinched. I really didn't know what to say. I must have had a look of dread on my face as I tried desperately to deflect the conversation from the questions that I knew were coming.

Me: Don't you remember? We saw some of Degas's ballet dancers at the *Jeu de Paume.* But Degas was not a friend of Lautrec.

G: So, how are ballet dancers like prostitutes? What are prostitutes? Why did Toulouse always paint these prostitutes? What is the *Moulin Rouge*? Can we visit there? Is it a museum like the *Jeu de Paume*?

As she pummeled me with these questions, all I could think was how much I wished Nicole was there to answer them for me. But strangely enough Nicole actually came to my rescue. Reeling from Grace's questions, I still had the presence of mind to ask myself the one simple question that had governed my life since Nicole's death: *What would Nicole do? How would she answer Grace?*

Just tell her the truth but in a gentle way, a voice whispered to me from somewhere inside my memory.

Me: Prostitutes are women who ask men to pay them money to make love with them. And so, ballet dancers are not like prostitutes. Ballet dancers are highly trained artists. Toulouse just copied the style and the situations of Degas in painting women.

Of course, my last little lecture on Degas influence upon Lautrec's style was meant to distract Grace from her focus upon prostitutes. But no such luck.

G: Is making love like a lot of kissing and hugging we see in the *parcs* as we walk around.

G: Yes, exactly, that's it. (And I thought I was out of the woods, off the hook, home free, but like all of those clichés, it just didn't work. Grace was relentless,)

G: Are all those women we see kissing and hugging getting paid money for doing that?

Me: No, not at all.

G: So then the prostitutes are different?

Me: Yes, they are professional love-makers. (Even as I said it, I realized how stupid it sounded).

G: So did Toulouse paint these prostitutes because he really liked their love-making and paid them both for that and to model for him to paint them?

Me: Yes, probably. I don't really know.

By the grace of God at that moment a long tour boat filled with sightseers emerged from beneath a bridge and Grace ran to the railing of the *quai* and waved hard at them. Most of the passengers waved back and Grace returned to me on my bench by the waterside smiling at her accomplishment of getting so many of them to acknowledge her.

Soon after, we did indeed visit *Montmartre* and *Pigalle.* I showed her the *Moulin Rouge* by day. Somewhat of a mistake, as she was intrigued by the pictures of the Can-Can girls bent over and showing their knickers in the lobby cards around the entryway. Actually, we started there. We talked some about Lautrec, how his own table was always held open for him, how his posters and paintings adorned all the walls along the sides and back of the showroom. And from there we set out to explore the rich history of *Montmartre.* Instead of a taxi which was just too expensive, we had taken the *Metro* to the *Boulevard de Clicly* in to *Pigalle* where we saw the *Moulin Rouge* with its red windmill on its roof. From there we climbed up into *Montmartre* with the Basilica of *Sacre Coeur* reaching above its houses as our focal point. *Montmartre* in the eighties up there on its high hill had an almost bucolic country village atmosphere in contrast to the growing urban sprawl of Paris down below. When we reached the top, the three domes of the *Sacre Coeur* looming above us, we were provided with panoramic views of all of northern Paris.

Everywhere we turned in *Montmartre* we seemed to encounter the *cottages* and *ateliers* of Paris's artists. For Paris *Montmartre* is not at all about the Gothic martyrs of its name, but rather is all about art itself, the artists who lived and worked and drank and ate and made love and above all made their art. In *Montmartre* art is everything and Grace, already captivated by the artists she had discovered in the *Jeu de Paume,* was drawn to the rich art history of that quaint village on the hill. Her guide book was always at the ready as we walked those bohemian streets and stumbled upon the landmarks of imagination and beauty that were created there. The *Bateau-Lavoir,* named for its shape after the laundry boats that used to ply the *Seine,* became the artists' hostel of the Post-Impressionists. At one time or another, Picasso, Dufy, Gris, Modigliani, Cocteau and many others slept and painted in its squalid cold-water studio-flats. As we walked through the *Cimetiere de Montmartre* Grace read to me from her little guidebook about the residents beneath its famous gravestones—Degas, the dancer Nijinsky, and her favorite, Le Goulue (Louise Weber), who was the model for many of Toulouse Lautrec's paintings and the most famous of the 'Doriss girls' who created the *Moulin Rouge*'s Can-Can. Turning a corner off of a busy shopkeepers' street, we came upon the *Rue Lepic* that Grace's little book told us was where Vincent Van Gogh and his brother Theo lived for two years. Van Gogh was one of Grace's special favorites from the

Jeu de Paume. We ate lunch in *Au Lapin Agile*, the rustic café that was *Montmartre's* version of *des Deux Magots* and the favorite meeting point for *Montmartre's* artist community led by Pablo Picasso. *Montmartre* got to be a sort of fine art overload for both Grace and I. We finally had to say our *adieaus* to its attractions and, staggering under a kind of aesthetic inebriation, retreat back to our home on the Left Bank.

Through the eyes of a precocious childlike Grace, all of these artists, their paintings, their hunger for light and color and originality, were like a powerful source of inspiration, a clarion call to beauty and creativity. In her classes at the *ecole* she started to draw pictures in her notebooks. Soon after she asked me if on one of our walks we could stop at an art shop and buy some oil paints and brushes and water color dyes. She took them to *ecole* and negotiated with her teacher to let her spend some of her class time actually painting. I bought her some small canvases and her teacher let her paint while sitting on the floor in a corner of the classroom. When she told me about this, I went out and bought her an easel and she clapped with joy. After another negotiation, her teacher allowed her to set it up in the same corner of the classroom which under the teasing of the other girls became known as 'the artist's corner', Grace's own personal *atelier* or studio. Then, on weekends, she would pack up her easel and paints, cart them to our *appartement,* and set herself up to paint in her own little artist's corner at home, her other *atelier.* But those were not the only places that Grace, now Grace the artist, would paint. Soon, on our weekends, in the best traditions of Seurat and Monet and Van Gogh (even Lautrec), she would carry her easel, brushes, and paints down to the *Seine*, in front of buildings on the streets of *Sant-Germain des Pres*, beside tables in our cafes in the *Latin Quarter*, on the greenswards of Paris' famous *parcs.*

Ah, the *parcs.* For me they had become, when Grace was in school and I was a solitary *flaneur*, my retreats, my resting places, my meditation zones, the places where I could sit in silence and turn my Eidetic Memory loose, calling up my whole life, unthreatened, often in tears and regret, thinking constantly of Nicole. Paris' *parcs* certainly were green and usually peaceful, often happy with the gleeful shouts of children playing, or melancholy with the sun setting and dark settling over their artfully aligned trees, always abundantly furnished with benches for sitting and watching, and shady nooks between bushes for spying, hourly populated with all species of interesting people and their intriguing interactions, from young lovers embracing on the grass to pensioners feeding the pigeons to painters at their easels to writers at their notebooks to strollers in berets with gargoyle headed canes or in bright straw boaters or in petite feathery *cloche* hats to young women in summer dresses to shop girls in modest kilts to mothers pushing babies in *la paussette* to all manner of people to watch going about their daily lives.

Good lord! What a sentence that was. I'm sorry. I really haven't gotten a good handle on this writing thing that I'm working at. It was, however, pretty much in Paris' *parcs* back then in the eighties that I first started toying with this idea of trying to write something. I had no idea what, but the Paris that Grace and I were exploring (and that I was aimlessly wandering on my own) seemed to be such a city of great writers, not only the French ones but the expatriates too—Hemingway, Fitzgerald, Joyce, Stein—all of who seemed to be jumping out of Grace's little guidebook everywhere we went, that it just seemed like I ought to be trying my own hand at it too. Earlier I mentioned the notebook that I had taken to carrying with me, mostly following Graces's example. Sitting on a bench in one of the *parcs* or nursing my morning espresso in a café. I was constantly thinking about Nicole, my infallible memory projecting a technicolor sense of our life together across the *cinematique* of my mind. Slowly but surely I started to embrace the idea of writing those memories down, not for myself for I would always have them clear and vivid in my memory, but for Grace to read some day in the future and help her remember her mother and our lives together. Thus. I got into the habit of carrying my notebook and a pen with me on my walks. I soon discovered that sitting on a bench in the quiet of a Parisian *parc* was the perfect place to write my memories down. A stop in a *parc* to write unfettered became a part of my daily diet of *flaneurie*.

The Luxembourg Gardens were the closest *parc* to our little *appartement* in the 6th. But the *Place de Vosges*, which in time became my favorite of the many Parisian *parcs*, was a walkable distance from our lodgings. To get to *Place de Vosges* demanded a stroll down to the *Seine*, across a bridge in the shadow of *Notre Dame*, into the Right Bank world of runaway Capitalism and voracious Consumerism. In the midst of all that, closed in by red-brick mansions, the *Place des Vosges* was a tiny island of green relief and peaceful solemnity, a perfect little square set off from the bustling outside world. Actually, I didn't mind the long walk at all because I knew that at its end lay my ideal *parc* that was like walking right into the middle of a Seurat painting.

But the Luxembourg Gardens, due to their proximity, was the *parc* I probably benched myself in the most often. If the *Place des Vosges* was a Seurat, the Luxembourg was like being cast into the strange weird world of a Dali. Its eclectic mixture of sculptures feverishly decorate an otherwise green, pastoral, rather heavily forested, very spacious urban *parc*. Stone stallions rear up over its walkways. Naked nymphs cavort around its fountains. Half-dressed lovers embrace and paw each other atop stone pedestals. Erect obelisks watch over the lovers like aroused voyeurs, perhaps inept chaperones intentionally enjoying their charges' couplings. The Luxembourg Gardens is the Parisian equivalent of New York's Central Park, only much more artsy or kitschy or kinky, though equally heavily wooded. Both *parcs* (parks) luxuriate in forested walkways that suddenly open out to more public areas that are much more densely populated. I can't tell you how many of my weekday afternoons I spent anchored to a bench in the Luxembourg perfectly happy just watching the world go by. If the Luxembourg Gardens is as heavily populated as New York's Central Park, the *Place des Vosges* is the total opposite. Small, enclosed, peaceful, it is a meditative retreat from the urban chaos all around. It is a perfectly symmetrical green space of grass and trees and bubbling fountains.

Our Left Bank had so much to see and do that Grace and I rarely ventured any further than the *quais* of the *Seine*. In that first year our excursion to *Montmartre*, plus a long walk from the *Tuileries Gardens* down the *Champs-Elysees* to the *Arc de Triomphe*, and my visits to the *Place des Vosges* and the *Moulin Rouge* night club were really the only times we left our own neighborhood.

One other place, however, that we pretty thoroughly explored was *Montparnasse*. If *Montmartre* was the gathering place for French artists, *Montparnasse* was the preferred residence of not only French writers but the expatriates as well. And its attraction for us was like the Luxembourg Gardens, its proximity to our own lodgings. Both Hemingway and Fitzgerald wrote novels in *Montparnasse* in between drinking and partying in its bars and cafes. *Shakespeare and Co.*, where James Joyce and Sylvia Beach conspired to get *Ulysses* published despite the censors, is close by.

But right now, I am not remembering (or trying to write about) *Montparnasse* for its literary history or it touristy attraction, rather it was on an evening in a café in *Montparnasse* that my own Parisian life,

which to that time all through that first year and a-half had been almost completely taken up with Grace, began to take a turn. Probably
the most famous celebrity to every take up residence in *Montparnasse*
was Hemingway. I had never really liked Hemingway's writing that
much, but one of his short stories, "A Clean Well-Lighted Place," that
night really struck home for me. It was simply about a man alone at
a table in a café. I realized that then, there, at that particular point in
the evolution of my life, that man was me. As time had passed, with
Grace in school five days a week, I had certainly become used to being
alone, but it was that night thinking about Hemingway's short story
and applying it to myself that loneliness became real for me as it never
had been before. I was that man in Hemingway's story, alone, sitting
at a table in a café watching the world go by, immobile, my life going
nowhere. But I wasn't completely lost because that night I actually took
out my notebook and wrote a memo to myself to read Hemingway's
story again in the light of day. I came to look at that night in the café
in *Montparnasse* as an important turning point for me. I started to realize that I needed to start living again or else I'd end up like that poor
lonely man in the story.

But about the same time another somewhat troubling circumstance was beginning to capture my attention. After my visit to the
Moulin Rouge I must admit, actually quite guiltily, I was starting to
feel just the slightest return of urges, sexual urges, that I hadn't felt for
a long time, well, you know, since Nicole. I didn't do anything about
them. In fact, I tried very hard to resist them. But nonetheless they
were there and they were troublesome. One night, midweek, alone,
curious to compare it to the *Moulin Rouge*, I took an omnibus to the
famous (or infamous), *Crazy Horse* night club. Grace and I had been
in Paris about two years and we both had taken to riding an omnibus
back from the terminuses of our longer walks. We both enjoyed sitting
atop the omnibuses. They were a delightful way to see Paris. The city
seemed to flow by us like a painted canvas on a roller. But I digress. I
took an omnibus to the *Crazy Horse*, sat at the bar at the back of the
showroom away from the stage because I was alone, and tried to convince myself that I was there merely for comparison purposes like men
insist that they only read *Playboy* magazines for the excellent short stories by name writers. My first impulse as I watched the stage show was
actually comparative. The *Crazy Horse* was completely different from
the *Moulin Rouge* and its frenetic Can-Can. The *Crazy Horse* dancers

were elegant and synchronized and so very professional They were the Parisian equivalent of the Radio City Music Hall's Rockettes... only naked! I couldn't take my eyes off of them. And the production values were the equivalent of a Las Vegas stage show. As they moved though their professionally choreographed minuets, formed their perfectly disciplined bare-breasted kick lines, colored lights danced on their naked bodies in dazzling, shifting, erotic waves. They were truly a feast for my starving eyes and I came away that night feeling for the first time as if I had finally chosen to join the passionate world of Paris that had been all around me since we arrived.

If there could possibly be such a thing as a sexual transubstantiation then I was entering into it. I felt my body coming back to life and my blood heating up. Who knows? Perhaps it was the naked *Crazy Horse* girls? Or perhaps it was simply all of the Parisian lovers that I stole voyeuristic looks at every day in the *parc*s? Or maybe the elegant *Parisiennes* that I passed every day on the streets? Or the ever-present *desmoiselles* who approached me in the evenings as I sat alone in the cafes? Who knows? But it was happening and it was real and I was feeling urges that I hadn't felt for years since Nicole's death. And that led me to a further realization, not a sexual one, but an existential one. I realized at long last that here, in Paris, it was as if I was on the verge of entry into a whole new life, as if I was changing into a whole new person, a kind of existential transubstantiation.

As you may have noticed as I have been writing about all of Grace and my *flaneur* excursions around the city, Parisians are not naturally outgoing or smilingly friendly like American midwesterners are. HenceI spent a great deal of time alone, sitting on benches reading or sitting in cafes drinking whether it be coffee or something stronger. Paris is sort of like a secret society that is very hard to join and has a rather strict and difficult initiation process. By now it was 1987 and Grace and I had, at least in our own estimation, become Parisians. We could, like Nick Carroway in Fitzgerald's *The Great Gatsby*, give accurate directions to lost American tourists with the best of them. Grace was now fifteen years old and, I felt, mature beyond her years. She was an accomplished artist, a diarist like Anais Nin whom she had discovered and idolized, an excellent student, now totally fluent in French, and, with me, a Parisian *flaneur* of the most knowledgeable bent. I might add that she no longer engaged me in any awkward conversations about sex. My guess is that she expended them on her weekly schoolgirl friends. Anyway, it was on a typical day for me—late afternoon, sitting in *des Deux Magots* having just ordered my second *aperitif*–that an extraordinary thing happened.

I saw a woman approaching, a blue package of *Gauloises* cigarettes at the ready. *Another Parisian whore*, I immediately presumed, primed to accost me and deliver the most cliched of all the come-on lines that these whores who worked the cafes used. Of course, she was going to ask me for a light, then engage me in conversation, then make her tired proposition. It had happened to me many times since I was always alone. I was inured to it. I was always polite in my refusal, my rejection of her sales pitch, her pleasant offer of her body for the evening. But it turned out this time this was no ordinary Parisian *desmoiselle*. As soon as she opened her mouth, I realized that she wasn't a whore (or if she was, she was plying her trade an awfully long way from home).

"Excuse me, do you have a light?" she popped the expected question, but not in French. Rather in an accent more Iowan or Hoosier than Parisian.

She was unmistakably American, probably midwestern, and she sounded actually a lot like me. *An American, how funny*, I thought. Needless to say, I was a bit taken aback, "flustered" might me a better word for it.

Me: Sorry, but I don't smoke.

Her: Oh, I guess I just thought that everybody smoked in Paris. (she laughed and smiled)

Me: I used to smoke grass (I offered unsolicited information), but I gave it up when I came over here.

Her: You're an American like me.

On impulse, acting the gentleman I guess, I got up and borrowed a match from a man at an adjoining table. When I got back to my table, she had already sat down. I bent to her, lit her up, and she sent a puff of blue Gauloise smoke out over her left shoulder.

Her: Mind if I join you? (which was a rather unnecessary question since she already had)

I don't know what made me do it, but for some strange reason I immediately consented.

And so, we sat there for a long awkward moment, she meditating, puffing, me awkwardly tongue-tied.

Her: (finally) I'm Wendy from Chicago. I work here in Paris.

At that, I immediately wondered what work she did, hoping beyond hope that she wasn't a prostitute.

Me: I'm Michael. (and I stuck out my hand for a shake, then when she didn't take it withdrew it quickly realizing how dumb it had looked)

W: (leaning into me across the table) I have a confession to make. I didn't really need a match. I just heard your American voice when you ordered and I thought how nice it would be to talk to an American for a change. Homesickness I guess.

Well, I just sat there all star-spangled, busted by my American accent. She seemed a rather nice enough woman. About my age, quiet, attractive in an aggressive sort of way, an open face and a winning smile. *So why not I thought*, No harm in chatting with her for a few minutes. Better than just sitting here alone.

Me: Well I can certainly accommodate you there. And talking to another American sounds quite good to me too.

W: Stay right here while I go get my stuff. I'll be right back.

It was only then that I realized that this Wendy person had come a quite long way from her spot on the other side of the café. When she sat back down, she started right in.

W: I noticed you writing in your notebook. It ticked my curiosity. Are you a writer?

Me: Oh god no! (I laughed nervously) I just write things down. Who knows what I'll ever do with them. Just memories, observations, you know, stuff, stuff I think of.

W: (now leaning across closer, pretty clearly interested in me, god knows why) Yes, I do know. I'm a writer too. I do much the same thing.

After that we seemed to just drift into a conspiratorial ease of conversation. She told me that she was a journalist and worked for the International Herald Tribune. It was the only English language newspaper in Europe back in those days. Writing seemed to be the doorway that our conversation led us through that first day in the café. She told me about her writing for the newspaper, how sometimes they sent her out with specific assignments to cover events or celebrities or the new films exported from America. She was actually a part-time film critic and that immediately captured my interest. We talked about films, about the kind of access she had to theatres and social events and all sorts of goings-on around Paris. But what was really more interesting, she told me, was when she wasn't on a specific assignment, she still prowled around Paris keeping her eyes open, and her ears evidently, for the odd story or interesting situation that she could write about.

W: And I jot them down in my little notebook just like you were doing.

So she laughed and described herself as a writer who worked even when she wasn't working.

W: But aren't all writers like that? Look at you. You are sitting here writing things down in your notebook that you say you have no intentions for. They are not notes or anecdotes or scenes or characters for your novel or your short story or your memoir, yet you are writing them down anyway, supposedly to no purpose whatsoever, yet you are keeping them in your notebook all safe and sound for your future use. Oh, you're a writer alright Michael. You just don't know it yet.

Wendy was like an indomitable force. Once she latched on to an idea, mounted the horse, so to speak, she rode it out until it was broken. I think now, as I look back at it, that it was Wendy that day in the café who first planted the seed in me, made me actually think about being a writer. Maybe she was right. Maybe all of the things I was writing down in my little notebook were, even if I hadn't acknowledged it yet, destined to end up in some kind of written form bigger than just random notes.

W: So, what do you write about?

It was an innocent enough question. She had told me all about her writing job for the newspaper. Simple *quid pro quo*. I've shown you mine now you show me yours. But for me it really wasn't all that simple.

Me: Actually, I really don't know. Just memories, I guess. The things I think about when I'm sitting here alone. Writing them down sort of feeds the illusion that I'm doing something and not just wasting time, treading water, drinking coffee.

W: What sort of memories?

It was then that I realized that I was sitting across my café table with a professional interviewer, someone experienced in drawing other people out, making them reveal themselves in somewhat intimate ways. What she was doing actually frightened me. I don't think she really meant anything by it. Drawing people out was just a habit with her, a reflex, something she did just as a matter of course because her job had inured her to doing it. But I must confess that as she questioned me I began to get a little nervous. I think I just wasn't ready to start giving up information about myself to a perfect stranger. When I didn't answer her right away she took another puff (she was on her second cigarette since she had sat down) and pressed on.

W: Memories? Do you only write about the past? What about the here and now? Here in Paris?

Me: Oh, I do. I often jot down my reactions to the things I see and hear as I walk around Paris. The sights, the buildings, the people I see in the parks and on the streets. But yes, mostly memories.

W: What sort of memories? Good memories? Bad?

This was really getting personal, I felt, but for some strange reason I was rather caught up in my conversation with this aggressive woman who had dropped down out of the sky and landed at my table.

Me: Oh, good memories mostly.

And that gave me pause for just a moment because, suddenly, I realized that for my special case in the light of my own very special memory that this whole conversation was really pretty absurd. I felt that I really needed to explain myself. I didn't really want to but as I looked across the table at this Wendy person I saw in her face, her eyes, that she was really interested in me, that her questions weren't meant to intrude but rather were just the emanation of a healthy curiosity. It had been so very long that any woman had shown any healthy interest in me at all that I really felt almost compelled to explain to her.

Me: You see, I have this memory problem. Well, not really a problem, rather a special skill, some would call it a gift. I remember everything. I can never forget anything. My whole past is always there, imbedded in my memory. It's called Eidetic Memory. If you don't believe me, you can look it up.

W: So then why are you writing your memories down?

Me: I don't know. Maybe I'm afraid that some day I'll wake up and this special gift of mine will be gone and I won't remember anything.

W: Wow, that's really weird.

Me: Yes, it is isn't it.

W: Well if you ask me, and I know you haven't, but I'm going to tell you anyway, writing in this notebook of yours is the first step to being a writer. Am I going to find my way into your notebook after today?

Me: Yes, I think so.

W: Good. That means I have made a good first impression and haven't succeeded in scaring you off which is often the effect I have on men.

Me: No, not at all, I've really enjoyed our conversation.

W: In that case maybe we can do it again. I've got to run now, but I like this café. You know that Sartre and de Beauvoir were regulars here don't you? And Albert Camus?

Me: Oh yes, that is one of the major reasons I come here.

W: Films. The Existentialists. Writing. We do have a lot in common I'd say. OK, I'm off. (and she hoisted her postman's bag over her shoulder) I have Mondays and Tuesdays off and that's when I usually come here. If you see me, let's talk again.

And with a wave she was gone.

After she left, I must admit that not only did I sit there for quite a while thinking about her, rerunning our conversation in my mind, but I sat and wrote about her in my notebook. Then a strange thing happened. As I was walking back to our little *appartement*, I started having pangs of guilt. *What would Nicole have thought of that?* That same old haunting question assailed my consciousness. I felt as if that day's Wendy entry in my notebook was a kind of evidence of infidelity against me. To this point, besides the random observations of Paris life and the Paris cityscape that I had written down, I had filled my notebook with my memories of Nicole, of our life together, of her existence in every possible way that I could conceive her. Now I realized that in this odd way I was trying to keep her alive, share Paris with her, working some strange sort of word magic on her lost being. Now this Wendy person had broken that magic spell, had intruded herself into my consciousness.

As the days passed after that I couldn't stop thinking about our café conversation. I tried to close it out of my mind, but it kept coming back. I had to admit that I had really enjoyed talking to her. Especially the writing part of our talk. Perhaps that day, in that clean, well-lighted café, was when I first started thinking about trying a writing project. I was pretty sure it was something I would never do, or if I tried would never be able to finish. But this woman had planted the seed. Who knows?

What I did know, however, was that the following Monday I was back at my table in *des Deux Magots* hoping that on her day off Wendy would appear again… and she did. Jumping off of an omnibus, stopping to look around, her eyes fixed on me and she came straight to my table.

W: Hi Michael. I'm so glad you are here. I was hoping you would be.

She was like a whirlwind, sitting down and parking her bag before I ever even had a chance to rise and greet her.

I too had hoped that she would return and sit to talk with me. That was why I had been back here on her day off, why I had thought of almost nothing else for the last week or so. But now that it had actually happened, I was typically tongue-tied. As she arranged herself across from me, I just stared stupidly at her. She lit a cigarette, puffed, exhaled a bluish cloud, then sat back with a bemused look on her face, and waited.

Me: Yes. Me too. (I finally found my tongue) I remembered that Mondays were your day off. I was hoping that perhaps you'd show up today. I really enjoyed talking to you before.

W: So, did you write about me in your notebook?

She had this mischievous look in her eye. As I thought about it later, I speculated that she had rehearsed her opening gambit—similar to her previous "do you have a light" charade—as she rode toward me on the omnibus, her strategy for drawing me out, another of her professional interviewer tricks. Of course, it worked, just as the other had. We were playing a rhetorical tennis game and now the ball was in my court.

Me: Yes, well actually I did. I think you would really laugh at what I wrote.

W: Oh, I don't know, try me.

Me: I'm not sure you'll like it.

W: (cajoling) C'mon, tell me.

Me: OK. I wrote about when you first approached me. I thought you were a *desmoiselle*, a prostitute.

W: I know what a *desmoiselle* is. (she laughed)

Me: Sorry.

W: No, I think it is rather funny. A kind of compliment actually. Maybe we should explore that first impression a little further. Like how much do you think I could command on the open market?

Now I was totally embarrassed and she was totally amused. I had managed to talk myself right into a corner and she was delighted to keep me trapped there.

Me: Well, as soon as you opened your mouth, I realized that was surely not the case.

W: Please don't call me Shirley.

She couldn't resist throwing off a line from a recent Mel Brooks movie that it turns out we had both seen, she in French, me in American, but it made me see just how much fun she was having at my expense, with my embarrassment.

W: So (and she arched an eyebrow at me) do you have a lot of experience with our Parisian *desmoiselles*?

Me: (now totally flustered, her sadistically amused) Oh god no. No. None at all. I've been here years and I 've never touched one of them (talk about 'he doth protest too much').

W: (perhaps deciding that line of conversation had run its course) Years? So, you are not just some American tourist? Just what are you doing in Paris?

Me: I have a teenage daughter. (I blurted out) My wife died five years ago. I just had to leave the States, running away I guess. My daughter Grace is in school here. She boards, then spends the weekends with me.

W: (that stopped her dead in her tracks) Omigod Michael, I'm so sorry. (she was clearly moved, all of her playfulness abruptly stopped)

Me: No. It's OK. I've sort of come to deal with it. I probably never will. But I don't really want to. It's Ok. You know, I've been here for years and you are the first person I've even mentioned her to. Her name was Nicole. A very French name.

W: Nicole… yes… Nicole.

I could tell that she was pretty visibly shaken by the turn this conversation had taken. I don't know why I had felt compelled to blurt Grace and Nicole out at her like that. Maybe I wanted to get back at her for teasing me the way she did when she first sat down. Or maybe I felt some guilt about not having mentioned Grace and Nicole at all in our first conversation the week before. Not guilt for not telling her, but rather guilt for inexplicably keeping Nicole and Grace hidden from her. Oh, who knows what my motives had been then, but now they were out in the open and I felt as if a weight had been lifted.

As for Wendy, she was just sitting there, her eyes down as if she was afraid to look at me.

As for me, I too was in a minor state of shock. My revelation had yanked our conversation into a deeper level of intimacy for which neither of us was prepared. I don't know why I had felt compelled to confide those simple facts of Grace and Nicole. I now was thinking there was some sinister reason I had held them back the week before. And Wendy, I think, was just sort of stunned. Our conversation thus far had been light and theoretical, about writing mostly, but now I had made it somehow personal, had dragged reality into our harmless café conversation. All these thoughts raced through my mind in a matter of mere seconds as the brief awkward silence hung between us. Up to this point we had just been two Americans bumping into each other in a foreign land. But now it was as if I had put Grace and Nicole down on the table between us and made things much more complicated.

Thankfully our awkward silence didn't last long at all. True to the straight-forward, no-nonsense self that I would become accustomed to in the next three years, Wendy attacked the silence head-on.

W: Well, (she gave me a tight smile as she reached for another cigarette) you are just full of surprises today, aren't you?

Me: Yes, I guess I should have mentioned Grace before…

W: And Nicole…

Me: Yes, Certainly, Nicole too. She died in an automobile accident.

Now I felt as if I was just spewing forth information that I didn't need to offer. But Wendy had somehow drawn me into her confidence. I was confiding the darkest reality of my existence to this perfect stranger I had met in a café.

Suddenly, Wendy stood up and I thought she was going to grab her bag and flee. But instead she gave a commanding wave to the waiter.

W: Oh Michael, I think we need something a lot stronger than coffee right now.

When the waiter arrived, she ordered two double whiskeys, sent him away, and sat back down.

W: Well, this explains a lot. Since last week I've been wondering about you. Why is he in Paris? Why is he alone? Divorced? Gay? Running away from something? As it turns out it was sort of all of those things. When I saw you writing in the notebook I thought 'oh, another writer, an American come to Paris to try to relive the expatriate dream' but then I found out that you weren't a writer at all. Just a random scribbler. So, I kept asking myself all week that question. Why is he here? Actually, that's probably what brought me back here today looking for you. Now I know that it is a lot more complicated than I thought. And you are a lot more interesting that I had imagined.

This Wendy certainly didn't pull her punches. The drinks she had ordered came and as we took our first sips, she re-entered her personal interviewer mode.

W: So, what other surprises do you have for me. Tell me about your daughter.

And I did. As the afternoon unfolded around us, different shades of sunlight filtering through the tree's leaves and casting delicate shadows on our table, moving to a second double whiskey, I told her about my married life with Nicole and painted a picture of Grace. I held back all the earlier stuff before Nicole. I had mentioned it before, as I had my Eidetic Memory. But I didn't want her to think I was some kind of freak (which I was). But deep down I knew that sooner or later she would draw it all out of me. As the whiskey took hold and the afternoon waned around us, I realized that this was the first time since Nicole's death that I had talked to anyone about her. And I realized that I felt good doing it, unburdening myself. I imagined that this might be what psychoanalytic therapy must be like, the old talking cure. Maybe. I doubt it. All I knew was that I was starting to like talking to this Wendy Person. Her last name was Porsek by the way. Polish. From South Bend, Indiana. But she wrote under the pen-name Wendy Masters. "Much more nonthreatening," she said, "or maybe not," she laughed.

We were both a bit drunk when we decided that it was time to go. Wendy was standing with her bag over her shoulder as we stood to say goodbye.

Me: Thank you Wendy. You are a good listener.

I really meant it from somewhere either deep in my psyche or deep in my heart. I'm afraid the two of them were pretty mixed up back then.

W: Look, I'm off work pretty early on Sunday. Can I meet you and Grace here? Around four. I'd love to meet her. Please. This is like a two-for-one-deal. An American I can talk to and an American girl to meet. Say yes. Sunday. Four.

She said that last in a sort of *faux*-begging, playful tone of voice.

Me: Yes, sure, it will be fun. I'll bet Grace will be surprised. I mean, an attractive Parisian woman actually talking to her father. Wait 'til you meet her. She is annoyingly curious. She'll have all kinds of questions for you. Your job especially. A journalist. She will be very impressed.

W: Good. Then it's a date. (then, realizing what she had said, she reflexively took a self-conscious step back) Well, not a date. I didn't mean…

Actually I had to laugh at that. She had sort of flustered herself over her word choice.

Me: Don't worry. I knew what you meant.

She turned to leave, but I stopped her.

Me: Wendy, I've really enjoyed talking to you here, these two times. Especially about the writing part. Yours, and even mine. You've actually got me thinking about why I'm carrying this notebook around. At first, I thought it was just to impress Grace, because she carries one. But now, after talking to you, well… I don't know.

W: Good. I've enjoyed it too. We'll have to do more of that.

As promised, that Sunday Grace was with me in the café when Wendy jumped off the omnibus lugging her ever-present leather bag. I had forewarned Grace that we were meeting someone in the café. A friend I had recently met I told her. I don't know why I just said friend and not 'woman,' probably my survivor's guilt again, but I did. Of course, Grace had asked "who" since in all the time that we had been in Paris we had never had anyone else sitting at our sidewalk table with us. Then, when I introduced Wendy to her and Wendy sat down, Grace was certainly taken aback.

W: Grace, it is great to meet you. Your father has told me so much about you. (a bald-faced lie) You are about all he ever talks about. (her pants totally on fire)

Wendy really did have a way with people, seemed to know exactly the right things to say. Grace immediately warmed to her. Soon the questions started to spew out of Grace. Ironic. An interviewer interviewing an interviewer. I just sat back and took in the show. They were two women talking and I wasn't really in their league. I did notice that Wendy wasn't smoking. Probably didn't want to set a bad example. Anyway, it really went well. I admit that I came into this meeting with some unspoken fears. *Would Grace feel I was cheating on her dead mother? Would Grace and Wendy not hit it off, hate each other? Would the whole meeting just be an awkward bad idea?* But five minutes in, all of my baseless fears were completely allayed. Grace had to be back at school at six-thirty so after two hours of the two of them quizzing each other I had to pack her up and go. As we were leaving and Grace was starting away, Wendy touched my arm and silently mouthed "Tuesday" to me. You know, her touch and her silent command, the brief intimacy of it, totally cast a spell on me. For the next two days all I could think of was meeting her in the café.

When that Tuesday came around and she sat down and immediately lit a cigarette, I just couldn't resist.

Me: You didn't smoke at all on Sunday.

W: God, I know. I don't know how I did it. I lunged for one the moment you guys were out of sight.

We both laughed over that and the ease of our conversation was again afoot.

Me: Well, what did you think?

W: Oh Michael, she's fabulous. Smart. Curious. Articulate. Oh, she's a good one. I really like her.

Me: She's pretty special I think, but then I'm totally biased.

W: She may be fifteen years old but she can carry on a conversation more interesting than ninety percent of the adults I have to talk to every day.

Me: Yes, you two really hit it off. I'm glad.

At that Wendy didn't really reply right away. She puffed, and I could tell she was thinking about something.

W: I'm glad too (she finally said) and do you know way?

Me: No why?

I had just answered without thinking and I immediately regretted it.

W: Oh, you stupid American men. You are so slow.

I just looked at her. I guess she was right because I had no idea what she was talking about, where she was going with this.

Me: Slow?

W: Yes, slow. Good lord Michael, a Frenchman would have seen what was going on between us right away.

Me: Between us?

W: O god! (and she stubbed out her cigarette in frustration) Look, I enjoy talking to you. I really enjoyed meeting your daughter. But there can be a lot more for us than just sitting in this café talking if you would just wake the fuck up and start paying attention.

That major curse word, actually the first of its type I had ever heard her utter in any of our conversations, really did catch my attention and, in fact, started all kinds of wheels whirling, thoughts dancing, lights flashing, in my mind. Suddenly I realized that Wendy actually was doing what I thought she was doing, talking about what I thought she was talking about, intimating something that had crossed my mind a number of times since I had met her but that I hadn't taken seriously because I never thought it could happen.

As all these thoughts whirled chaotically in my brain, Wendy just sat there staring at me, never even blinking, with this silly grin on her face, totally proud of herself for opening the doors and driving the huge Mack truck into the room.

Me: You mean… (I stammered)

W: Of course I do you idiot. I've been thinking of making love to you ever since that first day we met. Maybe the most attractive thing about you is that you're not a Frenchman.

Me: Oh Wendy, I don't know…

W: And you never will unless you try, Right now. Our first time. Let's go to my flat. We'll have all night. Just us. Neither one of us alone.

Without another word we just got up. I put my notebook in my pocket. She shouldered her bulky bag. Then after only a few steps she took my hand, leading me. It was the first time we had really touched, that I had felt her skin. Then a few steps later she pulled up short, reached up and put her arms around my neck, pulled me to her, and kissed me hard full on the lips. Then, on our second kiss, right there in the street, everybody watching, our mouths opened and our tongues caressed each other. Then, on our third kiss, flocks of pedestrians swerving around us and smiling right there on the sidewalk, our faces pressed into each other and our tongues penetrating our mouths in a kiss so sensual that I don't think either one of us ever wanted it to end. Even today, thirty years later I think that would qualify as some major PDA.

W: Oh wow, Michael. Oh. I just thought we needed to get that out of the way. I didn't think it would be that good.

Me: Yes, Oh yes. I'm so stupid. I'm so sorry it took me so long to see you, really see you. I'd be lying if I said I wasn't attracted to you all along too. I was just afraid of ruining such a good thing. I just so enjoyed being with you. Until I met you I hadn't really thought too much about being alone but then…

W: (she put a finger to my lips, shushing me) Enough. No more talking. No more thinking. You come with me now.

And so I did. We took a taxi to her flat. We made love voraciously. I thought I'd be afraid, feel guilty, maybe even impotent after so long away, but that certainly was not the case. It was as if our bodies had found each other at the perfect moment in history, our histories. We entwined naked with each other, we deep kissed more and more and then more, we caressed every inch of each other, we met and penetrated not only each other's bodies but each other's deepest desires. We made love only as two lovers surprised by the depth of their passion can make love, no words, only the language of our bodies in perfect conversation.

I quickly realized that making love with Wendy was totally different and new for me. Making love to Nicole had been like two adoring lovers enjoying each other on the grassy bank of a woodland stream with a gentle breeze caressing them, coaxing them into each other's bodies. Quiet, relaxed, silken. Making love with Wendy was like riding a freight train. She would start out slow, climbing steadily, then, picking up steam, she would pull you with her to the top of a high hill, and then suddenly plunge hard and full speed down the other side, unleashing all the power of her sexual engine, the wind in your face, the pressure of the plunge torqueing your body, all your senses, into an utterly explosive release. Nicole was a waft of clean fresh air. Wendy was a powerful pulse of steam.

Wendy in Paris, in bed, opened up a whole new world for me. She was a creature of constantly creative sexuality. She prided herself on offering a *charcuterie* of sex that promised to be different every time we shed our clothes and sampled each other's bodies. Right away we were eager, hungry lovers. We devoured each other unabashedly, erotically. From the very beginning Wendy stressed, *faux*-begged, laughingly taunted, sternly commanded, me to do absolutely anything, ANYTHING, I wanted with her body. She tried to make me understand that she was open for anything. But I don't think I ever really got it. Of course, she was a much more experienced lover than me. Oh, there had been the hippie girls in Berkeley, and Victoria, and of course Nicole. But Wendy was totally different from all of them. She had no boundaries. No hesitation, no denial. She would initiate or participate in any sexual act that the two of us together could imagine. This, I think, could only happen in Paris. Back in America Nicole (she of the sexy French name) and I made love frequently, enjoyed each other immensely, produced Grace as the perfect culmination of our lovemaking. Our American version of sex was as wholesome and healthy and fun filled as an Indiana State Fair with Grace as the midway prize. My and Wendy's Parisian lovemaking was as different from that as the languages we did it in. Perhaps 'making love' is not really the proper word at all for what we were doing. Our Parisian lovemaking was much more naughty, even playfully dirty, mildly kinky, unashamed, often openly public, always romantic and wonderfully satisfying, It was pure sex at its most personally heightened. There is a definite reason that French kisses are called French kisses and that cunnilingus is the favored language of Parisian lovers. Who knows, perhaps for the French the tongue is the most sensual and erotic sexual organ. Wendy even taught me a few words that I had never heard before.

Yes, Wendy certainly was a creative lover, an adventurous lover, but she could also be a very philosophical, theoretical, analytical lover in the best tradition of Simone de Beauvoir and Anaïs Nin and George Sand. We didn't use our tongues only for the bvedroom. Before, during, after, and even apart from, we spoke the language of sex to each other. In fact, Wendy loved to expound on it. Listen:

W: You American men! You think everything has to make sense, to mean something. You are always, like the Militant Capitalists that all you American men are, trying to find the worth in everything, what its value is. Even in sex.

Me: In sex?

W: Yes, you spoil it by trying to analyze it — determine its value. Look, there are three kinds of sex. Procreational sex really does have value. It produces something that is rather valuable. Procreational sex is perfect for you American Capitalists. It produced your Grace. She proves the great value and profit of Procreational sex. But for us Michael, ours is purely Recreational sex. Play. Fun. An ongoing game that we play with each other's bodies. It can be competitive. You know, who orgasms first, or better, or the most times. Who is on the top and who is on the bottom. Or it can just be a carefree game like playing cards or throwing darts.

Me: But what about love?

W: Love or lust? Personally, I like lust better.

Me: But love is important, right?

W: Of course it is, and we have it, and that is why we are having so much fun.

Me: So you said there are three kinds of sex. What is the third kind?

W: The third kind is Power sex. Believe me honey you don't ever want to go there.

And with that she laughed and stuck her tongue in my mouth successfully cutting off any more questions. That was Wendy. Oh yes, she could be sexually creative, adventurous, playful. But she was also a very serious person, adamant in her beliefs, thoughtful in her views of life and the world around her.

As Wendy and I fell deeper and deeper in lust (a kind of love perhaps) with each other, I realized that she was working a kind of sweet magic upon me, another secular transubstantiation of my body and my blood into her lover, her friend, her student, her companion. Very quickly we had built a substantial relationship with each other, mainly through sex, but in other ways as well.

Don't get me wrong. Wendy and I did all kinds of things other than having sex. For example, we went to the movies together. Our shared love of film had been one of the things that had driven our conversation that first afternoon when we met in the café. She had mentioned that one of her assignments for the International Herald Tribune was writing film reviews. One afternoon (okay, after we had sex) we decided to take in a film. It was 1988 and the hottest film that spring in Parisian cinemas was *The Unbearable Lightness of Being* about the Communist repression of the so-called 'Prague Spring' in Czechoslovakia. It was a good first film for us to see together because it was actually in English with French subtitles. But its value as our first film together was even better than that. It triggered a café conversation afterwards that stripped bare Wendy's political orientation, something we had never really discussed. Just from her no-nonsense directness, her constant effort to control her life (Okay, her always wanting to be on top), her fearlessness, her dedication to her job, I figured that she was a feminist. No deep perception on my part. Her whole bearing shouted it! But as we talked about that film, I realized that she was a radical leftist who despised the Communist repression that flexed its military muscle all over Eastern Europe. As time went on and Wendy chose movies for us to see, I realized that most of them were tailored to her personality and her political beliefs. *Gorillas in the Mist* about the fearless anthropologist Dian Fossey. *The Accused* about a vicious gang rape. *And God Created Women*, either the least or the most feminist movie of them all. But not all the films we saw were of the political, feminist ilk. That year we saw *Frantic*, a thriller set in Paris, and *Dirty Rotten Scoundrels*, a comedy set on the Riviera. But the one thing that going to the movies with Wendy did for me was greatly improve my French pronunciation. Very few of the films were in English and I, of course with my memory had a full mastery of French, but I found myself picking up just by watching them the pronunciation of what was being said on the screen.

We sometimes went out to dinner together. After she would have a hard day at work I would splurge and treat her to a romantic candlelit dinner in a clean, well-lighted place. Our favorite eating spot was a tiny eight-table restaurant near the Herald Tribune offices called *Francoise' and Yoyo's*. We went so often that we got to know the owners Francoise a Parisian and Yoyo an Algerian, and their large, lazy, black Labrador who habitually slept under our table as we ate.

One day, surprising me, Wendy even organized a picnic for us. She actually emptied her large leather bag of all of its notebooks and pens and womanly detritus and filled it back up with wine and cheese and *baguettes* and a blanket. Then she walked me down to a small *parc* on the *Seine*, spread the blanket, and laid me down. It was like being right in the middle of the famous Seurat painting. Before I knew it, right there on the grass, we were embracing, entwining, kissing, making out for everyone to see like a couple of horny teenagers. I must admit that since I had been in Paris, I had always wanted to do that. Before I met Wendy, always alone, walking the city, everywhere I went it seemed, I saw young lovers wrapped in each other's arms, making out unabashedly in public. I guess I was jealous of them, their unbridled happiness, because I was so alone and missing Nicole so much.

Me: You know, (I said to Wendy when we came up for air) you are fulfilling one of my favorite Parisian fantasies.

W: I am? What's that?

Me: Making out in a *parc* in public.

W: It doesn't take much to please you does it? (she laughed)

Me: I guess not, but you certainly know how to please me. (and saying that I dove back in for another round of kissing and light humping)

When we tired of molesting each other, Wendy laid out our picnic between us on the blanket. As I looked at it, as we broke the bread and uncorked the wine, I realized that there it was once again. Bread and wine, our bodies and our hot sexual blood. Wendy had worked a very different kind of transubstantiation upon me, changed the whole substance of my being. Needless to say, when the sun set on our *Seine*-side picnic, we went straight back to Wendy's bed. Although, the first thing she did when we entered her apartment was repack her big leather bag.

But not all of our excursions out of our bedrooms and about Paris were as satisfying as our film-going or our romantic dinners or our picnic by the *Seine*. One evening Wendy had worked late and we hadn't eaten until after nine. It was nearing midnight when we left the restaurant, a cloudy night, pretty much pitch dark between streetlamps. We were wending our way to her flat when out of a side alley a dark shadow ran at us and grabbed at Wendy's precious leather bag. Luckily it was hung securely on her shoulder and its strap was strong because when that thug grabbed at it Wendy caught the strap and grabbed back. A brief tug of war ensued between them. I don't know what got into me, but all of a sudden my old Secret Service training kicked back in after all those years. Without thinking I crooked my arm and hit him square in the face with the sharp end of my elbow. It was exactly how my instructors had told me how to break an attacker's nose. The mugger went down like he had been shot and without hesitating I kicked him hard and we ran. When we got back to her flat, totally breathless, we burst through the door and literally fell across her couch.

Me: Are you OK?

W: Yes, I'm fine.

Me: Thank god.

There was a long silence between us as we caught our breaths. Then she looked at me with a strange look on her face.

W: Michael, what was that all about?

Me: What?

W: You totaled that guy. You hit him once and he fell right down. You looked like you had done that before, like you knew exactly what you were doing.

Me: Really? Did I?

W: Yes. You did. I've gotta say that I was impressed. Where did you learn to do that?

I knew her well enough to know that she wasn't going to let it go. She would keep picking at me until I confessed. So, I told her right then and there.

Me: I guess I never told you anything about myself before I met Nicole and I went and became a professor. I was in the Secret Service guarding President Kennedy.

W: Yea right. (she scoffed) Sure you were. And I'm Martha Gellhorn.

Me: Who is Martha Gellhorn?

W: Not important. Look, you really cleaned that guy. I'll bet you learned karate when you were a kid. Right?

Me: Yea, that's it. I earned a black belt when I was in high school.

Actually, I was delighted that I got out of that conversation so easily. I even felt good about it. I tried to tell the truth and she laughed me right into a lie. I just let it all go. I guess I didn't feel like Wendy needed to know all of the details of my past life. I was actually proud of some of it, but there were other things I wasn't so proud of. Nonetheless, after that night, I think Wendy had a new kind of respect for me.

A lot of the time on weekends, Wendy and my forays out into Paris included Grace. And this happened often enough that I was sure Grace knew that there was something more than cups of coffee in sidewalk cafes going on between us She was a now a sixteen-year-old in a boarding school among other sixteen-year-olds so I am pretty sure that sex was no longer a puzzling topic of conversation for her. Who knows if she suspected that Wendy and I were sleeping together. If she did, who knows if she approved or disapproved. She certainly didn't begrudge Wendy my company. In fact, they seemed to get along famously. I think Grace sort of thought of Wendy as this sort of woman of the world that someday she, Grace, wanted to become. They would sit in a café and Grace would quiz Wendy on her job, what stories she had covered that week, where Wendy had to go, what interesting people she had interviewed. One day, probably echoing some assignment she had been given in school, Grace asked Wendy:

G: Who is your heroine? Who would you like to be like?

W: (she thought for a long moment) Martha Gellhorn.

I of course, was eavesdropping on their conversation and that name rang a bell in my head. Wendy had mentioned that name before.

G: Who is she?

W: She was a very brave journalist. She lived right here in Paris when she wasn't off in a war zone right in the thick of it.

G: What war?

W: The Spanish Civil War was her first.

G: I don't know anything about that.

W: Look it up when you get back to school.

G: What other ones?

W: World War II. She was here in Paris when the Americans liberated us from the Nazis.

G: Aren't you American?

W: Well yes, but now I think of myself as a Parisian.

G: Martha Gellhorn, I'll have to look her up.

W: I don't think you'll find her under her own name in the encyclopedia.

G: How come?

W: Encyclopedias just aren't interested in women unless they're Queens or wives of famous men. Martha was married to Ernest

Hemingway for a while. Look under his name and maybe you'll find her there.

One day Wendy and Grace and I were having lunch in *des Deux Magots* when a tall thin man with a camera stopped and asked if he could take our picture. Well, not all of us. Just Wendy and Grace. Who knows why the two of them together caught his eye or what he had in mind for that photo. But after taking it he bowed politely, thanked us, and handed me his card. After he left, I handed the card to Wendy and asked:

Me: What was that all about?

Wendy looked at the card and her mouth dropped open in a GASP!

W: Omigod! Omigod! Henri Cartier-Bresson! Bresson!

Me: What is it? Who is he?

W: Only the most famous photographic artist in all of Europe. Oh, I wish I had known. I would love to have interviewed him.

G: But why did he take our picture.

W: I don't know. Probably because you are so pretty in your little schoolgirl kilt and cardigan. Oh Grace, maybe he'll put our picture into one of his published collections.

G: What's a published collection?

W: A book of famous photographer's best pictures.

G: Wow. That would be pretty cool.

It always surprised me how Wendy seemed to know everything about Paris: its history, its celebrities, its secrets, its customs, its complete landscape, its triumphs and tragedies. F. Scott Fitzgerald once wrote: "There are no second acts in American lives." He was dead wrong. As time went on, I fully realized how very lucky I had been to meet Wendy when I did. She hadn't made me forget Nicole, but she certainly had given me a new life at a time when I was pretty much lost.

Wendy and I communicated well both in bed and out. I don't want to leave the impression that sex was what it was all about between us. But something else equally important was going on between us during those idyllic Paris years. Yes, sure, we made love every chance we got, but the rest of the time we mostly talked about writing. Spurred by Wendy's enthusiasm for her profession and the drive to write at the most explicit and articulate and informative level in the most expressive words and sentences she could muster, and the encouragement she repeatedly gave me to write down my perceptions in my little notebook that I carried, I actually started thinking more seriously about perhaps someday writing something more than just random scribblings in my notebook.

I was pretty good with words. How could I not be? Thanks to my relentless memory, words really came easily to me. In fact, I think I've remembered every word I've ever read or even heard spoken. What Wendy taught me was how to think about putting words together, how to make them work as part of a larger structure. Of course, all of the conversations that we had about writing were from a journalist's viewpoint. Wendy was already a professional writer immersed in a journalist's stylistic agenda that was all about directness and clarity and information dispersal. But as we talked over a long period of time, together we hit upon something that subsumed or overarched those pragmatic journalist's goals. Wendy finally hit upon it:

W: In order to be a great journalist like Gellhorn or even Hemingway, good writers have to develop a style of their own. They have to find a way to 'own' their words.

As I look back on it now from this far horizon of 2019, it was in Paris in those café conversations with Wendy that I first got the idea that someday (this day I guess) I might actually write something bigger (this memoir I guess). A memoir, I guess that is what this is. Actually, I don't really look at it that way. It is, perhaps, a memoir about memory. Not just my memory and its impact on my life, but also of my memory of all the history around me whether in Cuba or in Dallas or in Berkeley or in Paris or wherever. A memory history. Maybe that is what this is. Funny, though I didn't really know it at the time. I guess I got the idea for this book some thirty years ago in those writerly conversations with Wendy in Paris. And now I'm finally getting around to writing it. I've been working on it for almost a year now and I have often asked myself why am I doing it?

There are a few people who know that I'm doing it, whom I've confided in, and I'm sure they suspect that I'm writing it all down because my memory is starting to fail me. No way. My memory is every bit as Eidetic and responsive as the day way back on that bike ride when Lenny named it for me. No, I think it is more complicated than that, more cultural, more a reaction to this 21st Century age of the computer, the web, social media, and the instant availability of information. Historical memory, per se, just isn't functional anymore. Facts, people, places, landscapes, don't exist in peoples' memories anymore. They live in that huge ocean of memory called GOOGLE just waiting to be instantaneously hooked, reeled in and repeated for the edification of all around as if we actually owned them. Computers, mobile phones, tiny hand-held cameras, have replaced so much of our brain function that we are actually turning into a civilization of robots. Believe me, on this topic I really do know of what I speak. But that is the material of the next chapter which I haven't written yet. Suffice to say though, it was in Paris with Wendy that the first seed for this book was planted.

But as they say, all good things must end. Wendy and I were together for three years. The sex was absolutely amazing, the conversation intelligent, politically enlightening, opening my eyes to all sorts of new possibilities (like writing for example), the companionship (perhaps the most valuable aspect of our whole relationship) satisfying, fulfilling, life-changing. I was no longer alone.

But Grace was about to turn 18 and ready to go to college. Our time in Paris had already decided her field of study, Fine Arts. She had already absorbed all of the Classical, Renaissance, Impressionist, Post-Impressionist Art that Paris had to offer. Yes, we had become Parisians, but we were still very much Americans. She needed to go back to the States to go to college. I knew it and she knew it too. I encouraged her and she applied to colleges back home. She wasn't a school girl anymore. She was smart, motivated, articulate, bilingual, and her drawing and painting had matured into a real talent. Paris had been an amazing teacher for her. I was so proud of her when she was accepted into the Art History program at Georgetown, my own far-off *alma mater*. My only real problem, regret, even guilt, was how to tell Wendy. Oh, I guess I could have stayed in Paris, sent Grace back to Georgetown, Washington, America, to study. But I just couldn't bear the idea of her being so far away, of us being separated from each other, of me being left alone again. I was forty-nine years old. I had stretched my money fairly thin living but not working in Paris for those last five years. I guess I rationalized that perhaps I needed to go back to America too. Washington wouldn't have been my first choice. It was a mine-field of bad memories for me. I worried that everywhere I stepped there the past would come back to haunt me. But that was Grace's destination and that meant that it had to be mine too.

As it turned out, telling Wendy of our plans, our leaving, wasn't the terrible ordeal that I had imagined. We were sitting on a bench in the Seurat *parc* on the *Seine,* our picnic *parc*, when I got up the nerve to tell her. I told her about Grace going to Georgetown. I told her I just had to go with her. I even asked her if she wanted to go with us, but I already knew the answer to that question before I even asked it.

W: Oh Michael, deep down I knew that this was coming.

Tears were in her eyes. I knew she was trying to hold them back. One escaped and ran in a pitiful thin line down her cheek.

W: I knew that you and Grace were going to have to leave sometime. (she gave me a weak smile and a little laugh) I don't know which of you I'll miss most. Just kidding, I'll miss you the most.

She leaned back against the bench and took two or three deep breaths like she was trying to gain control of herself, her thoughts. Finally, she turned back to me and put both of her hands on my knees, holding me still for what she had to say.

W: When we started, when you told me that you had lost your wife, I tried to warn myself off of you. 'You don't do reclamation projects,' I told myself. Oh Michael, I think I knew right away that I could never replace your Nicole. But then I met Grace and then you and I just got along so well, and you never once got in my way of doing my own thing, and we were so good in bed with each other. And it all just got away from me, from us. We were perfect for each other in this time and this place. Neither one of us was in for the long term and there was a kind of safety in that.

I remembered that I uttered a couple of farewell clichés. Actually, I don't remember what I said. (Imagine that!) And so we parted, friends I think, lovers always, confidantes (a good word for each of us).

Afterwards, Wendy did really well for herself. About two years later, winter 1991, Grace and I were having lunch in a Georgetown pub when suddenly Grace pointed to the TV set overhead and literally gasped, "Omigod Dad, there's Wendy!"

On the TV she was reporting from what looked like right in the middle of Desert Storm, the invasion of Iraq out of Kuwait. American tanks were rolling by behind her. Helicopters were blowing sand up around her. And there was Wendy, in a khaki jacket with the collar pulled up around her face. Clearly, she had given up print journalism and opted for the more glamorous land of television where she could be where the action was.

The first thing that came to my mind was that Wendy had actually found a way to live out her Martha Gellhorn fantasy. *Wow, good for her*, I thought. In fact, I think I even felt a little bit jealous. She looked like she was really having fun. It was almost like a replay of Gellhorn being there when the Americans marched into Paris in 1944.

It's funny. Once one starts thinking about doing this writing thing, your life starts to sort itself out into chapters. The Wendy chapter or Paris chapter or flight from Nicole's death chapter had come to an end. So Grace and I were off back to America to start another chapter. Grace's chapter was pretty well defined, four years of college in Washington, D.C. My chapter? I had not the slightest idea what it was going to be about.

CHAPTER 9: THREAT INTELLIGENCE

There was a world of difference between the sidewalk cafes of Paris and what Georgetown had to offer for the people-watching *flaneur*. Washington, D.C. in the nineties was as different from Paris as the politics of the two countries—people-focused Socialism vs. the belligerent buttoned-down Conservative Republicanism of the coming-to-an-end Reagan/Bush era. In Paris the sidewalk cafes offered a wealth of tables open to the air and street. Sitting in a Parisian sidewalk café, the whole world of the particular *arrondissement*, of the street, moving past you, around you, even joining you, was decidedly *al fresco*. The *desmoiselles* wouldn't even hesitate to walk right off the street and join you at your table. Not so in Georgetown. It was, still is, a neighborhood of coffee-shops, upscale restaurants, and *faux*-English and Irish pubs. If any of them had an outdoor, street-side patio at all, it was three or four tiny tables lined in a narrow row against the outside wall of the building cut off from the street by a chest-high black wrought-iron fence. Nonetheless, while drinking my coffee and eating my muffin, in good weather, I still liked to sit outside near the street and pretend I was still in Paris even though all I had left behind there I knew only existed in my overactive mind.

Of course, once again I was alone. Not a day went by that I didn't think of Wendy, where she was walking with her big leather bag, what stories she was covering, what movies she was seeing, who she was sleeping with. I had been in Georgetown almost seven months. Cherry blossoms, Spring, all that Washington clap-trap, was unrepentantly ushering in the decade of the nineties. Reagan was gone, Bush was mustering the nerve to go to war for oil in the Middle East. Russia was no longer a Cold War threat. America no longer held much interest for me. I was only here because Grace was here. She was a happy coed studying Art History and living in a dorm on campus. I was wedged into the cheapest efficiency apartment I could find in Georgetown trying to figure out how I was going to pay Grace's next semester's tuition.

I was sitting at one of those fenced-in patio tables looking at the job listings in *The Washington Post* one Spring afternoon when out of nowhere Lenny materialized back into my life. It was as if a spectre out of my distant past had come back to haunt me.

Me: What the hell?

L: Mikey, how ya doin'?

Me: What are you doing here? How did you find me?

L: C'mon Mikey, I've always known where you are. I've tracked you all the way from Indiana to France and back. I never connected with you in Paris, but I always knew where you and Grace were if I needed you.

Me: Needed me? What do you mean?

L: Oh, just in case I needed to get in touch with you.

Me: Why would you want to get in touch with me?

L: C'mon Mikey, you're my best friend. We've been like a team since high school. Sure, it has been a while, but now here we are. And I need to talk to you.

Me: About what?

L: Not here. Too public.

And he turned and pointed to the street beyond the black fence. No, we weren't in Paris anymore. I immediately had the sick feeling that I was being drawn back into Lennyworld. Lenny was pointing at a large black sedan parked illegally at the curb with dark tinted windows and the looming shadow of a driver behind the wheel. It had CIA written all over it. Just using his cajoling voice and preying on my curiosity, Lenny lured me into the back seat of that car. I instinctively knew that I shouldn't follow him, but nonetheless I did. Because he was right. He had always been my best friend. Years before I had read an existentialist novel that I had identified with titled *The Magus*. As I settled into the plush cushions in the back seat of that car (clearly a government car of some sinister identity) I realized that my Magus had once again walked into my life.

In the car, behind the dark glass, just me and Lenny and his large driver, I realized that nothing was changed. Lenny was still a spy, some sort of government agent, a clandestine fixer, a military troubleshooter, CIA, Secret Service, FBI, it didn't matter, Lenny was a spy agency unto itself, just as he had always been, going all the way back to the sixties, our twenties. As we settled in, out of the public view, he got serious.

L: Mike, you're not going to like what I've done, but I've been checking up on you. I even had my people follow you around a bit. I know that you are truly alone except for Grace. You don't have a job.

You tend to walk a lot, even in the snow. You are running out of money.

He paused then, his confessional set-up complete, and turned to his sales pitch. It was vintage Lenny. The same Lenny as ever who was an expert at dangling carrots in front of me and leading me like some horny virgin down the primrose path.

L: I want to offer you a job. I know you need one. You were just now checking out the job ads in the newspaper. I can offer you a job that will pay ten times, twenty times, hell, countless times what you will find there. It will be much more than you need to pay all four years of Grace's tuition. It will move you out of that one-room chicken coop you are living in and into a Georgetown penthouse if you want.

Me: Terrific. Who do I have to kill?

Lenny got a good laugh out of that.

L: Here's the deal. I'm starting a new company, a company that I'm going to build that does a job that nobody else can do or even knows how to do. I want you to help me run it. Knowing all about your special gifts, and, most important, knowing that I can trust you, I've decided that you are the perfect fit for this job.

Me: What's the job?

L: Well, that question raises a momentary problem.

To say that I was suspicious and growing more so every minute would be like saying the CIA stood for "Cookies In America,"

Me: What "momentary problem"? What does "momentary" mean?

L: Well, you see, I can't really tell you what the job is until you tell me that you will take it.

Me: Let me get this straight. You are offering me a high-paying job that I'm supposed to take totally on faith, knowing nothing about it except that you think I'm perfect for it.

L: Yes. Exactly. You've got to trust me on that.

As I paused to consider his blind offer, I realized that pretty much all of my life I had never been able to decide whether Lenny was my nemesis or my salvation. The best I could figure out was that he was probably both. I thought about the absurdity of this conversation for a long minute and then, against all of my better judgement, like some poor doomed bull facing a matador with a handful of swords, I charged right into Lenny's red cape.

Me: OK. I'm in. You're right, I need the money. So, what's the job?

Lenny let out a large exhale of relief, like air rushing out of a dangerously overinflated balloon. An excited grin burst across his face that for the briefest moment projected me all the way back to high school when Lenny and I would come up with some genius scheme to rule our adolescent world of sports or girls or cars or teachers or parents.

L: Excellent Mikey, absolutely excellent. C'mon, I'll show you our office building.

And that government issue spy-mobile sped off out of Georgetown toward Foggy Bottom. As we drove, Lenny started the unveiling, began with some background.

L: About two months ago I was running an operation out of Langley. Someone was jamming these new machines, computers, that we had installed about ten years before to replace typewriters. Hackers. That's the name the computer nerds used. They said that someone had hacked into our systems and were raising holy hell with both our data collections and computer filing. Well, at first, I didn't know what they were talking about and all the spooks wanted was for me to find these hackers and stop them. But then I sat down with one of the computer nerds and he talked me through what was actually going on. Then he did a really cool thing. On his computer screen he tracked all the incoming channels that these hackers could use and found a pattern of what he called "virus infected" emails coming from a location in Alexandria. Bottom line, we staked out the building and when we were sure that we knew who they were, me and my guys broke in and took them down.

Me: So now you've got your own platoon of thugs?

Lenny sort of chuckled at my sarcasm.

L: Sort of. But here's the kicker. We didn't arrest those guys. We turned them. Told them the only way they stay out of federal prison was they come and work for us, working against hackers rather than as hackers.

Lenny's narrative ended as the dark spy-mobile pulled up in front of a nondescript, three-story, windowless brick building in Alexandria. I followed Lenny inside to find an almost totally unfurnished, open-space first floor. A desk and three straight-backed chairs populated one corner. On the desk was a rather large and boxy entity that I mistakenly identified as a TV set. On another wall were three more desks similarly supporting three more of these *faux*-TV-sets. Of course, they were computers not TV sets, but at the time I really didn't know the difference.

L: Do you remember Director Turner, Stanfield Turner? You didn't know him. I think you were off at Berkeley at the time. Late seventies. I was working for the CIA, the FBI, whoever. Anyway, a really smart guy. I worked for him the whole time he directed the CIA. Took me under his wing pretty much. My mentor I guess you'd call him. He was a real intelligence theorist. Forward looking. He saw all the weaknesses in our intelligence community in the seventies and eighties, all the bumbling mistakes we made in Iran, the whole Middle East and in Central America. I learned a lot from him and this company is going to be built on his principles.

Me: Great, but just what is this company I'm going to be working for. Am I your only hire so far?

L: No, you're my fourth. I hired my computer nerd from Langley who helped me find my other two employees, the turncoat hackers I busted. They are going to be the nuts and bolts of our company and you are going to ride hard on them, the General Manager or whatever you want to call yourself, President, Chairman of the Board, King, I don't care. You'll be in charge of overseeing all of our operations.

Me: Lenny, c'mon, I don't know shit about computers.

L: Hell Mikey, no one does. And you will soon, certainly with your special powers, learn them a hell of a lot quicker than the average nerd.

As we stood in that large flat nearly empty space in that empty building all of this was coming at me really fast. I waved my hand at Lenny to signal a time out, crossed the room and collapsed pretty much overwhelmed into one of the chairs. Lenny took his seat across from me at his desk behind his computer. We just looked at each other for a long moment. I think he sensed that I was on the verge of walking away before we had even begun. So, he changed the whole tone of his sales pitch. He went all theoretical on me. As I think back on it now, I'll bet he took this tack in the voice of his spymaster hero, Stansfield Turner.

L: Look Mike, our government, all the branches of the military, the intelligence gathering community, have been getting more and more dependent on computers. It's the nineties Mike and pretty soon computers will be taking over everything. That's great. They are wonderful machines. But there are real problems too.

Me: What problems?

L: We have all sorts of vulnerabilities in our computer systems, especially in our government and military facilities. And who knows, down the road, when our public utilities, our banks, our airlines and railroads, when everything is computerized, some whacked-out computer guy, some hacker, or worse some country like Iran or China or certainly Russia, could attack our computer systems and raise holy hell with the country's whole infrastructure.

Me: Whoa. You're making it sound like Armageddon is coming at the hands of a bunch of TV sets.

L: Jesus Mike, they're not TV sets! The computer age is upon us and the government especially needs to face up to the threat. We really need to close up all the holes or some really bad shit could happen.

I must admit that, as he talked, at first I thought that he was suffering from an acute case of some sort of science-fiction paranoia like an alien invasion from outer space. But quickly I realized that he was deadly serious, that he saw us looking for a way to save the world.

Me: And we, our company, (even as I said it I realized that I had just expressed my commitment to Lenny's vision) is going to solve these hacker problems?

L: I hope so. America is just not prepared for what could happen. The threat is out there, believe me, and we've got to find ways to combat it.

Me: OK. Fine. So what is this company that you think I'm qualified to run.

L: I don't really know yet. But I do know that nothing like it exists so far. 'Threat Intelligence.' That is going to be our product and the government has already committed to being our biggest customer. That's where the start-up money is coming from Mike.

Me: So what is this "Threat Intelligence"? Is it just another form of CIA intelligence or FBI intelligence?

L: No. Completely different. Well maybe not completely. Intelligence for a whole new world order.

Me. What's this 'new world order.'

L: The Internet and now, just in the last three years, the World Wide Web.

Me: Time Out! Internet? World Wide Web?

L: I know. It's complicated. For the last ten years a bunch of computer professors, here in America, in England, in France, have been working to line up all the computers in the world. It all started with our government's project called the ARPANET and that developed into the Internet and then finally three years ago this English guy turned it all into a workable global system he called the World Wide Web.

Lenny saw the wide-eyed look of curiosity, wonder, confusion, intellectual engagement, on my face and I think that is the moment that he knew he had me.

L: Yeah, pretty cool huh.

Me: Yes, I guess so. So where do we come in? This new company we're starting up.

L: We're going to be the first of its kind, a 'Threat Intelligence' company. In the next couple of years everything, our government, our military, every new business in America, is going to become dependent on computers.

Me: What's wrong with that? It sounds like the impact that the invention of the telephone or the automobile had.

L: Nothing. Computers are… like magical. But just like the telephone bred all kinds of fast-talking scammers and automobiles bred generations of car thieves, the World Wide Web is already turning out a new breed of criminals. We call them Cybercriminals.

Me: And we're going after these computer bad guys who exist out there somewhere in the wires of these machines?

L: Exactly.

Me: So our company… does it have a name?

L: Not yet.

Me: (sarcastically) Terrific.

L: I know. I haven't gotten that far yet. You can name us. That's the first thing you can do on the job. But don't go hanging up any signs on the building. We are going to be strictly under the radar.

Me: (again sarcastically) Terrific.

Strangely enough, Lenny and I had fallen right back into the kind of dialog, the challenging back and forth, that we had always had from high school all the way up through college and our old Washington days. It was as if the twenty-year hiatus in our friendship, our spymaster relationship, our Magus journey, whatever, had never happened and we were back to sparring verbally and intellectually with each other as we always had.

Me: So our company (I began again) is going to be some sort of computer-world, sci-fi, detective agency?

L: I guess you could say that.

Me: And you would say…?

L: It's more complicated than that, more sinister, spookier. These two guys that I busted in Alexandria are just one example of these cybercriminals. They actually turned out to be pretty harmless, just two nerds screwing around with their computers.

Me: And now they work for you.

L: Yeah, they were easy. They hacked into the Pentagon data base. We scared the shit out of them. I even told them we could hang them for treason. They folded like underwear out of the dryer.

Me: So what's the big threat if now you know how to find hackers like them.

L: The problem is that we're the only ones who know how to do it, and we're only about a couple of months into finding that out and we know there have got to be a lot more dangerous hackers than these guys out there.

Me: How dangerous?

L: My two guys told us that there's a whole other network out there of only these cybercriminal bad guys. They operate on something called 'the dark web'. That's something like a cyber underworld, the refuge and attack headquarters of the cybercriminal elite. Nobody knows very much about it.

Me: Sounds like how the Mafia used to be

L: Yes. That's where we're going, to penetrate this so-called 'dark web' like the old spies did with Russia during the cold war. Hell, like you did in Cuba and Berkeley.

We'd only been talking for about thirty minutes and I was on information overload. I got up out of my chair and walked all the way across that big empty room just to get away from Lenny and all of his cyber mumbo-jumbo. Nice try. He just got up and followed me. Pretty soon we were pacing back and forth beside each other. I broke the awkward silence.

Me: OK, I said I was in. I'll work on this with you even though I don't understand it yet. Just tell me what you think we are going to do in the very simplest terms you can come up with.

L: (he stopped pacing and turned to me while, for a long moment, he worked at carefully choosing his words) Our company is going to specialize in providing cyber security and hacker investigation to whatever government and military entities that are threatened.

Me: OK. Fine. But just one more thing. Why me?

L: That's easy. When we came up with this idea, I thought of you right away.

Me: Whose 'we'?

L: Not important. Mike, you have these peculiar gifts. You can do stuff that nobody else can do, like Sherlock Holmes or Chuck Yeager or Elvis or Hank Aaron. C'mon, I know what you can do. You speed read a book and can remember every word.

Me: But like I said, I don't know anything about computers.

L: But the one thing I know is that you are one really fast learner. You can master these computer machines in no time. Besides that freaky memory power you've got, you're also a forensics expert. You are perfect for this job. Hey, we could name our company "Cyberforensics." That's pretty catchy, huh?

Me: (dripping sarcasm) Yeah, really catchy.

L: I want you to get hands-on and learn everything you can about what a computer can do. Our computers are the best, the most advanced ones out there. I know it won't take you long. Then I want you to find out everything you can about this 'dark web', about hacking, about cybercrime. Only then can our company go to work. My nerds will help you get up to speed. Mike, don't you see? You're perfect for this job.

Me: OK. OK. I'm taking the job. Actually, the more you talk about it the more interesting it seems.

L: I know. It is. We'll be cutting edge. But there is more to it than that.

Maybe it was the slightly lowered tone of his voice, the kind of tone people instinctively fall into when they decide to impart a secret, that immediately made me suspicious. *Oh, oh, here it comes*, I thought, *there's always a catch. Nothing is ever what it initially seems where Lenny is concerned.*

L: Here's the deal, Mike, I don't want to keep a lot of records of our company's dealings. Who our customers are. What our projects are. Who and how much we are spending and getting paid. Basically, how we operate. We will be security consultants to a number of government agencies, some clandestine, some every bit as dark as this so-called 'dark web.' We will specialize in political and military espionage. That's where you come in. You'll be my traffic manager. You'll keep all of our doings in that amazing Eidetic Memory of yours. I don't want any paper trails. No files. Zero accountability.

As he talked, I realized that I had stepped into a field of quicksand and was being relentlessly pulled down into Lenny's spook world and he would be my only lifeline, the only one who could pull me out.

Me: Jesus Lenny!

L: I know. But you can do it. Don't you see Mikey? If I have you, I never have to write anything down. That is a tremendous advantage in the business you and I are going to be in. Nothing written down equals no evidence, no paper trail, no complications, no targets for other companies to pursue, no oversight. We can deal with whatever comes our way any way we want.

As Lenny spoke, his voice dropped almost to a whisper as if he was afraid that someone was listening in.

Me: So, I'm to be some sort of walking file cabinet for you and our company?

L: Oh no, much more than that. Not only will you gather all this information but you'll be the policy-maker who decides how we use it. For each threat we encounter you will be the one who focuses us, who can sort all the intelligence we gather, who can file it in that magical memory of yours and apply it to how we make our operations work. We will very likely have multiple operations, cases, going on all the time. That's why I called you a 'traffic' manager. We're not just going to have computer nerds sitting in front of screens here in this building. We're going to have a group of special agents at our disposal to carry out operations against any threats that we uncover. You'll also be the commander of that cadre of operations. You'll dictate the scenarios that we will use to counter the hackers that we find.

Me: So, we won't just be identifying the threats to our government entity customers, we'll be moving against those threats for them.

L: Yes, so there will be no evidence to link them to our operations as well.

Me: So, nothing we do can link us to them or them to us. Like nothing that we do ever exists except inside my head. Is that it?

L: Yes, don't you see Mikey, you are the only one I could ever trust with this job. Hell, you're the only one I could ever trust to tell you what I've told you so far. I said, 'darker than the dark web,' 'under the radar.' We'll be like cyberspacemen going into a dangerous black hole.

As I look back on it now, I should have run as fast as I can back to academia or to Paris or to anywhere as far from this cyberspook scenario that Lenny had laid out for me.

Yes, I definitely needed the money. But my motives for staying were much more blameworthy than just that. This company, this job, this dawn of the computer age, all captured some strange sense of ex-

citement for me. I had always been a fan of *Star Trek* where every week
for an hour the crew of the *Enterprise* explored new frontiers. I fanta-
sized I was going to be Mr. Spock to Lenny's Commander Kirk. No,
better, it was like Lenny and I were setting out to confront what my
idol, President Kennedy, had called 'the New Frontier.' We weren't going to the moon, but we were definitely aiming for another version of
deep space. In other words, every bit as much as the money, the idea
attracted me to the futuristic vision of it.

And then, there was one other little thing. For just a brief minute, a
flash in my consciousness, my old theory of secular transubstantiation
raised its hoary head. I was ripe for a change. I needed a completely
new life because the one I was living since we left Paris was totally
empty. Of course, I sensed that I would probably live to regret this
particular transubstantiation as I did everything that happened when
I threw in with Lenny, but I rationalized that so far I had survived his
Magus ministrations. And besides, the money was really good.

And so we began. My first three months as General Manager of
our 'Threat Intelligence' company was spent in learning to operate the
computers, reading every article I could find on the history of cyber development, peering over the shoulders of our in-house hackers, learning the ins and outs of computer hacking. The first day at my request
Lenny left me alone in the building. I just wanted to get the lay of the
land. The ground floor had a door to the outside and that was it. It was
basically a windowless cave for computer troglodytes to work without
the chance of distraction from the outside world. I climbed to the second floor and it had four small windows in its square of walls—East,
West, North, South. I decided that this second floor would be my office, my General Manager's work space, above and away from the drone
hackers down below. I picked the North window looking out across the
blue waters of the Potomac to Capital Hill. Within a day Lenny had a
desk, a computer, some office chairs, a conference table and some floor
lamps in support of inadequate ceiling lighting of this loft. The only
thing missing were file cabinets. But it was while picking my workspace
that I came up with another idea that both Lenny and I agreed was
necessary. We installed hidden cameras, the kind they had in Las Vegas
over the gaming tables. We put them in the ceiling over the first floor
so that I could (via two TV screens sitting on my large desk next to my
computer all behind a wall that made my office private) keep an eye on
our hackers down below. Our reasoning was that if we could turn these

cybercrooks to work for us, why couldn't someone else turn then back to work for them. These cameras had a really sensitive zoom capacity that allowed me to actually look over our hackers' shoulders and read their screens. When Lenny told me that our company would be supplied with the very latest technology, the fanciest gadgets, he was right on. Once I got the building squared away to my satisfaction, I settled in to do the grunt work of learning everything I could about computer hacking.

For the next three months I read (and of course memorized) every computer manual I could get my hands on. I sat our three hackers down around my conference table and made them spill their guts about their hacking careers, their techniques, their pathways into this mysterious 'dark web'. These guys were all in their early twenties and had gotten hooked on computers only a few years before when the Internet and the World Wide Web were just coming into existence. I spent hours and days sitting on their shoulders watching them manipulate the material on their screens. The first time I sat down with them at their computers, before I had even sat down at my own, I noticed that a short wire ran out of the computer to a small oval-shaped object on their desks.

Me: What's that thing that looks like a mouse with a tail coming out of the computer.

The three of them looked tight-lipped at me, then at each other, then almost in unison broke out laughing.

Them: It's actually called a mouse. Yes it is.

Me: Oh yeah, so that's it. I actually read about that.

That little exchange, however, proved pretty useful. First of all, it broke the ice between the four of us, me as their boss them as my happy henchmen. But more importantly, it signaled to them the very high level of ignorance that their boss possessed and I think gave them motivation to bring me up to cyberspeed as quickly as possible so we could get on with the actual business of our start-up company.

Mentoring me, they started with the very basics of computing, gave me a whole history of the computer revolution, its functions and then, most important of all, its burgeoning capabilities. We literally spent hours sitting around that conference table talking about computers and hacking. They were really proud of some of their hacking exploits which were mostly pranks that got out of hand, things that they did just for the fun of doing them, for the satisfaction they got out of flexing their cybermuscles. What I realized as the four of us sat around talking was a sense of what this company that Lenny had envisioned could do. We were going to be a sort of cyber detective agency and my nerds were like those old keyhole-peeping, compromising-photo-taking, divorce-work detectives who got their rocks off spying on cheating spouses for the voyeuristic fun of it.

Out of those talks all sorts of useful things emerged, and the nature and goals and policies and procedures of our fledging company began to take shape. One of the first things I did for my own education was learn their language, the language of computer hacking. I compiled a whole dictionary of hackers' terms. It became our 'Threat Intelligence' lexicon: Malware, Ransomware, Worms, Viruses, Cyberattacks, Process Doppelganging, Cross Site Scripting, Hactivision, Browsers, Routers, Backdoors, Firewalls, Crypto-jacking, Website Rerouting, Industroyers. Actually, it was from this list and the definitions we worked out in our conferencing that I found the name for our company. One day it just jumped out at me. MALWARE. INC. It had a ring to it that I really liked. It reminded me of "Murder Inc." from the old gangster movies that had been some of my favorites. Of course, adhering to Lenny's desire to stay 'under the radar,' it was a company name that would never go on the facade of our building or on business cards, but it was a name that both Lenny and I liked and the way we would refer to our business between ourselves and our more clandestine customers from then on. For our business cards Lenny and I came up with a meaningless, unintelligible name for our company. We called it "THRINTEL." We figured that was less attention-grabbing than MALWARE, INC.

After about three months of cramming and actually working hands-on with my nerds, Lenny and I sat down to put our heads together and actually define the direction that we wanted our company to take. I hadn't even seen much of Lenny those first few months when I was getting myself up to speed. But finally, I went to him and told him that we had to sit down and actually figure out what we were doing. He was more than ready. In fact, I got the sense that he had just been waiting on me. I also got the sense that he had been where I had gotten to before he ever went looking for me. And so the brainstorming sessions began.

L: Mikey, the first thing we have to do is figure out just what our version of 'Threat Intelligence' is going to be.

After about three months of self-educating myself I thought I had a pretty good handle on what we needed to do.

Me: OK. As I see it, in the office on the machines we'll be tracking down the threats. Then, in the field, either on the computers or actually going after the hackers, we'll be neutralizing the threats.

L: Yes, that's a general view of it. But it's a lot more complicated than that. Sure, we will specialize in TI. You'll be the point man for harvesting 'dark web' information right off the computers here in the office. But we won't just be a bunch of cyber Peeping Toms. Your memory will photograph everything as you monitor the 'dark web' and then you'll put it all together and come up with an action plan. You'll make all the right connections just like you did way back with the Cuban Missile Crisis.

Me: But what do you mean by 'action plan'?

L: Sure, we'll supply TI feeds to our customers, but we'll also provide them with what I call 'anticipatory action'.

Me": Dammit Lenny, speak English.

L: Right, in other words, we'll find the hackers and stop them before they can strike. We'll track them on the 'dark web' and then go after them with either our own cyber weapons, our anti-hackers, or our less sophisticated field operation agents. Our overriding goal will be to neutralize, in some instances really take out, the enemy hackers that are screwing with our customers.

Me: And our customers are?

Lenny: Right now they are different government entities: NSA, CIA, FBI, the military branches. They are our only customers now. Down the road I think we'll have a lot more: corporations, financial institutions, all sorts of businesses, anything that depends on a computer to operate. Mike, we really are a cyber detective agency. We'll collect evidence and use it to destroy the bad guys.

As he talked, direct, unblinking, I found his vision totally enervating. We were entering a whole new realm, a new age. As I look back on it now, as I look all around me from my desk in 2019 with my laptop in front of me, my cell phone sitting right beside it, my I-pad on the other side, music streaming into my pure sound headphones, my flat-screen HD Smart TV hanging on the wall, I still feel that cyberexplorer Star Trekish rush that I felt way back then listening to Lenny describe his vision for our company.

Me: OK, but I still don't fully understand what my job is going to be. How do I fit into all this.

L: I want you to be my 'risk management leader,' my final solution analyst.

Me: You used the term 'traffic manager' earlier.

L: I know. But that was too simplistic. You are going to be more than that.

Me: How so?

L: Your Eidetic Memory will be invaluable in collecting, analyzing, and making the kinds of cyber connections that we need to make for keeping our clients safe. Your ultimate purpose will be to orchestrate that appropriate action based on your analysis that will solve our client's computer security problems,

Me: You keep talking about action. What kind of action? Is this going to be physical action, the dangerous kind of detective work? Or just pressing keys on our computers? You said you had some operatives, agents. What is their role here? How am I going to be involved with them?

For a couple of weeks Lenny and I had these sorts of brainstorming sessions where I bombarded him with questions like this. I have to give him credit. He answered all my questions unwaveringly, straightforwardly, not pulling any punches.

L: Mike, we'll customize our services directly to the needs of our clients. In other words, we'll analyze our clients TI needs and then choose the TI tools at our disposal to protect our client's threat vulnerability. There are a whole range of TI use cases that we will be engaged with—'dark web' monitoring, phishing investigations, information hacking, security telemetry augmentation, cyberattack group tracking, tactical intervention and neutralization.

Me: Lenny, again in English. What do you mean by 'tactical?'

L: I can't sneak much by you can I? OK. There will be times when neutralizing an attack group will have to be handled hands-on.

Me: By hands-on do you mean hands with guns in them?

L: Possibly, but I doubt it will ever have to come to that. But, right now, any tactical use of outside agents will be much more subtle. We will try to infiltrate hacker groups as a means of undermining them and turning receptive hackers to go to work for us. Certainly, we are interested in site takedowns, but we'd rather turn some of these sites to our own uses.

That particular answer to one of my many questions didn't really put my mind at ease. But this wasn't my first rodeo with clandestine, hush-hush government work so I certainly wasn't surprised.

Me: Takedowns?

L: Sorry. Poor choice of words.

Much more interesting, as our orientation talks progressed, was the theory behind our product that Lenny had obviously very carefully worked out. As we talked, I came to renewed appreciation of how smart Lenny really was and how immersed in the complexities of this whole new approach to detective work and security that he was.

L: Look Mike, yes, a lot of this is definitely rocket science and you need to be conversant with that science, but your job is putting that science properly to work.

Me: That's my 'traffic' function?

L: Yes, right. TI is evidence-based knowledge. It includes CONTEXT (the client's needs), MECHANICS (our cyber platforms), ACTION strategies (how we neutralize threats). All of our energy is aimed at protecting our clients from an existing or emerging hazard to their computer systems. Again, that's where you come in. 'Intelligence' isn't just a series of data points. It is a process. Yes, we will collect a lot of data, but your job will be to take that data, analyze it, and make the connections that will enable us to productize this process and deliver it to the clients. Again, your memory will drive this whole process.

Me: Jesus Lenny, 'productize' is not a word.

He had to laugh at that.

Me: So, our services provide info about the identities, motivations, locations, targets and methods of the attackers?

L: Yes. This info comes from network traffic, 'dark web' monitoring, and malware detection, as well as human sources such as your analysis. Oh yeah, and one other thing. Your facility with languages will also be important because we suspect that potential attacks will probably emanate from hostile foreign sources like Russia, China, Korea. There may well be times when we will need to monitor chatter in other languages. Or even go overseas.

Me: Who is paying for all of this?

L: The usual suspects. NSA, CIA, FBI, blah, blah, blah. I mentioned them before. They are our only customers right now. We'll be positioned for a ton more commercial money later as I see it.

Me: What do you mean 'commercial'?

L: Mike, like I said before, computers are going to take over the world. Not just these government entities. Banks, corporations, airlines, healthcare, oil, gas, energy, all the utilities, manufacturing, retail stores, any entity dependent on computer information.

Me: Really?

I was pretty stunned by this vision of the future that Lenny had just hit me with. My 'Really?' was a sincere expression of my realization of the seismic change that Lenny saw coming and my realization that he might just really be right.

L: In a very short time, probably in the next few years, certainly by the end of the nineties, almost every large enterprise in America will be hacked by these 'dark web' cyberbandits. More and more these large enterprises are going to need TI services to protect their systems and their client information. Right now we are going to start developing the TI platforms that will build the programs to stop those threats. We'll be the only ones in this field. The government is paying for all of our R and D, research and development. Down the road we stand to make a fortune. It's a really sweet deal.

Oh Lenny, who would ever have guessed that you were such a visionary, and such a greedy capitalist, and such a ruthless violent spy-master, and such a persuasive salesman, and such a thoroughly corrupt and cynical public servant, and such a pseudo-patriotic shadow enigma. I had to hand it to him. Since high school and college and our Washington back in the sixties, he had evolved into a real piece of work. And, yet again, I had listened to this Prince of Darkness and let him seduce me into his own personal version of the 'dark web' world.

After two weeks of these sorts of brainstorming sessions with Lenny I just had to get away, take a break from his intensity, his drive to get our company underway. Grace had a five-day Fall break from Georgetown. I rented a car and collected her on campus and we drove up to the Jersey Shore for a long weekend of sun, sand, toffee and cotton candy. Grace was thriving in her Art History Studies. No mystery there. She was indeed a very serious young woman. But after our *flaneuring* idyll on the boardwalk, driving back, she blindsided me with yet something else for me to try to process, every bit as stressing as my last few months of cyber assimilation. She had acquired a boyfriend. She gleefully told me all about him as we drove back to D.C. I gnashed my teeth all the way, managing (but barely) not to explode with suspicion, dire warnings, unspeakable sexual fears. Ultimately, I just ended up feeling sorry for myself. Lenny had me tightly in his grasp and Grace was growing up and growing away from me who had been the only man in her life for so long. To put it in the most vulgar of terms (but perhaps the truest) it felt like both of us were in the process of losing our virginity.

When I got back to Washington and re-immersed myself in my work and started acquainting myself with our clients, another idea started nagging at my consciousness, my somewhat bruised identity. It was that old transubstantiation issue, my concept of secular transubstantiation, that sense of persistent existential change that I had come to accept as the arc of my life. All of this concentration upon this on-rushing computer age, on this total change in our way of life, exhumed that idea, theory, belief, whatever, that I hadn't really thought about during all of those lost years in Paris with Grace and Wendy when I was certifiably happy. The more I got into our computers, the more I began to understand what they could do, the more I accepted Lenny's confidence that these glorified TV-sets were going to completely change the world, the more drastic change seemed to be bearing down upon me. After weeks of listening to Lenny spin out the vast array of possibilities for our company in this impending new age, I realized that it wasn't just my life that seemed to be an ongoing exercise in transubstantiation, but the whole world was caught in this process of cyclical change, that the body and blood of the whole world was being changed by this new and powerful force, this deity of computerized intelligence. For me, transubstantiation became a world metaphor for a universal existential change. Oh yes, Jesus at the Last Supper certainly was a poet, a maker of powerful, long-lasting metaphors. His 'body and blood' metaphor was his most enduring, more powerful than his parables, his miracles, his preaching. It was a metaphor that embodied the inevitable experience of change that inhabited every second of human existence. Jesus' metaphor of transubstantiation wasn't just a Last Supper poem that Jesus the poet composed on the spot. It was an idea about the inevitable certainty of change that has endured for two thousand years. As I learned more and more about computer memories, and as my own memory went back along the passageways of my own life, my secular existential version of Jesus' poem came to define all of the changing stages of my life just at this point when I was preparing to enter yet another new stage. But this time it wasn't just me. If Lenny was to be believed, pretty soon the whole world would be transubstantiated.

That was my state of mind as Lenny and I got down to business. Everyone remembers their first time, the first time they had sex with someone other than themself. My first time was with Melinda Bowser-man during County Fair week right before our junior year in high school in mom and dad's barn. We had been prowling around and petting each other up for all of two weeks when we (actually she) decided it was time to do it. To say that Melinda was one of the easier girls in our high school would be vastly understating the fact. We ducked out of the Fair the afternoon of the rodeo. We knew that our parents would certainly be staying for that, the bronc riding, the bull wrestling, the calf roping and all that country kind of fun, well into the evening. We hightailed it back to our barn. We weren't nearly brave enough to go in and do it in the house. We pawed each other out of our clothes and went at it with gusto. Oh yeah, I can describe that first time in two words: clumsy and prickly. "Clumsy" because I am pretty sure the first time is like that for everyone, and "prickly" because we made the uninformed decision to do it in the loft amidst the bales of straw. Melinda was a tall and gangly farm girl, strong and pretty, and pretty assertive. I started out on top but she quickly demanded that we change positions so she could mount up and ride me like those cowgirls that mom and dad were watching back at the rodeo. Pretty quickly I realized why she insisted on being on top. Every time she bucked down on me I was impaled in the back and the butt by dozens of tiny spears of straw. Well, my point is that if you are running a new world detective agency like I was then your first case is like that, totally memorable but hopefully neither as clumsy nor prickly. Of course, since I remember everything, that first shouldn't have been any more memorable than all the rest, but it was because, like that first sex in the barn with Melinda, I had no idea what I was doing.

The first case that came across my desk was from the Air Force. They had installed computers to clarify their radar tracking reception and suddenly all of their screens had gone offline as if someone had just cut the main electrical cord (which of course did not exist) to all of their control towers. I was sitting at a computer console with Tommy when Lenny burst in on us with this urgent S.O.S. from the Air Force.

[Digression:] As I am writing this I just realized that I haven't yet introduced my three hacker-nerd partners in crime. Tommy was the original recruit that Lenny had lured away from the Pentagon. He was absolutely your protype computer nerd who had taught himself to process, program, code and below-the-surface compute (a.k.a. 'hack') before he was even out of high school. The military snatched him out of M.I.T. in the middle of his sophomore year. It was Tommy who the first thing he did upon coming aboard with Lenny had downloaded TOR to our office computers. TOR stood for "The Onion Router" and was developed by the U.S. Navy in 1990 as a way for intelligence agents overseas to communicate with their handlers back here in the U.S. It was a software that gave us access into the 'dark web' as regular users. And soon after that Tommy had also acquired 'Spy tech' software for us. All of this was in place before Lenny had even brought me on-board. Ernest and Ralph were older and much shadier than Tommy. Both of them had for a time attended R.P.I. (Rensaeleer Polytechnic Institute) in upstate New York, drinking heavily, smoking pot constantly, and pretending to be Computer Science majors in one of the first programs of that sort in America. Despite their stoner lifestyles and in the interstices of being drunk or toasted, they actually acquired enough computer facility to penetrate the 'dark web' and thrive therein. Tommy had been instrumental in initially busting them, and Lenny had been the mechanism for turning them. And thus we all found ourselves working together at Malware. Inc. (or our cover name THRIN-TEL). [End digression]

But now back to Lenny bursting in on us with our first case. Tommy immediately called the contact number that the Air Force had given Lenny and got the access codes and the universal passwords for the network that had been blown out. Once we got that, my three hackers hit the accelerators on their computers and started driving the cyber highways like it was a drag race and fire was coming out of their exhaust. It took them almost two days but Ernest finally came to me with a lead that held some promise.

Ernest: Boss, I came across some chatter that sounds like it might be our guys. Here, I wrote it down.

He handed me a coffee-stained piece of paper with two lines of text scrawled across it: "Yes! Their screens have gone black and they've got no clue where their planes are." God bless Ernest, pothead alky that he was, for finding the needle in our first hay stack.

Me: Do you know where it came from? Who these guys are?

E: Tommy's our tracker. He's working on it now. I'm going out for a smoke.

I watched him as he left, extracting his cigarette pack out of the rolled-up sleeve of his heavy metal Megadeath tee shirt, and marveled at the combination of cyber expertise and nonchalant slovenliness of my company's help.

An hour later Tommy came in, grinningly proud of himself, and much more serious and formal and focused than Ernest had been (or ever would be). Ralph was right behind him.

Tommy: We got them, Mr. Edwards, whoever they are.

Ralph: Yep, found 'em. Bunch of dumb asses.

Tommy proceeded to lay out a much more detailed analysis of the situation than Ernest had (or ever would have) ventured.

T: They are calling themselves SPECTRE 94 like they're out of some James Bond movie. We tracked their signals to Philadelphia. Ralph is right. They can't be too smart because they were so easy to find. We are pretty sure that they have planted a simple virus in the Air Force network. I'd call it a 'switch virus' because all it really can do is turn things on and off. It'll take a little work but I think I can find it and disable it. That should get the network back online.

I sent them off to work on that and called Lenny with the news. He was excited, but after thinking on it for a minute he decided that we were only halfway home on this case.

L: Now we have to find them and put them out of business before they do any more damage.

Overlaying one computer-generated map of Philadelphia over another and another and another into the dozens, my nerds narrowed down the location of the home base of SPECTRE 94 to a gentrified neighborhood of coffee-shops, bookstores, ethnic restaurants and designer label clothing stores. We were pretty certain that we were dealing with some upscale Yuppie hackers. One thing I learned while working with my three hacker-nerds on that first case is that if you are going to build a viable start-up company the first thing you should do is hire people smarter than you are or at least people who have the experience that you don't. On that first case I spent hours looking over the shoulders of my people trying to absorb all of the moves that they were making on their computers. I did have my Eidetic advantage to help me along of course. By the time we put that first case to bed, I had learned more about how to work both the 'dark web' and the available map coordinate systems than I had learned in the last few months of reading all the manuals and clicking on my mouse.

But once again I get ahead of myself. Right in the middle of our labors at tracking down the SPECTRE 94 hackers, Lenny burst in upon us all hot to join in the fun. We had just pinpointed the neighborhood that the SPECTRE 94 probes were coming from when he arrived. Tommy took the point and said that he could shut down their computers right from our office by inserting a 'switch virus' in the electrical company's main feed into the four square block area from which the SPECTRE 94 chatter was emanating.

L: No. Don't do it. I don't want to tip them off yet that we are on to them. You've got the Air Force network back online already haven't you.

T: Yes, they're back up.

L: Good, the four of you drive to Philly and comb that neighborhood until you find them. Say you are census takers or vacuum cleaner salesmen or fucking Jehovah's Witnesses, but go door-to-door until you find them. Mikey, once we know who they are, I want you to do a full background check on them. I need to know as much about them as you can find ASAP. No reports or anything. Just read anything you can find on them and tell it to me over the phone. Before we shut them down, I want to know if I can turn them.

So off to Philadelphia in our government issue sedan we went to start our search. By the time we were no more than a half hour into our drive we all wished that Ernest had taken a bath that week.

In Philadelphia we did our door-to-door diligence. Now that was the kind of old-fashioned detective work that you read about in mystery novels. On the second day of knocking on doors and ringing door bells we hit pay dirt. In the car driving up, Ernest and Ralph had decided to pose as gas company repairmen looking for a dangerous gas leak in the neighborhood's apartment buildings. "It will just take a second, we just have to check your stove and heater hook-ups" they assured whoever answered the door. Finally, in a third-floor apartment in an upscale building with an elevator, a young woman, blonde, dressed in jeans and a PENN tee shirt, answered the door and let them in. As she escorted them through the apartment to the kitchen, a voice from behind a half-open door asked, "who's that hon?" She answered, "Gas company inspectors" and jumped to close the door, but not fast enough to keep Ernest and Ralph from seeing a table with two computer consoles much like the ones in our office with a man sitting at them typing and clicking away. After they left that apartment, they got the tenants' names from the super and we were in business.

Turns out they were Nancy and Carl, recent graduates of the University of Pennsylvania fledgling computer science program, unmarried, both from wealthy Main Line families, she working in a bank designing a computer system for her employer, he working in his father's Big 5 accounting firm doing the same thing for them, both making more than enough money to afford the best electronics available in those days. When I gave my report on them, Lenny's eyes must have lit up like the headlights on a fourteen-wheeler. I couldn't see his eyes over the phone, but I could hear the excitement in his voice. He told me to send the others back to D.C., but for me to watch the building until he got there. Good old detective novel surveillance. I loved it. I sat in a coffee shop across from their building the better part of that day watching and waiting, but Nancy and Carl never came out. Finally, Lenny showed up in his trademark large black, tinted-window sedan accompanied by two black-leather-jacketed men in sunglasses who had CIA written all over them.

L: Good work Mikey. We'll take it from here. Catch the train back to D.C.

And so, we brought our first "Threat Intelligence' case to a successful conclusion. The following Monday Lenny arrived at the Malware, Inc. office with my two new employees, Carl and Nancy a.k.a. SPECTRE 94, which was no longer in business in Philadelphia, but was very much in business working out of our office in D.C. We had our first mole on the 'dark web'. By threatening them with treason, federal prison, a firing squad, telling their parents, who knows what, Lenny had turned them to our purposes, turned them against their parents, convinced them to quit their jobs, pack up, and move into us. They knew that we owned them, and weren't all that happy to be working with low-lifes like Ernest and Ralph, but as time went on they learned to live with us. After all, their SPECTRE 94 misadventuring had really been just fun and games for these rich Yuppies and they could play out of our office just the same as they could in Philadelphia. And get paid handsomely for it.

As I look back on it now it strikes me that this time, the fledgling years of our company, was one of the wackiest and exciting times of my life. It was the Wild West. Lenny and my nerds were riding the 'dark web,' rounding up and hog-tying any hackers that might be messing with our immediate clients. Lenny would bring us problems and we would try to solve them. I remember the FBI was probably our most insistent customer in those earliest years of our company. They were in transition from J. Edgar Hoover's mountain of paper files to the computer filing of that old data and their new data. 'Dark web' forces were consistently hacking and rehacking into their network and trolling their data bases for whatever they could get. We kept building firewalls against these hackers, but they kept backdooring our walls and renewing their infiltrations. Finally, Lenny had had enough.

L: Who are they? Find them and give them to me.

It turned out they were a group of hackers calling themselves LAZARUS in celebration of their particular breed of malware that they had imbedded in the FBI's network that was actually capable of regenerating itself when it was blocked. This posed a problem that we hadn't dealt with before and was one we couldn't really solve with our usual anti-malware strategies. What we could do, however, was track the malware to its source which turned out to be a warehouse in New York City, more particularly in the south Bronx.

What we didn't know was who or how many these LAZARUS hackers were, so Lenny sent me to the Bronx to surveil them, get their numbers, and find out just who they were. I spent three days watching the building and noticed that two types of people seemed to be coming and going. There were 4 people, all male, who looked like very ordinary hacker types—all in glasses, jeans, tee or polo shirts, working regular eight-hour shifts. Then there were three sets of two men each on 24-hour duty in the building, one of whom was always on the door and visible to me when it opened and closed. I decided that I needed to get a closer look so I hit a used clothes store, got myself up like a wino, complete with a bottle of Ripple in a brown paper bag, and lurched drunkenly up the side of the building, sat down about ten feet from the door, and started drinking. I wasn't there two minutes when one of the door guys, large, muscle-bound, in a black leather jacket, burst out of the door and kicked me right in the leg. "Move it asshole!" he ordered and I ran for my life, leaving him laughing in my wake. From the brief encounter, I surmised (quite accurately I might add) that the LAZARUS hackers were in the employ of a criminal organization that had hired these thugs to guard them. When I reported my observations back to Lenny, he didn't seem too surprised.

L: Who else would go to great lengths to hack into the FBI? Gotta be organized crime. A crime family. Maybe Mafia or Russians, maybe even a drug gang.

Two days later the FBI raided that warehouse. Shots were fired. Two members of the Borgiano crime family were killed and the four hackers were arrested on the spot. Lenny made no attempt to turn those LAZARUS hackers. He marched two of them into our building in handcuffs a day later and ordered them to talk our hackers through the disabling of their FBI malware. He had plea-bargained those two into helping us, but he had no interest in them working for us. It struck me as sort of strange that organized crime hackers really held little interest for him. As it turned out he had bigger fish to fry then just run-of-the-mill American gangsters.

One of our early cases that is worth telling you about was our first experience with Ransomware. Can you believe it? Some greedy hackers actually tried to get the political campaign of Bill Clinton in 1996 to pay them five million dollars to unhack their computers. It was sort of the cyber equivalent of Watergate back in the seventies. These Ransomware hackers had planted a worm in the Clinton campaign's servers that did two potentially damaging things, things that could completely cripple the operations of political campaigns at a crucial time in the election year. First, it just blacked out all of their computer screens connected to the main data storage server. Second, it breached that server itself and diverted all of the traffic that went through it to them: emails, voter data, speechwriting texts, strategy papers, donor lists, everything.

As soon as it happened and the cyber hijackers contacted them for ransom, the campaign went to Lenny and he brought their problem right to us. That's when the whole affair went all cloak-and-dagger. These hackers probably realized that they sooner or later could be tracked through cyberspace. This was before the time of online bank transfers to offshore accounts. Therefore, all we got from them was a plain old telephone number that we called to set up a good old-fashioned, traditional kidnappers' hands-on money drop. What these cybercrooks didn't know was that through our computers, the time and place for the drop was cyber-booby trapped. We turned all of our gadgets loose on them. We put censors on every inch of the drop zone, cameras on every street corner leading in and out of the drop zone, of course tracking devices in the duffel holding the money. But to my mind the sneakiest part of our set-up was a clear, thin lamination inside the money packets themselves that held miniaturized tracking components in the form of almost invisible transmitting wires. This last was one of Carl's ideas who had been playing with all sorts of miniaturization techniques. What he referred to as "nano crap."

Of course, Lenny picked me to make the drop. I don't think he felt he could trust putting five million in cash in the hands of any of our other employees (except perhaps Tommy who was such a straight arrow that William Tell could have trusted him). But of course, as always, Lenny had a stronger reason for picking me. I was to be his on-site back-up. His directions to me were to commit to memory every single detail of the drop zone, its occupants, all movements within it, and to alert his spotters via a hand signal the moment I saw the pick-up swing into motion. Actually, it reminded me of my job way back when, riding point on President Kennedy's motorcades. So, I went and sat on a park bench on the mall about halfway down between the Capitol Building and the Lincoln Memorial directly across from the trash container into which our duffel bag full of money was to be deposited. I didn't have to wait long. After I put the bag in the trash can, I crossed the mall, exited the area, then immediately reentered wearing a different jacket and a baseball cap. I wasn't sitting on my bench for more than five minutes when a messenger on one of those thin-tired English bikes pulled up to the trash can and pulled out the bag of cash. I gave my signal and the biker pedaled away. That should have been it. One of Lenny's thugs was stationed along the sidewalk that the biker was riding on ready to intercept him, but about twenty yards down the path the biker messenger flung the bag into a stand of low-standing bushes. From behind a tree a man in a hooded sweatshirt stepped out, grabbed the bag, ran to a car parked at the curb on the adjoining street (a grey, utterly non-descript, at least 10-years-old Dodge Charger) got in and drove off. What these bad guys didn't reckon on was me. I watched it all and got the car's license number and conveyed it to Lenny's spotters via my walkie-talkie. They picked up the car within two blocks of the drop zone and the rest was history. The messenger turned out to be just a pawn, given $200 to pick up the bag and toss it into the bushes. Lenny let him go. Lenny's spotters followed the car to a garage all the way up in Baltimore where they took four hackers into custody. Under Lenny's familiar threats of federal prison, gang-sodomy, public hanging, drawing and quartering, and whatever other horrors he could come up with, these hackers talked our hackers through the necessary steps for freeing the Clinton Campaign's computers.

As time went on, our 'dark web' monitoring and cyber signal tracking capabilities increased exponentially. We added four more hacker-nerds that Lenny judged harmless enough to turn. The government agencies who bankrolled us updated our computers about every six months to a year as new better devices came on the market and cleverer auxiliary gadgetry became available. Then came the PC explosion, first desk-tops and towers, separate screens and keyboards, then laptops became staples in offices, banks, hospitals, businesses, everywhere, and soon after almost every home in America had a PC or a MAC, and then came the wireless revolution. Wow, talk about transubstantiation! The bodies and circuits of the computer industry seemed to be changing identities almost day-to-day.

But once again, I've gotten overenthusiastically ahead of myself. Throughout the late nineties, during that developmental time, as our company evolved and our capabilities became more and more sophisticated, I also tended to all of the mundane workings that were essential to any start-up and then highly successful business. As General Manager of THRINTEL (nobody but Lenny and I and Tommy every referred to it as Malware Inc. anymore) I handled payroll, purchasing (office supplies, new computers, banking, everything including toilet paper for god's sake), scheduling of our hacker employees (all of whom were held captive, unable to look for other jobs or leave the company for any reason, but whose personal lives we decided to accommodate the best we could with flexible hours). I never could figure out why hackers so liked to work in the middle of the night fueled by gallons of coffee. We also gave them liberal vacation time, and even Christmas bonuses. All of this to keep them happy even though we were keeping them prisoner. And finally, I was also in charge of internal affairs (it was paramount to my job to make sure that none of our turncoat hackers turned on us).

As for this last, I had to keep an eye on them both inside and outside our building, making sure they weren't meeting outside the building to sell our secrets or warn our targets. Admittedly, my nerds were a pretty shady lot, but Lenny had put enough of the fear of god into them that they stayed loyal. And besides, we were paying them very good salaries that they certainly couldn't get in jail. I only had two breaches of security in those early years. One was just a careless sexual liaison with a 'dark web' spy, a honey trap that my compromised nerd became suspicious of and actually brought to me. The other was a deliberate sell out, a mole situation that I should probably tell you about. One other aspect of my job that made me a bit suspicious right away, but that I ultimately chose to ignore in the best tradition of the military's 'no see, no tell' policy toward homosexuality in that era, was my bi-weekly expense reports. I simply gave them to Lenny and the funds needed to pay the bills, often inflated above the requested figures, magically appeared in our business bank account within a day or so of their submission. I suspected that it was Lenny who inflated my figures, and it all seemed a bit shady to me. I even asked Lenny about it once. He assured me that it was just appreciative money coming from satisfied customers and all was on the up and up. I never broached the subject again. But again, I am getting ahead of myself.

While all this was happening, my life was like that of a cloistered monk? I threw myself almost completely into my work. No longer the Parisian *flaneur*, my footsteps beat a path in the morning from my new apartment in Alexandria to our office and back in the evening to home. Some nights I ate alone in front of the TV set watching the national news and wondering which of our clients would be covered that night. As for the job itself, over time I inured myself to the monotonous handling of all the petty details of running what day-by-day, month-by-month, was becoming a very successful, busy, in-demand enterprise. I must admit that I really liked the idea of being in charge, though that was an illusion that I willingly fostered. Even though he wasn't seen here all that often, Lenny was really the one in charge. Two or three times a week, he would show up in this black, tinted spy-mobile and check in on us. But at other times he would sweep into the office when a more urgent hack of one of our clients that needed immediate tending too. I sensed pretty quickly that our THRINTEL business was not the only operation that Lenny was carrying around on his dance card. I firmly believe that already back in the sixties when we were both in the Pentagon that Lenny was an Intelligence Community fixer-in-waiting and that, over the years, while I was hiding in academia and then in Paris, that he had ascended to a position of fixer-extraordinaire in charge of whatever sinister plots the American spy community happened to be hatching at the time. Since going to work at THRINTEL my chosen literature for reading myself to sleep at night became spy novels. I rather quickly dismissed the ridiculous exaggerated pulp of Ian Fleming but soon opted for the much more sophisticated and well-informed novels of John Le Carre. In fact, I started thinking of Lenny as our American version of Le Carre's George Smiley.

Lenny and I didn't have any sort of social life. Heck, I didn't have any social life at all. We didn't go out to bars for drinks or watch football games together. We did sit down at my conference table at least once a week and have his version of heart-to-hearts. He would make polite inquiries about Grace, her studies, her interests. He would ask repeatedly if I like the job, was enjoying the work, if there were any problems around the office that he could help me out with. He always would end our conversations by telling me what a great job I was doing, how I was making his life quite easy, how I was the one totally responsible for the success of the business. Of course, it wasn't difficult to build a successful business when Lenny kept bringing in new projects and new clients every week, when the coffers kept filling up with large checks from any number of money laundering sources, when all expenses were paid out of the OMB which was the government's main money laundering source. In reality, the government just sort of kept us on retainer as their go-to destination whenever any computer system threat reared its ugly head. But Lenny was right in one sense, and he had been right all along ever since he had recruited me. I was pretty invaluable to him because I had no problem at all running the business and running it without the slightest threat of oversight or political probing or public media investigations. Ever since we opened up for business, I had kept THRINTEL 'under the radar' as Lenny had requested and that was probably what him and our spy-ware clients valued the most.

The only real break I got from my monastic life at THRINTEL was the increasingly rare time I got to spend with Grace. She was a very busy young woman. Though she didn't talk much about it, I was pretty sure that she was splitting her time between her studies as a junior in Art History at Georgetown and her young man who after months of hiding him from me finally surfaced at a dinner we had scheduled in a pub just off the campus. Over the shepherd's pie and the fish-and-chips she introduced me to him. We made awkward small talk for an hour until the two of them fled to an evening lecture on Monet or Seurat or some such Impressionist, post-Impressionist or French painter whose name I didn't really care about. Of course, I immediately ran a computer background check on her beau, his family, his studies, his finances, his friends, and his dog. Actually, he didn't have a dog, but if he had I would have checked Fido out too. That done, sanity returned, I calmed down, decided that it was a situation I need to graciously live with. But, nonetheless, all the time in my heart of hearts I was hoping that it was an infatuation that she would ultimately get over.

Strangely enough, a number of times at the end of my strategy sessions with Lenny he seemed more concerned with my utter lack of any social life than I was. A couple of times, politely, he asked or offered: "Are you seeing anyone?" or "Mike, you need to get out a bit more" or "I can get you invitations to some lobbyists' dos or embassy parties. You could meet some people, a lot of girls are loose here in D.C." Challenged social mixer that I was (ever since my disastrous days at Berkeley), I managed to avoid his social overtures. I think he was only making them because we had been friends for such a long time and he genuinely wished for me to be happy. The strange thing about all this extracurricular concern on Lenny's part was that I knew very little about his own social situation. I knew that he wasn't married. I was pretty sure that he was a confirmed workaholic of a similar species that I had become since coming to work for him. But that was it. I knew he wasn't gay, but yet he never gave any mention of a woman in his life. He didn't live in his black spy-mobile, but he didn't live in a suburban mansion either. With no factual evidence I envisioned him going home at night to a bachelor apartment much like my own. In other words, except for our collaboration in our business, Lenny was as much an enigma to me as were the spymasters in the novels I was reading.

It was almost three years in as the General Manager of THRIN-TEL when I found out why Lenny had really hired me, come after me and not some other, more experienced, more computer conversant manager who could probably do the job I was doing just as well. You could never really trust Lenny to tell you all that was going on. With Lenny I always suspected that nothing was ever really what it seemed. He hadn't really hired me to be simply a manager. He had come after me and my Eidetic Memory that had lain dormant for so long to be a spy, a field agent, a Pathfinder like I had been back there in Cuba in the sixties, a valuable asset that he could turn loose when a really dangerous threat needed to be evaluated and resolved. I've described already some of our early cases while THRINTEL was getting underway. But as our business grew some cases came along that were different or tougher or even more dangerous than some of the others. Many of our cases we could just resolve in-house via the computer savvy of our hackers. The GRU/KGB case was certainly not one of them.

It all started with Lenny double-timing it into my office and shutting the door decisively behind him. Clearly, he had something to tell me that he didn't want any other of our people to hear. It was one of those 'loose lips sink ships' moments when Lenny, who was usually as cool as a jazz sax player, gave in to a four-alarm panic. I'd only seen that look of pedal-to-the-floor urgency on his face once or twice since I'd come to work for him so I knew that something important was in the works.

L: Mike, the fuckers hacked NATO.

Me: (bemused) What fuckers?

L: (calming somewhat) We don't know. We just know NATO has been hacked. We don't know who. Probably the Russians. Maybe the Germans. Maybe both. We don't know how they did it. Get your people working on that. We really need to find these guys.

Me: (messing with him) The fuckers?

L: (catching on) Dammit Mike, this isn't funny.

Some background. It's late 1994. Since the Berlin Wall had fallen and Germany had been put back together, and since the U.S.S.R. had fallen and had not been put back together, Eastern Europe and the rest of Europe and even us in America had been operating under the illusion that the Cold War was over. Not so fast! The fuckers were still out there. The Russians, the KGB spy intelligentsia, weren't giving up as easily as Gorbachev had to Reagan and then Bush. The KGB and their German counterparts the GRU were still spying, but with the ascendance of computers that spying had taken on a whole new texture, a whole new kind of intelligence threat. And now this data breach of NATO. Lenny was certainly right to be concerned.

I put my hackers to work on their hackers right away. As it turned out, their hackers were good enough to plant a virus in the NATO system, but weren't really good enough to cover their tracks. My guys followed their digital footprint to an area in Berlin that had formerly been East Berlin. It had been a major data breach. We were sure the Russians had done it. They had stolen the contact information, passport numbers, airline, rental car, hotel purchases, phone logs, of everyone who had passed through the NATO purview in the last three years since NATO's computer network had gone on linc. It was all ultra-valuable information that could be used for espionage, the tracking of military and government officials, the movement of troops and equipment over the breadth of Eastern Europe, all extremely sensitive data of great interest to nation-state spy agencies like the KGB and the GRU. Lenny was back in the office the next day for my report. Yes, definitely the Russians I told him. KGB military intelligence agents working out of Berlin under the protection of the German GRU.

Me: We're working to disable them now. They used a Crypto Jacking Malware to get into the NATO system. We're setting up a threat confrontation between our Fire Eye disabler and their Stalin Locker VPN Filter Malware.

L: What?

Me: We're stopping them. Shutting them down for now, but the damage has been done and it will be only a matter of time until they get in again. They seem to have a pretty elaborate computer station manned by a cadre of experienced hackers. Pretty much just like us.

L: Terrific. I need to think about this. I'll be back.

And he was gone.

But not for long. He was right back that afternoon. I got the feeling that he had just left so that he could consult with someone further up the chain of command than him, maybe get the go-ahead for further action. The meeting in my office with the door closed that we had next proved that was the case. He came right to the point.

L: Mikey, I need you to go on a reconnaissance trip to Berlin. You can't just do this job from your desk. We've been authorized to be America's answer to these hackers except nobody can know that it is us. Hopefully these Russian pricks have no clue that we're on their trail. They'll know something is wrong when their data stops coming in. Maybe we've got two or three days before they get antsy.

Me: And you want me to do what when I get to Berlin?

L: Pin them down. Locate them. Watch their comings and goings. See if you can find any security coverage. Find a way that we can get in and take them out. We need this kind of intelligence so we can move.

Me: Take them out?

L: Yes.

Me: Just what do you mean 'take them out'?

L: Destroy their computers. Neutralize their hackers.

Me: Neutralize?

L: Mike, you've done this before, back when you were sent into Cuba. While you are getting this intel I'll be assembling my team here and joining you in Berlin. All you have to do is brief us and your job will be done.

Me: But why me? Why not some professional CIA spook?

L: All kinds of reasons. Nobody knows who you are. Nobody at NATO, the GRU, you've never even been to Berlin before. And I can trust you, you and that magical memory of yours. I know that your information will be precise and accurate. And there will be no record of it. When my people hit this hacker station nobody can know who we are or where we came from. It might get rough. We can't afford an international incident. We are in fucking *détente*.

As he talked, worked his seduction, I felt this strange pulse of *deja vu* going back some forty years to my brief Pathfinder incursion into Cuba. But back then my information had helped President Kennedy in his decision-making. This assignment that Lenny was pressing upon me, however, came with much more sinister overtones. Clearly, I was going undercover in support of some sort of paramilitary action. Lenny kept cajoling.

L: Of course, you'll get a nice bonus for doing this. Hazardous duty pay.

Me: Hazardous?

L: No. Not at all.

Me: I've got more money than I need.

L: I know. Sorry. It's not the money, I know. It's just that I've got to put together this whole operation fast before these guys get away. I know you can get us a wealth of information in a short time and deliver it to us in person right away as soon as we step off the plane. Mike, you've got powers that no one else has and you are the one that can make this work.

So there we are. That evening I was on a plane to Berlin. No cover story. Using my own identity. A tourist, I guess.

Berlin in the winter of 1994 wasn't really a major tourist destination. It was a city in recovery. Recovery from years of military occupation. Recovery from years of economic isolation from the amenities of the Western World. Recovery from the absence of freedom—to come and go, to speak out what you think, to imagine a life beyond the wall. When I landed the city was coated in a dirty grey snow, the air was cold and cloudy, the streets were dimly lit and cheerless. My hackers had given me an address where they thought their hackers were housed and, before I did anything, I took a cab there. I had landed at 9AM after a long night flight, but Lenny's sense of urgency precluded me getting a hotel room and going straight to bed to combat my jet lag. Instead, I set myself up in a coffee shop across the street from the address I had been given. I was amazed at how much their building resembled ours. Brick, almost completely windowless, one front entrance door.

After a while I struck out for a walk in the neighborhood, made my way into an adjoining street behind the building and saw that it had a back door where people periodically came out on a small loading dock to smoke. These smokers opened and closed the loading dock door with keys. They always locked it behind them when they came out and I presumed locked it from inside when they went back in. What this told me was that there was no security guard at the back door. If there was, he would have let them out and back in and been in charge of the door. I also made a mental note that two of the men's wives or girlfriends or whatever drove right up to the loading dock and brought their men their lunch. I made a mental note of the makes of these two cars and even their license plate numbers. I also, of course, counted how many of these men, who I presumed were the hackers, came out to smoke. Five of them. Of course, there could be some non-smokers in there too, so my count might not be fully accurate.

Back having another cup of bitter German coffee across the street from the front door, I witnessed what I thought might be the changing of the guard. A large, black-leather-jacketed man arrived in an equally large black sedan and went into the building. The car waited. Minutes later another thuggish-looking character, also in a black leather jacket, came out, got in the car, and they drove off. *Black leather must be the uniform of the local GRU*, I thought. *One guard on the door changing at 3PM,* I made another mental note.

By late afternoon, around 5PM, I was beginning to doze off from watching the building when my cigarette smoking hackers started to come out, but only three of them. All I could figure was that the hackers didn't work on a regular 8 to 5 schedule. They probably came and went as they pleased. So, I couldn't really give Lenny a read how many people would be in the building at any one time. But one thing was certain. There would be a guard on the front door for twenty-four hours probably in three eight hour shifts: 7-3, 3-11, 11-7. It was security, but it was pretty light security. I had also noticed that there were security cameras mounted on both front corners of the building but none on the back of the building.

By then it was 6PM, a gloomy fog had settled down on the Berlin streets and I was exhausted. I found a cheap, nondescript hotel nearby and booked a room. I didn't care how dirty it was. All I wanted was a bed. But before I climbed into it I checked out the hotel room. My eyes swept in a 180-degree arc in front of me. Double bed. Floor lamp with a yellow shade. Small desk with just one drawer. Lounge chair with the stuffing coming out of it. No sign of any cameras in the ceiling or on the walls. One picture hung over the bed, a pastoral scene with a cow. It looked to be OK. There was no telephone. Perhaps I was being paranoid. But it was Berlin after all. Funny, but the one thing that after almost thirty years now that sticks out in my mind about that room was that stupid picture. I took it down off the wall and looked behind it, but there was no bug. That done I fell into the bed and slept the sleep of the dead. As I fell asleep Lenny's words as he sent me off echoed in my mind: *"you can't do this job from your desk. Mike, you can see things that other people can't see. I'm counting on that."*

I awoke before dawn, that is if there even was a dawn in that dingy, gloomy Berlin of those days. I was back at my post drinking coffee before seven o'clock when the morning changing of the door guard took place right on schedule. Then minutes later a man on a bicycle pulled up, leaned his bike against the front wall of the building, knocked on the door and was admitted by the door guard. The bike hadn't been there the day before. I thought on that and decided that this hacker either had taken the day before off or had worked different hours from the others or just hadn't ridden his bike that day. I watched the smokers' loading dock until about 1:30 and the same two cars pulled up delivering their lunches. That done, I had another idea that I thought I would try that afternoon. I had pretty well surveilled the outside of the building, Now I wanted to see if I could get some info on the inside.

On the plane flying in overnight, I had looked at some street maps of Berlin, actually quickly memorized them then threw them away in a waste bin at the airport when I arrived. That afternoon I told the cab driver to take me to the city hall where, from the maps, I knew the main registry office was located. Luckily, the clerk on the desk spoke English. I had been worried that I would have to communicate with him in my rusty Deutchlish. But he was very organized, very what I imagined a German might be. With little fanfare he directed me to the second floor library where the property logs were shelved. I had given him a three-line story of how I was an American interested in finding a building to buy in the street where our KGB hackers were housed. Very accommodating. He even plucked out the specific volume that held the address I wanted. Again, luck was with me. I found the address and it not only had notations about the sale of the building two years before, but it had a contractor's floorplan of improvements to the building done after the sale. It took me about three minutes to memorize that floorplan, turn the book to the shelf and leave. I can't imagine that even the most curious of cameras might get suspicious of someone taking that miniscule amount of time looking at a dusty library book. Lying in my bed in the pitch dark that night, over and over I traversed the hallways on both the first and second floors of that building, opening doors, climbing the stairs, imagining how each room was furnished. By one in the morning I felt as if I worked there.

Lenny and his troops arrived the next morning. He walked down the street past our hackers' building at precisely ten o'clock. When he turned back on the other side of the street, I stepped out of my look-out post in the coffee shop and hailed him. Of course, this means of our meeting had been pre-arranged at the airport in Washington when he saw me off three nights before. He didn't join me, rather just kept walking on the other side of the street and, surreptitiously, with one hand signal, motioned me to follow. Around the corner he bundled me into a small, four-passenger German car of some miniature make that I didn't recognize and drove me to a small house in a residential area in what used to be West Berlin. I learned later that it was a CIA safe house left over from the Cold War eighties. Counting Lenny, there were eight of them. I speculated that they were private contractors, probably ex-military, and heavily armed with their ordinance strewn around the room on tables, desks, and beds, all manner of sawed-off shotguns, hand guns, grenades, whatever, weapons of individual destruction and mass confusion that I couldn't even identify. I briefed them all after-noon, every detail of what I had observed in my two full days of sur-veillance. They had a small chalkboard and I even drew them a map of the interior hallways and layout of the building. By seven o'clock that evening I was back at the Berlin airport boarding a plane for Washing-ton. All the way across the Atlantic my imagination nagged at me with images of what Lenny and his thugs might be doing back in Berlin and my partial responsibility for whatever that was.

Lenny got back two days later and bounced into my office like he was the Easter bunny come to deliver colored eggs.

L: Mikey my boy, the operation went off smooth as silk and your information was totally invaluable. Well done.

Me: What happened?

L: Not important. If the Russians are smart, nothing.

And that was the total extent of the debriefing that I got. It was a graphic, totally non-informational, lesson in spookology. See no evil. Hear no evil. Tell me no evil. I got on my computer and for a week combed the Berlin newspapers for any news of Lenny's attack on the Russian hackers. Nothing. I even looked on the 'dark web' to see if there was any chatter there. There wasn't. The closest I came to anything resembling what might have happened was a Berlin Police report of an act of vandalism in a building (no address given) in the neighborhood where I had been staked out.

Lenny's raiders in black ski masks drove up to the back loading dock of the building in two cars identical to those of the women who brought the lunches. They overpowered the smokers, opened the back door with the smokers' keys, and stormed the building. At the same time Lenny rode up on a bicycle to the front door of the building, knocked, and when the leather guard opened it maced him. Having gained entrance, the raiders went through the building room by room terrorizing and tying up the hapless hackers as they went, collecting bags of paper and files and demolishing every computer that they encountered. They took an axe to the central servers on the second floor. Then they sat all the hackers in a line against one wall, turned the shotguns on them, and threatened to execute them if they didn't give them all the information they had on the NATO hack and any other projects they had underway. The terrified hackers spilled their guts into a recorder and the raiders left with the material to set Russian computer hacking back years.

That is my imagination's construction of how Lenny's raid went down. Sorry readers but that's the best I can do. There was certainly no real information forthcoming. Notice however that my version is a completely bloodless one. I'm not sure Lenny's version, the real version, was.

After my incursion into Berlin went off well. Which, granted, was an emergency action. Me being thrown into a pool without benefit of water wings. After Berlin Lenny got all mushy over my contribution to the operation's success via my Eidetic reconnaissance skills. Not only was I rewarded with a pile of happy horse shit praise from Lenny, but also with a nice pile of laundered money from our benefactors in spookworld. All along I had been banking most of my high six-figure salary, living a monastic life, paying Grace's tuition, spending very little on myself, not even taking vacations. I was again totally alone. What did I have to spend money on? This extra bonus made me twice a millionaire. I dreamed of a rosy wealthy future for Grace and I. Oh the best laid plans! In 1998, a year from finishing her Ph.D., Grace decided that she wanted to get married. Not until she finished her degree, but nonetheless I began to feel a large hole beginning to open in my life.

Also, after the Berlin adventure, Lenny felt overly comfortable sending me on other recon assignments. As these recon missions became more frequent, I realized that the company I was running for Lenny was a lot more than a computer-based, 'dark web' monitoring, threat intelligence detecting agency. It was, in fact, a complete specialized spy cell within the other military and intelligence communities of our government. THRINTEL was masquerading as a bunch of computer nerds, but really, we were a bunch of enablers of an army of spooks engaged in a whole new form of cold war stretching all the way across the globe. After Berlin, Lenny had no qualms about sending me on other reconnaissance assignments. Over the following years I did short stints in Amsterdam, Beirut, Tehran, and back to Berlin where in 1998 Lenny finally succeeded in getting me shot.

But again, I am getting well ahead of myself. First things first. I had to deal with our mole. It was actually me who first sensed that something was wrong. Each Monday I held our hackers' organizational meeting. I insisted upon these meetings and they usually lasted about two to three hours. Our business had grown and prospered. Paying lip service to our cover as a Threat Intelligence agency, we had taken on a number of commercial clients besides the government intelligence agencies who owned us and were always our first priority. These commercial clients were banks, hospitals, any business that dealt in personal data that needed to be protected, even one intriguing on-line sales enterprise calling itself, facetiously I thought, AMAZON. Driven by this growth, our number had grown to nineteen full-time hackers, most of them hired right out of burgeoning Computer Science programs in major universities across the country. We still, every once in a while, turned a cybercriminal or a hacktivist to work for us in lieu of going to jail, but they had to be either too good at their hacking to turn down or too promising in the loyalty sector of their psychological profile to waste. Tommy ran these weekly meetings now and I sat in on them listening intently, filing in my memory what was going on with each member of our hacker staff as they presented their weekly reports orally to the meeting at large. It was in one of these meetings that I got my first whiff that something was wrong. Four of the nineteen one Monday morning reported that the projects they were working on, all cyber incursions of Mystery Bot, a newly emerging triple threat Malware especially attractive to Ransomware cyber incursion and a potential threat to our bigger commercial clients, had gone dark. In our meetings, over a number of weeks, these hackers had warned that if this particular cyber threat was turned loose it could raise havoc especially with financial institutions. Then suddenly this Ransomware attack group who called themselves the Shadow Brokers just shut down and disappeared, probably to reincarnate themselves in a deeper receptacle in the 'dark web'. As they delivered their report, our hackers couldn't understand why this had happened. They were certain that they had covered their tracks, that the Shadow Brokers didn't know that we were on their trail. And yet they were gone, and we would have to start all over in tracking Mystery Bot.

This caught my attention. My suspicions led me to talk it over with Lenny and it was he who almost immediately figured out what had happened.

L: Somebody tipped them off.

Me: But who? My guys are pretty good about not leaving footprints.

L: I think we've got a mole. Someone inside who found them, clued them, probably extorted money from them, sold us out. Or maybe they infiltrated us, turned one of ours via blocking email, a honey trap. Or planted someone with us that we hired. A long game mole.

Of course, Lenny gave me the job of ferreting out this traitor and it wasn't a fun one. In fact, the mole chapter in the saga of THRINTEL turned out to be a sordid little sex story that made our whole company feel dirty, but taught us all a valuable lesson.

The first thing I did was to do away with our Monday hacker meetings. At this point I think I didn't really believe Lenny's conviction that we had a spy in our midst. In fact, I really hoped that his whole mole theory was just a superspook's paranoid fantasy. So, Tommy and I started receiving our hackers' weekly reports, interviewing them individually, in my office behind closed doors. We made up some lame excuse that we wanted to get more personally involved with their work, that we needed a closer synergy with the individual responsibilities and projects that they each were running. In actuality, I just wanted a closer look at each of them, turn my Eidetic eyes loose on their body languages, their facial tics, their hands, their tells, as if these meetings were a poker game and they were sitting across the table from me nervously fingering their cards.

Before we met with each of them I carefully shuffled through my memory files of their original background checks when they had first come on board our operation. It was as if I was actually turning pages in a file and sentences were streaming out in front of me. As I called each file up, I marveled at how accurately I remembered each hacker's background, education, personal life, finances, job interview evaluations, and varied circumstances that brought each one into our purview. I actually surprised myself. I hadn't been challenging my Eidetic Memory that much for a while so it was good to feel its strength again. Nineteen hackers, nineteen different life styles, nineteen different areas of expertise, nineteen on-going cyber projects, nineteen (and actually many more) connection paths into the 'dark web', the hacker underworld. The more I thought about it, the more I realized that all nineteen of them were associating with cybercriminals on a daily basis as they prowled the 'dark web'. Every one of them every day witnessed criminal activity, data theft, virtual kidnapping and ransom schemes, treasonable incursions into classified government secrets, identity thefts, dirty money changing hands and being laundered, all taking place on the mean streets of virtual reality. I quickly began to understand how the temptations of all this criminal activity observed and traced and monitored on their computer screens could eventually get to them, turn them to the dark side. For, after all, we were the dark side too. We were a semi-clandestine operation functioning under the radar in close association with the spookworld of Lenny and his CIA/NSA/FBI and global cohorts.

If we had a mole…and even as the individual interviews started, I still hoped that we didn't, that one of our own people hadn't turned on us, that Lenny was wrong. But, if we did have a mole, I figured that this rather big and sudden change in our weekly operating procedure might spook him or her, flush this villain out, cause him or her to run or at least to stop the selling of information that seemed to be going on. In these interviews my memory, my Eidetic powers of observation, my superpowers (according to Lenny), were functioning as a sort of human lie detector. Only it was one much more accurate than the real, questionably accurate, lie detectors of the 1990s.

Out of these interviews, Tommy and I came up with four viable possibilities, all personnel who at one time had crossed cyber trails with the Mystery Bot virus or tracked the 'dark web' chatter of the Shadow Brokers group. It took about four weeks of these Monday one-on-ones to settle on these four: three male hackers and one young woman right out of the Michigan State cyber forensics program that had grown out of the original program that had been the role model for my own Purdue University forensics program way back in the seventies. Tommy and I presented our suspicions to Lenny and he told us to sit tight and he would get back to us. Two weeks, then a month, went by and Lenny didn't get back to us. Our weekly Monday one-on-ones went on. In that time, our hackers reported two more of our on-going cyber surveillances suddenly shutting down, probably relocating to different orbits in cyber space. Two of these reports, however, actually came from two of the hackers that we had put under suspicion, thus probably clearing them from any mole-suspicion (unless of course their report was just another layer of misinformation designed to shift attention away from their own molishness). In truth I began to look at the whole affair as an exercise in black comedy, us stumbling around trying to bring ourselves, our own operation, to some climactic revelation, a kind of cyber masturbation.

Lenny finally came back to us and, in the best tradition of most conspiracy theories, the truth looked like it lay much more on the surface than in the darkness of the cyber underworld. In the best tradition of old-fashioned Cold War spying, Lenny had put tails on the four suspects we had presented to him. They had eliminated two of them right away. One was a twenty-four-year-old dweeb who lived with his mother. He spent all of his free time in a teenager's arcade playing video games, (which were just coming into existence as a craze). He seemed congenitally nervous (a condition that would later be acronymed as ADHD) which had initially caused us to identify him as a possibility. The other quickly eliminated suspect was the girl from Michigan State. She turned out to be a burgeoning religious fanatic. When she wasn't at work for us, she was atoning for her cyber sins on the 'dark web' by living in a computer -generated virtual world called SIMS where she had created an avatar for herself as a nun able to work chartable life-changing miracles for virtual homeless people, potential virtual suicides, and virtual lost pets. Lenny quickly deemed her much too bat-shit crazy to be our mole. The other two suspects proved much harder to eliminate so Lenny, naturally, sic-ed me upon them using his same old—"Mike, you see things that other people don't"—line that he had been using since high school to get me to do things for him that I didn't want to do. Once more I was out of the office doing the old-fashioned kind of detective work.

I took turns following my suspects, always using disguises in the best Sherlock Holmes tradition, mostly just hoodie sweat shirts, sunglasses, baseball caps and other non-office-professional clothes. In my memory I noted where they went, who they met with, what they did, what patterns emerged in their life-style, their choices, even how they dressed for different occasions. I was after whatever secrets they might have, whatever perhaps they were trying to hide, whatever they did after looking over their shoulders to see if anyone was looking.

One of them turned out to by gay. He had a live-in male roommate. At first that made me suspicious. I was thinking that he might be a good target for blackmail if he wanted to keep his homosexuality secret. But he just didn't seem to be hiding it. He and his roommate rarely left their apartment, except once a week my hacker would go out, usually on a Friday night, to a nearby gay bar. There he would drink, hang out and make conversation, before picking someone out and going to the men's room with him presumably for his weekly blow job probably both giving and receiving since he would be in there a pretty long time. But another pattern of my gay suspect's out-of-the-office life was the driving of his roommate, whose face I never really saw because he was always bundled into an oversized grey hoodie, to doctors' appointments usually followed by pharmacy stops. It didn't take me long to figure out that this hacker was functioning pretty much full-time in his out-of-the-office life as a caregiver for his partner who was afflicted with the plague of the nineties, AIDS. Once I realized what was going on with those two, I quickly lost interest in that suspect as our potential mole. Actually, instead of considering him a traitor, I started thinking of him as a kind of saint.

My other suspect was a harder nut to crack. He seemed to be living a perfectly normal life outside of the office. In fact, he was actually pretty boring, except for one thing. His clothes all came from J.C. Penney. He drove a five-year-old Chrysler compact. He ate in fast food joints, didn't drink much, never gambled, really boring. Except he had a smoking hot girlfriend who seemed to move in and out of his life at random times as if she contacted him on weekends when she came back into town off the road. A statuesque blonde at least three inches taller than him dressed in designer clothes wearing spike-heeled 'fuck me' shoes stacked like the guns of Navarone and with a face right off the cover of *Vogue*, she was way, way, way out of his league .And yet she kept showing up and shacking up with this utterly unremarkable computer nerd. There was no doubt in my mind that he was our mole caught in a really obvious honey trap by this uber-sexy seductress. I took my certainty back to Lenny and he thought for no more than thirty seconds before sending me back out.

L: Forget about him, Mike, take two weeks and follow her. Find out who she is, who she works for, where her contacts with these 'dark web' guys live. She's milking information out of our guy and passing it on.

And so, the second stage of my mole surveillance took on the cliched shape of a retro Cold War scenario—follow the *femme fatale*. At least on this assignment I didn't have to worry about being recognized by one of our own, hence I didn't have to concoct any disguises. Meanwhile, as I was off following her, Tommy was back at the office monitoring every online communication of our nondescript little mole. As it turned out he wasn't doing anything suspicious at all online. The information he was supplying, it seemed, all took the form of pillow talk. As for our honey trap *femme fatale*, she never left Washington at all as I had suspected. That was probably just some cover she told our guy to confine her seductions to weekends so that she would have a good parcel of time to screw information out of him. Of more interest was who she hung out with and where.

On her typical day she arose late, elevenish, got brunch at a bakery around the corner from her very upscale apartment building, then filled her afternoons with shopping, pedicures and manicures (what would later come to be known as mani-pedis), sometimes a movie, sometimes a museum, sometimes a run to keep in shape, or just a long walk along the Potomac in the sunshine. Following her I concluded that her weekdays were just killing time until the weekends that she spent screwing our nondescript little hacker nerd. In other words, she seemed to be living the life of a high- class prostitute who only had one client. Except for her Mondays. Both Monday afternoons during the two weeks I was following her she took a cab to a brick building two blocks off Columbus Circle and spent a couple of hours inside. I figured this was where and when she was reporting the fruits of her weekend's information gathering on her back.

Reverting to my own Holmesian fantasy identity I knocked on the door of that building posing as a Jehovah's Witness complete with a handful of official-looking white pamphlets. Immediately, I was greeted and turned away by a security guard. But as I was talking to him, I looked inside and, sure enough, there were desks with computers sitting along the wall with users conversing with keyboards and screens very much like our hackers in our offices at THRINTEL. It was the lair of the Shadow Brokers I was certain.

While I was doing this, Tommy was back at THRINTEL planting a faultily encrypted alert concerning the whereabouts of the Shadow Brokers on our mole's project wall. Lenny figured that Miss *Femme Fatale* would screw this cyber footprint out of our mole on the weekend and report it to the Shadow Brokers on the following Monday. He set up a raid on their building for Tuesday morning. His operators hit them on their loading dock as they were packing all their computers into vans. Lenny's thugs destroyed all the machines with fire axes, then called the FBI. All the hackers were detained in the building until the FBI's paddy wagons arrived and carted them off to be charged with cyber extortion via Ransomware. When they were arraigned at the end of that week, pursuant to a plea bargain, the main witness against them was Miss *Femme Fatale*. Turns out she was about more than just a prostitute. She was a hacker herself, but because she was so gorgeous the Shadow Brokers saw much more value in her operating in the real world of sexual seduction than in the virtual world of the 'dark web'. They had identified THRINTEL as their hacking nemesis and assigned her to infiltrate us. Once she had seduced our dweeb, she cajoled pillow talk about his job, his projects, out of him. She photographed any printouts in his briefcase as he snored in post-coital bliss. She even got into his laptop and surfed for anything about THRINTEL she could find there. After that, when Tommy and I reintroduced our weekly hacker meetings, her tactics were the first, and certainly the most lurid, topics of discussion. As for our hapless mole, after we threatened him with jail until he signed a non-disclosure agreement, we fired him not so much for cause as for stupidity and an ungovernable dick.

Of course, that whole mole episode made Lenny and I much more conscious of security, both virtual and real. We double-banked our firewalls online and we put guards on our doors who searched all of the backpacks and brief cases of our hackers going out. We cautioned them to report any new romantic connections that they made so that we could background check their lovers. But mostly we just cautioned them not to talk about their worklife outside of the office at all. Our mole experience was indeed a lesson learned that helped us build what we hoped was an impenetrable firewall around THRINTEL's business. Our company was growing by leaps and bounds as the internet gained more and more influence. Data (both governmentally strategic and commercially profitable) became the most valuable and 'dark web' marketable quantity in twenty-first century existence.

As our Threat Intelligence company and our hackers and their machines approached the universal virtual threat of Y2K, our business continued to grow and prosper. Hackers of every imaginable ilk proliferated faster than we could even identify them. Teenager computer geniuses entertained themselves by hacking into shoddily secured networks. 'Dark web' profiteers hacked into personal computers and commercial businesses and sold whatever data they harvested. Nation states—Russia, China, North Korea, Iran, Israel—set up fully equipped hacking stations manned by their best and brightest hacker nerds armed with the latest, most sophisticated, electronic weapons. As Y2K bore down on the world, a new version of the Cold War came into existence, and THRINTEL was one of the strongest forces on the virtual front lines. As all these threats grew up around us, our company also became more and more sophisticated and heavily armed. In-house, we could scrub any virus, ferret out any worm, disable any Malware, shut down any Ransomware, monitor any transaction or cyber plot or incursion strategy on the 'dark web', and track and locate any individual hacker or hacker group like a cyber bloodhound hot on the trail. But we also quickly learned that all of those were only temporary solutions.

Over time, as the need for and practice of Threat Intelligence grew, what Lenny had said initially, going all the way back to our first case— "You can't just deal with these problems sitting at your desk"—proved abundantly true. In order to really put a hacker or a hacker group out of business, we had to leave the virtual world and engage them physically in the real world. That was the job of Lenny and his small clandestine army of ex-military contractors. Old habits die hard and Lenny certainly was no exception to that rule. I don't think he was ever able to shake the techniques or objectives of the old Cold War spy plots. He firmly believed that true intelligence work (a.k.a. spy craft) could only be done by "leaving your desk" (in our case, our computer screens). And so, when a particularly vexing set of circumstances took hold on our computer screens, he would send me out into the street, often in some foreign country whose language he expected me to learn on the run. As time went on, I became the bridge between the virtual trackers in our office and Lenny's raiders. I was like the cavalry scouts in the old west or the point men for the platoons in the jungles of Vietnam. After that first reconnaissance assignment in Berlin, I did similar in-and-out stints in Moscow, in Tehran, in Israel (which was supposed to be our ally), in Amsterdam (which for some reason, maybe the easy availability of pot, became a late-nineties hotbed of hacker activity), in Prague (hack central of Eastern Europe), and even in Berlin once again.

To tell the truth though, I really got to not so much mind being sent off on one of Lenny's recon missions. It got me out of the office and into the real world, a place that I was more and more losing touch with since I was spending less and less time with Grace. It broke up the boredom and drudgery of managing what by the late nineties had become an international resource company doing multi-millions of dollars of business per year. And the recon work I did really wasn't very hard at all. I actually got pretty good at it, confident in my spy craft (perhaps overconfident). On most of the jobs, all I did was walk around and take it all in, watch the people I was directed to watch, collect license numbers, residence addresses, observe the comings and goings of everything from personnel to deliveries to repairmen in and out of designated buildings. I would map the layout of my target area's work spaces: entrances, exits, possible escape routes. My Eidetic Memory made it all pretty ho-hum spy work. All I had to do was look at things once and I could totally reproduce them in a report to Lenny and his operatives. Nothing to it, until one of those recon assignments got me shot!

It all started when Lenny showed up in the office with one of the big-wigs from the FBI. When they came in, this suit had smoke coming out of his ears and a head about ready to explode. I think Lenny brought him along so that I could calm him down. We sat him down and he commenced raving about how some hacker group had attacked the national data center right here in Washington and had gained entry to innumerable government websites.

Suit: Jesus Christ, we sent men to the moon. Why can't we keep a bunch of hippie hackers out of our computer business?

Me: We can sir, but they have to poke their heads up out of their virtual dens before we can track them down and neutralize them.

I refrained from telling him that we went to the moon thirty years ago and hippies were a species of an equally distant past. Anyway, we calmed him down and immediately set about exploring the incursion and instituting cyber damage control. From the very beginning we suspected the Chinese.

This FBI suit gave our guys access to the national data center's networks and they set to work. First, they traced the hacker activity through code patterns and recurring anomalies that we had already logged over years of monitoring as familiar to Chinese actors. Following the trail, we detected a fully functioning worm with its tentacles slithering across all of the data center's networks and harvesting data from all of its data bases. Who knows, this worm could have been working for years or it could have been inserted and lain dormant waiting to be activated when the time was right, when the national data center got all of their data bases up to speed and felt overconfident and safe in their security. In reality, all of that cyber data turned out to be only loosely guarded and utterly vulnerable when the Chinese hackers decided to activate their worm. We traced the hacker activity to the sub-basement of the Chinese Embassy in Washington. By the time the FBI suit got to us, these Chinese hackers had already made a huge data take and transmitted a mountain of priceless information to the Chinese Ministry of State Security Servers in the Embassy sub-basement. We determined that this mega-hack had garnered a wealth of information that would prove invaluable to the creation of a counterintelligence data base: personnel forms, passport information including numbers, photos and listings of all border crossings, financial data, security clearances, family information (spouses, children, even romantic attachments), corruption investigations, equipment purchases, contacts inside China itself. We decided that their worm was their tool of a broad-ranging spy campaign to collect a huge pool of data that could cripple American intelligence operations for years.

Once we figured out what the Chinese were doing and had pinpointed that basement hacker station in their Embassy, we (Lenny, Tommy, me) decided that we had to counterattack them on two fronts. The first part turned out to be not all that difficult. We set our hackers on their worm and within a day they disabled it and stopped the flow of information. The second part of our counterattack wasn't quite so simple. We had to somehow get to their servers there in the sub-basement and destroy them and the data bases that they held. Clearly, we couldn't mount an all-out commando assault on a foreign country's Embassy in the heart of downtown Washington. Instead, we decided on a flood.

Lenny sent me on yet another of my routine recon walk-throughs. Disguised as a homeless wino, bottle in a brown paper bag and all, I circled the whole building twice, mentally noting and diagramming every aperture, window, grate and passageway into that sub-basement. Then, using the cover of an academic with a Fulbright Grant preparing to spend a year in Beijing, I entered the Embassy right at five pm and wandered the first floor in a bumbling search for the visa desk. In doing so, I witnessed the hackers leaving work for the day exiting through a single basement doorway. I measured the distance from both the main entrance and a back entrance to the building. I also noted the meager security on those entrances consisting of one guard for each door carrying only a single side-arm. Our plan really went off quite well but for one small glitch, me getting shot.

Two AM, dark in the alley behind the Embassy, the only light dimly seeping back to us from the street. Lenny and I directing his operatives to the grating over a window well into the basement. Silently removing the window glass with a diamond headed cutting tool and suction cups, we breached the basement. Attaching a fire hose to a nearby hydrant, we ran the hose through that window into the basement hacking station and turned it on full blast, our way of faking a burst water main. *Viola*! Our flood.

We let the water flow silently into the basement for about ten minutes before we called in the rest of the cavalry. They arrived, lights flashing and sirens screaming, in a Washington D.C. fire engine disguised as firemen in full turn-out gear. The lights and the siren shrieks flushed the security guard on the back door out into the alley leaving the entrance door open behind him. Our fake firemen leaped down off their truck, axes in hand, hoses uncoiling, and rushed the open door. One occupied the security guard, pretending to explain what was going on with no success due to the language barrier, but with great success in distracting him as Lenny's raiders rushed through the open door and down the steps into the by now half-flooded hacking station.

Oh yes, I forgot to mention that Lenny and I were also in fire department uniforms. We went in with the *faux*-firemen in a pseudo-supervisory capacity. Once in the basement, knee-deep in water by now, I directed our men to the servers and they smashed them to shreds with their axes even as their cohorts were spraying everything in the room with the hose that had uncoiled down the steps from the trucks. It all took a matter of mere minutes. When Lenny and I determined that we had caused enough damage to destroy not only the stolen data bases but also all of the hacker station's equipment, we made our escape up the stairs to the truck. By then, the security guard had gotten suspicious, broke away from the fake-fireman who was distracting him, and ran to the top of the stairs to confront the havoc we had wreaked upon the basement he was supposed to be guarding.

Lenny and I were the last ones to jump on the rear running board of the firetruck as it pulled away down the alley. Hanging on for dear life, we pulled past the basement doorway just as the Chinese security guard ran out with his pistol drawn. As we sped away down the alley, he raised his gun and fired off a volley of shots. Luckily, he was either a poor shot or our firetruck was moving too fast for him to draw an accurate bead on us. All of his shots missed our fleeing truck. All that is except one. All of a sudden I felt a hot burn below my waist. My right buttock was on fire. I had heard the rapid-fire gunshots as we turned out of the alley. *Terrific!* I thought. *I've just been shot in the ass.*

CHAPTER 10: READING AND RETREATING (AND 'RITHMATIC)

A s I lay in that hospital while the doctors were stitching my butt back together and then IV-pumping me full of pain medicine and anti-biotics, I had plenty of time to think. I always seemed to get a signal when it was time for me to undergo a new transubstantiation in my existence, time to throw off the essence that had been growing on me like mold. Admittedly, this most recent signal was the most direct and painful one that I had yet received. A bullet to the butt really burns a message into you.

I'd had other such signals before. Certainly President Kennedy's death. Victoria's hateful stare of betrayal. Even getting knocked off the railing by that lightning bolt at the Grand Canyon. By far the worst signal of all was Nicole's death. All really painful signals. But there had been good, non-painful signals too. Nicole picking me up at the Grand Canyon and then making me fall in love with her in Las Vegas. Grace being born. Wendy asking me for a light. And then, of course, there were all of the mixed signals every time Lenny showed up in my life. His appearances out of nowhere always signaled change for me, for the better or the worse. I never knew which until it was too late it seemed. Nevertheless, I always seemed to follow him down the primrose path to perdition that he led me on. But getting shot in the ass was argu-ably the most non-subtle example of just such a signal. It never would have happened if Lenny's (and the CIA's and America's and Russia's and China's et. al.) old Cold War habits didn't die so hard. Despite the fact that THRINTEL was becoming well known as the premier online Vi-rus, Malware, Ransomware disabler extant, our company still at times felt compelled to resort to the old spy craft, to physical surveillance and interdiction, in other words, to muscle and firearms and home invasion and blackmail and all manner of similar spookworld tactics. That stubborn adherence to the past is exactly why I caught that bullet in my butt.

And so, lying in that hospital bed, I started thinking seriously about where my life had been and where my life was going next. Having a bullet burn through your butt really tends to catch your attention and like all these other signals it can head your life in a whole new direction. I was almost sixty years old. Y2K was rapidly approaching to possibly ignite a firestorm of cyber chaos all around the world, and it suddenly occurred to me that it was the perfect time for me to get out. I computed the arithmetic of my last nine years with THRINTEL and the sum of it all was this bullet in my butt (plus, of course, a lot of Uncle Sam's laundered money, probably more that I would ever need).

Lenny, of course, came to visit me every day in the hospital. I think he felt a kind of guilt (that is if he was capable of feeling guilt) over this whole butt-shot affair. We purposely kept Grace out of the loop. She was used to me going off for days at a time as part of my job. Actually, me and Lenny and Tommy were the only ones who knew about me getting shot. Lenny's team of thugs who got me off the firetruck and hustled me into the special government section of Bethesda didn't count because they were faceless and didn't really exist and butt-shot comrades were probably fairly common to them. I had been in the hospital for four days when I finally was far enough out of my pain medicine haze to break the news to Lenny.

Me: Lying here, I've been thinking a lot and I want out.

L: We'll get you out of that bed and on your feet again as soon as the doctors say it's OK.

Me: No,,No. I mean I want out of THRINTEL. I'm just tired, done. Cyber-terrorists, cyber-spies, cyber-crime, data collection, getting shot in the ass, I'm sorry Lenny but I'm not coming back.

L: You and me we are THRINTEL. You can't pack it all in over something like… Well granted, getting shot is a really serious thing but… (he was starting and stopping as if he was in heavy traffic, trying to find an argument)

Me: I'm sorry Lenny, I'm done, out, not coming back.

L: But we need you. You're the key to everything. This is just a pothole in the road. (Then Lenny realized what he had said). Well not a pothole, a bend, a… (his voice trailed off).

Me: (I cracked up) A frigging bullet hole you mean! A lot more serious than a pothole.

L: Oh boy, a really bad choice of words. Really bad.

Me: Look, every day managing THRINTEL I've got so much stuff coming at me that I feel constantly on edge. I'm almost sixty years old. So are you. Hasn't it ever occurred to you that we're just getting too old for this Cold War shit? It was fun while it lasted, but I just don't need all of the craziness anymore. It's been nine years since we, no you, came up with the idea for THRINTEL. I'm sorry, good friend, but I've just had enough.

Lenny saw that I was deadly serious. He got up and started pacing the room, trying to find some way to change my mind. The problem was that Lenny was pretty much right. Together we had built a great company. Thanks to my Eidetic Memory we had avoided all of the political oversight that Washington since Watergate had become so famous for. We had left no paper trails. As far as everyone knew we were just a bunch of computer geeks who never got up from their screens. After three laps around my hospital bed, Lenny finally gave it up. He still hoped that time and healing (of my butt) would change my mind. But he didn't really hold out much hope for that. So, he backed off, gave his life-long best friend the benefit of his doubt.

L: OK, I understand. But you know you will always have a place at THRINTEL if you change your mind. I mean, have you really thought this through? What are you going to do?

Me: Nothing. I don't have to do anything. From the very beginning our spook sponsors have been paying me too too well and I've hardly spent any of it. Grace is on a teaching assistantship now which means no tuition. She's even working part-time at a gallery at the Smithsonian for her spending money. Hell Lenny, I've damn near rich. I've got hardly any expenses. I can certainly retire with no problem.

L: Retire? Are you kidding me? You'll last one, maybe two months. You can't tell me you're going to give up all the action.

Me: Action smaction. I just got shot in the ass thanks to your action.

L: OK, OK, I get it. Once you are back on your feet we'll talk again. I just can't believe that you can just walk away from what we built together. But if you don't change your mind, we'll still talk. If you get bored you know that I can get you any job you want in Washington. You'd make a great security guard in a parking garage or a janitor in a government building. Geez!

Me: Who knows? We'll see. If retirement doesn't work, I may take you up on that. Maybe I could be a crossing guard at an elementary school or a receptionist at a church rectory. Probably not much chance of getting shot in the ass in jobs like that.

Four days later I left the hospital, but it took another good month for me to be able to sit down comfortably. A few days after that Grace came to visit me at my apartment wondering why I hadn't called her when I got back from wherever I had been, then wondering why she found me in bed in my pajamas at four in the afternoon, then wondering why I hadn't gone back to work when I got back. So many questions requiring so many lies. I really hated lying to her but figured I really had no choice. I told her I was laid up with a bad case of sciatica in my right hip and I didn't really want to bother her with it and I was taking a leave of absence from work until it cleared up. After a couple of weeks of her visits and her questions I confessed that I had been enjoying retirement so much that I had decided to make it permanent and had quit my job. Good daughter that she was, she took all of my lies at face value and pretty soon stopped peppering me with questions about my health and my precipitous decision-making. By then I was up and walking around pretty comfortably, at least for short intervals.

One of the first things I did when I got myself out of bed was limp into the university library. Lying there all day had started me reading again. That was fine for the first few weeks I was laid up, but rather quickly I realized that all the books I had on my shelves in the apartment I had already read years ago and knew by heart. Over my nine years at THRINTEL I hadn't read a single book outside of computer manuals and case intel. In fact, the last books I had read were my Existentialist philosophy books that I had collected in Berkeley and then in Paris. I just hadn't had the time or the energy in the last nine years, since Paris really, to actually read anything other than *The Washington Post*.

Out of the hospital and confined to my apartment for that month of recuperation, I was thrown into a kind of hermetic life of reading. My re-immersion cast me backwards in time and served to buttress my conviction that leaving THRINTEL was the very right path for me to follow. My reading triggered my dormant thinking about Sartre, Camus, Existentialism, all that, but I quickly realized that they were my past and I needed to look to my present and even my future. On that first trip out of my apartment, on that foray to the Georgetown University library, scanning the shelves in the Philosophy section, I came upon a book titled *Simulacra and Simulation* that struck me as something I might be interested in. It was written by another French-man, Jean Baudrillard, which was a good recommendation for me. It was dumb luck, I think, that I picked it up and checked it out. Little did I know that as I read it, this Baudrillard guy's vision of the modern world of the nineties confirmed some of the doubts I harbored about the upcoming twenty-first century. During my years at THRINTEL, as computers became more the standard of contemporary life rather than the anomaly, I had begun to see the downside of the cyberworld. Baudrillard saw how at the end of the twentieth century nothing any longer was real, that all was just simulations passing themselves off as reality. After nine years working at THRINTEL, his thoughts on the contemporary world really struck a chord with me. In a sense he had made a logical move from my familiar Existentialism. He saw that the new technology of the computer was on the verge of taking over the world just as the Nazi collectivism and the technological warfare of World War II had back in the forties when Existentialism was formu-lated as an antidote to those dehumanizing forces. I realized that the whole computer dominated universe had imposed an almost robotic essence upon me and it had taken a bullet to bring me back to life.

One other thing that my bullet had brought me back to was my Catholicism. I hadn't been a good practicing Catholic for a long time. Oh, I went to Mass with Grace every once in a while, maybe once a month when she dragged me out, certainly on holidays like Christmas or the anniversary of Nicole's death, but my heart, or soul, whichever, wasn't really in it. But after I was ambulatory again, one Sunday I took myself to Mass without Grace. Maybe it was a renewed sense of my own mortality that did it. Or maybe it was guilt that I had drifted away from something that had been a formative part of my identity which I was re-discovering. Or maybe it was something as simple as wanting to get out on a Sunday morning and be with other people in familiar sur-roundings and not be alone. Who knows? But when I got in the church and the old familiar ritual started unfolding before me, I realized why I was there. It was time for my body and blood to transubstantiate once again. Actually, it was kind of funny, really rather ironic, that this time my major life changing was actually precipitated by the shedding of my own blood.

And so, I healed up and retreated into a reading retirement, and was perfectly happy out of the mainstream of American life. Y2K came and went without even a flicker of concern on the part of the world's computers. They handled Y2K's minor annoyance with aplomb. The world didn't end, the clocks didn't stop, the computers hardly even blinked.

As I said, I was perfectly happy, and then Grace walked in on my increasingly contemplative life and dropped her bomb.

G: Dad, I'm going to get married. I'm going to marry Martin. He asked me yesterday and I said yes.

Me:_____.

I literally had no response. I couldn't think of anything to say. What she announced caught me completely off guard like walking into a clear glass door that you thought was open. One minute I was talking to my daughter, the most important person in my life, and the next minute—BAM! I was stunned, unable to even speak, shaken with incomprehension, standing there feeling like a complete fool. When I finally found my voice, I still didn't know what to say.

Me: He? Who is he? This Martin.

It was the best I could come up with. That is how at sea I was. It was, of course, the worst response I could have made. What kind of a father has no idea whatsoever who the boy that has just asked his daughter to marry him is?

G: It's Martin, you silly. I've been dating him for more than a year.

Me: Yes, Martin, of course. The tall one.

G: OK. Yes, sort of tall.

Grace was getting suspicious that I really had no clue who we were talking about and she was right. I still couldn't picture this Martin. I had gone out to dinner with Grace and a couple of her boyfriends over the last few years, but none of them had made enough of an impression on me to remember their names much less tell them apart. So much for the magical powers of Eidetic Memory.

But as I thought more about it I realized that this memory lapse was probably much more complicated. I had probably intentionally blocked out the existence of Grace's boyfriends due to a subconscious terror of losing her, of some other man being in her life and coming between me and her. Like another glass door hitting me in the face, I suddenly realized that I still thought of my Grace as that little girl back in the farmyard in Indiana with me and Nicole. I panicked. Nicole was gone forever. And now I feared that Grace would be gone from me as well. It was all just another indication that I was deeply mired in the past and badly needed to move on.

Grace was looking at me funny as these thoughts roiled around in my mind. She was probably trying to understand why I was so thunderstruck. Maybe she was anxious about what a strange reaction her news, her presumed joyous news, was occasioning in me. I'm sure my wide-eyed, open-mouthed, speechless reaction had given me utterly away. She tried to bring us both back to reality.

G: Martin wanted to ask you first, but you were sick in bed and we wanted to get married as soon as we could because we've got graduation coming up.

Me: What's he graduating in? (I must confess that I was still trying to place this Martin fellow)

G: He's getting an MBA and he already has a job here in Washington. And I think the Smithsonian is going to offer me a full-time position when I graduate.

Getting married, graduating with advanced degrees, holding jobs, it was all crashing down on me much too fast. But I also quickly realized that I was totally failing Grace. I was ruining her ecstatic news. I was short-circuiting her joy. In no way was I reacting the way that a good father should to his daughter's exciting sharing of perhaps the most momentous decision of her young maturity. She so wanted me to be happy for her and this Martin person. I suddenly realized that I had better get with the program really quick or I might lose her forever.

Me: Oh Grace, that's fantastic, wonderful, I'm so happy for you. Wow!

Even as I uttered the words, I realized that I was reading a total lie from the centuries-old script that every other father of a beloved daughter had read from going back to the inception of the other clichés of bended knees and engagement rings and breathless "will you marry me's," I said it, but I didn't mean it, but it was exactly what Grace wanted to hear.

G: Oh Dad, we're going to do it in the summer after our graduation. I can't wait.

I immediately computed my time left with her. All of these years it had just been me and her. We had gone through so much together, tragedies and triumphs, the two of us against the world. And now along comes some faceless guy named Martin and ruins it all for me. But even as that thought worked its resentful way across my mind, I realized the clear and present flaw in my whole reaction. "Ruin it all for me" echoed in my consciousness. IAAM – "It's all about Mike!" I was making this whole turn of events about ME and it was really about HER. Grace was in love; Grace was all grown up; Grace was asserting her freedom and stepping out into the next phase of her life; Grace was breaking away and the major part of her emancipation was leaving me behind. The words of my co-conspirator, Sartre, echoed in my inner ear. I wanted to continue to impose my essence upon her existence. And those times had just come abruptly to an end.

She waved her ring finger at me and the jewel on it flashed in the sun like a period on a sentence. She was going to get married. It was a *fait accompli*. Not a thing I could do about it. No choice for me. I had to swallow that bitter pill, cut my losses, try to salvage something, anything out of the whole situation.

Me: Grace honey, I'm so happy for you. It's a beautiful ring. I can't wait to meet your fiancé.

As soon as the words left my mouth, I knew that they were wrong.

G: Oh Dad, you've met Martin. We went to dinner a couple of months ago before you got laid up.

Me: Of course we did. I didn't mean "meet." I meant I was eager to see him again, congratulate him on marrying the most wonderful girl in the world.

It was a pretty good save.

After Grace left and I sat there alone thinking about it, I realized just what my almost total immersion in building and running THRINTEL had robbed me of in the last nine years. Good lord, Grace was eighteen when we came back from Paris and now she was twenty-seven and about to be married and be gone from me forever (and with some guy named Martin who I couldn't even place). Those years had all flown by us so fast and my job (and her studies) had robbed us of so much time together, time that I longed to have back as I sat there alone feeling sorry for myself when I should have been feeling happy for my daughter.

I took then both out for dinner a couple of days later, for two reasons. Of course, to celebrate complete with chocolate mousse and French Champagne, to congratulate them and offer all my blessings. But mostly I wanted to get a look at this Martin, to see if I could recognize him. Turns out he seemed a really nice, clean-cut young man and it was clear right off that he adored Grace (as well he should!). He even started off our dinner once we were seated in the restaurant with what seemed a heartfelt apology.

Martin: Mr. Edwards, I really meant to meet with you and ask for Grace's hand but when I had bought the ring and was ready to give it to her she told me that you were sick in bed and it wasn't a good time and besides I wanted to surprise her though I'm pretty sure she suspected and I knew we both didn't want to wait and we wanted to get married right after graduation and so I went and asked her.

He delivered that apology all in one sentence and probably in one breath. Actually I found his breathless race to conclusion quite convincing.

G: Oh dad (Grace gushed and bragged), it was so romantic. I was working in the portrait gallery in the museum right under a portrait of Franklin and Eleanor Roosevelt. He walked right up to me and went down on one knee and held out the ring and asked me. Of course, I said yes right away. There were some other people in the gallery. They clapped for us. Oh, it was so cool.

As it turns out Martin was two years younger than Grace and was getting an MBA at Georgetown. He had already lined up a job with a Washington investment bank. Grace was also ready to graduate with her Ph.D. in Art History. As I listened to them over dinner as they unfurled their plans for their future to me, I thought *wow, these two are ready and eager to take on the world.* What continued to stab at the back of my mind was that those plans had very little to do with me. But I had already resigned myself to the reality that Grace's (and her soon-to-be husband's) plans really didn't include me. What did include me, unfortunately, was a whole other set of plans, plans from planning hell, THE WEDDING!

After a wonderful dinner and rich dessert plus a bottle of Champagne, as we were sipping Irish Coffees in a state of bloated tipsy receptiveness, they mentioned the tentative date of their wedding. That was when I blundered blindly into yet another fatal mistake. I told them that I would pay for their wedding. Even as I made the offer I could see their eyes spark with both appreciation and greed. I didn't realize it at all, but I think they were actually aware that I had just saved them thousands of dollars in wedding debt. What did I know about weddings? Nicole and I had gotten married by a priest in a small country church in Indiana with Grace already on the way. What I didn't realize was that by offering to pay for their wedding Grace and Martin decided that I had to be included in all of the logistical decisions that accompanied a twenty-first-century version of wedding spectacle. Oh, I had no problem with the money. I had plenty of that. It was their gratefulness and their feeling that I should be consulted on every wedding detail that was the problem. Never had I so wished that Nicole was still here with us. The Card Shop. Save Your Date cards (whatever they were). Invitations. Stationary colors and textures. The wedding dress. The church. The music. The reception. The food. The reception music. Why did they feel that they had to solicit my opinion on everything? I wanted to run away to somewhere safe where they couldn't corner me and ask me what color flowers should make up the centerpieces on the tables or what font should be used for the place cards. Just shoot me!

The wedding was supposed to be a small affair. Martin was an only child and, of course, Grace and I only had each other. His parents were coming down from Connecticut for it. I invited Lenny and Tommy from THRINTEL. Nevertheless, some fifty invitations went out, mostly Grace's and Martin's friends from Georgetown. One of Grace's girlfriends from her *ecole* in Paris even flew in. It actually turned into a nice medium-sized party. Both Martin and Grace were Catholic, his mother evidently devoutly so, so they were definitely committed to a Catholic church wedding. Actually, they had met in church. Well not exactly in the church, but at some church function at the Newman Center on the Georgetown campus, probably a pancake breakfast or a Food Finders fund-raising walk. The date for the wedding seemed like it was rushing at us, bearing down on us like some unavoidable reality. I actually thought about asking Grace if she wanted to take a long weekend, just the two of us, and fly to Paris. I guess I wanted one more walk along the Seine with her, one more visit to the Musee D'Orsay where her life-long love for art had been born, one more climb up to Sacre Coeur and Montmartre, one more visit to her young life when it was just the two of us trying to recover from Nicole's death, looking for ourselves, her growing up, me running away. But I knew that wasn't going to happen so I never even brought the idea up. You can't recapture the past and you certainly can't use the past as some sort of reassurance that the future could possibly be endured without the life, the people, who were gone.

Giving Grace away was perhaps the hardest thing I had ever had to do. Walking her down that aisle I felt like a condemned man being led to the electric chair. Handing her over to Martin was like losing Nicole all over again. With each step down that aisle toward the black tuxedoed line of groomsmen and the brightly colored trail of bridesmaids flanking the smiling priest and his attending altar boys, I felt my eyes starting to well up, my throat tightening, my elbow shaking against Grace's steadying hand. Grace felt it too. "Daddy, it's OK. I love you," she whispered. I managed to hand her over to Martin. I even shook his hand totally unconvincingly. Then I retreated to the pew and it was over in so many ways.

Catholic weddings and the full Mass that accompanies them can be interminable things, especially if all you want to do is escape the whole situation. As the Mass unfolded and I sat and stood and knelt according to rote, all I wanted to do was run, get away from it all, escape the ritual simulacra that everyone in the church was just mindlessly following along. But then, there it was, the old familiar transubstantiation poem again, the words, the idea, that always caught my attention. Every time I heard its words intoned by the priest, every time the raising of the host and the chalice popped up in my line of sight, every time the body and blood underwent their sea change right before my eyes, it always made me think of my own predicament, my own potential for change, made me wonder if there were any possibilities left for my own battered body and blood. That point in the wedding mass renewed my consciousness of my own theory of secular transubstantiation which I had nurtured philosophically over so many years. It triggered a flicker of hopefulness, as had happened so many times before in my life, that perhaps a new existence, another chapter, was out there waiting for me, waiting to raise me, phoenix-like, out of the ruins of my world as it had been and into a brand new, brave new, world that I hadn't even yet imagined.

As I write about all of this now from my distanced perspective, I realize that Grace's marriage was just another signal that time was starting to close on me like a runner coming up from behind in a distance race that I was doomed to lose. But what I also sensed back there at Grace's wedding was that my competitive nature was kicking in, that I wasn't quite ready to lose the race just yet.

I started writing this book from a vantage of sixty some years going all the way back to 1962, but now it is 2019 and I'm writing about events that happened only about fifteen years ago. I guess that signals that now not only have I pretty much run out of time, but I'm rapidly running out of material for this book as well. But not so fast reader people. Back then, that wedding reminded me that transubstantiation was not just a ritual, a moment in the Catholic Mass, a prayer, but

rather was an invocation of magic, a poem, an idea that could be embodied in all of our lives. One clean, well-lit evening in a café back
there in Paris so long ago talking to Wendy I remember quoting a line
I had run into while I was reading F. Scott Fitzgerald. He wrote that
our lives are but "one-act plays and we need to live them to the fullest"
(or something like that). But he was wrong. Many lives are two, three,
five, seven-act plays. Some, certainly not all, possess the capability of
constantly reinventing themselves, secularly transubstantiating. Who
knows, as I knelt there at Grace's wedding watching the bread and wine
change to body and blood right before my eyes, maybe I was just kidding myself, but suddenly I felt this surge of expectation, of wondering
just what the future held in store for me.

  After the wedding, I retreated back to my condo and my books.
I had given Grace and Martin a honeymoon in Paris and after their
graduations and the wedding they took it. After all, Paris is where
Grace and I had gone to try to find our new life after we lost Nicole.
When they got back they were literally aglow with all the excitement
that had been packed into their magical summer. As for me, my life
drifted into a kind of relaxed limbo of reading, *flaneur* walks around
Washington, coffee in coffee shops along my way. But suddenly all of
that disengaged, uninvolved, irresponsive, meaninglessness of retirement was shattered by 9-11. Mine, and everyone in America's, complacency was shaken to the core. Our supposedly safe world was exploded
in a firestorm of embedded airplanes and toppled skyscrapers. Even the
pentagon near me in Washington was hit. On 9-13, while the rubble
was still being sifted, Lenny came back at me.

  L: Mikey, you need to come back to THRINTEL. We're at war
now. We've got to find Osama Bin Laden and take out Al-Queda. We
need you back to coordinate this operation. Our government friends
have given us *carte blanche* to find that bastard and shut him and his
terrorist army down.

  That did it for me. If I ever needed a signal that it was time to
transubstantiate into a new life that was it. Everything about my life
in Washington, hell in America, just added up to disaster existentially.
For the first time over the course of my whole old life I resisted Lenny's
temptations. On 9-14, I turned the key in my condo door and ran. But
where to?

CHAPTER 11: A SAFE HAVEN

In the cab on the way to Reagan International Airport, I still didn't know where I was going to run to or whether mine was going to be a permanent retreat or rather just a temporary sabbatical from my old life until things cooled down and I could come back. I also hadn't decided how I was going to handle the problem of telling Grace and Martin that I was going on the run, "in the wind" so to speak. I got lucky. The first thing I did when I got to the airport was call them. And I got their answering machine which was perfect. I didn't have to explain myself to them at all.

Me: Hi guys, just wanted you to know that I'm going on vacation for a while. Talk to you later.

After getting that phone call out of the way so easily, I sat down in front of a large departures board and tried to figure out where I wanted to go, plot my escape route. I knew I couldn't go back to Indiana. There was nothing there for me but too many good and bad memories. Paris wasn't an option either. Too many good memories that I didn't want to spoil. What was coming upon me as I sat there was this strong sense that I shouldn't retreat into any of my old lives. That was why I was leaving Washington in the first place. Going backwards would defeat my whole purpose. In contrast, I had this vague sense that wherever I went it had to be somewhere new where once again I could completely start over from scratch, anonymously, undetected. I mean, I was already pretty much alone in Washington, being an invisible man somewhere out of the way wouldn't be that much of a leap. However, I also was pretty certain that Lenny had all the tools he needed to track me, would always know where I was if he wanted to swoop back in and prey on my life once again. But I also knew that if I got in any kind of trouble that I couldn't handle that Lenny would be there for me, that I could "call in the cavalry" so to speak. But I also rationalized that I was presenting myself with a valuable opportunity. *It is the 21ˢᵗ Century* I reasoned. *A brave new world. Sure, it has its problems: 9-11, terrorism, all that. But I am sixty years old and I'm a long way from giving up on life.*

Actually, sitting there on that bench staring at the departures board,

I felt like smacking myself on the side of the head. *Sixty years old you dunce, and you still haven't engaged with who you are and what you really want out of your life.* That was my dilemma, cluelessness, anti-existential cluelessness. If I had possessed a dart at that moment, I could have pegged it at that departures board and let it make up my mind for me. Instead my eyes scrolled down to the "Qs" (which had always been one of my favorite letters) and I got up, walked to the desk, and bought a one-way ticket to Quebec. I'd never been there. In fact, I'd never ever even been to Canada. So it seemed like a new place that offered me a chance to start over.

Unfortunately, when I got to Quebec, after a week of wandering around there, I couldn't help but feel that it was too much like Paris to work for me. London was my next stop. Really crowded. Tourists everywhere, all speaking English, glutted with Americans. I was looking for somewhere unfamiliar, quiet, safe, and that sure wasn't London. I didn't even last a week there. You've heard about the Wandering Jew? Well I guess I was the Wandering Catholic. Maybe it was my equally vague sense of Catholicism, or, even more farfetched, maybe some spiritual force out there that planted a transubstantial whisper in my consciousness. "Go west young man" somebody once said long ago. I decided to flee London and see if Ireland might work for me. Dublin was terrible. A dirty industrial city on a fetid river whose greatest accomplishment was the invention due to a brewer's mistake of a black beer having the consistency of motor oil. I passed through Dublin like a fugitive and fled further west by train. At this point I was actually considering going all the way west back to America since my escape route was proving such a bust. But my train stopped in the town of Galway on the west coast of Ireland and my transubstantiative quest took a turn for the better. Of course, Miss Maeve Gallagher had a lot to do with that. But then, I am getting way ahead of myself again.

Galway in 2002 was really a small university town not yet corrupted by the ravenous economy boom being fed by American technology that came to be known as the "Celtic Tiger." Where that name came from I have no idea, but it had totally changed the makeup of much of that small country. In the mid-nineties, Ireland had been an economic disaster. Jobs were disappearing. Education was limited to the very rich. The government had no money to prop up the hemorrhaging economy. But then, as the twenty-first century bore down, American white knights, heavily armed by the computer boom in the US, rode in in the form of extensive technology investment in Irish manufacturing. Read computer chip factories. Suddenly there were jobs for everyone. Construction, both industrial and residential, boomed. Wisely the government pumped some of this new found wealth into education for its young people to go to college. Almost overnight immigration from Ireland (mostly to the US) turned into emigration into Ireland (mostly from third world countries). The young stopped fleeing the country and the disenfranchised started coming in. But when I got there in 2002 Galway hadn't yet been changed by the roaring "Celtic Tiger."

I was only there a few days when I realized that Galway could suit me really well. Immediately two things convinced me. Galway was a peaceful place and the people there, the Galwegians (what a funny name—like something out of a sci-fi movie or *Lord of the Rings)*, really liked Americans. They had actually re-named their town square from Eyre Square to Kennedy Square in honor of our President who had spoken there back in the early sixties. Ronald Reagan too had spoken at University College in 1983 and used his famous Irish charm to win over the whole population. And their most recent American hero (somewhat surprising in such a strongly Catholic country considering his sexual history) was Bill Clinton who had brokered the Irish Peace Accord, known as the Good Friday Agreement, in 1998. Good lord, when I got to Galway even the IRA was at peace! And I have to say that it even made someone as cynical as me proud that an American President had been a major factor in bringing peace to what had been one of the most violent and contentious countries in the world. My very first day, just off the train, the publican in the first pub I stepped into, as he was pouring my beer, said" "You're a Yank aren't ye? You Yanks are alright with us." He didn't buy me my pint, but the sentiment impressed me nonetheless.

And so, I decided to settle, at least for a while, in Galway. The next day I found myself a cheap, one-room, immaculate flat on the second floor above another pub overlooking the broad walkway of Shop Street, the main commercial thoroughfare of Galway. Shop Street was, and I'm sure still is, the very hub of Galway life. It runs in a straight line from Kennedy nee Eyre Square all the way to the bend of the River Corrib. That pristine river, before it meanders out into the famous Galway Bay of sentimental song and the Atlantic Ocean, flows right through the center of Galway City. Unlike the scum-coated Liffey in Dublin, I really enjoyed walking along the sparkling Corrib. It was so clean that fly-fishermen in hip boots stood right in the middle and caught pink salmon the size of hurling sticks. But back to my base of operations on Shop Street. The first day that I walked the whole street I counted seventeen pubs. There were probably more on the side streets feeding in but I didn't get to them that first day. After that it took me a good two weeks to explore all of Shop Street and, as I did, almost every store clerk, every bartender, every pensioner sitting at a street side table gave me a smile and a wave. It was pretty much a *flaneur's* utopia. As I walked, I also realized that Galway was a city of churches, most of them Catholic, some of them having a remarkable history. The Galway Cathedral had at one time been the site of the city prison. Another church had been badly defaced and turned into a stable for his men and horses when Cromwell had invaded Ireland.

At that time, when I landed in Galway, I didn't really acknowledge it but I was not just wandering around from country to country. I was also circling around and around this existential idea of secular transubstantiation that I had started toying with as far back as my flight out of Berkeley in the late seventies. Perhaps that was another reason I felt immediately comfortable in Galway. It wasn't just the peace of the place, but I liked the unashamed Catholicism of the place. I was looking for something to believe in and these Galway people (sorry, but I just can't call them "Galwegians") were a whole city of believers. Set down in this Catholic country in this Catholic city, sitting in a coffee shop watching most of Galway's population file in and out of Catholic Churches on Sunday mornings, I finally decided "oh what the hell" and started going to Mass again.

I tried Sunday Masses to begin with, but they were always pretty crowded and pretty fervent, zealous. But I went to a couple of weekday Masses and really liked them much better. They were short and to the point with terse, straight-shooting sermons that reminded me of Hemingway sentences. In fact, I was sitting in the cathedral on a rather gloomy Wednesday when the priest quoted a Joyce Kilmer poem about that American Catholic's love for Ireland:

Romantic Ireland is not old.
For years untold her youth will shine.
Her heart is fed on Heaven's bread,
The blood of martyrs is her wine.

There it was again. The bread and wine, the body and the blood. Each time I went to one of those weekday Masses, I would wait with my own version of fervent expectation to hear those magic words of Christ's poem of transubstantiation and to see the symbolic raising of the host and the chalice. It was truly a magical moment and there in Catholic Galway I became sort of lightly addicted to it. I only went to one of those brief weekday masses about once a week, if that. But, when I went, I always waited in expectation for that particular moment, those words, that simulacra of change. It was in Galway that I became convinced that my own life was a flesh and blood motif of ongoing transubstantiation. My own body and blood seemed to be shapeshifting at a rather alarming rate. I sensed that Galway had a new identity in store for me, just waiting to happen.

I had been in Galway for about five months when the Galway Arts Festival for 2002 got underway. It's a yearly two-week long *ménage* of plays, dance productions, live music of every genre, operas, street spectacle, visual arts, lectures, an outpouring of artistic zeal. Talk about fervent! I didn't know anything about it that first year, but all of the chatter both in the pubs and on my brand-new Euro-data'd lap-top were talking the Festival up as the best thing since St. Patrick and Michael Collins. "The Festival opens with the parade," my bartender in *Neachtain's* insisted, "do not miss it." So, on a warm but cloudy July evening I joined the crowd at the head of Shop Street waiting for the Arts Festival Parade to step off. And quite a Parade it was. A regimental band with three bearded drum majors in kilts wielding long batons with round ornamental heads led it off. The band was followed by a long, rolling, rainbow-colored dragon that would put any Chinese competition to shame. The dragon was followed by colorfully frock-coated, high-hatted, face-painted visions on stilts towering above the crowd and navigating the cobbled-stoned streets with the adeptness of ballet dancers. Then came the acrobats and the jugglers and the clowns and the fire dancers and the flag wavers and the baton twirlers and the mimes and the slithering bouncing leaping tumbling dancing elaborately costumed, face-painted, crazily-behatted, army of Dionysian, Mardi-Grasian, Carnivalian, Mummerian, marchers. Next came the mythic characters: Aengus the god of love and poetry, Cliodhma queen of the Banshees, Queen Mav, Grace O'Malley the Pirate Queen (lots of queens), Gaillinch the Goddess of the river for whom the city of Galway is named, all mixed in with an army of leprechauns and faeries and the ghosts of drowned fishermen. Believe me, I didn't know about any of these figures but in answer to my question a chap next to me as we marched gave me a running commentary on them. He also told me to follow all along with the parade to the huge bonfire at the terminus. It was the St. Patrick's Day, the Thanksgiving Day, the Christmas Parade all rolled into one. As you can probably tell from my description, I was really quite impressed. I fell in with the crowds along the streets following the revelers and really getting into the exhilaration, the unbridled exuberance of the Parade. But then, to everyone's chagrin, the heavens opened up and the thousands of revelers were treated to a quiet typical Galway downpour.

My first thought was to get undercover and keep myself dry since I didn't have an umbrella. So I ducked into the doorway of a shuttered shop. My second thought was of the threat this rain posed for the great bonfire at the end of the Parade. I thought about how appropriate that bonfire probably was, reminiscent of some old Druidic Irish tradition. As I stood in the shadows looking out at the rain, it was getting dark and the Parade was forging ahead despite the soaking it was receiving. I was sure that all the revelers were supremely confident that it would stop raining by the time they reached the bonfire. These pelting rains tended to show up in Galway almost every day, but they didn't last very long. Anyway, the Parade marched resolutely on, but I didn't. Only moments after I ducked into the shelter of that doorway I was joined by another person, clad in a rather bulky Macintosh and wearing a floppy rain hat. "Beastly Galway rain," a laughing woman's voice declared from out from under the hat when she noticed me lurking in the shadows. It was a rather congenial way of breaking the ice and it brought a quick smile to my face as she flipped up the wide bill of her rain hat and smiled back at me.

Me: Yes. It certainly is.

She: Too bad for the parade. Let's hope this stops soon.

Me: Yes, definitely.

She You're a Yank.

Me: Yes, I am.

She: Good to that. I'm glad to see that you are at our Parade. It is one of the real highlights of Galway's year.

To this point in our conversation I had responded more or less like an inarticulate moron whose vocabulary consisted of no more than three "yeses" and a "definitely." Nonetheless the woman seemed nonplused as she took off her rain hat and shook the water off of it. Then, looking back at me, was a quite attractive woman of about my own age, sixtyish perhaps, with what in the gathering darkness looked to be a ready smile.

She: Are you in from America for the Arts Festival?

She didn't seem the least bit timid about starting up a conversation with a complete stranger in a dark doorway in a rainstorm. So, I followed her lead and found my voice.

Me: No. Not at all. I've been in Galway for this whole year. Renting a flat in Shop Street.

She: Really. Brilliant. You must enjoy it here.

Me: Yes. I really do.

She: So, what do you do?

Me: Well, that's a good question. Walk mostly. Go to the pubs. Read a lot.

She: So nothing.

Me: Pretty much. I'm retired.

She: What I really meant was what is your occupation, your work, your job. But obviously you no longer have one so that is a perfectly silly question. Sorry about that.

Me: No. Not at all. It's the kind of thing you ask of a perfect stranger now isn't it. My name is Michael Edwards. Yours?

She: Maeve Gallagher.

I have to say that I really liked the lilt in her voice from the first time she opened her mouth. She pronounced her name "Gallahheer" leaving out the hard "ag" that we would grunt in the States. The rain had suddenly let up and the moon was actually out from the clouds and casting a gentle silver light over the shiny wet streets. The parade had passed us by and our meeting in the doorway seemed to be over. But this Maeve person didn't seem to want our conversation to end.

M: Are you coming along to the bonfire, Michael?

She really caught me off guard, addressing me directly by name like that when she had only met me mere minutes past. And no one ever called me "Michael." In America it was always "Mike." Lenny always called me "Mikey." I have to say that I really liked her "Michael," its congenial formality, its full-length intimacy.

Me: Yes, I'd like that. Will you show me the way?

M: Oh, we'll probably catch up with the Parade before they get there.

Me: That rain won't spoil it, will it?

M: Oh no, lord no. When they light it, it will stretch all the way to the sky. It will light up the field as if it was day. And there will be music and dancing. The best craic of the whole summer.

Me: It sounds like a pagan revelry, quite a party.

M: Oh, it is. It's our celebration of the Old Ireland, the tribal Ireland that Galway once was.

I have to say that she really caught me up in her enthusiasm. There was just something about her that attracted me. She seemed like someone that was worth spending time with, smart, easy to talk to, enthusiastic. Sixty years old perhaps, but full of life, outgoing. I'd only known her for about a half an hour and yet I really felt very comfortable with her. Actually, felt, as we walked, to be lucky to be in her company.

M: So you are a reader you said.

Me: Yes, it is my greatest pleasure and time-filler these days.

M: How long have you been retired?

Me: Just this year.

M: What sorts of things do you read?

Me: Anything and everything that comes to hand and catches my eye really.

I didn't spring my Eidetic Memory on her right then. That would have been way to crude. I definitely felt it better to keep my secret powers to myself in case she might think me some delusional superhero wannabe like a kid in Batman or Spiderman costume at Halloween.

M: Really: Well you will need to visit my bookstore someday soon.

Me: You own a bookstore!

The whole situation was getting to be too good to be true.

M: I certainly do. You must stop in sometime. It's on Abbeygate Street just off of Shop Street. Probably quite close to your flat, though rather tucked away out of the bustle.

And she handed me her card.

I still sort of marvel at how it happened, me falling in love with Maeve. It had been years, ever since Wendy, since I had been interested an any woman. After Nicole, and even Wendy, I just never seemed to encounter any woman who matched up. But this Maeve person, in a gentle, open, outgoing, just really friendly way, had somehow gotten into my head. That night at the bonfire she had drifted off to join some friends, but before she left, I told her that I looked forward to exploring her book shop. She just smiled, sort of enigmatically, and waved as she went. She was probably thinking *Well I'll never see him again.* The whole rest of the weekend she kept popping up in my mind until I realized that she held some sort of different kind of attraction for me. I think it might have been that she was just so easy to talk to. Who knows, maybe it was as simple as the books that we shared. By Monday I was champing to find her bookstore. I held off until afternoon, not wanting to seem too eager (or even creepy), but when I walked through the door and Maeve got up from her desk to greet me, she was a true revelation. I had only seen her in the shadows the night of the parade She had been my "dark lady" so to speak all weekend. But here, in the daylight of her sun-splattered shop, she radiated a beauty in the way that only a 60-year-old woman of grace and substance can. Maybe, no probably, no certainly, now that I remember it, it was her smile that struck that small spark of love within me there at the very beginning before I even got to really know her.

There was just a touch of gray in her hair and a few tiny wrinkles around her eyes, but her face was striking in a way that I had never imagined was beautiful before in any other woman. It was her smile. When she smiled her whole face went open and welcoming, beckoning you in. After she greeted me and we shook hands, her mouth drifted into a small grin that had a quality of bemusement or irony about it as if she knew exactly what I was up to and was amused by my presence in her bookish world. From that first moment that we actually met in the light of day, I have since enjoyed tracking the oh-so-subtle shifts in her enigmatically expressive face.

(I really need to digress here a moment and confess that women, even Nicole, then Wendy, recently Grace, have always been a complete mystery to me—and now Maeve. Hell, I wouldn't be surprised if I didn't speak for all men. In fact, I'm pretty sure that any man who thinks he knows what a woman is thinking or is up to is severely deluded.)

But back to Maeve's face. Oh, she was beautiful alright, but not in the deceptively innocent, clear-eyed, clean-skinned way that younger women can be. Rather, as evidenced by small subtle shifts in her face, she was always thinking, wondering, speculating, evaluating, deciding. In other words, her face radiated a kind of quiet intelligence that constantly made me wonder what she was thinking, where I stood in her estimation:

What does she think of me?
Does she like what I am saying.?
Am I pleasing her?
Is she laughing at me? With me?
Agreeing with me?
Tolerating me?
Liking me?

All of those thoughts danced in my mind with just the simple shift of her mouth from the radiant smile to the enigmatic grin, from the total openness to tight-lipped irony. Maybe that was it? She was this woman of mystery to me. A gentle *femme fatale*. And I was trying to solve her.

And then there were her eyes. Bright (quite appropriate since she was Irish) green! Not a jealous green, or an aging green, but a verdant green, the kind of green that surprises you when through your airplane window you first spot the shore of Ireland as you are heading for a landing at Shannon. And wide! Looking right at me, her eyes, unblinking, spoke torrents:

I'm totally taking you in, all that you are, you can't hide from me, I know what you are thinking, and I understand you. I can see your emotions, your needs, your desires, your secrets that you are longing to express.

Her eyes could be totally hypnotic.

That was it for me. There, at the beginning, she totally unmanned me. Right then I already knew that Maeve was different from any woman I had ever encountered before, had an attraction for me that was new and irresistible. Victoria had been an evil queen. Nicole had been the warm and innocent love of my life. Wendy had been my great adventure, alive and exciting and courageous. But Maeve was different from all of those. More experienced and analytic than Nicole. Less romantic and driven than Wendy. More mature in more ways than just age. As I wrote before, going all the way back to that first night at the Parade, I was comfortable with her. Unpressured. She radiated peace, and peace was what I needed at that time in my life. My need for peace was why I had once again run away from America. Peace was why I had settled in Galway. I had been at war for a long time. I'd like to think that she understood what I needed, what I was looking for, and that was why we hit it off right away.

Her smile, her grin, her eyes, her mystery, her peace. All of that was my first impression, my mind racing in the futile chase after her essence, her inner self. It was all my attempt to understand my attraction to this woman my age in this foreign land in this friendly world. But lest you think that Maeve is just a creation of my overactive imagination, be not deceived. In the light of day that afternoon in her shop she was every bit the flesh and blood woman that Nicole and Wendy or even the wicked Victoria had been. Although I must confess that at that particular point in time, I was not yet really sexually attracted to her. Not to say that I didn't notice that she was tall and slender in a figure nicely tucked into a pair of rather tight jeans ending in a pair of little grey ankle boots of the kind that elves might wear, sans the upturned toes. Oh yes, one other thing. Maeve, as it turned out, was a devout Catholic. When I found this out, I was already pretty much in her clutches. Who knows, not only did I fall in love with her peace, but perhaps I also saw in her my salvation.

Maeve's bookstore was a bookstore in the narrowest sense of the word. It was all books, very little else—a desk with a cash register, two straight-backed chairs. As retail shops go, it was probably at least three centuries past its prime and behind its times. If I were to try to find words to describe the shop's identity, they would be "claustrophobic," or perhaps "airless," or, maybe better, "cave-like," or "dust-bound," or certainly "suffocating," It was simply books and shelves, rough floor-to-ceiling bookcases, on a worn wooden floor, under a low dusky beamed ceiling. It was dimly lit by an inadequate chandelier in the shallow front room just inside the door plus bare bulbs hanging from the ceiling at irregular intervals down the narrow aisles. The front façade of the shop consisted of two rather large glass windows opening on the street. These windows were spotlessly clean (as if she washed them every morning) and might have admitted in a good deal of light if not for more shelves of books with their titled spines facing the street which blocked out much of any available sunshine. In other words, it was a pretty dreary and gloomy place. Maeve, with her ready smile, was the only real beacon of light within.

When I first entered the bookstore, Maeve was sitting on a straight-backed chair at the desk. On the desk sat a cash register that would have been old in the 1950's. She greeted me with her best welcoming smile: "Why hello. You're the Yank from the Parade. I'm glad you stopped by." She immediately got up and extended her hand. I gave it a gentle shake and swiveling my head about 180 degrees took in the layout of the shop. The shelves reached back into the depths of the store like the walls of the catacombs. My face must have given away my first impression of surprised disappointment because she immediately changed the unspoken subject.

M: As you can see, we have a really large selection of books, certainly the largest in Galway. Larger than the public library even.

Me: Wow. Yes. I can see that.

I tried to dispel my initial unimpressed reaction with a burst of unfelt enthusiasm.

M: Everyone who comes in is free to browse as much as they want. I'm sure you'll find something that you will want to read.

Me: Yes. I'm sure I will.

I think my clumsy reaction had put her off, but she hid it well. Nonetheless, a rather awkward moment came down like a curtain between us. I decided to break the brief silence with a somewhat confessional lie.

Me: Since I've been in Galway this year, I've been reading the few books that I brought with me and books I've bought at Easton's, but their offerings are pretty slim and pretty much just best-sellers from England published in the last couple of years.

M: Yes. I know. They're not really a bookstore. They're more of a card shop and souvenir emporium. Their shelves are stocked with more gimcracks than books. The real readers in Galway come here.

When she said that, my body betrayed me once again as it turned ever so slightly to affirm the emptiness of the shop. If this was the store of choice for Galway's "real readers" none of them were anywhere in evidence in her store this afternoon.

Me: Oh, I'm sure I'll find something I'll want, probably lots of good titles. I can't wait to start browsing.

At that she smiled warmly, extended her hand back toward the dark depths of her cave and expressed her hospitality in the age-old words:

M: Oh, by all means, be my guest.

I wandered around in the dimness for about an hour, and even found two books that I had always wanted to read but had never seen in any of the bookstores back in D.C. *The Quiet American* by Graham Greene (a Catholic writer I had heard about) and an Irish novel that looked good, *The Railway Station Man* by Jennifer Johnston. In fact, I saw a lot more books in her dim and dusty aisles that I could have fun reading. Her bookshop was actually quite an eclectic collection of literary titles. I had always liked bookstores like this because they were a great place to exercise my Eidetic Memory. I, long before, had invented a game that I used as a way to give my memory a workout, take it out for a spin so to speak. I would go down an aisle of books in a bookstore and then stand back, close my eyes, and try to remember every title in the order I had seen them. It was a tremendously reassuring game. Every time I did it, I was reassured that my special powers were still intact. Some people lift weights, I walked aisles and memorized titles. The only difference is that the barbells can be set aside and forgotten. That wasn't the case with all my titles.

As I said before, I prowled her aisles for about an hour and in that whole time not another customer came in. Granted, it was getting late in the afternoon, but it seemed sort of sad to me that she had so little business. I took my two books up to her to pay.

As she rang me up, I looked around and knowing that there were no other customers for her to deal with I pulled up the only other chair in the shop and decided to engage her in conversation. I started out by telling her what a great collection she had and how now that I had discovered her shop I would be buying all of my books here in the future. I showed her the two books I had found and she nodded her approval:

M: Ah, Jennifer Johnston. You have good taste. She's one of our very best Irish writers. You are a serious reader indeed. You will enjoy both of those.

We talked for a while. I asked her how she had gotten into the bookstore business.

M: My family. My da owned this building. There are three flats upstairs. Our family lived in one of them and we rented the other two. I still live in the other one up there. My da started the bookshop business way back in the forties. I've worked in this shop off and on since I was about ten years old.

I loved the way she just opened up to me like that. I think she was happy to have someone to talk to on such a slow business afternoon. I didn't have to do a thing. Such a deal! She just kept rambling on.

M: Mom and Da finally passed away and my sister had long since married and moved over to England. So, the shop just became mine by default.

Even as she talked, new questions, almost all of which I judged too intrusive to ask her, kept popping up in my mind. We must have just talked about the bookstore, its evolution over the years, for about a half hour before I got up to pay and leave as it was nearing closing time.

Two days later I decided I had waited long enough to not appear creepy or stalkish and dropped back in professing to need more books, which was certainly true but was certainly not an emergency either. This time around, there still being no customers in evidence, instead of disappearing into the aisles first off, I pulled up a chair again and engaged her in conversation right away.

Me: What kinds of things do you really like to read? Do you have any favorite books?

I was an American after all and we are well known for being pushy and interrogatory so I didn't feel too bad about trying to talk to her about herself, trying to find out more about her. To my great surprise and even greater relief, she wasn't put off at all, wasn't the least bit hesitant about talking about herself. Of course, I didn't ask her some of the more personal questions that I wanted to ask her: *Have you been married? Are you in a relationship with anyone?*

OK, BUSTED! Yes, from the very first I was attracted to her. Early on I had started thinking about her as certainly a friend, but perhaps more. For the next couple of weeks, I dropped in on her during my walks in the city. Not every day. Maybe twice or even three times a week. About all we talked about was books. She was almost always reading when I would wander in. From all appearances she had plenty of time for it since there were rarely any customers in the shop when I dropped in. I really began looking forward to seeing her on a regular basis. And, as I walked toward her shop in the afternoons, they were not the only time I was thinking of her. She was so nice, so friendly, and I loved talking to her. But I also caught myself thinking about her at other times, while lying alone in bed at night staring at the ceiling, while sitting alone in a pub with happy couples chatting, flirting, laughing away around me. I realized that in no time at all Maeve and I had moved from being mere acquaintances to becoming friends. I wasn't just a visiting Yank, but a Galway citizen (notice I didn't write "Galwegian").

For weeks we had just been talking during business hours. Infrequently a customer might stop in and interrupt us, but not very often. Then, one afternoon when I came in late, near her closing time, I decided to up the ante just the slightest bit.

Me: Hi. I was reading and lost track of time. Meant to stop by earlier to find a good book for the weekend. Too late now though, I guess.

M: Oh Michael, no bother. It is almost closing, but I can stay around as long as you like until you find something.

Me: I have a better idea. (OK, BUSTED again. I had actually been rehearsing this little scene for about a week)

M: Oh?

Me: Would you like to go out for an early dinner? It seems like the only place we ever see each other is here amongst all the books.

Her reaction to my cautious invitation was not what I expected at all. She laughed, a small laugh, sort of a laugh of relief, accompanied by one of her all-out smiles.

M: Yes, definitely. I would love to go out for dinner. I've been waiting, quite patiently I might add, for you to ask something like that. And I always thought that you Americans were so confident, so forceful, so, well, racy.

To be honest, I was for a moment struck dumb by her light-hearted reaction. I had really been afraid that she would want nothing to do with such a further intimacy. So my response was both stunned and stupid.

Me: RACY?

M: (she laughed again, smiling all the while) No, not really. Bad choice of words. We're just going to have dinner. Not racy at all. You are so right. The two of us need to get out of this dusty old place for a change.

With that she grabbed a cardigan sweater out of one of the desk drawers, buttoned it up, collected her umbrella from its place next to the door, turned the door sign to "closed," and ushered me out. She took me to her favorite restaurant, a fish house named *McDonagh's*. Of course, it was early, so there were only a few other people in there. But as soon as we walked in and I looked around I realized there was no bar. She noticed me scanning the place, perhaps read my chagrin on my face, and laughed again. It struck me that ever since the moment I had asked her to dinner she had been laughing at me. She sat me down at a table but she remained standing.

M: Michael, I'll make you a deal. You invited me for dinner so you get to pay for that, but I'll stand you the pints.

Me: What pints? There is no bar here.

M: No problem. The bar is the pub across the street. A long-standing partnership. *McDonagh's* just takes the pint glasses back across at the end of the night.

Me: That sounds like a real win-win.

The whole time I lived there, over and over, I would run into examples of how easy-going, sane, downright functional Irish society could be. Of course, the Troubles denied those impressions, but for me Galway was probably the most friendly and accommodating place I had ever lived.

Maeve was clearly well-known, a regular, at *McDonagh's*. We were treated like V.I.P.s by all the servers and even the owner who came over to say hello to who they termed "our favorite customer." As I was soon to learn as Maeve and I in the ensuing weeks took in first a film and then a play then a couple more dinners then even a drinks and dinner party at one of her friend's homes, she was pretty much a "favorite" wherever we went in Galway. A number of evenings after our film or play, whatever, we would stop for a nightcap in one of the Shop Street pubs, *The King's Arms* or *An Pucan* or *The Other Door*, listen to some music, before I walked her home. Before either of us really noticed we were sort of dating. Everything was totally above board though. We always stopped to say good night at the foot of the stairs that led up to her flat above the bookstore. Then one night, both of us rather tipsy from our stop at the pub for a couple of pints, as we shook hands Maeve leaned into me and gave me a gentle kiss. Not on the lips, on the cheek, a laughing tipsy kiss, not serious at all. But after that, at the foot of her steps, when she took my hand she also pecked me on the cheek, except the third time she did it I turned and our lips met.

About a month into our hanging out like this together, as we sat in a pub over pints, she informed me that she had been quite entertained when one of her friends in group conversation somewhere had referred to me as "Maeve's Yank."

M: We seem getting to be quite the item.

Me: Really? Well, people will gossip.

M: Yes. I know.

Me: I'm sorry if I've put you in an embarrassing light with your friends.

M: Actually, I'm pretty hard to embarrass and in this case I am finding their curiosity rather flattering, entertaining.

Me: Curiosity?

M: Oh, I'm sure that they all think that we are lovers.

Me: They do? (now I was the one embarrassed, trying to find a suitable response to this sudden revelation)

M: Well, aren't we? Sort of?

Me: Yes, sort of I guess, but not in the true sense of the word.'

And then she jumped in with both boots and turned both of our lives in a whole new direction.

M: Well that certainly is easy enough to fix.

Me: (Nerdishly. Sputtering) OK. Yes. Yes it is. Do you mean?

M: Oh good lord man! We've been circling around each other for nearly two months. Isn't it about time?

That night she took me by the hand and led me up the stairs for the first time.

We made love twice more that week and there was absolutely no doubt in either of our minds that we were totally caught up in it and each other. At the end of that first week, in her bed, both sated, relaxed, coiled in each other, wrapped in the first stage of falling in love, she reflected softly on what we had just done with each other's bodies.

M: Oh Michael, for a while I've thought that I probably was done with sex, that maybe I was too old to still enjoy it.

Me: I know. I think we're just about the same age and, oh Maeve, I am really enjoying it. I had almost forgotten how it was when I used to have it, years ago.

M: I haven't had the opportunity for a number of years, at least with another person.

Me: Believe me, I know exactly what you mean (and we both cracked up).

M: It's like finding something you lost and thought you would never find again.

Me: Right now I'm thinking that we never really lost it, at least the need for it.

M: Funny that it took us so long to get around to it.

Me: Oh boy! I have to confess that I have thought about having sex with you from almost the first time we met, after maybe only one or two afternoons sitting talking to you in the shop.

M: Then why did it take you so long? Why didn't you try? Why did it have to be me leading you by the hand up here into our bed?

Me: I don't know. You've been so good for me. We were getting along so well. Yes, I thought of you in a sexual way, but I was afraid that if I acted on those thoughts it would ruin everything.

M: Oh, just brilliant. And everyone says that Americans are so pushy.

And so we became *bona fide* lovers in every sense of the word. Shortly after that Maeve sprang another surprise on me. She invited me to go to Mass at the Cathedral with her on a Sunday. It came as a surprise because, while I knew that she was a good Catholic like almost everyone else in Galway, I had never mentioned my renewed interest in my life-long religion to her. I never revealed that I went once a week to a weekday Mass, that I had developed a whole existential theory of secular transubstantiation around my special part of the Mass, that Ireland, Galway, this Catholic country, had awakened a renewed sense of religious consciousness in my soul so deadened by all those years as an adjunct to banks of computers. In the Mass I found moments of welcome peace, of acceptance, even community, especially for someone like me, a stranger in a new land, alone. Maeve proferred her invitation late one Saturday night as we were lying in bed afterwards in each other's arms.

Me: Do you go to Mass every Sunday?

M: Yes, pretty much, definitely lately.

Me: Why lately?

M: (her ironic grin stretching tightly across her face) Because I need to seek forgiveness for all of the week's mortal sins that I'm committing here in bed with you.

Me: Mortal sins? You don't really think…

M: Of course not, you idjit. What we're up to is too good to be sinful.

Me: (getting into the spirit of the exchange) Or maybe it is so good because it is so sinful. So that makes me an "occasion of sin" for you (I teased her, remembering that phrase from my distant Catholic childhood).

M: Oh, indeed you are, and a quite fine one if you ask me.

Me: Wow, you make me feel really dirty.

She: One of your best qualities.

So that Sunday I picked her up at half-eight and we crossed the stone bridge over the Corrib to go to Mass together at the Cathedral for the first time. As I knelt in the pew next to her, I started analyzing, probably overthinking, why I was there, not so much with her but for me. Probably my going to Mass, even before she ever took me, had to do with my starting to realize just how old I had become. Before I retired, while working at THRINTEL with all of those young people, I never once thought about my age. But now, since I retired, I was suddenly aware that the years had flown by and I was running out of everyone's most valuable commodity, time. My memory, which could play back all of those years in cinematic detail, was little consolation anymore. I had always seen my memory as a means of resisting the deaths of others, especially Nicole, in my life. But now I had started using my memory to push back at my own thoughts of death. It's complicated I know. But as I sat there in that pew next to Maeve it was those kinds of thoughts about why I was there and how this Catholicism which I now shared with another with whom I was rapidly falling in love figured in the whole delicate equation. We were both in our sixties and time was rushing past us at high speed. We were two very different people from two very different worlds, and the calculus of the whole situation was indeed complicated. Thanks to my memory I was pretty much a whiz at Math, but this was a problem I hadn't yet worked out.

When it came time for the transubstantiation ritual, my magic moment of the Mass, my whole attention was glued to the altar. It was that way every time I went to Mass in those days. The words, the raising of the host, the magic of the bread and wine changing, had become a weekly fascination for me, probably my main reason for going to Mass. I saw in my own life that power of transubstantiation and I think I was seeking the reassurance that it was still going on and I could still experience it. And so there it was. Maeve and I met each other. We became friends with each other. We started making love with each other. We ended up going to Mass with each other. And that first Sunday, as the transubstantiation unfolded on the altar in front of us, I suddenly knew, as if an angel had delivered the message, that Maeve had gently, unknowingly, led me not only up her stairs to her bed, but through a door to a whole new existence of Irish friendship and late-in-the-game love. I, and she, kneeling beside each other at the communion rail that first time at Mass together, had no idea that there were going to be yet a few more steps in our transubstantiation together.

As time went on, almost as it had with me and Wendy in Paris, Maeve and I drifted into what I guess would be called a dating relationship. Afternoons in the empty shop, dinners all around Galway, music in the pubs, plays, films, of course making love a couple times a week. She even got me Irish dancing one night at *Murphy's White House* pub across the river. One thing bothered me though, but I put off raising it with her for the longest time. So few customers actually came into her shop. At most she might sell twenty books a week. And she wasn't buying any new books. From surveying the books in the front windows, I speculated that she hadn't bought any new books for about five years. So she knew the bookshop really didn't have a future I realized and I immediately wondered why she kept going to work every day.

This whole situation nagged at me, When I stopped by in the afternoons, we would sit and talk almost undisturbed by any customers, even browsers, coming in. It took me months to get up the courage to finally ask her about it. I was afraid my American pushiness would strike a raw nerve. When I did finally bring the subject up, she wasn't perturbed at all.

Me: Does it bother you that you have so few customers?

M: No, it doesn't really bother me. Not so many people are avid readers anymore as you and I are.

Me: I know, but you are just not selling hardly any books.

M: Yes, business was much better back when my father was alive. I've been working here in the shop all my life. My father's life work was these books. He was educated and very well read. He loved introducing readers to these books.

Me: So, you keep the bookshop as a kind of memorial to your father?

M: Oh no. For me, it's much more than that. We're one of a kind. It's the only real bookshop in all of Galway.

Me: Well, you've certainly got that right.

M: You've seen the other stores that sell books. They only sell best sellers from England and America. Or travel books on Ireland, every one with a photo of the Cliffs of Moher on the cover. Or novelty books. Good lord, they even sell whole books with just blank pages. All of their books are brand new. They don't carry a single author published before 1990. Really, they are just greeting card shops.

It wasn't a rant that she delivered at me, but it was a defense of her idea of what a real reader was and needed and she was the only one supplying. After taking a deep breath and thinking a moment she looked up at me, a kind of realization in her eyes.

M: Maybe you're right. I've never seen my shop as a memorial to him, but my da collected these books. Maybe for some strange reason I don't want to let them go. They were his life, his pride and joy. They are all I have left of him.

Her saying that decided me that I was on the verge of going too far. I changed the subject, decided it was none of my business, let it go.

Soon after that Maeve decided that I should move in with her above the bookshop. I was spending most of my nights there anyway. So I did. And then I got the letter from Grace announcing that she was pregnant. When I told Maeve, for a moment it stopped her dead in her tracks. But quickly she summoned her radiant smile and told me how wonderful that news was and how happy I must be. I laughed and she called me "Grandpa." Which was all well and good, but I didn't believe a word of it. I had caught that moment of hesitation and it bothered me. A day or so passed and I couldn't get it out of my mind. So I asked her. As soon as I broached the subject she burst into tears. It was the first time I had ever seen her cry.

M: Oh Michael, yes. I'm afraid you'll go back to America to welcome the baby and you won't come back.

Clueless, baffled by women as usual, dunce that I am, her fear of abandonment actually surprised me. Sure, I had thought about going back to Washington to see Grace's baby, but I had never thought of anything more complicated than buying the plane ticket. The last thing I had even considered was giving up Maeve. She was just too good for me, perfect for me. We were so good together. I had realized long before this that I was deeply in love with her. To my credit, without even thinking, I blundered into saying exactly the right thing.

Me: Why don't you come with me?

M: (With her smile suddenly beaming right through her tears, I was really surprised that a rainbow didn't immediately arc across her face) Oh Michael, really, I can go? Oh Michael, I love you so.

Thinking back on that whole conversation from here, so many years after, I just have to shake my head at the charmed life I led. Go figure where saying exactly the right thing at that time in that place would come to a feckless sort like me. But it did, and five months later, before Grace was due to deliver, Maeve and I flew off to America.

That is not to say that the preparations for our journey were uncomplicated. More than once Maeve worried herself into an Irish tizzy:

M: Oh Michael, I've never been out of Galway except for Dublin a few times.

M: Oh Michael, what will I wear? I'll look so dowdy next to your smart American women.

M: Oh Michael, do you think Grace and her husband will like me?

What if they don't?

And then the real stunner:

M: Oh Michael, what will they think of us? Will your daughter think I'm your Irish whore?

That one almost made me choke on my Guinness.

Me: Maeve love, if they think that it will certainly make you about the most elderly whore in Ireland.

That got me a good, hard loving punch to the biceps.

I think I spent most of my time in those months before we left assuring Maeve that everyone in America was going to love her just as much as I did. I remember remembering how in Paris after Nicole's death when Grace was only twelve or thirteen when I had taken up with Wendy how the two of them became fast friends, co-conspirators, confidants.

Me: Maeve, look, it is going to be fine. In letters I've already told Grace about you. She can't wait to meet you.

That was a bald-faced lie, but the very next day I wrote that long letter telling Grace all about Maeve.

When we got to America I was absolutely right about Grace. She accepted Maeve whole heartedly—open arms, feel my baby jump, so glad you are here for the big event, all that kind of stuff. I actually sort of thought that Grace was laying it on pretty thick. As usual, I had no idea what was going on with Grace until one day it all just came flooding out:

G: Dad, your lady, I like her. She's really nice. Quiet. Gentle. Smart. I can see that she makes you happy.

Me: I'll confess I have been a little worried about how you would react to her.

G: You two seem really good together.

Me: And it's Ireland too, Galway. I'm really comfortable there.

G: (seriouscr and seriouser) I've always felt guilty about how we left Paris.

Me: Paris?

G: I know you did it for me. And I know you had to leave Wendy to come back to the states with me. Over the years I've thought about that, what a sacrifice you made, giving her up. That had to be really hard. I was too young to understand at the time. But since… well, I feel really sorry about that.

Me: Don't! What Wendy and I had was never anything more than temporary. Wendy was special, absolutely. She was driven. She was going to be a real journalist come hell or high water. Boy, that woman could really write! She could make the world come to alive in words. But we were never going to have a relationship long term. She was way out of my league in terms of ambition. Yes, we were pretty good together, but there was no way I was going to send you off to the states to college on your own. I loved Wendy. I love Maeve. But you are my daughter, mine and Nicole's, you two are the loves of my life.

Whew! That was a really long speech for me. Grace was totally in tears by the time I was done. But they were good tears, "tears of love" she called them.

But just to put my life in those days before Grace had the baby in perspective, let me put that conversation with Grace next to a similar conversation I had with Maeve at about that same time.

M: Grace is still Catholic, isn't she?

Me: Yes. They're already planning the baby's baptism.

M: Do you think that she thinks that you and I are living in sin?

Me: I don't think so. People in Ireland may still think like that but I don't think they still do in America.

M: (quite quizzically) What?

Me: I'm joking. And we're not living in sin anyway, in Ireland or America or Timbuctoo. We're living in love. Whole different thing. It makes everything that we're doing completely alright.

M: Oh Michael, you always say just the right thing.

Yeah right! Like I had any idea what the "right thing" was. But you see my problem. I was trapped between two utterly disturbed women.

We were in America for two full months. The baby came right on time. A gorgeous girl who Grace named Nicole. Maeve had just put a "CLOSED" sign on the bookshop door in Galway and didn't seem the least bit worried about it. Oh, she might have had two or three customers who missed the shop, but Maeve didn't really seem to care. Little Nicole's baptism came and went and we were packing for our return to Galway when Maeve caught me completely by surprise.

M: You know Michael, I like it here, in Washington, in America. There is so much to do. And Grace and Nicole. You know I've never had family like that all these years. I know you'd like to watch your granddaughter grow up, be able to have Sunday dinners with your daughter's little family. Let's just stay here.

I thought that she was kidding, just indulging in a flight of wishful thinking. But she was deadly serious. In bed that night we talked about it. Of course, we couldn't stay right then, this time over. There were things in Galway that needed attending to. But she was serious. She had clearly been thinking about this for some time.

Me: But what about the shop? It's not as if you can just sell it. It's hardly a going concern.

M: The shop. Oh lord no. Nobody would buy it. But you forget that I own the building. Over the years a number of developers have approached me with offers, handsome offers.

Me: But the books. You love the books. Your father's books.

M: Oh yes, I'm going to miss the books. But then you can't have everything.

Me: Love, it's a really big step.

M: I know. But maybe it is time for me to have a change of scenery from Galway. Start a whole new life in a whole new world like all those Irish did during the famine. I could pretend to be little Nicole's grandmother.

Me: You'd be the sexiest, smilingest, most beautiful grandmother in all of Washington.

M: And you're more full of it than any resident of Blarney Castle ever was.

And so, back across the ocean we went, bent on coming back to America as soon as we could. Actually, it turned out to be not that big a deal. It took only about two months for Maeve to sell her building. The buyers had no interest in the bookshop. They were going to totally re-hab the building into high-end urban condos. Thank you Celtic Tiger!

As soon as the deal was underway, I started thinking more seriously about our other problem, our books. I say "our books" because I realized that those books had pretty much come to mean as much to me as they always had to Maeve. And the bookstore had been what brought Maeve and I together. It had been our safe harbor where we could sit and talk away the afternoons, get to know each other, fall in love.

Me: Have you thought about what you are going to do when we get to Washington?

M: Well, I don't know. What retired people do I guess, whatever that is.

Me: You're too young to retire.

M: Michael, I'm sixty-two years.

Me: What would you think about starting a new bookstore, you and me, partners?

That sort of threw her. Long pregnant pause. I could almost see the wheels turning behind her eyes.

M: Oh Michael, wouldn't that be a pretty big undertaking? I mean, in America. Wouldn't it be awfully expensive?

Me: I think as equal partners we could swing it. You're going to make a bundle selling your building and I've got THRINTEL. Equal partners, you and I. And we've got half the battle won because we've got all your father's books to stock our new bookstore shelves, at least some of them. Why don't I run it past my financial advisor?

M: What's a financial advisor?

Me: Not important. I'm excited about this idea. I'm certain we can swing it.

M: But what did you mean about Da's books?

Me: I've got a few ideas about them. Just leave it to me.

As it turned out, all that remained was simple logistics, something my years at THRINTEL had made me pretty adept at. When Maeve's real estate deal was signed and sealed and we were ready to vacate, I hired a boat container and found four hardy lads to pack it for us. We loaded all the books and shelves on a cargo ship bound for Norfolk where they would be dropped on a truck and delivered to our new bookstore's address. Now all we had to do was find that address.

As soon as we got to Washington, I started combing the city for our potential bookstore, looking at existing bookstores that might want to sell and vacant retail spaces that might serve our purposes. In one weekend I visited every bookstore in the D.C. area, talked to their owner, pitched my idea. No luck. Then I looked at vacant buildings and available rental spaces and totally hated those alternatives. The buildings were spectacularly overpriced and the rents were so exorbitant that they pissed me off. Maeve could see my frustration and consoled me by just suggesting we drop the idea. I was not consoled!

Then we caught a break. The owner of a bookstore in Georgetown near the campus called me. I had talked with him once already and he said he'd like to meet and talk some more. His bookstore, like Maeve's had been in Galway, was an old one (like its owner) and hopelessly out of date. Worse yet, a large Barnes and Noble was going up about two blocks away that he was sure would make his store obsolete. He wondered if I was still interested. His building was old and square and flat-roofed and ugly, but it was located on a corner on a busy street just off the campus. It also had a dry basement which really attracted me. And we could afford to buy it which had not been the case with so many other vacant buildings around Washington. So, we did.

Our building was separated into two large rooms, plus my basement for which I had definite plans. We did a complete re-design of the previous bookstore. Getting our bookshop just the way we wanted it harkened me way back to when in one of my previous lives I had created my Forensics Lab at the university. *Funny isn't it*, I thought at the time, *how you change whole lives and yet those lives tend to interchange. And it is memory that ties them all together.* Yes, I had designed work spaces before, at the university, at THRINTEL. That experience served us all well now. But I also remembered something Maeve had said about the old bookstore back in Galway, that it was "the only one of its kind," the only "real bookshop," all the others were just "card shops." With that in mind, we set out to make our bookstore completely different from all the others, especially the big bad Barnes & Noble The first thing we decided on was our name. Maeve insisted that it be Irish. I insisted that it be strong enough to compel people to come in. So, we stole our name, *James Joyce and Company*, from the most famous bookstore in all history in Paris. Okay, yes, it was pure plagiarism, but we just didn't care and it wasn't actionable, only suggestive.

The two large rooms on the ground floor we painted bright white and we installed two skylights to give them an airiness and easy reading light for both browsers and relaxing readers. One corner of the front room right inside the front door was our coffee bar. One whole wall was devoted to newspapers from all over America and all around the world in both English and a multitude of foreign languages. After all, Washington might well have been the most polyglot city of readers in America back then in 2009. The coffee and newspapers were aimed directly at attracting regulars in the same way that a bar and friendly bartenders do in Ireland. Pursuant to that same goal, we furnished the front room with comfortable furniture, stuffed armchairs and a few sofas against the walls, plus stools under the windows.

The large back room was totally devoted to books, as were four tables in the center of the front room. The books in the back room were set aslant, spines up, on shelves no higher than six feet so that they were easily accessible to all the customers. No rolling ladders or claws on the ends of poles for us. We hung these two high-ceilinged, sky-lighted rooms on the main floor with Impressionist prints and famous black and white art photographs. We didn't foresee it then, but over time we would actually fill one whole wall with autographed photo-portraits (shot by a self-taught Maeve who became quite the artistic photographer) of the famous writers who chose our shop to do their book launches and signings. Finally, the basement was my personal bailiwick. It was all of our used books from Galway, both hardbounds and paperbacks, plus the best used books culled from the inventory of our predecessor's bookshop. I didn't realize it at the time, but my basement would not turn out to be just a storage area. It became especially attractive to students and other readers on book budgets who would haunt its shelves and find excellent bargains especially in the classics. Everything we did was aimed at making ours the most customer-friendly and congenial bookshop in all of Washington.

Probably our most inspired and perhaps creative contribution to our ambiance appeared to us one morning on the sidewalk as we were walking to work. A young woman was down on her knees painting a colorful apple-blossomed, very Impressionist, Washington street scene on a cleared-off section of sidewalk. A tip jar flanked her painting. We passed by her, but then Maeve stopped me and led me back.

M: (addressing the young woman and tipping her a fiver) You are quite good.

She: Thank you ma'am (and she went back to her street painting).

But Maeve pressed on.

M: Can you paint on glass?

That was when what Maeve was up to suddenly dawned on me. It was brilliant, Maeve looked at me and I smiled my assent to her idea. Maeve hired the young artist on the spot to come and paint her pictures on our front windows—murals, portraits of famous people, city-scapes, landscapes of America the Beautiful and other countries as well. She painted a new mural on one window every month. They were sort of like the window displays in department stores at Christmastime. They signaled that our shop was an artist's haven, a cultural meeting place. But best of all, her murals totally distinguished us from the Barnes and Noble big box down the street.

I did something else that Barnes and Noble never thought to do. I made the rounds dropping off business cards to all the professors at Georgetown University that I could track down (and believe me, tracking down professors is no easy task). I solicited their textbook orders with promises of hands-on, high-quality service and ordering the likes of which no other bookstore in the city could match. A lot of them bought my pitch and we installed a whole textbook corner in the rear room of the ground floor.'

And so, we built it and people came. W. P. Kinsella wrote that line in his novel *Shoeless Joe* which became the movie *Field of Dreams*, but it happened for us too. Readers. Hard-core Bookies (not the betting sort). Students. Retirees. People in search of the great god Wi-Fi. Eccentric retro-people seeking writers like Sterne and Fielding and Dickens and Flaubert and Sand, certainly Joyce, and Fowles, and so many others that the millennium has left behind (but that Maeve's Da always kept in stock). *Flaneurs* (like I had been in Paris) looking for a cup of coffee, a warm seat, a friendly newspaper. Tourists (attracted by our shop's name) to see how it compared to the original in Paris. All sorts of eccentric birds. And we welcomed them all in, greeted them with Maeve's radiant smile.

It strikes me that I have made Maeve and my D.C. bookshop project sound like all giggles and bubbly. But don't be deceived, starting any new business has its chuck holes, its growing pains. It took us almost two years to get our bookshop up and running, functioning the way that we had envisioned it. But indeed, ultimately, Maeve was the Queen of her castle and I was the jolly troll in the basement shelving used books and helping customers browse my personal little catacomb. I had some regrets leaving Galway (and I'm sure Maeve did), but the joys of emigrating back to D.C. outweighed them. Starting our business and watching it grow and flourish. Seeing baby Nicole grow and flourish. Watching Grandma Maeve take too and spread her love to her new found family.

After a while, after I had memorized all of the aisles of books in my basement, after I had put to memory all of the spreadsheets and tax forms of the bookshop's administration, after I had committed to memory all of the books for thrcc-ycar-olds in baby Nicole's library (who was hardly a baby anymore), after all of those Eidetic gymnastics, my memory was getting bored, lazy, unchallenged, whatever. Admittedly, for better or worse, blessing or curse, my Eidetic Memory, the chronicler of all my diverse lives, had provided a constant source of amusement to me. I started seriously thinking of a way to put it back to work.

CHAPTER 12: WRITING

It wasn't more than a month after Maeve and I returned to D.C. that Lenny showed up just like the proverbial bad penny, though graying at the temples, no longer shiny. We had just moved into our building and were starting to remodel it. Then one day as we were working, he just appeared out of nowhere. He came through the door like he had just seen me the day before (though it had been the better part of four years), pulled up a chair, and watched me work until he was shamed into picking up a paint brush and pitching in. "Oh, what the hell," he said to no one in particular, "why not?" Maeve had never met him and was really quite amused by his just swooping in and joining the party. I think she liked him from the very beginning. Showing up like that was just like Lenny. He seemed to move in and out and back into my life at random like a good or bad memory that persists in haunting you.

Actually, that was indeed just like Lenny. After all, he was my life-long best friend. But he was also Lenny the spook, as ungraspable as water through your fingers, and, knowing that, I was naturally suspicious. *What primrose path is he going to lead me down this time? What scheme is he putting together that he needs me and my magic memory to make work? How is he going to complicate my life now?* But, as it turned out, this time Lenny was pretty much OK, on the straight and narrow, the up and up, sort of, maybe, I hoped. As for Maeve, she thought Lenny was charming. Oh, good lord!

Me: How did you know I was back?

L: (He laughed heartily at that.) Mikey, I've known exactly where you were every day. I'm retired, but I'm still on the board at THRIN-TEL and I have the run of the place.

Me: Yeah, I figured you did. I even checked my clothes, my bags, my shoes for a GPS tracker you might have planted.

L: C'mon Mikey, I've got much more sophisticated methods of tracking people than that. But in your case there was nothing sinister about it. I just wanted to make sure you were safe.

Me: Why? Did you think I was some kind of target?

L: No, not at all. In fact, when I saw you had settled in Galway and things were going so good for you. With Maeve and all. Well I was really happy for you, hell, envious. And then Grace had her baby. My god, you're a Grandpa.

Me: Why didn't you come see the baby?

L: I wanted to, but I was out of the country. But I must say that I was really surprised when you went back to Ireland and then right away packed up and came home.

Admittedly, all of this was encouraging, and Lenny was all "hale fellow well met," but I was still suspicious. By now we had put down the paint brushes and were sitting on some straight-backed chairs facing each other. Maeve was off making tea in what was going to be our coffee corner.

Me: Fine, you know everything about me. What about you?

L: I'm retired.

Me: Yeah, right! Like Mafiosos are retired.

L: No, really. I'm out of THRINTEL. Well mostly.

Me: What does that mean?

L: I turned it over to Tommy and the Millennials. Of course, they'll fuck it up and you and I probably will have to go back in and clean up their mess.

Me: Not going to happen, Lenny.

L: I know. Just kidding. Really, I'm retired. All I do is a little harmless consulting work, strictly off the books, sometimes even for free. Totally untaxable. Gee Mikey, you and me, we're almost seventy years old. You're a grandfather.

It was the word "harmless" that made the sirens go off in my head. If you have read this whole book, traced Lenny and my friendship through all these years and all these pages, then I think you will understand that I didn't believe any of this manure he was shoveling, not for a second. Lenny was no more capable of retiring than Mickey Mantle was capable of taking better care of himself or Yogi Berra was capable of making sense. At any moment I expected Lenny to break out in an attack of spycraft like other people break out in hives. *Once a spook always a spook* was the mantra I kept chanting in my mind as Lenny and I supposedly, "harmlessly," hung out with each other.

My circumstantial evidence:

1. Nobody ever retires from the kind of work Lenny had done all his life.
2. He claimed he was in "partial" retirement, some consulting work. For who? The government? The CIA/ NSA? Black ops? Satan?
3. He claimed he had been out of the country when Grace's baby was born. What kind of work takes someone like Lenny out of the country? I asked him. He changed the subject.
4. He admitted that he always knew where I was, what I was doing, that I was safe. His implication was that he could protect me in Galway if I was ever threatened. I mean, did he have one of those drone things hovering over me as I walked down Shop Street.

Lenny my friend, thou doth protest too much. All of you out there reading this can certainly see why I didn't believe a word he said. As it turned out though I was wrong, well sort of wrong. What I had left out of my case against Lenny was that he really was my best friend, and he really was interested in my well-being, and he really had taken care of me all of my life for better or for worse (although he did get me shot in the ass). But the very best thing in that dumb ass's favor was that Maeve and he became fast friends. Good lord, from the very first he charmed her right out of her Irish Macintosh and galoshes. So, anyway, just like that, Lenny was back in our life.

But don't get me wrong. I really enjoyed Lenny coming around on a regular basis. Admittedly, every time he dropped in I expected him to spring some shady scheme or unholy proposition on me. But time, quite a bit of time, passed and my fears never panned out. Lenny became Maeve's confidant and she his. He flirted shamelessly with her right in front of me and she loved every minute of it. He became Grace's funny Uncle Lenny and Nicole's second Grandpa. And he and I regularly enjoyed our pints of Guinness at the Irish bar right in the neighborhood. It was a lot like old times, like we were high school buddies again only older and grayer and street smarter, not Indiana farm boys anymore. The only interruptions in our return to friendship were Lenny's occasional trips out of the country. "Consulting" he started off calling it;" then "repping for an import/export company," he vaguely described it; then a "sales agent and negotiator" for an international consortium. I suspected that he was an agent alright, but I don't think it had anything to do with either a "company" or "sales" at all. I tried to get him to talk about his trips overseas, but he danced around those conversations like a prima ballerina. He did, however, bring back presents for Maeve and Nicole, from Russia. He never brought anything for me. He probably didn't want to give me any conversation pieces concerning his trips. Then, about three years after we had been back, when the bookshop under Maeve's leadership was running like a utopian world unto itself, the whole focus of my life and my dormant memory changed. And Lenny played a major part in it.

One afternoon as Maeve and I were sitting on a couch having our afternoon cup of tea, a little old Jewish man walked into *Joyce and Company*. Maeve got up to greet him as she did for almost everyone who came through the door. I sat and watched their animated conversation until Maeve pointed me out, took him by the hand, and led him over to me for an introduction.

M: Michael, this is Mark Harris. He's a novelist. He's in town to give a lecture. He's also a professor. But he heard about our shop and he decided to stop in and look us over.

I shook hands with him, His name set off a jingle as if from a little bell in my mind, and then the old Eidetic kicked in and I placed him, much to my delight.

Me: Mr. Harris, of course, you're the baseball writer.

Harris: Yes, that's how everybody thinks of me. But I've written other things too.

Me: Of course, you've got to come with me. I want to show you something.

Straightway I led him down into the basement and straight to the "Hs" and there he was, a third of a shelf, four copies of *Bang the Drum Slowly*, his other baseball novels, copies of his other books, some in paperback, some in hardbound. He seemed almost visibly moved by his shelf.

H: None of the big new bookstores stock my books anymore. Most of them are out of print. The only place people can find them are in libraries.

When we got back upstairs Maeve had a cuppa waiting for him and we talked away the rest of the afternoon. Then, over time, whenever he came back into town he would stop in for a chat. He loved it when I told him that I had sold a couple of copies of his books and that I had managed to replace them with more copies that periodically showed up on the internet. We talked about everything on those visits. Yes, we were both baseball fans, but he also seemed interested in hearing about some of my adventures, especially those from the spook years with Lenny.

H: I'd sure like to meet this Lenny sometime.

But most of the time, as he and I and Maeve would sit around and talk, he would reminisce about his life as a writer. And that was what got me thinking for the first time.

H: You've got a lot of good stuff there young man.

Of course, I was hardly young. I was pushing seventy, but I guess I was young to him.

H: Good stuff, and memoirs are all the rage now. You should write it all down.

The next time that Lenny and I were sitting in the pub I told him what Mr. Harris had said. He thought about it for a long minute, turning it over in his head as if he wanted to see what would come scurrying out from under.

L: You know, we've done a lot of wild shit Mikey.

Me: You've got that right.

L: You should do it. Like he said. Write about us.

Me: Me? Why don't you write about it? You were a lot more spookier than me.

L: I can't write. I can barely read.

Me: What makes you think I can?

L: With that memory of yours. C'mon Mikey. I bet you'd be a hell of a writer.

Me: So, in this book, what would we be?

L: "You just keep thinkin' Butch. That's what you're good at." [quote from our all-time favorite movie]

Me: No, you'd be Butch.

L: No way Jose. You've always been Butch.

Me: No, you should be Butch.

L: Oh, for god's sake, write the damn book!

Soon after that, and with Maeve agreeing that it was a great idea, I signed up for a Creative Writing class in the Adult Education Program in the Georgetown Night School. I wasn't nearly as sure about the whole idea as Maeve and Lenny seemed to be, but I decided to give it a try. Our assignments were to try our hands at short stories. I wrote a couple of them and they got at best a lukewarm response from the

other people in the class. They were writing stories that were real poetic, flowery I thought, highly metaphorical. I was writing stories that
were factual, boots on the ground, straightforward experiences stated
straightforwardly, no frills. I quit the class halfway through. I was convinced that for me it was a waste of time. I could never write like those
people did. But the idea, Mr. Harris's idea, Lenny's idea, Maeve's idea,
that I could be a writer stuck with me. I decided I had to read more, the
best writers of the twentieth century, paying attention to how they do
it—their styles, their structures, their narratives, how they create their
characters. I read novel after novel, memoir after memoir, for probably a full year, and as I did, I became more and more convinced that
I could do it, write it all down, and do it my own way. So that's where
all these words came from, the start of this book that I've foisted upon
you and am soon coming to the end of.

When I decided to try and write this memory book, I didn't know
right away how very different my life was going to be, how my perspective on almost everything was going to change, if I actually followed
through with it. Up until I started writing this, my whole life had been
spent out in the world, outside of myself, working for others, dealing
with others, spying on others, loving others. But as I wrote I realized
that I was descending into an interior world that only existed in my
memory. I was embarking upon my exploration of the past aboard the
vehicle of words, fleshing it out in sentences. Before I started writing,
the closest I had come to that interior world had been when I found
peace in Galway. Maeve had been a big part of that. Now I was going
to try to become a writer like Mr. Harris. *We'll see* I thought as I sat
down to write.

And so I started writing. I decided to take it from the very beginning, me and Lenny back in high school in the fifties on the farm in
Indiana. But that didn't work at all. I wrote about eight pages, read
them over, and threw them away. They were really boring. We were
just like pretty much every other kid in Indiana in those days, pretty
boring. Then I remembered something that Creative Writing teacher
at Georgetown had stressed. He said that every story needed a "hook,"
something to right away catch the reader's attention, pull them into the
story. When I started thinking about it, hooks started coming at me
faster than foes in a video game. The missile crisis was the most obvious
one. My Eidetic Memory went right along with that and I quickly realized that it would be a major contributor to the book I was plotting to

write. And then there was the structure that this "hook" consciousness generated, a series of chapters each dealing with a different event or period or setting in my life. They were real episodes that I had lived, but they, at least some of them, were set against the backdrop of history, or my own personal history. And so, I sat back down and started writing again. When Maeve read the first few pages, she smiled her radiant smile and gave her rather witty evaluation of my prose.

M: I like it Michael. It is very down to earth. In fact, it is probably the first novel I've read that begins with ruts in the mud.

Even as I wrote that first chapter, I began to discover my narrative voice. I realized that my book was going to be a conversation, an ongoing exchange between me and Lenny and Nicole and Wendy and Grace and myself. That conversational idea certainly took the form of dialogues between me and my characters, but it also took the form of ongoing conversations, maybe commentary is a better word since you can't really answer back, between me and you readers out there. My book was certainly going to be a memory piece in terms of the describing of the events of our lives. But in terms of this conversational narrative voice, it was quite naturally going to be a kind of confession, sort of like the old Roman Catholic cleansing ritual that has so regrettably fallen out of fashion. As I plotted out the events, the stages of my life, I also realized that my book was going to be about life-altering change, that I had moved from one life to another like some disgraced criminal fleeing his past. Or better, like that shape-shifting guy I just Googled, Proteus. Or better yet, like a quote that I once saw in Paris long ago in the great cathedral of Sant Sulpice from blessed Jean-Jacques Olier who entered the clergy after going from "conversion to conversion, birth to birth." Exactly, my life had been like that and now I was working at being reborn as a writer.

Finally, I realized what Maeve had seen right away. My book was going to be a novel. Not a memoir, not an autobiography, but a novel where I could describe the events and people and worlds of my life just as I imagined them as if they were characters and places in one of Hemingway's or Proust's or Fowles's or Mark Harris's books, the writers I had decided I wanted to be like.

But there was one problem that Maeve and I hashed over *ad nauseum*. As I just said, we had decided that my novel was going to be about the themes of memory and change. Maeve and I were in complete agreement about that. Then one day my novel's title came to me like an injection right into my brain. *Eidetic Transubstantiation.*

M: Oh good lord Michael! That is the worst title I've ever heard of.

Naturally I was stunned by her immediate negative reaction, her adamant rejection of what I thought was the perfect embodiment of the themes we had agreed upon. Maeve insisted that no one would ever read a book with a title like that. Stubbornly, I held firm and the two of us would argue about that title all across the years that it took me to write this book and bring it to press. OK, maybe I was just being stubborn. Probably Maeve was right because the title certainly is a mouthful. But I really felt my title captured what my book was really about.

My Eidetic Memory was my main qualification for writing this book in the first place. It gave me the power to graphically, accurately, vividly, recapture in precise detail those events, both historical and personal, in my life, recreate the settings where my personal history had played itself out. As I wrote, the people and places of all the stages in my life came back to me as if my life was a train. All my characters were the passengers. The cities and jobs and changes were the stations. And this book was the stationmaster responsible for keeping it all on track: Lenny, Victoria, Nicole, Wendy, Grace, Maeve, moving from Washington to Berkeley to Indiana to Paris to Cyberspace to Galway to right now. ALL ABOARD!

And then of course there were the philosophers. They were a different kind of passage on that train. Perhaps they were the books one packed to fill the time between stops: Sartre, Camus, Kierkegaard, St Paul, Jesus, Mr. Harris. These people, these thinkers, somehow crossed the tracks of my life at just the right times and gave me the help I needed, the impetus to understand. Maeve was reading this as I wrote and her favorite poet was the Englishman William Wordsworth. She said that my book was sort of like his famous poem, *The Prelude*, where he argued that the meaning of life is found in "spots of time," pieces of memory that we "recollect in tranquility" and they connect us all to the truths of our inner selves. Her saying that in turn reminded me of a book I had read during my reading year and really liked, *Winesburg, Ohio.* It was written by a Midwesterner like me and was just a series of episodes that came together to reveal the truth of that small town's life.

Sorry, got a bit side-tracked by my train metaphor, exactly the sort of thing I vowed to avoid when I quit that Creative Writing class way back then. But back to my book title that Maeve disliked with such a passion. Perhaps as you have been reading my book you have wondered, perhaps even questioned, my burgeoning interest in religion, in going to Mass, in going back to my Catholic roots. Actually, if you have been paying attention, my interest was not really in religion but in the secularization of a central Catholic Mass idea, transubstantiation. Believe me, I was nowhere near becoming a devout Catholic, but I had become as I got older curiouser and curiouser and more and more involved in my own interpretation, secularization, of the whole transubstantiation thing. I will definitely acknowledge that the ritual of the Mass held a real attraction for me that kept drawing me back into churches to observe it. The raising of the wafer of bread and the chalice of wine were an unchanging invocation of a kind of transubstantive magic. The fleshing out of my own personal idea of secular existential transubstantiation was fed by these forays into Catholic ritual and my own life's layering out into Maeve's "spots of time."

Transubstantiation is a big word made up of three interlocking parts. At its center is *substance,* the basic make-up of the self. The *trans* is the principle of change that is the potential embedded in every substance. And the suffix, *ation*, is the action, the catalyst, that sets the substance off on the track of change. A full transubstantiation is a wholesale change in existence—a new life, a new world, new ideas, new triumphs, and if one is lucky, perhaps a new love. As I wrote I realized that like the proverbial cat I had a whole procession of lives and my book was going to go back through them and try to understand how they formed me, shifted the shape of my life time after time. Back when Grace and I were in Paris, we went to the Louvre and traversed its maze of rooms and hallways hung with hundreds of oil paintings of biblical and religious figures. What struck me was how many of these saints and repentant sinners and early prophets painted by the Old Masters were looking to heaven with a kind of ecstasy radiating from their faces. A Rubens painting of *Saint Ignatius of Loyola*, a Francisco de Zurbarian painting of *Saint Francis in Prayer*, their faces were bathed in religious feeling as they looked up to heaven as if they had shed their earthly selves and were being drawn to another world, another life. They seemed moving on a pathway of transubstantiation.

But there is also a quite palpable desperation involved in my decision to sit down and write this book. It is because I am starting to dread not only the attacks upon memory from within that happen to people my age, but also the attacks upon the whole function of memory from without by the technology of the 21st Century. Right now, it is 2019 and I am almost to the end of this book. I am almost 75 years old. I can't help fear that sooner or later my memory will begin to fail as it already has for so many people around me my age. Maybe it has already begun for me. I've noticed lately that my Eidetic Memory, always so accurate, so reliable, so taken for granted, has started telescoping. That is, at times it goes to fading in and out, sharp as a blade one moment, then weaker, slower, the next. So that is why I want to get all of this down before I start forgetting.

But perhaps even more troubling, because this threat to memory is more universal, global, a creeping affliction of all age groups not just old people, is the growing dependence upon Google and Bing and all the invasive species of their sort. As I sit here in 2019 writing this book about memory, it frightens me that the very idea of memory, even my brilliant Eidetic Memory, is growing less and less functional in society. Oh, my memory still works every bit as good as ever (at least for now), but nobody, not even me, needs memory anymore. The world has Google and Alexa and Siri. Homo Sapiens can still use their genitals and their voices and their legs and arms, but nobody really needs memory any more. What in the past could be done with my freakish Eidetic Memory can now be done with AI, Artificial Intelligence. The original invention of the computer was based completely upon the scientific study of memory, but now computers are rapidly replacing that very human function that gave them birth. Google has become our memory, Wikipedia our reference book, Technology our hand-held religion literally worshipped absolutely everywhere you look. I'm betting that the world will not end in fire or flood, in nuclear war or global warming, but by cell phones that will turn us all into thumb-driven, inarticulate, cyber-glazed robots. But these are the fears and rants of an aging man. Enough. Don't count me out just yet.

And so this writing thing had finally come to this. I've pretty much written myself right up to today, into a corner so to speak. As I sit here wondering what might be my next transubstantiation, I suddenly realize that perhaps it has already come and I've landed myself in this new world of words. Therefore, the most appropriate thing that I have left to say is simply "read this in memory of me."

OTHER ANAPHORA LITERARY PRESS TITLES

The History of British and American Author-Publishers
By: Anna Faktorovich

Notes for Further Research
By: Molly Kirschner

The Encyclopedic Philosophy of Michel Serres
By: Keith Moser

The Visit
By: Michael G. Casey

How to Be Happy
By: C. J. Jos

A Dying Breed
By: Scott Duff

Love in the Cretaceous
By: Howard W. Robertson

The Second of Seven
By: Jeremie Guy

CPSIA information can be obtained
at www.ICGtesting.com
Printed in the USA
LVHW091519030320
648853LV00008B/156

9 781681 145150